MW01137854

THE
SATISFACTION CAFÉ

A Novel

KATHY WANG

SCRIBNER

New York   Amsterdam/Antwerp   London
Toronto   Sydney/Melbourne   New Delhi

Scribner
An Imprint of Simon & Schuster, LLC
1230 Avenue of the Americas
New York, NY 10020

For more than 100 years, Simon & Schuster has championed authors and the stories they create. By respecting the copyright of an author's intellectual property, you enable Simon & Schuster and the author to continue publishing exceptional books for years to come. We thank you for supporting the author's copyright by purchasing an authorized edition of this book.

This book is a work of fiction. Any references to historical events, real people, or real places are used fictitiously. Other names, characters, places, and events are products of the author's imagination, and any resemblance to actual events or places or persons, living or dead, is entirely coincidental.

First Scribner hardcover edition July 2025

SCRIBNER and design are trademarks of Simon & Schuster, LLC

Simon & Schuster strongly believes in freedom of expression and stands against censorship in all its forms. For more information, visit BooksBelong.com.

For information about special discounts for bulk purchases, please contact Simon & Schuster Special Sales at 1-866-506-1949 or business@simonandschuster.com.

The Simon & Schuster Speakers Bureau can bring authors to your live event. For more information or to book an event, contact the Simon & Schuster Speakers Bureau at 1-866-248-3049 or visit our website at www.simonspeakers.com.

Interior design by Hope Herr-Cardillo

Manufactured in the United States of America

10 9 8 7 6 5 4 3 2 1

Library of Congress Cataloging-in-Publication Data has been applied for.

ISBN 978-1-6680-6892-2
ISBN 978-1-6680-6894-6 (ebook)

for Vivienne and Daniel

THE

SATISFACTION CAFÉ

I

THE TRICK TO A GOOD MARRIAGE

CHAPTER ONE

Joan Liang's life in America began in Palo Alto, where she lived in the attic of a two-story home on Azalea Street. Joan did chores for the widow who owned the house in exchange for reduced rent; she never could have afforded such a nice neighborhood otherwise. She lived in that attic until she was married, and she was married for only six weeks before she stabbed her husband. Joan was twenty-five and had lived in the United States for two years. The year was 1977.

Joan had not thought she would stab her husband. It had been an accident (sort of). Afterward she was disappointed that marriage had not turned out as she'd imagined. She had thought it would be wonderful. It had been, actually. Until it wasn't.

Though later, Joan would wonder why she'd ever thought marriage would be so special. As a child in Taiwan, most of the married women Joan encountered were melancholy, if not outright miserable; throughout her childhood, Joan's own mother had on occasion risen from the kitchen table without warning to cry with showy force into her hands.

"You've ruined everything!" Mei would shriek if any of the children came near, and so they soon learned to keep away, which only worsened Mei's despondency. At least every other Saturday, Joan's father, Wen-Bao, spent the night across town in Shilin, where he kept a two-bedroom apartment for his mistress. Joan's mother was haunted by the two bedrooms; it drove her nuts, Mei said, to think of so much empty space.

"Can you imagine," Mei would remark, legs crossed as she sat before her vanity, "how much *lust* a man must carry inside, to furnish such a large place for one woman? When all six of us are crowded in the same square footage? Do you understand the scope of his betrayal?" At this point Joan's brothers usually wandered off; they were bored by this conversation, which repeated itself every few months. Only Joan would remain at her mother's feet, where she watched Mei sit with perfect posture before her mirror and pluck white strands from her hairline.

After moving to California, Joan established the routine of calling her parents every Sunday evening Taipei time, during which Wen-Bao, if he'd visited his mistress that weekend, would have already returned home. On these calls, Joan's parents performed the same interrogation: how her studies at Stanford were proceeding, if there was any chance to graduate early from her master's program so that she might begin to earn money. Money was key. Joan had three brothers, each of whom by various rights (older, male) should have been sent abroad before her. Two had been disqualified by their academics, whereas the top candidate, Alfred, had been surprised by "issues" (his girlfriend was pregnant), and so at the last minute Joan was sent instead.

Through her father's job at the electric utility, Joan's parents had saved three thousand dollars for Alfred to begin his life in America. Out of this three thousand they spent five hundred on a plane ticket for Joan and repocketed the remainder. For this Joan was grateful, as she was a girl and thus not entitled to anything. At dinner her father took the first cut of meat; he also ate all the yellows from eggs. After her father, the meat went to Joan's brothers, and then to her mother, and then to Joan, by which time there was usually nothing. So just because Alfred was supposed to have gone to America didn't mean Joan would. Mei and Wen-Bao, however, had been *nervous*—having already fled the Communists once, they preferred to settle a child abroad, an international insurance policy drawing Western wages.

On their calls, Joan's parents never inquired about her romantic life. If she were to, say, divulge that she'd kissed a man, or even dined alone with one, such news would have been met with recriminations followed by punishing silence. A husband, naturally, must be found at a certain point. A husband was part of the scaffolding upon which all the family's dreams—money, safety, education—would be constructed. But Joan's parents did not want to know anything of the process; the eventual union with the man you slept with each night should be accomplished without sex or romance, at least if you were a good, responsible girl. And for her entire life thus far, Joan had been a very good girl.

————

The man Joan married was named Milton Liu. He was, of course, Chinese—aside from her landlord, Joan socialized only with Chinese people. Milton, who was studying architecture, was tall and well built, with elegant long fingers. He played piano, which Joan liked; she possessed no musical ability, but one of her first splurges in America had been a record player and a few LPs of Bach and Chopin. Milton had an easy way of speaking and excellent cheekbones and a gentle, sleepy expression, which was what had attracted Joan in the first place: besides being handsome, he also looked *nice*. Because her parents were mean, Joan was drawn to this sort of appearance.

When she had an open afternoon between classes and her job as a hostess at Lotus Garden, Joan liked to sit and daydream on one of the benches within Stanford's campus. That such splendor was free for the general public to enjoy seemed to her a uniquely American miracle. After she met Milton, she asked him about the school's architecture. He told her the style was Mission Revival.

"It's incredible that one man could create such a majestic place, all in the name of learning," Joan had remarked. It was their first real date. Their previous encounters had all been group outings: weekend hikes or evening potlucks, since no one had enough money to host a real dinner party.

Milton informed Joan that Leland Stanford had used Chinese labor to build his railroad fortune, millions of which he spent constructing the school. "Many Chinese died," he added. "The men were blown up tunneling through caves." They were at Harbor Place in Chinatown, where the specialty was shrimp noodle soup. Around them sat slouched men wearing padded jackets, sipping tea, and slurping broth; outside, knots of similarly attired men were huddled on the sidewalk, smoking and arguing in Cantonese.

"Did he go to jail?" Joan asked.

"What? Of course not."

Joan ate some more noodles as she considered this. She usually vowed not to drink the soup due to its sodium but couldn't help it—and Harbor Place had such *good* soup, the bits of roasted duck and chopped scallion and fried onion all melding into a layered broth. It was always served near scalding; on the off chance that a white person came upon the restaurant, the waiters would shout, "Careful! Very hot!" as they set down the bowls. She swirled the noodles into an oval on her spoon. In the middle of the spoon, she placed a shrimp dumpling, soggy enough now that its skin was beginning to disintegrate.

Joan tipped the spoon into her mouth and closed her eyes. The bite went down smoothly, the heat and texture and salt playing together in pleasant symphony. Due to the expense, she didn't often eat at restaurants. Joan liked to believe she could make the same food at home for less money, but the reality was the meals she made herself, well—for some reason there wasn't any soul. She assembled another spoonful, and by the time the bowl was empty, she'd decided she wouldn't think of Leland Stanford any longer. Weren't vicious men a given in this world? Ultimately it was pointless to try to keep track of them all. Stanford may not have built his splendid university with its towering eucalyptus groves for people like Joan, but the fact was that she was indeed here, and he was long dead, and thus she needn't think of him any longer.

CHAPTER TWO

The wedding was simple: the courthouse followed by sheet cake and fruit punch in a community room at the YMCA. Being an adult was delightful, Joan thought. Each new milestone was remarkable and thrilling.

Shortly after they were married, Milton took Joan to a video store. The store, which specialized in Chinese titles, was near downtown. Milton was excited, exclaiming he couldn't wait to show her someplace new, though the store had not, in truth, been new to Joan. She'd first visited on her own a month earlier, in search of a historical miniseries she'd watched in Taiwan, *The Supreme Kingdoms*. The shop owner, a Beijing native with tobacco-blotched teeth, had an arcane filing system he refused to explain to customers, which meant Joan had to ask for the series (all episodes but the pilot had been out on loan).

Weeks later, the same owner watched Milton escort Joan into the store, raising a few fingers in tepid greeting before returning to his newspaper. Once inside, Milton wrapped his arms around her from behind, resting his chin on top of her head. Joan blushed; she was not used to public displays of affection. She liked the feeling elicited by Milton holding her, a contented pleasure which spread from the center of her body—but that she did enjoy it so made her feel as if she were showing off.

Joan was only just learning how to manage a husband. Her best friend, Kailie Chan, whose wedding dress Joan had borrowed for the ceremony with Milton, had told Joan the trick to a good marriage was to award your spouse a victory each day. A man's ego was like a baby, Kailie said. It required constant feeding.

"Isn't it incredible," Joan said upon Milton ushering her farther in, "that there's a shop right here in California just for Chinese videos? I wonder what Americans think when they walk past."

Milton beamed, and Joan felt the brief thrill of checking an item off her to-do list. She had already delivered to her husband his victory today.

It was midday, the sky cloudless. The light streamed milky yellow through the window, settling into rainbows on the ground. Joan wandered to the shaded half of the store. She examined a series that looked to be about the Japanese occupation of Manchuria. Did she want a sad story? She didn't think so, but most of the historical dramas she favored seemed to have tragic endings, and even if they didn't, you couldn't help but recall what had really happened in the end.

"What're you looking at?" Milton asked.

"Hmm? Something on the war, I think."

"Come here," Milton said. He stood by a dark curtain that separated two shelves from the rest of the store. He smiled impishly, motioning to the area beyond.

Joan didn't move. She knew what could be found behind the curtain. She had glimpsed the space on prior visits, though always with her face in motion, as if performing a greater scan of the area. As if what lay beyond held no interest.

Pornography! Joan had no experience with such material, although at least to herself she could admit she was intrigued—yes, she was interested, she wanted to know! The human body, so mysterious, soft and malleable and sticky—she was both intensely curious about its abilities and squeamish over the possibilities. As a child, Joan had occasionally spotted photographs of nude women: a scattering of magazines at the newsstand in Taipei, carelessly stowed behind the candies and cigarettes. The covers were always large—too large, it seemed, for the gray plastic sleeves they were to be contained within—the oversize font running across the women's permed hair; inches of milky cleavage, shoulders exposed.

As Milton beckoned, Joan could feel the owner's gaze on her. Were she to look back, she was certain she would find his face set in the same dour cast that to certain Caucasians might sound a warning, a signal to brace for rocky service ahead: definitely no speaky English, a laggy response time, perhaps a mentally slow second uncle who slept in a back room? But Joan knew such a man must contain multitudes: English lessons on the weekends; revenue figures scrolling past expenses in a ceaseless ticker inside his brain; the cash he secreted from the wasteful hands of the IRS; a few failed business deals already under his belt; relatives who'd starved back in China and a disappointed wife and unappreciative children at home. Such a man might believe Joan decent, but the moment she went through that curtain he would recategorize her as that *other* kind of Asian, the wanton sort, uneducated and shameless.

It was Joan's first real experience choosing between embarrassment and preference. She did not turn away but instead straightened her back and followed Milton.

They were the only customers in the aisle. The videos were crammed in the same random fashion as in the rest of the store, but here there were only two rows of shelves facing each other, extending nearly to the ceiling. Milton had recently detailed to Joan each of California's major fault lines, and she could not help but imagine an earthquake now, the tapes falling onto her and Milton, all the naked men and women crashing to the ground.

Milton perused a display at eye level. Something in his manner, a hint of sly familiarity, prompted her: "Have you been here before?"

"All men do it," he answered naughtily. "What do you think?"

Joan forced herself to look at the videos. Alone with Milton, her embarrassment was quickly overrun, and she greedily took in her surroundings. She was surprised by the number of titles, which appeared to offer settings of greater diversity than the imperial dramas that ruled the rest of the store. There was also *racial* diversity: white people, and what looked to be a Mexican man on one cover, a woman in a red dress beside him, shoe straps dangling from her fingers. And here was a Black man and an Asian woman, actually, *two* Asian women and *four* Black men, and several Japanese titles, one of which she dared wedge out with her finger—the translated copy promised a story of betrayal and gangsters, of steamy encounters and possible blackmail.

Blackmail!

A man pushed aside the curtain and, upon seeing Joan, spun around and left.

"Have you found one?" Milton whispered.

Joan hadn't known she was expected to pick something. Conscious of the possibility of another customer entering, she hastened to choose. She reached for the video directly facing her, which had on its cover an Asian woman with her face cupped in her hands. Joan liked the woman's expression, which looked serious, as if she were about to review a grocery list or discuss an unfair medical bill. This particular actress had her long straight hair swept behind her back rather than in the usual tight curls.

Once Joan held the video, however, she regretted her choice. She wished the male actor were on the cover as well—the man should really bear some of the pressure of expectation, she thought. The back also bore frustratingly limited copy: it described only a sexy "high-stakes" situation. But what *was* the situation? And what about it was high-stakes? There came at that moment the chime of the bell—another customer— and so Joan quickly dropped the video into Milton's outstretched hand and went outside, where she waited for her husband.

————

They returned to the store two weeks later. Joan had spent the morning packing the rest of her belongings to move to Milton's apartment. For nearly two years Joan had woken up at five to prepare a fiber-rich breakfast as well as a lunch to be reheated by her seventy-four-year-old landlord, Iris Mahoney; Joan also was responsible for changing the litter box of Felix, Iris's bad-tempered tabby, and cleaning the house. The Craftsman bungalow was technically three bedrooms, though Joan didn't live in one of the three. She was instead allowed use of the non-permitted attic. The space was narrow, asymmetrical, with unpainted walls; when she lifted her arms, her fingers grazed the ceiling.

There were some books left to pack, as well as her favorite green wool coat. Joan had left the coat for last, as she knew she wouldn't forget it. On the desk were some items she had purchased when she'd accompanied Milton to the university art shop earlier that week. She'd been entranced by the supplies, their breadth and specificity, and thus had allowed herself a rare splurge: a stainless-steel protractor and calipers set *and* a matching mechanical pencil *and* a Staedtler eraser and two pads of gridded paper.

Joan dropped the pads into her tote and the rest of the supplies into its large pocket. She then packed the books and green coat in her duffel. After she finished, the room was empty of her possessions. As was her daily custom, she went to the chest at the foot of the entrance and removed from it a rag and wiped the dust from the furniture.

"I wish you weren't leaving," Iris said when Joan came downstairs.

"Me too," Joan said, but this was only to be polite. Iris had been nice enough, but she'd also been unfair. The attic had been advertised as a stand-alone unit with bathroom attached, and the cleaning characterized as "light straightening"—all false claims. Joan thought she understood why, as Iris lived on a fixed income and didn't seem to have family nearby, but at the very least her rent should have been lower.

"Was it because you had too much work? I should have had you manage less. You do get used to the assistance." Iris coughed helplessly.

"No, no. It's just I'll be moving in with my husband."

"Keep in touch, *please*." To Joan's surprise, Iris grabbed her hand. Joan couldn't recall Iris touching her before.

"I will, Mrs. Mahoney." As she waited out front for Milton, Joan waved to Iris, who stood in the window; she wore her red velvet robe and looked especially diminutive from the street.

She's not so bad, Joan thought. She met me, and reckoned she could get more from the situation, and so she did. I suppose it's human nature.

Milton drove up in his yellow Volkswagen, and together they placed her suitcase in the trunk. There was a celebratory feeling between them; they had spent nights together, but now she would truly be moving in. To mark the occasion, they drove to a Chinese deli downtown and bought takeaway boxes of fried pork cutlet and shredded pickles and rice dotted with black sesame seeds. They ate at a table outside, with sodas Milton had brought from home. After they finished, Milton checked his watch.

"Let's go to the video store again," he said. "We can walk."

This time Joan studied over a dozen options before deciding. Her final selection was titled *Swedish Hostilities*, though this might have been a mistranslation—the font was light pink, and the cover reflected a distinct Victorian air, the men in morning suits and women in pastel gowns. The film promised an intricate plot: the woman's father owned a steel company, and she had recently started working at the factory as well. There, the woman discovered that her father was actually a gangster, with debts to powerful mafia men.

An unexpected liaison . . .
A man as charming as he is dangerous . . .
A woman as innocent as she is sensual . . .

Joan would have read on, but she and Milton were no longer alone; another customer had slipped behind the curtain. She could see in her periphery that the man was nearing, and she was moving away when Milton laughed.

"Joan," Milton said. "Joan! This is Kenny. He's a friend."

Joan stopped and turned. Kenny smiled at her. He had slick black eyes and a long, anemic mustache.

"Come say hi."

"Hi," Joan said. Kenny took her hand. His fingernails had dark half-moons of dirt and Joan thought she could discern a hot, oily scent from either his clothes or his skin.

Kenny commented to Milton how attractive she was. "So fair-skinned. And she's taller too, not one of those who disappear if you stand straight."

"Oh, she has a presence," Milton agreed, laughing.

"Are you from Stanford?" Joan was prepared to force herself to like Kenny if so. She was a snob about Stanford, which she wholly adored (her ardor had survived her learning of the moral transgressions of Leland Stanford, whom she'd now forgotten about). There was just too much to admire about the institution (the buildings, sculptures, and gardens), and by extension she loved the people who learned and taught there too.

"No, we met at work." While Milton studied for his architecture license, he worked at a lab, where he did something with mainframe computers.

"Oh."

"Kenny," Milton said, "is single."

"Do you want me to introduce you to someone?" Joan silently went through her list of contacts. For the best chance of success, it would have to be a person not so beautiful and not so smart—either one and the woman likely would not enjoy Kenny, and would possibly be upset with Joan for the match.

"Sure," Kenny said. He seemed to be waiting for something.

"Well," Joan said lightly, "it was nice—"

"I told him," Milton interjected, "how we like to watch videos."

Only a second passed before Joan understood Milton's meaning. Once she did understand, she was so stunned by the casualness of his disclosure that her mind could only return a numb blankness. Appalled and dazed, she exhaled and took a step back.

After all: it had only been little over a month since Joan had sex for the first time. She'd lost her virginity on the wedding night and judged the initial experience between neutral and unpleasant. On Milton's double bed, examining the goose bumps on her arms as her new husband loomed from above, she had bled, and afterward suppressed her impulse to immediately soak the sheets, as Milton was already snoring. With more iterations, however, more nights and some weekend afternoons, Joan began to enjoy lovemaking. When Milton started to play the videos, she watched with an out-of-body detachment, though once he'd turned them off (they didn't always watch to the end), she found herself left with a vague discomfort, this tension slowly giving way to a searing, urgent internal focus that had been missing in prior encounters with Milton.

So this is why people go crazy over sleeping together, she'd thought. This is why they make reckless decisions and ruin perfectly good plans.

Back in Taiwan, it was because Alfred had impregnated his girlfriend that Joan was allowed to emigrate. Thus, sex had even brought her to America.

Though things weren't perfect. Days earlier, Joan had edged painfully close to a UTI; there were also certain aspects of Milton's performance, even with the videos, that had left her with the distinct impression that *more*—though she was not clear what *more* entailed—was possible. But who was to say Joan wasn't lacking herself? She knew nothing of sex; her education matched that of the other students of Taipei First Girls' High School, in that they were merely informed sex was a tawdry act conducted by the base and uneducated, a group certainly not to include graduates of the number one girls' school in Taiwan. She'd never had a class on sex education, never seen a man's private areas, until their wedding night.

Kenny released a fake-sounding cough. "Kenny said he can watch with us," Milton said. He was gazing upon Joan frankly—lovingly, she thought. "And stay for whatever happens after."

Joan looked at Kenny again. He had dark raised moles on the side of his neck, and his eyes were like little black marbles. These features, combined with his mustache, lent him the appearance of one of the unhealthier catfish in the tanks at Lotus Garden.

"I don't think so," Joan said faintly.

"Don't be a tease," Kenny moaned. He moved toward her, and she shuffled back. There'd been a ding-ding of the bells earlier, of the owner going outside to smoke, and from Joan's prior visits she knew he would be at least ten minutes.

She crossed her arms. "I don't think this is appropriate."

Kenny sighed in Milton's direction. Between them there passed a silent exchange Joan couldn't decipher. Milton turned to Joan. "Sweetie," he said.

"I don't like this," Joan blurted. Out of instinct she hit Milton, on the side of his shoulder. Joan had never hit anyone before. Though as recently as a few years earlier, Joan had been smacked, quite often, by her mother. Mei had a habit of silently stewing and then, without warning, suddenly losing her temper and striking.

When Milton didn't respond, Joan prepared to slap him again. He caught her by the wrist. "I love when you fight back. You always fight. That is, at first."

Joan gasped. These were private matters! Activities between a husband and wife, ones not to be shared! Her indignation broke her fugue, and she righted herself and pointed at Kenny. "I don't want him here." Kenny wet his lips and leered.

"Now, come on. Kenny is my friend."

"He makes me uncomfortable. I don't *like* it." To her surprise—as Joan wasn't normally a crier—her eyes began to water. Kenny at least had the decency at this point to look ashamed. He went to the end of the aisle and began to examine a stack of videos.

"Won't you at least consider it?" Milton said gently. He stroked her cheek with his thumb. "You might like it. Isn't everything worth trying at least once?" Joan shook her head.

"I know you are nervous. You *are* nervous, aren't you?" It was only once Milton began whispering that she realized how loudly he'd been speaking before. "Sometimes I forget how inexperienced you are. I will tell Kenny to leave."

Relief swept through her. "Thank you."

"But in the future you'll have to listen to me, eh? I'm your husband. I understand things you don't—I know about the world."

Joan tilted her head up at Milton. He was so elegant and handsome, even in that harsh fluorescent light; though Joan wore heeled sandals, he was still nearly a head taller. His shirts, even his T-shirts, were always pressed. His eyes, his mouth, his soft colors, all reminded Joan of the husband of her favorite aunt in Taipei. The aunt who, with her heart-shaped face and full lips, was the sort of beautiful to regularly have her looks remarked upon by strangers, and smart to boot (she too had gone to Taipei First Girls' High School), had married well, her husband a naval officer from a well-to-do family. The man went abroad to work and died shortly thereafter, and for the rest of her life Joan's gorgeous aunt had remained a widow.

Joan had not thought this unusual at the time. You married, and then there was no more. Sometimes the outcome was lucky and sometimes unlucky, but either way, once married you were done.

There were many women who'd been interested in Milton, Joan reminded herself. She recalled her triumph the first time they'd held hands in public. The thrill of his touch as he tugged her, gently, toward him for her first kiss.

And now here, in the dim light of the narrow aisle, her future unspooled before her—the larger apartment to which they'd eventually move, which Milton would select; the jobs Joan would work, the paychecks she'd earn, to be deposited straight into Milton's outstretched palm. The house they might buy, the midlife crisis she would tolerate (a new car, a girlfriend) once Milton reached a certain age and was disappointed in his imprint so far on the world. Everything in her life would come from Milton. There would be more Kennys, and here finally Joan forced herself to acknowledge that sex was indeed part of it, that Milton would shape its form and frequency to his desires, and it wasn't so bad, because so far she did enjoy it, but now there was a rotting part of her she would have to endure, and slowly it would gnaw at her pleasure until there was none. This was the choice she had made, and surely there were worse.

There were absolutely worse outcomes.

"No," she said.

Milton blinked at her. His eyes were not so unlike Kenny's, although they were larger, and Milton had smooth skin, which made all the difference. What if Kenny had been born with big eyes and a few extra inches of height, Joan wondered—would he still be lurking in dark corners of video stores, waiting to watch other people have sex?

Kenny was observing them with open interest. Milton held her and pressed his mouth to her neck. "It's okay," he whispered. His breath hot against her skin.

There was none of the earlier pleasure of being held. Now in Milton's arms she felt suffocated, as if he were draining something vital. But when Joan tried to pull loose, Milton only tightened his grip, until finally she yanked free. She then shoved him hard, with both hands. He stumbled backward, knocking into a shelf. He righted himself and came toward her.

Milton's slap was lazy, easy. Afterward he let his hand dangle in the air with his thumb to his mouth. Joan felt the area of her cheek he'd struck. It was warm, and she pressed the tips of her fingers to it.

The two of them stared at each other. Joan thought she could discern in Milton's round eyes an apology being assembled, and had the urge to impede him from actually saying sorry. It was fine, she'd likely reply if he did. She'd been trained her whole life to forgive a man like him.

She put up a hand. "I don't want you to touch me."

"Of course I can touch you." Milton laughed. "I'm your husband!"

"You disgust me. Looking at you right now makes me sick."

There was a sharp intake of breath. This time, when Milton hit her, it was harder—much harder. Her head made a harsh sound as it bounced against the wall. The pain followed a second later. Her ears rang, and in the distance Joan thought she could hear Kenny speak, but she wasn't paying attention to Kenny any longer, she was directing all her faculties to her bag. She could not see well—her vision was still a blur, her head filled with tiny stars—but she shoved her hand in her tote and grabbed the first item she touched, the protractor. It was only after she'd swung that Joan realized what she held were actually the calipers, which had fallen out of their rubber casing.

The calipers, with two adjustable legs to measure area, were a precision product, made from carbon steel. Given their height difference, Joan managed only to make contact with Milton's chin and the bottom third of his cheek. On the downward arc, the sharpened tips sliced through his shirt and into flesh, where they left a ribbon of crimson. While the greatest damage was to his shoulder, it was Milton's cheek that bled most.

Milton touched a hand to his face. His fingers came away slick with red. He screamed.

Joan wiped the calipers against her pants and dropped them into her bag. She then strode out of the store. She had nearly reached the parking lot by the deli before she realized she didn't have the car keys—well, of course she didn't, the Volkswagen was Milton's.

Flummoxed, she stopped and set down her tote. She'd happened to stop at a row of parking meters and pondered her next move as she stared at the printed warnings of expiring time. Should she turn back? Or flee? Would the police arrest her? And *then* what would she do?

All her life, Joan would be one to face a difficult problem fully and plainly—this was a characteristic those close to her would by turns admire and loathe. And so after another minute she picked up her tote and reversed her path; as she rounded the corner, she saw Milton outside the store with its owner.

Milton held a cloth to his cheek. Joan identified the makeshift bandage as Kenny's windbreaker, though she didn't see Kenny anywhere.

When Milton spotted her, he backed away. "Call the police!" he shouted.

The shop owner was still smoking. "Did you do this?" he asked Joan.

"Why are you asking her?" Milton hollered. "Of course she did! You think I would do this to myself?"

"I don't get involved in domestic affairs," the owner said.

"This isn't a domestic affair, for God's sake. She *attacked* me!"

Milton's chin had begun to drip; he pressed the other sleeve of the jacket to it.

"I only believe what I happen to see with my own eyes."

Milton moaned and clutched his shoulder. "You don't happen to be blind, do you? Because there's blood all over!"

"I did attack him," Joan said. She thought it only fair to be truthful; she was beginning to feel a little sorry for Milton.

The owner glared at the two of them, his eyes darting back and forth. He went to Milton and examined his chin, evaluating the injury from multiple angles. The owner, named Terrence, had once imagined he'd be a doctor—his uncle was a dentist in Sacramento and lived in a beautiful brick house. Occasionally, as Terrence reshelved videos, he pretended he was a surgeon in a major hospital. This patient will die unless his heart's fixed, the nurses screamed. Someone, hurry, call Dr. Terrence! He had not been pleased when Milton came rushing out of the store, interrupting his smoke break—in real life, his day-to-day life, in which he was the owner of a video store and a half acre of undeveloped land in North San Jose—Terrence did not like the sight of blood.

Terrence puffed his cigarette and then let it drop to the ground, stamping it under his foot. "I don't want either of you to come back here," he said angrily. "I have too much stress already." He returned to the store, leaving Milton and Joan on the sidewalk.

Milton pointed at her. "You're a crazy person."

"No," Joan said slowly.

"Of course you are. Who stabs someone over a video? What kind of civilized person conducts themselves this way?"

"I didn't want Kenny there. I didn't think the situation was appropriate."

"You crazy bitch, you could have done a better job of telling me that. Civilized people use their words! Do you think any normal marriage functions like this?"

He was panting now, and as Joan regarded her new husband, she held her breath. She tried to pretend the afternoon had never happened, that she still found him the most exciting, the most gentle, the most desirable person in the world. But it didn't work, not even a little; all she saw was the beige windbreaker splattered with blood. On impulse, Joan bent and retrieved the owner's discarded cigarette from the ground. It lay flaccid in her fingers, its warmth already gone. "I want a divorce," she said.

CHAPTER THREE

As far back as she could recall, Joan had suspected her parents did not like her. This feeling had been more puzzling to young Joan than upsetting—she couldn't figure out *why*. She was female, always a liability, but she'd come after three boys, so it wasn't as if she'd compounded some great disappointment. Joan believed she did most things well or at least serviceably; she was certainly better at school than her brothers. Alfred had been closest to her academically, but then Alfred had impregnated his girlfriend. The girl's father had sworn he'd kill Alfred if he refused his responsibility, and it was rumored the family had connections with Triad gangs in Hong Kong and California.

Had someone threatened to kill Joan, she knew Wen-Bao and Mei would not have reacted with sympathy. They would have said it was a problem she'd brought upon herself, and then slammed the door to keep her from infecting the rest of them. Growing up, Joan had never regarded herself as in need of careful handling; she was not like her brothers, who were treated as a precious resource, investments to nurture and grow. She had not been sent to any form of schooling until she was nine. Her clothes were shabby, castoffs from older relatives, while Mei visited the tailor each season for new coats and dresses.

The day after Joan stabbed Milton was Sunday. As per routine, Joan called her parents. She informed them of the dissolution of her marriage. Following this, there was such a long stretch of quiet she thought they might have been disconnected. "Hello?" Joan asked.

There came on the line the sound of heavy breathing. "You can't get divorced," Mei said.

"I am."

"That's impossible. No one gets divorced. What does your husband say?"

"He wants it too."

"You can take these things back."

"Milton *hit* me," Joan said plaintively. She omitted that she had stabbed him; while compulsively drawn to honesty, she felt this detail would not accurately reflect their circumstances.

"We have a wedding banquet planned for November," Mei said. Joan and Milton had already had their wedding, but that was the American one; the "real" celebration was to take place in Taiwan. Joan knew her parents were anticipating the red envelopes filled with cash, gifted by relatives and friends, which would go toward a new car for Wen-Bao.

Joan wiped her palms, which were beginning to sweat, against her jeans. "The banquet won't happen."

"Yes, it will. We've already told our friends."

"Well, I'm sure Milton's already told *his* parents. So I'm telling you, it's off."

This was not only the most direct but also the most disobedient Joan had been with her parents. Joan could not recall having ever said no to Mei and Wen-Bao—she must have done it at some point, but not in recent memory. Joan suspected that no matter how much Milton might smack her around, her parents still would have proceeded with the banquet; it was only the idea of Milton's parents not playing along, and inflicting upon Mei and Wen-Bao an even greater face loss, that gave them pause.

Mei's voice returned on the line. "So much trouble you've caused. You should feel such shame. I want you to say it. That you are ashamed. That you are a disappointment."

"I am a disappointment," Joan murmured. This was something she'd done since a child: whenever Mei was unhappy, Joan apologized and atoned. Mei's approval had always mattered greatly to Joan; at night she would lie awake and consider how she might please her mother, conjuring up elaborate fantasies of discovering valuable jewels on her walk home from school.

As an adult in California, however, Joan found the psychic force of Mei's rage blunted by distance; as she evaluated her situation an ocean away from Taiwan, Joan realized she was *not* disappointed. She had extricated herself from an unsatisfactory marriage; she had taken charge and left a mean-spirited man who likely would have only become meaner. When she thought about things this way, why—Joan was quite pleased!

"I don't understand what we could have done. To deserve such a bad daughter. When you called, I thought you might be saying you were pregnant."

"I certainly *hope* not," Joan blurted. Mei gasped and hung up.

Joan stared at the receiver and waited for the harsh clang of a broken connection. As was her routine when her mother hung up on her, she called the house again. She did this even though Mei never answered, and indeed the phone rang and rang. The following Sunday, Joan called her parents at the usual hour, to no response. She tried again the next weekend, and the weekend after that. She didn't yet know it, but Joan would not speak to her parents for another two years.

CHAPTER FOUR

Aside from her parents, Joan did not inform anyone of her divorce. She hated to be the subject of gossip—and oh, how people would gossip! She and Milton were the first Chinese couple she knew of to actually divorce, in a community where even a broken engagement could fuel speculation for months. Joan hoped withholding comment would be her best defense against rumors; deprived of oxygen, the topic would naturally wither.

Milton, however, was not so discreet, and quickly and widely aired his side of the story. Joan realized too late the tactical advantage she'd allowed. Soon those whom Joan had believed her friends began to avoid her on campus; she was still invited to the larger Chinese gatherings, but Milton attended nearly all of them. Milton was also far better at working a crowd than Joan—a storyteller, a presence, beleaguered at the moment, sure—but still a winner, always a winner, and most of the Stanford Chinese Student Union, as it turned out, preferred to stick with winners. Only Kailie stayed loyal, meeting Joan when she could.

They had lunch one afternoon at Lotus Garden, when Joan was on break, and Kailie shared her news.

"I'm four months along," she said. "I have no idea what to do with a baby."

"I'll help," Joan promised. "I can babysit."

"You're such a good friend," Kailie said. But Joan could see how Kailie's hand hesitated over the minuscule slope of her stomach; Kailie's husband, Anthony, was friends with Milton. The next time Joan asked Kailie to dinner, Kailie paused to speak with Anthony, her voice muffled as if a palm were over the phone. When Kailie returned, she asked for a rain check. "I'm so tired these days."

Of course, Joan said. She understood. Joan had some pride—she tried to keep her voice from trembling.

Joan's world, already small, shrank to school and work. She'd returned to her original lodgings in Palo Alto, though Mrs. Mahoney neglected to decrease Joan's chores—either Iris had forgotten or was simply reneging on her word.

Each morning, as she had before, Joan prepared Iris's breakfast and lunch. After school she manned the hostess stand at Lotus Garden before returning home. Saturdays, Joan worked an all-day shift; on Sundays, she was off, as Sam Wu, the owner of Lotus Garden, closed the restaurant each week for what he called the "Sabbath" (but was in fact an illegal card game held in the banquet rooms).

Before, these Sundays had not been a problem. Joan had used the time to run errands, take the bus to Chinatown, and once she'd met Milton, well—Sundays were for him. But now Sundays represented hours of torpor, of endless time used poorly. Of the minutes crawling as she wandered the discount grocer and couples and families whizzed past, everyone already grouped off, assured of their place.

In short: Joan was lonely.

Outside the main entrance of Hoover Library was a cork bulletin board edged in steel. This board had been useful to Joan over the years: it was how she'd discovered the Chinese Student Union and her room at Mrs. Mahoney's. Departing the library one afternoon, Joan stopped and looked at the board; her gaze lingered on the bottom corner, which advertised community classes.

Bike repair and safety course, she read. *Learn Spanish in three months. Ping-pong. Beginners' cooking. $20. $10. Free. Free.*

She started small: a public speaking course, dropped when she learned she'd be required to make a speech in the style of Abraham Lincoln. Then a glass workshop, in which she made a ceiling lamp. There was no space to hang the lamp in the attic, so it sat in a padded box in the corner. Next Joan enrolled in a painting course. For her first project, she painted herself.

At the end of the first week, the instructor approached Joan. Charisma had long white hair that she kept in a bun, and she wore a silver chain with a dangling amethyst that Joan liked to look at. Charisma stood behind Joan and examined her portrait.

"Why are you older in this? Are you portraying your future self?"

Joan looked at the painting. She did appear old, she realized—she had painted herself with short permed hair, which resembled her mother's, and wearing a long floral dress. Joan had not worn this dress since she'd left Taiwan. It had once been her "fancy" dress, a hand-me-down from her beautiful aunt.

"I don't know," Joan said. "I suppose I didn't realize." She tried to keep her voice from wobbling. She had paid twenty-six dollars for the course, and now all she had was a painting in which she looked old.

"You can change it," Charisma said. "This needn't be final. You can add some length to the hair. And adjustments can be made to the clothing." Joan made some tentative strokes with the brush.

"And the background. The yellow, it's a harsh contrast. That is, if there isn't any cultural significance to the color yellow," Charisma added hastily. On weekdays, Charisma was a graduate student at Berkeley; she had enrolled last semester in one of the country's first Asian studies courses. "Or you could simply *like* the color yellow! I hear describing your favorite color is like describing your favorite flavor of ice cream! Could you describe vanilla? It's hard, isn't it?"

Joan didn't like vanilla, or ice cream in general; she began to boldly paint over the background. The greens and taupes she chose cooled the portrait, as did the flowing black hair she allowed to curve into waves at the bottom (her own hair was stick-straight). After Joan finished the portrait, she hung it on the attic wall, where it was of comfort—the painting was as real as could be, a marker of her time so far on earth. Were she to disappear tomorrow, Joan imagined Mrs. Mahoney would just leave it on display for the next tenant.

After the painting class, Joan enrolled in a small-business course. She would have liked to continue in the arts but was running out of storage. Also, there was the not negligible issue that art courses cost money, and Joan was in a financial position where she tried not to part with money unless necessary. In fact, she not only wanted to spend less, she also wished to earn more—it was *always* good to have money, she was beginning to understand. While she did not miss Milton, she did miss certain aspects of him, specifically the use of his VW Rabbit. Aside from the usual conveniences, Joan had felt safer with a car. Lotus Garden was located in an old strip mall that was decent by day, but the nights could be treacherous. After dinner shifts, one of the bus boys usually walked Joan to her bike, but Hugo and Quan weren't always available. Twice there'd been strange men who appeared as she pedaled around the corner. "You bitch," one screamed last week after Joan failed to stop at his command. "You goddamn sneaky bitch!"

The business course was free, run by a national nonprofit out of a classroom in the biology building. Inside, next to enlarged prints of the human heart, students proposed jewelry stores and home repair businesses. The volunteer mentors, three men, gave feedback and taught them to draft business plans.

Joan did not have a business idea but enjoyed the classes. Participation was voluntary, so she could simply observe. A fidgety woman with short curled hair wanted to open a dog grooming shop—Joan remembered her because she looked like a poodle. There was an aspiring carpenter who crafted beautiful end tables; Joan appreciated him because of his calm, monklike air (Devin was usually on mushrooms).

After class, Joan would buy a cup of coffee and take it outside to a group of benches in a small grove. There was a man who set up a blanket in front of the grove each Sunday, known locally as the Screamer. While she sipped her coffee, Joan would listen to the Screamer rave about Communists, chemicals in the water, the aliens at Area 51; he especially hated groups of young men and would direct his raving at any who crossed his path. "Virgins, oh, check out this pack of *virgins!*" he would yell, pounding a drum. Joan was interested in the Screamer, whose ravings she found a little too observant for a presumed madman. She'd heard that on the weekdays he had a job, a regular office position where he filed papers and spoke politely to others. If the rumor were correct, Joan wondered which the Screamer considered the true heart of himself: the office worker Monday through Friday, or the man who shouted on weekends.

After a few weeks Joan became aware of a man who watched the Screamer at the same time she did. He sat on the opposite bench and was thin and tall, with a sharp nose and a shock of gray-brown hair. As the weather had cooled, he almost always wore a navy coat. It was the coat Joan noticed first; the material was thick and beautiful.

Eventually the man introduced himself. His name was William Lauder, but he was the sort of William who insisted that people call him Bill. Bill was interested in Joan—he asked about Taiwan and how she had come to California, what her life was like now, all questions she answered while omitting the more complicated details (estranged parents, Milton). In turn, Joan asked Bill about himself: what he did (business), what he was doing on the bench (he'd gone to Stanford; it was his habit to walk his dog on campus, but then his dog had died, and Bill kept walking). It was only years later that Joan would realize she'd happened to meet Bill at a very specific time, when he was both single and feeling open and generous toward the world. Later, reflecting upon the situation, Bill's family would characterize this as an "optimum" period; they would not intend the word "optimum" positively.

When he met Joan, Bill Lauder had been divorced three times. Only a certain sort of man is still wealthy after three divorces; Bill was *quite* wealthy. He'd had children only with his first wife; his second marriage, which took place in Vegas, had been quickly annulled. His third lasted five years, and now he was single again. He was still working, though not very much, and with more free time on his hands, he was beginning to feel restless, although restlessness for the wealthy is an altogether different proposition than it is for the poor—it was a *relaxed* sort of restless.

Joan did not know any of this when they met. She knew only that Bill was an older man who wore a beautiful coat and shoes—and clothes can say a lot about someone, but not everything. She didn't know Bill's age (fifty-one) or his lineage (Irish and German); she had no idea where he lived or if he had a bad temper. She did, however, sense one thing about Bill: he was the sort of man who did not like to be alone. He'd been the first to broach conversation, and after he learned she came to the grove each Sunday, he did too, and made it clear he was doing so to meet her. On their sixth encounter, he brought her a potted orchid and asked her to dinner. Their tenth meeting, Bill asked her to spend the weekend with him.

Right away Joan understood this as a request to sleep together. Earlier, she might have been insulted, but thanks to Milton she no longer regarded sex as a singular milestone (and certainly *Milton* had not thought it so precious!). But while she enjoyed Bill's company, Joan felt that to be intimate so quickly after her divorce would be a dangerous acceleration. Bill was different—not just from Milton but from any other man she'd ever considered. It wasn't only his age. Bill was white, a big distinction, and had adult children (another big one). Joan had never imagined she'd encounter even one of these complications, and thus to be dating someone with both made her feel not only reckless but unbalanced, as if she'd lost her inner equilibrium. Bill mentioned family holidays and school vacations as past lived experience; he referenced summers in Maine and spoke of Europe as if the continent contained the whole world.

"Why not?" Bill asked when she said no.

"I have work on Saturday." She hadn't told Bill where she worked, only that it was a Chinese restaurant. He had asked if it was Lucky Lin's, the restaurant most Caucasians knew of in the area. She'd said no, and he hadn't inquired further.

"You can ask for a day off, can't you? If you give enough warning."

"Saturdays are very busy."

"Well, all right." Bill laced his fingers behind his head. In the sun, she could see his freckles; his tortoiseshell glasses looked almost clear. "I'll come to you, then. I can pick up dessert and then swing by your place Saturday evening. You've got Sunday off, haven't you?"

"I don't live alone," Joan said quietly. "I rent a room in a house. The landlord is older, and conservative." Thankfully Mrs. Mahoney was older than Bill. Joan would have found dating him difficult had they been the same age.

"Oh?" Bill sounded amused. "I didn't mean to stay at your place. Though I would like to see it. I intended for us to go over to mine, just to be clear."

Joan didn't know if she wanted to go to Bill's house. She knew it would be large, and likely grand; by now she had discerned that Bill was successful in a manner unfathomable to her. Her own existence was similarly foreign to Bill, though she knew he was ignorant of the gulf between them; that whatever he might claim, he could not comprehend the rough low ceilings of Mrs. Mahoney's attic, nor her work at the restaurant. The oily chaos of the kitchen, the unsanitary presentation of condiments; the thick, sticky odor that she felt clung to her clothes and hair even after she'd showered.

She wedged her hands underneath her thighs. "How old are you, anyway?" They had never spoken of their ages. There was the brilliant sweep of a hummingbird in her periphery, and she raised a hand as if to tempt it to her. It flew off.

"I'm fifty-one." When she didn't say anything, he added: "In my circles, that's not too bad. Some might say it's pretty young."

"Oh." Joan didn't think fifty-one was young. She was twenty-five—the difference between her age and Bill's was longer than she'd been alive.

CHAPTER FIVE

Joan first slept with Bill in Carmel. He'd suggested Napa for a weekend, but Joan wasn't a big drinker. Her face flushed when she consumed alcohol, and it wasn't a rosy pink but a full-throated red, and soon after her head would pound. She only ever experienced a few minutes of exaltation when she drank, a thin fizzy feeling that quickly evaporated.

Joan was pleasantly surprised, once they finally slept together, by Bill's body. She realized subconsciously she'd feared Bill might resemble her father, who had a wide droopy belly and raised liver spots all over his back. But Bill was fit in a manner Joan would later recognize as if not entirely inhabited by Californians, then at least well represented by them: a combination of trim and clean and sunned. Over their time together, she had begun to understand why some women prefer older men, or at least a certain *sort* of older man: the kind with maturity and taste and means. Yes, the means! Their hotel in Carmel was the most beautiful hotel Joan had ever seen, each room an individual cottage set amid lavender fields. Even sitting in Bill's car, being moved from A to B without having to dodge traffic on her bicycle—oh, Joan could see the appeal! But on those drives with Bill through Stanford's campus, she would occasionally glance out the window at the runners on the dirt side path; she would see the lustrous taut skin of men in their twenties, the sharp cut of their faces and bodies, and a fresh anxiety would bloom.

But. Here in Carmel there was only Bill. In bed he had none of the urgent jerkiness of Milton, the arrogance and desire to try anything, prove everything. Joan had the sense that not only did Bill know what he was doing, he'd been *told* he knew. Their first night together, she reached out and stroked his shoulder, and he grinned because he thought it an intimate gesture, but for Joan it was more than tenderness. She wanted to touch someone who'd traveled along life's arc with such good fortune; she wanted to feel his flesh, stroking it over and over as you might a charm, hoping some of its luck will pass on to you.

———

"How do you speak English so well?" Bill asked their first night. In bed together, after, he emitted a swirl of lazy contentment and triumph that Joan was startled to recognize from her time with Milton. He wrapped an arm around her.

"I learned it in school in Taipei."

"Does everyone?"

"Everyone in a good school," Joan said. She'd gone to the best college in Taiwan but knew it meant nothing to him; she could try to explain, but he wouldn't understand.

———

"You know, I really haven't been married that many times," Bill said the second night.

His expression was serious, so Joan was careful not to laugh. She considered three quite a few times to be married. Although I've been married too, she recalled with surprise.

"The first one counts, of course. That's when I had my kids. You can't regret children. I suppose some do, but not me." Bill bent his arm behind his head. The hair on his chest was sparse and light gold. He described his first wife as *difficult*.

"What makes her difficult?"

"All sorts of things. You know what a WASP is?"

"No."

Bill explained, though it still didn't make sense to Joan.

"They're repressed, that's all. Old money—they've got hobbies and jobs and ways of living they deem acceptable, and everything else is 'gauche.' When the kids were young, Agatha and I would take them to a certain restaurant for their birthdays. After the cake came, I'd ask the waiter to take a photo. Agatha hated that. She said it was rude, that it called too much attention to us. For Christ's sake! It's a child's birthday!"

"Really," Joan said with genuine attention. She was interested in snobs. It wasn't that she admired Bill's first wife, but she did want to know how such a woman inhabited the world, how she ate and dressed and traveled.

"Marriage isn't always an ideal state," Bill said.

Yes, Joan agreed. It really wasn't.

———

They were supposed to spend only two nights in Carmel but extended it to four. Joan called in sick—her first time doing so—to Lotus Garden. She also used the hotel phone to call Mrs. Mahoney, to simply check in. Joan knew Iris was terrified of falling and dying alone in the house; it was one of the reasons she rented out her attic.

Joan and Bill spent their last day in Carmel by the pool. The resort had a lovely pool, sparkling clean and with enough loungers that one never had to wait for a seat. As soon as a guest rose from a chair, attendants would rush forth, refolding towels and clearing away drinks.

Joan owned one bathing suit, purchased her first month in America, a blue one-piece she'd thought perfectly acceptable at the time but now, in such lush surroundings, found drab and old-fashioned. The fabric was starting to pill, and she was self-conscious next to the rows of women in their brilliant bikinis, toned legs glittering in the sun. She'd brought one of Bill's shirts in her bag, and after she toweled off, Joan quickly buttoned it over herself and joined Bill at his table in the shade.

"Is that my shirt?" Bill asked.

"Yes. Is that okay?" She had not asked him for permission, knowing he wouldn't mind. Bill's clothes were all beautiful, and he treated each piece as if he had an infinite supply, using his arm to wipe wine spills.

"Of course. It looks better on you than on me."

She stroked the cotton. It was cool and tightly woven, so much so that it felt like silk.

"It's from Charvet," Bill remarked. He was eating a banana, as she'd recently told him he should consume more fruit.

"Charvet," she repeated.

"A store in Paris. My girlfriend at the time chose it."

"Oh."

"You're not upset when I talk about past girlfriends, are you? You don't seem to have any curiosity about them."

"I'm very curious," Joan said honestly.

"Ask me something, then."

There was so much she wanted to know: what languages they spoke, whether they wore flats more or high heels, the color of their hair. "Have all your girlfriends been younger than you?"

"Not all." He stroked her cheek. "You are beautiful, just absolutely lovely."

"Have they all been Caucasian?"

"Yes. Some Europeans. And a Cuban."

A short distance behind Bill, a thin blonde shrugged out of a caftan and piled her hair high up on her head in an elegant fashion Joan knew she could never replicate with her own slippery locks. "Why do you like younger women?" Joan asked, looking at the blonde.

"Wouldn't you?"

"Ha ha," she said, though a part of Joan wished Bill hadn't stated things so plainly. Being young wasn't the same as being smart or clever. There was an expiration: one day you had youth, but eventually it went. She had it now; Bill had *had* it, she thought a little sourly. Still, at least he was honest.

The blonde made a splash as she dove into the water, and at the shallow end two swimmers emerged and strode to the hot tub. Joan thought she could feel the eyes of the other guests on her. What were they thinking? That she was young, maybe, and that Bill was old, and all the associated inferences. That she didn't belong here, and they were wondering how she had come to be at such an exclusive place. Joan didn't know either. Had it really begun on that bench at Stanford? It seemed incredible that luck could be distributed not only so randomly but also *exponentially*—that a different bench, an alternate Sunday class, might have meant her never experiencing this hotel as long as she lived.

Bill smiled at her, his eyes friendly. How lucky Joan was, to have met someone like him. He knew so much of the world; he was cultured and smart and kind. She reached, and he caught her hand and bent over her fingers and kissed them. "I am so happy," he said.

CHAPTER SIX

Bill's family met the news of his engagement with surprise. They hadn't known he was dating anyone, as in the past he had at least brought his girlfriends to a family gathering before deciding to marry them. The revelation that his latest betrothed was a twenty-six-year-old Chinese woman brought an additional level of shock and (some thought) sordidness to the matter; there were phone calls made, neglected correspondences reignited. Letters were sent to lawyers and financial advisers. Especially panicked were Bill's two children, Juliet and Theo.

"You know she's basically our age," Theo said to Juliet on the phone. They were twenty-four, fraternal twins. Their mother, Agatha, had divorced Bill when they were nine, after which she'd moved to a townhouse in Pacific Heights. Theo and Juliet had lived with her during the school week, shuttling down to Palo Alto on weekends.

"I know." Juliet was in her apartment in Nob Hill, half a mile from her mother's place. She had taken a break after college and just begun medical school. When her father had shared his news, for some reason she'd immediately pictured the cadaver from a recent anatomy lesson.

They had not been allowed into the actual room for the dissection, only observed the gray and withered body from above.

"How do you know?" Theo asked.

"I had lunch with them."

"When? Why didn't you tell me?"

Classic Theo: always nosing around other people's business. He was, however, not the most forthcoming himself. He was calling from Maine, where from Juliet's understanding, he was currently sponging off his newest girlfriend, whose family owned a vacation home in Kennebunkport with panoramic ocean views. "You weren't here," Juliet said.

"What's she like?"

"The same as the others. Young. She's Asian, though. So that's different. Dad's branching out, racially at least."

"Does she speak English?"

"Yes, though not perfectly. She appears sane, but it's never a sure thing. You know how Dad is."

Theo did know. There'd been the two wives after their mother, who had been awful enough, but then also the interests before and after and in between. A British woman named Fanny, a snob with an unusually high forehead who liked to comment on how Theo cut a steak; an extremely angry yoga instructor who, for years after Bill dumped her, continued to write to both Theo and Juliet, holding forth on what she described as Bill's "flexible relationship with the truth." When Theo was younger, he had almost admired his father for the profligate dating, but this admiration had long since slid into embarrassment. Of all the women, there'd been only one Theo liked, a family friend named Gloria. If Bill were to marry again, Theo hoped it'd be to someone like Gloria—she had no kids of her own (and was part owner of the Toda Group, which operated luxury resorts around the world). But Bill had only dated Gloria a few months; he claimed he hadn't felt any *spark*. As Theo recalled Gloria's departure—her disappearance from family lunches, the abrupt cancellation of spring break in Bhutan—Theo's fury at his father's irresponsibility, his lack of consideration for his children's feelings, bubbled into a nasty rage.

"I fucking hate him. I truly, truly hate him!"

Juliet was silent. She regretted having worked Theo up like this. His outbursts had worsened in recent years, though their mother still insisted on referring to them as his "little whims"—as if the destruction of furniture, a lifetime ban on United Airlines, and three totaled vehicles all constituted a mild personality quirk, like being messy or disliking vegetables. Theo had nearly been kicked out of Duke for academic non-performance, until their father had agreed to pay for the renovation of the law center, and last year Theo had been accused by an ex-girlfriend of stalking. But then Wendy had been a dramatic bitch, Juliet thought.

"Where did they even meet?" Theo's voice was lower now.

"Stanford." If only Bill didn't walk all the time. He'd first started after Juliet and Theo bought him the poodle, which they'd really purchased to give him some companionship *other* than a woman.

"Is she a student?"

"I think she's in graduate school." As if that made things better. One would need quite the extended postdoctoral career, Juliet mused, to make an age-appropriate match for Bill.

At least their own mother had been Bill's age *and* his first marriage; Juliet may not have known much about Chinese culture, but she did instinctively grasp the strategic advantage afforded first wives versus subsequent concubines. Juliet could still picture Evie's tight little dresses, her hand yanking at the hem as she poured wine while teetering on absurdly high heels—toward the end Bill's third wife had been desperate to learn all of his favorite dishes, as if the perfect roast potatoes might preserve her position in the house, the house Juliet had grown up in, the great Falling House, and all that came with it. Nearly all of Bill's girlfriends had proved disposable, but that was simply the fate of certain women, wasn't it? They had nothing else to offer. Juliet glanced at her shelves filled with textbooks.

"He can't have children with her," Theo said.

"He doesn't like kids, remember? He barely liked us."

"He didn't have them with Evie," Theo mused. "And you know she wanted them."

"Right. So don't worry. Go make yourself a drink."

"I can tell when you want to hang up. What are you doing? Probably getting ready for Paul. I hate that name, by the way."

"What's wrong with the name Paul?" Juliet studied her nails. "We're going for Thai."

"Do you think she knows how to cook Thai? Our future stepmother."

"I think she's from Taiwan, not Thailand."

"What's the difference?"

"I don't know. Something with the spices, maybe." There was a honk from the street, and Juliet went to the window. She watched Paul light a cigarette as he sat in his convertible. "Don't think about it."

But Theo ranted on: at one point he spat something that sounded like "cunt," which she found unbearably crass, though likely that was the point.

"Hello? Are you listening? *Hello?*"

"I'm listening." Juliet could tell something about Joan particularly bothered Theo. Was it that she was Asian? There *was* something unseemly; Juliet had felt it in the restaurant, the way they appeared as they walked in. Joan, so much smaller and younger, hand in hand with Bill; it had reminded Juliet of some of those Vietnam War veterans she encountered while volunteering at the VA. The American soldiers went and fought in countries they knew little about, and then they came home and brought with them these Asian women, all dark hair and no English. Inside the hospital the wives were mostly silent, pushing wheelchairs and fetching from their totes containers of food that they fed to their husbands.

Occasionally there would be a loud one, harpyish, screaming in an awful accent: You go move car! What doctor say? Why you no pay attention to doctor!

Perhaps Joan had come from similarly rotten conditions. Why else would she want to marry an old guy like Bill . . . yes, that made sense. And that could have been Juliet, had fate swerved right instead of left, the same way her life would be different had she been born impoverished. But Juliet knew in her bones she was the daughter of a wealthy man; any other consideration was merely theoretical. And so, minutes later, when she hung up the phone, she went out to greet Paul with all the confidence of a woman who has the supreme advantages of money and youth and the conviction that things will always be such a way.

———

Back in Maine, Theo went downstairs for dinner. His girlfriend, Charlotte, and her parents were already at the table, and they were the sort to wait for everyone to be seated before eating. Theo's mother had once been like this, but after the divorce she'd abandoned such formalities. He wondered what Agatha would say about Joan. When he'd told her that Evie was moving out, all Agatha had asked was whether it was Bill who'd ended things.

"Yes," Theo had confirmed. "Thank God they had a prenup."

"It's not polite to talk about money," Agatha observed. Though, as Theo knew, his mother did care about it quite a lot.

"Is everything okay?" Charlotte asked now, as Theo sat beside her. Like most of his girlfriends, Charlotte was brunette and slim, and she gazed at Theo with what he liked to believe was worship. She especially adored certain aspects of him: that he was six-three and had won "best-looking" in high school; that he'd gone to Duke and grown up in a beautiful home in Palo Alto, a masterpiece by the architect Ava Castillo which had once been photographed for *Architectural Digest*, officially named by Castillo "Falling House." Charlotte even seemed to like that his parents were divorced, and that he'd split his childhood between Palo Alto and his mother's place in San Francisco: there was a messy, high-end quality to it that appealed to her. She had been searching for someone just like him, she'd once said, which seemed to Theo an incredible concession to make in a relationship—it was like telling the other person: I'll always love you more than you love me.

"I was talking to my sister," Theo said.

A plate of tri-tip was passed. They'd grilled on the deck just prior: fat steaks and halibut and striped bass from the local market. Charlotte's parents, Louis and Barb, ate like this every night. Theo was certain Charlotte had never eaten a convenience-store burrito alone in the kitchen, washing down the grease with expired milk and repeating the same for breakfast—all while her mother was having an impromptu four-day "overnighter with a friend."

And yet. The Kincaids assumed Theo was just like them. Functional. Rich. Well, he was, wasn't he? He'd had a bad run, that's all. The job at UBS, they hadn't understood his trading strategy. McKinsey, a bunch of entitled fucks. The table was discussing a vacation to Portugal.

"You'll come, right?" Charlotte asked. "Oh, Theo, you would love it. The siesta lifestyle."

"I wouldn't miss it," Theo said. He would call his mother or, better yet, visit her in person when he was back in California. He would tell her about Joan and ask her to write a check to cover his costs in Europe and rent through the rest of the year. Theo felt safe that Agatha wouldn't tell Juliet about his asking for money—he had his own relationship with his mother. As he did with his father.

———

And so that was Theo and Juliet: Bill's only children. There was his ex-wife, Agatha, who spoke to Bill a few times a year, usually about

Theo; his second ex-wife, Katrina, to whom he'd been married only three months, after a drunken weekend in Vegas (no one kept in touch with Katrina). And then Evie, the third wife, to whom he'd been married five years (no one talked to her anymore, either). There was Bill's brother, Henry, who had worked with Bill until he moved to Connecticut, where he now lived with his wife, Gillian; there was a sister, Bridget, who lived with her husband, Martin, in Ross. There was also their youngest sister, Misty (Joan would come to know quite a lot about Misty in future years).

Each of these people was complicated. Each of them thought mostly of themselves. But in this system of planets there was still the unspoken acknowledgment that Bill was the sun around whom they revolved; he was the oldest, the most successful. That he'd managed to retain this position amid multiple divorces gave him an air of impermeability—he was the titular "head of the family." Though there was resentment about this too.

Joan knew none of this when she agreed to marry Bill. She understood he was wealthy, but only in the manner someone with no experience might envision: no debt and a big mansion and ordering without consideration of price at dinner. Joan too was thinking mostly about herself, that she was making a choice that would cut her off, likely forever, from the life she had imagined. She was not marrying a Chinese man but rather a Caucasian one; she was not marrying a young man but instead an older one. Bill's family was a minor question, one unknown out of many. Besides Juliet, Joan had not met them; she would soon.

CHAPTER SEVEN

B ill had acquired his start the way so many of America's wealthy do: his parents had given him some money. His father, John, was the first to transform the family's generationally held apricot orchards into office buildings, and out of John's four children, it was Bill who displayed the most aptitude for real estate development. Bill was decent in business, and like all those with profound wealth, he had also been lucky. He was generous but not unwise; he liked luxury but not excessively; and, most importantly—given that three marriages are a financial toll no matter how moneyed the parties—Bill had a good lawyer.

Bill's lawyer was named Nelson Das. When Joan met him, Nelson had already known Bill for fifteen years. He'd started in litigation at Sullivan & Cromwell in London and later moved to San Francisco and joined a smaller firm's private practice. Nelson's mentor had worked for Bill, and when Phillip Stein retired, he referred the Lauder account to Nelson.

Nelson had not been surprised when Bill told him he was marrying (again). It was Nelson's experience that a certain type of man simply preferred to be married. Without a partner, nights and weekends were empty; they needed a wife the same way a child clutched a security blanket or craved ice cream. The thing was, you could get sick of a craving. When that happened, Nelson was there too.

Bill asked Nelson to connect with Joan, as it had become routine for Nelson to meet Bill's potential wives.

"Alone?" Joan asked when Bill presented the invitation.

"Yes, alone."

"Who is he again?"

"Just my lawyer."

They were seated in the kitchen. When Joan first saw Bill's home, she'd been stunned by the beauty of the place: the gently sloped ceilings above rooms of majestic height; the spaces flowing one after the other, any of which opened directly into nature. The house was modern but not overly angular, and what Joan really loved was the warmth she felt, as if it were a real live person wrapping its arms around her. She had spent a dreamy hour that morning hanging her clothes in the closet. This was going to be her home, her *life*, and she'd been happily floating along in this shimmering bubble of fantasy until it popped.

A lawyer! Well, of course Bill would want one; lawyers got involved when there was money, wasn't that so, and it seemed Bill had plenty. A lawyer would want to protect Bill's money—protect it from her, she supposed, if she tried to leave and take any.

But: who was going to protect *her*? Bill had three divorces to her one; what was Joan to do if he left her?

She kneaded her hands in her lap. "Do I need my own attorney?"

"Do you want me to get you one?"

Joan could tell Bill was surprised by her question. She'd asked it spontaneously, the word "attorney" rolling awkwardly from her mouth. Joan had first encountered the word in a mystery novel but had never used it in conversation.

"No," she replied after a moment. She didn't know what she would even do with an attorney if furnished one. She would be nervous; she would be deferential to their authority and eager to please. And she did want to please, she wanted *Bill* to be pleased by her—but this was how she'd felt with Milton. Just as Bill had learned from prior marriages, so should Joan.

She was pretty enough, Nelson thought, as they sat for lunch at the Fish Market, which he'd thought friendlier grounds than his office. There were elements to Joan's presentation that suggested she would not do well at, say, a charity lunch: her hair was slightly wiry and stuck up in small bits near her forehead, and while her shoes were neat, they were also inexpensive, and he could see they'd been polished and resoled. And then there was the fact that she was Chinese—*that* had been new. At least for Bill.

"You understand this is a friendly conversation," Nelson said. He directed at her his most benign smile.

She smiled back. "Yes."

The day's special, cod set against some limp asparagus, arrived at the table. "I hope you don't mind my being direct," Nelson started, and Joan nodded: she'd been waiting for this, he saw. But of course; what else to expect when your fiancé's lawyer asks you to lunch?

He sipped his coffee. "You are twenty-six. Bill is fifty-one. We hope the two of you stay married until the end—ah, the end of your lives. That is the optimal outcome. But, in life, sometimes there are less than optimal outcomes."

He'd thought he might need to explain further, but Joan understood quickly enough. She'd heard of prenuptial agreements, and so Nelson went through his questions: what would you expect, what is important to you? Nelson was not embarrassed to be asking such questions. These were *the* questions when someone like Bill married someone like Joan; when one party possessed resources and the other none.

"You should take some time to think—"

"What did the others ask for?"

He noted both the bluntness and the practicality of the query. Bill had told Nelson he should answer all of Joan's questions. Nelson should be *fully transparent*, Bill said. Well, Nelson would be the judge of that. Men always believed it was going to be different the next time around. Nelson's experience was that the wives might change, but the dynamics generally stayed the same.

"You should have that conversation with Bill. But remember, Agatha and Bill had children. And I can share that Evie received a sum." This had been the subject of some contention. Evie had not thought it enough compared to Agatha's; Agatha had not thought her settlement enough either. It was almost always never enough.

Nelson scanned the dessert menu. He was about to inquire if Joan liked lemon cake when she cleared her throat. "I wonder," she said slowly, "about the house."

Without realizing, Nelson bent the paper menu. The *house*? As in: Bill's house? Bill's home was no cookie-cutter mansion but rather a multiyear passion project commissioned by Bill's father from Ava Castillo, a protégée of the famed architect Yves Clark. When Ava was finished, she'd been so pleased with the result that she'd given it a name: Falling House, based on its sloped design, which from certain angles as the sun was setting, made it appear as if the structure were tipping into its shadows. The home sat on an acre and a half of prime Palo Alto real estate and had been professionally photographed multiple times, magazines making special note of its radial design and vast redwood beams.

"The house Bill lives in currently," Nelson confirmed. "Falling House."

"Yes." She flushed. "I need to feel as if it is my home too, at least somewhat. That it isn't Bill's to just take away if he feels like."

"It's a very expensive place," Nelson said pointedly.

"It could be a percentage earned each year we're married. I've seen sample agreements—I found them at the library."

"I see." Nelson pushed up his glasses. "And what if he didn't want to give that to you?"

"I would have to assume," Joan said softly, "that it would be, ah, indicative of some broader feeling toward me, and I would have to think about that." She flushed deeper but managed to maintain eye contact. Her hand didn't shake when she lifted her water glass.

Oh, she was cool. Very cool. Nelson bet she could be icy if it came down to it. Did Bill know she could be such a way? Some people went their whole lives without encountering certain aspects of their partner, and other times it was only at the end of a relationship that they finally did. I had no idea he could behave like this, they'd remark in wonder. I never dreamed she could be so uncaring.

Nelson set down his dessert menu, which by this point he'd folded into a little square. "Does Bill know your thoughts on the house?"

"He will when I tell him," Joan said. She looked surprised, as if she'd just decided this.

The next time Nelson saw Joan was at the wedding. It was a simple ceremony, held at the Palace of Fine Arts in San Francisco. Nelson was pleased to make the invite list, though during the reception he found himself cornered at the bar by Juliet and Theo.

They were so glad Nelson was there, said Bill's children. With Nelson around, they knew Bill wasn't being taken advantage of.

"A professional's watching out for the family's interests," Theo said.

"From a long-term perspective," Juliet added.

The bartender returned with a new bottle of champagne. "You're both very kind," Nelson said as glasses were filled, and then the children left, satisfied, though they were actually incorrect about one crucial point: Nelson's job wasn't to serve the family, it was to serve Bill. Theo and Juliet would learn this later; in fact, everyone would.

"The beef was delicious, wasn't it?" Joan's neighbor Inez asked. If Joan
ed her head, she could spot patches of Bill through Dina's enormous
pdragons down the table; he looked delighted to be next to Candy
, who had huge breasts and had inherited a majority ownership of
ockey team from her father.

"Yes, it was very tender," Joan agreed, slapping herself lightly on
 leg to stay awake. Inez could be dull, but she was also extremely
tty, which was likely why she had been stowed in social Siberia by
 cunning Dina.

"Everything is so pretty. The tablescape. I've always thought it'd be
e to be a floral designer. Though I wonder how they feel about all
ir work eventually dying." Inez patted her lips with a napkin. "What
 you do again?"

"I recently graduated." Joan had finished Stanford last month. That
 possessed a master's in mathematics and spent her days polishing
od and dusting drapes was depressing; it wasn't that she had to do
ch work, it was that she couldn't even do it well. Falling House was
timidatingly large, and as soon as Joan moved in, the housekeeper,
id, who under Bill had enjoyed a cosseted employment in which she
ent the majority of her days listening to talk radio and baking for
r grandchildren, had resigned. Joan had yet to hire a replacement—
e didn't know *how* to hire one. Until recently she had been a sort of
usekeeper herself; she had no idea how she could presume to exhibit
e gravitas of an employer.

"That's nice," Inez said. "To have graduated." A stretch of drunken
ughter erupted from the other end of the table. Inez blinked her big
es, waiting for a response, and now Joan would have to think of some-
ing, and the conversation would continue like this, lobbing tedious
ttle bombs back and forth indefinitely.

Oh, how did people do any of this? Sometimes Joan wished there was
place she could visit to feel less alone: a restaurant with very friendly

CHAPTER EIGHT

After marriage, Joan was dismayed to discover that
vert. He liked to go out: to baseball games, dinne
At parties, he'd promise to stay by her side, but soon t
hand on his shoulder, some acquaintance he hadn't seen ir
would be left on her own, floundering among strangers wi

In August, one of Bill's "good friends" (he had a lot (
a fellow real estate developer named Trevor Hall, turn
was a rather handsome strawberry blond whom Joan
prone to extended silences. Bill said Trevor was a hoot, y
him better, but she was doubtful.

Trevor's birthday party had been planned by his w
quent entertainer who almost exclusively wore one-sl
and believed in seating spouses apart at dinner. At th
their palatial home in Woodside, Dina placed herself ir
Keller, a thirty-one-year-old scion of a publishing dynast
Garcia, an architect who'd worked on their home in So
seated across from Dina, while Joan was at the far end.

"The beef was delicious, wasn't it?" Joan's neighbor Inez asked. If Joan tilted her head, she could spot patches of Bill through Dina's enormous snapdragons down the table; he looked delighted to be next to Candy Gill, who had huge breasts and had inherited a majority ownership of a hockey team from her father.

"Yes, it was very tender," Joan agreed, slapping herself lightly on the leg to stay awake. Inez could be dull, but she was also extremely pretty, which was likely why she had been stowed in social Siberia by the cunning Dina.

"Everything is so pretty. The tablescape. I've always thought it'd be nice to be a floral designer. Though I wonder how they feel about all their work eventually dying." Inez patted her lips with a napkin. "What do you do again?"

"I recently graduated." Joan had finished Stanford last month. That she possessed a master's in mathematics and spent her days polishing wood and dusting drapes was depressing; it wasn't that she had to do such work, it was that she couldn't even do it well. Falling House was intimidatingly large, and as soon as Joan moved in, the housekeeper, Enid, who under Bill had enjoyed a cosseted employment in which she spent the majority of her days listening to talk radio and baking for her grandchildren, had resigned. Joan had yet to hire a replacement—she didn't know *how* to hire one. Until recently she had been a sort of housekeeper herself; she had no idea how she could presume to exhibit the gravitas of an employer.

"That's nice," Inez said. "To have graduated." A stretch of drunken laughter erupted from the other end of the table. Inez blinked her big eyes, waiting for a response, and now Joan would have to think of something, and the conversation would continue like this, lobbing tedious little bombs back and forth indefinitely.

Oh, how did people do any of this? Sometimes Joan wished there was a place she could visit to feel less alone: a restaurant with very friendly

CHAPTER EIGHT

After marriage, Joan was dismayed to discover that Bill was an extrovert. He liked to go out: to baseball games, dinner, people's homes. At parties, he'd promise to stay by her side, but soon there would be a hand on his shoulder, some acquaintance he hadn't seen in *years*—and Joan would be left on her own, floundering among strangers with dazzling teeth.

In August, one of Bill's "good friends" (he had a lot of good friends), a fellow real estate developer named Trevor Hall, turned forty. Trevor was a rather handsome strawberry blond whom Joan found stiff and prone to extended silences. Bill said Trevor was a hoot, you had to know him better, but she was doubtful.

Trevor's birthday party had been planned by his wife, Dina, a frequent entertainer who almost exclusively wore one-shoulder dresses and believed in seating spouses apart at dinner. At the party, held in their palatial home in Woodside, Dina placed herself in between Miles Keller, a thirty-one-year-old scion of a publishing dynasty, and Antonio Garcia, an architect who'd worked on their home in Sonoma. Bill was seated across from Dina, while Joan was at the far end.

servers, perhaps, where she might order a bowl of spaghetti and casually surrender her insecurities. When she was little, she used to daydream of a place she named in her head the Satisfaction Café, which had friendly employees and nice food and pretty toys; even as a child, Joan's imagination had not stretched to fantastic outcomes but, rather, a reasonable amount of happiness. It seemed to her incredible that the world's collective adult population, with all its resources and understanding of loneliness, had yet to produce such a space—though in the absence of such, Joan wished she could at least speak to another wife, and specifically a younger one. The May–December pairing was common enough in Bill's crowd, and at some parties Bill and Joan appeared practically the same age, so extreme were other gaps. And yet at such events the wives seemed to shun Joan's attempts at contact—they murmured quick niceties and then edged away, back to their husbands.

Though, wait: Wasn't Inez married? Joan vaguely recalled Bill speaking of her husband, that he had some sort of business with chemicals. And Inez was certainly *young*.

"I've been having some trouble," Joan ventured. "Some trouble, ah, adjusting. To married life." Oh *God*, Joan thought. I said it wrong. She's going to think I want to have an affair!

"I understand." Inez smiled patiently. "Do you hate Bill?"

"No!" Why had Inez thought this? Now Joan was paranoid that she had been emitting some misleading energy—husband-hating energy, as it were. "That's not what I mean."

"Well, I hate Ronald," Inez said. "He's awfully cheap."

"Oh," Joan said stupidly.

Inez rested her chin in her palms. A pear-shaped diamond gleamed from her left ring finger. Her right hand featured a blue sapphire the size of a gumball, which mirrored her necklace and earrings.

Inez caught Joan's glance. "My own," she said, wagging the gumball. "Nearly all my good pieces are from my mother. Ronald would *never*.

He likes people to think he does, though. He wants me to wear them for precisely that reason."

"That's not very nice," Joan said, indignant. "I'm sorry he behaves that way."

"Oh, don't be. I wouldn't want him to buy any jewelry. He's got terrible taste, and he's cheap on top of it all. Even when he does give me something I want, it's rarely actually mine. The house in Napa, for example. Who found it, who renovated the whole goddamn thing? There's not a napkin or chair in there I didn't choose. But it's all in Ron's name, at least on paper."

"That's not fair," Joan murmured.

"True. But there are other entertainments." Inez nodded toward the center of the table. "Even if Ron's a drag, I find ways to make life bearable." Antonio, the architect seated by Dina, returned to Inez a private smile.

While Joan absorbed this, Dina rose and began to walk the table. She passed in a flash of gold—a squeeze on Joan's shoulder, "It's always so *nice* to see you and Bill"—and a square envelope was placed before each guest. From hers Joan pulled out a record, the seven-inch size, and then she recalled that Trevor liked music, it was the one thing she knew about him, that he spent his weekends going to concerts. She spotted him by the bar in a gray suit, laughing with his arms crossed. She hadn't spoken to Trevor at the party, not even to wish him happy birthday. Which was strange, wasn't it? It was his dinner. He was why she was here.

There was a clunk on the table. Dina had dropped another party favor: shiny chrome lighters with *40* engraved in elegant script.

Joan stroked the lighter. It was beautiful, heavy in her hand and sleek. Well, the whole evening was beautiful—the food and wine and flowers. The guests and decor. Though even among the splendor Joan found she preferred the simple round kitchen table in Falling House. Which was her house now too, at least a little each year, which she couldn't help but imagine in literal terms, Bill taking a saw and slicing off a bit of the sun porch, were they to ever divorce. She had managed that much with Nelson, though not before some uneasiness with Bill. "I didn't know you were such a little negotiator," he'd commented, and Joan had thought she might collapse from shame. But she'd held. And the awkwardness—though dreadful—had eventually gone. A lesson for her. Feelings pass. Decisions remain.

"Anyway," Inez said, downing the rest of her champagne. "All we can do is try, isn't that so?"

Yes, Joan agreed. She and Inez had made their choice, and now look how much surrounded them. Waking each morning to the soft light drifting in and great wood beams above; the lush boxwoods guiding her morning path, the stone terrace set by the Japanese maples. It was the sort of existence Joan would have thought pure fantasy only a year earlier, such an immense concentration of beauty as to be unfair, surely impossible. And yet it was possible. She lived it each day. She shouldn't take any of it for granted.

———

So Joan tried. She met the Rommels, Bill's elderly neighbors who always spoke of how much they'd loved Agatha, and gritted her teeth and asked for gardening advice. She attended school fundraisers though she did not have children and was not sure whether she liked them. She volunteered to manage the gift table at Dina Hall's own birthday party months later (it wasn't that Dina actually *cared* about gifts, but it was necessary to keep track for recordkeeping, didn't Joan agree?). And in November, when Joan was invited to the opera, she quickly accepted.

The invite had come from Sue Strong, another wife of one of Bill's friends, a former dental assistant with a fondness for Tahitian pearls. Joan suspected Sue had been prodded by her husband, Randy, into the invitation—Joan had caught Randy observing her at Trevor's birthday with what appeared to be light pity—but an invitation was an invitation. That the opera outing was "ladies only" was intimidating, but it was through such events that Joan believed she'd best integrate. Better to complete difficult tasks right away: after all, she had gone straight to stabbing Milton.

Joan had recently learned how to drive, in a little maroon BMW that had once belonged to Bill. She had all the same enthusiasm for driving as a teenager in fresh possession of a learner's permit, and the morning of the opera, Joan headed to San Francisco. She wished to arrive with plenty of time to first visit Chinatown: the herbal shop where she bought tea and dried mushrooms, the bakery, the jewelry store. When she parked and spotted those familiar apartment balconies on Kearny Street (the stalks of green onion in planters, the stiff movement of sun-dried undershirts on hangers), she was brought nearly to tears. What a relief to stroll alongside the old men pushing shopping carts, children chasing pigeons and throwing poppers—for Joan was rarely with other Chinese people anymore. The only exception was Betty Wong, a casual acquaintance of Bill's, but the woman was never friendly to Joan. Sure, Betty kept her hair dyed jet black and wore embroidered silk coats and brilliant jade bangles whenever she entertained— but she returned Joan's conversation with the curtest of replies, and the only time Joan ever really saw Betty smile was when she was with white people.

After a bowl of shrimp noodle soup at Harbor Place, Joan drove to a parking garage she had mapped near the opera house. She was still early and so browsed the neighborhood. There was a nut shop, a small dark place that reminded her of Chinatown, and she went in and purchased a bag of salted cashews for Bill. She envisioned her return, how she'd tell him what a nice time she'd had with Sue and the rest of the women, presenting him with the cashews at the end. *Just thought of you,* she'd remark. It sounded like something Sue would say, one of those lines like "my mister" or going "on holiday."

Joan dropped off the nuts in her car. The garage was underground, beneath a large lawn with an industrial-looking playground. As Joan ascended back up the stairs, she heard the laughter of children.

Ah, what a wonderful day to be in San Francisco. The sky was clear and bright. The locals, unaccustomed to sunshine in November, had responded with spontaneous urgency; there was a group of men in suits, jackets open, chatting and drinking beers. Next to them a knot of teenagers had stripped to bras and shorts. Joan was dressed for the opera, in a long navy dress and cardigan, and she moved to a shaded spot under a tree. She yawned. The sun caressed her shoulders.

The park up here was surprisingly large, with rows of cypress trees and soft grass. The greenery reminded her of Wen-Bao—on weekends her father had liked to visit such parks, though after a short walk he often spent the remainder of his time dozing on benches. If there was only a lawn, Wen-Bao would stretch out a blanket or just lie directly on the grass. Sometimes, if he were already asleep, Joan would sit next to him and gently press her palm to his back.

She yawned again.

Her cardigan, neatly folded, was a perfectly serviceable, if somewhat flat little pillow. She lay on the grass. The sun swept her face, and the heat again brought to mind Taiwan, the humidity each afternoon as she walked home from school. When Joan arrived at the apartment, she'd sometimes encounter her grandmother tottering in her bound feet. Joan had hated the sight of the feet, which were deformed and even in shoes emitted a foul scent. Contained within her memories, however, the feet were no longer grotesque; Joan couldn't recall the stench, only how her grandmother would slouch forward in the early evening as if her bones were made of jelly. Those peaceful dinners when nothing happened, when Mei was happy and Wen-Bao home, the long table of rosewood, a bowl of rice before her . . .

"Joan?"

Joan opened her eyes. Sue Strong stood over her.

"I *thought* it was you," Sue said. In her stiff pastel dress and matching pumps, she resembled a sturdy pink tent. She shielded her eyes with a hand. "I always park here. Did you take the stairs? They absolutely reek of urine."

"I didn't notice." Joan's mouth was furry from sleep. Had she missed the opera? But no, the sun was still overhead.

"You weren't sleeping, were you?" Sue asked. She moved closer, into the shade.

"I was taking a nap."

"Ah!" Sue fluttered a hand. "I know. It's exhausting, honestly."

What was exhausting? Perhaps Sue meant the drive—when there was traffic, it could be very tiring indeed. Joan floundered for what to say next. "*Tosca.*"

Sue looked startled. "What?"

"The opera. I've been looking forward to it. I looked up the plot at the library." Joan had expected an easy story, something light and airy like a ballerina's costume, and thus had been taken aback by all the murder and suicide.

"Right." Sue straightened. "Well, we ladies did make a vow to attend more opera and ballet. We do the fundraising and have fun choosing our outfits, but who of us actually pays attention once we're there? The arts are important, wouldn't you agree?"

"Should we go?" Joan picked up her bag and attempted to discreetly unfurl her cardigan. "We can make sure we pick good seats."

"The seats are assigned." Sue looked at her strangely. "I'm actually on my way to meet Dina. We have a committee meeting."

"Oh." Joan flushed and looked at her watch. They had another ninety minutes.

"But the seats will be good," Sue said. "Very good. It will be a lovely program."

"So lovely," Joan repeated. She waited until Sue left and then arranged her cardigan back on the grass. She lay down and stared at the sky, the laughter and screams washing over her.

———

"I hear you fell asleep on a bench," Bill said the following week. He had just returned from poker at Randy Strong's.

Joan was on her knees in the kitchen, examining the underside of the sink for the source of a ghostly drip which had taunted her since morning. "It wasn't a bench," Joan said. She came out from under the cabinet. "It was a nice spot of grass. And I used my sweater as a pillow."

"You don't have to go to the opera just to go, you know." Bill sat next to her on the ground. "I could have told you it was boring."

"It wasn't the *opera* that was boring."

"Now, now." Bill laughed. But he usually liked it when she was a little disagreeable, so long as it wasn't directed at him. "The part I don't get is the napping. Why sleep at a park? You do know the area is full of vagrants? You could have been robbed."

"I was tired," Joan said simply. Although it wasn't so simple. Her period was a month late, though she hadn't yet told Bill. After all, it could be anything: weather, sleep, stress, diet.

Although Joan suspected.

Would Bill be happy if she were pregnant? He'd never explicitly stated that he didn't want more children, or rather, he'd hinted at it but then done nothing in the way of trying *not* to have more, practically speaking. A child required parenting: *good* parenting, ideally. And what did Joan know about good parents?

"What do you want to do tomorrow?" Bill scooted closer. "I'm not working, so let's spend the afternoon. Something fun."

Fun, Joan repeated in her head. It was a cute word, so snappy and American.

He clapped his hands. "I've got it. Mini golf. Have you been?"

"No."

"Don't worry, it's nothing like regular golf. You shoot the ball through dragon heads and castles."

"I hope it's easier than ice-skating." Bill had taken her last month to a rink in Cupertino. She had slipped and fallen endlessly while handsome American couples glided past.

"You need to rest more." Bill kneaded her neck, his thumb moving up and down.

"I rest enough."

"I can feel how stressed you are."

"You're older," Joan said shortly. "So you need rest even more than I do."

"Not too old, I hope," Bill said, curling her closer to him. He pressed his mouth to her shoulder.

The next morning, Joan woke later than usual. She moved lazily under the sheets, the soprano's sweeping, wistful aria from *Tosca* stuck in her head. After she dressed, she went to the kitchen and filled the kettle.

"I thought I wouldn't wake you," Bill said. "You looked so peaceful. A very beautiful sloth."

"I was dreaming about a song," Joan said.

"Really? Sing it."

"I can't. I don't know the words."

"We should go to a concert sometime. Trevor and Dina are always asking."

On the stove, the kettle began to whistle, and Bill retrieved her favorite teacup from the cabinet. "What?" Bill asked when he turned. Joan was staring at him.

"Sometimes I wake up," Joan said, "and I can't believe this all began with listening to that man scream at Stanford. I can't believe that's what led to this life, right here with you."

"It's funny, isn't it," Bill agreed. "But isn't it *nice* all of it happened?"

As she sliced an apple, Joan agreed that it was very nice—and in another month she had confirmation of her pregnancy. Bill's reaction wasn't exactly as Joan had hoped: his congratulations was stammered, and for a while she detected a slight frostiness, nothing she could specifically name, but it was in the air all the same. She wondered if he'd expected her to spend the rest of her years doing just as he'd wanted, all her decisions tilted toward his implicit preference. It was a good question, really, but Joan never asked.

CHAPTER NINE

B y the time Joan gave birth, five days over the forty-week mark, she was sick of being pregnant. The nurse took away the baby, and then Joan slept, and when she awoke she was presented with a blue folder with forms to complete.

"Jamie. It's a girl's name," Bill said. "Isn't it?"

"You can call him James," Joan said. But she would never do so. She would always call him Jamie.

Jamie was a fussy baby. When he cried, his entire body went red as he wailed and shook. Joan slept very little, but it was manageable; she suffered, but the suffering was tolerable because she could see an end.

"It's because you're so young," Bill said fondly. To Joan's relief, his earlier reluctance around her pregnancy didn't seem to have lingered; he appeared as excited as a first-time father, though Joan had little idea how first-time fathers should be. Bill marveled at Jamie's tiny hands and feet and taught Joan how to change a diaper. They were sent gifts—silver rattles and soft animal-print shirts and pants that made Joan want to weep for how pure they were. A month after Jamie's arrival, Dina and Trevor visited with a big red fire engine.

"And you're doing well?" Dina asked. She seemed softer toward Joan now that she was a mother; the Halls didn't have children, but Dina seemed to know a lot about them, inquiring how Jamie was feeding and sleeping. Trevor had peeled off upon entering and now sat with Bill in his study.

"Oh, yes. A little tired." Joan blinked blearily at the fire engine. She'd once had a toy like that, she recalled. A blue wooden convertible with a long string attached to the back and wheels that clicked as it was dragged through the courtyard. Someone had bought that toy for her. Somebody, at one point, had cared enough for Joan to bring her that car.

"Is Bill helping? Men are useless at these things."

"Bill has been helpful," Joan said, still staring at the fire engine. "He even changes diapers."

"Oh, well," Dina said, "he's done this before, hasn't he?" Though Dina laughed, it didn't seem to Joan to be a completely *nice* laugh—but then Joan never knew how to interpret Dina. Dina and Bill had been friends for years; they had one of those intimate friendships that can sometimes unnerve spouses.

Joan left to feed Jamie in the nursery. When she emerged, she encountered Trevor leaving the bathroom. He had a fine, angular face with pink cheeks, as if he'd just come in from the sun. "Do you need help bringing the fire engine to the nursery?" he asked.

"No, no, I'm fine," Joan said, although it was quite heavy—the engine was metal and had a child-size seat. She felt milk dripping into her bra and crossed her arms. "I'm doing some sorting later. I'll take care of it then."

"It's a wonderful thing, to have a baby. You should rest. No one cares if the house is clean. They care that you're doing all right."

Why, he's *nice*, Joan realized. Or at least he can be, when he feels like it. She had the sudden understanding that all big men like Trevor and Bill were once little boys; that they had been babies, just like Jamie.

After the Halls departed, Joan washed the dishes and moved the fire engine to the nursery. She stroked its cool, smooth metal; it was a finer toy by magnitudes than the convertible she'd had in Taiwan. She wished, rather impossibly, that she had brought it with her to California. Joan could imagine giving it to Jamie one day when he was older. See, she could say. Here is my special toy, just like yours; I had people who loved me, just like you do.

In the afternoon, when Bill was out, Joan retrieved the cookie tin that held her old phone book and passport and went into the office.

"Is it a boy?" Mei asked. This was the most important question.

"Yes." Joan looked to her side. She had set up a small bassinet which she could move from room to room. Jamie was awake but calm, staring at the ceiling.

"Your husband is pleased?"

Joan took this as an inquiry as to whether she was married. "Yes."

"Where is he from?"

"He isn't from Taiwan." Joan cleared her throat. "He isn't Chinese at all, actually. He's American."

From the silence that followed, Joan knew she'd misjudged how poorly Mei would take this news. Growing up in Taiwan, Joan had often heard the saying that only those women who couldn't find a Chinese man had to marry another race—and white men in particular were known for their inability to judge quality or looks. They couldn't discern if your cooking was flavorful or if your family was decent; they couldn't tell if the university you attended was well ranked or even existed at all. In short: they didn't know *anything*.

"How old is he?" Mei finally asked.

"Older."

"How old?"

"Fifty-three."

"He must be rich," Mei said. "I can't imagine why otherwise. If you've already shamed yourself, you should have been sending us money."

Joan had in fact been planning to visit Western Union at some point; she'd been waiting for when she could leave Jamie for a few hours. "Is that all you care about? Money?"

"I hope you understand that you are selling yourself," Mei said, unbothered. "What I'm saying is, I'm just not sure if you're any *good* at it."

This time it was Joan who hung up. She waited a short while by the phone for the call she knew wouldn't arrive, and then went to the cookie tin and retrieved the checkbook for the bank account she'd opened upon moving to California. She kept her checkbook balanced, and the last figure was the remaining tally of all she'd saved from Lotus Garden. Joan crossed a line through the figure and netted the sum to zero. She would send her parents this much, Joan decided. But nothing more. Nothing of Bill's. She wondered if her parents would speak to her again once the money stopped.

Jamie made a noise, a small rustling sound, and Joan went to him. He'd spat up, and she ran a washcloth over his bib. The bib was blue, the same blue as her wooden convertible, and suddenly Joan recalled that the car she'd loved so much had actually been Alfred's, which had then been passed to her brothers. It had gone to her only after no one else wanted it.

———

Jamie cried to feed every two hours. He refused a bottle, and so at night Joan woke and fed him from the breast. Afterward he required rocking and humming before being placed back in his crib—if she tried to set him down too early, he would release a powerful scream. In the mornings, sometimes Joan was so tired she would fall asleep while brushing her teeth. She began to go to bed right after dinner.

"When are you getting a nanny?" Bill asked.

Joan didn't respond. She had not thought they would get a nanny. After all, she had no job herself.

"Of course you'll get one," Bill said. "Agatha had two. Besides, how would we ever go out?"

First Joan placed ads in the Chinese newspapers. *Seeking nanny. Live-in OK. No cooking required.* But she received few responses. Next she pasted flyers at the Chinese supermarkets, which met with more success—she received a steady string of calls. Her first hire, a twenty-four-year-old named Wendy who claimed to be from Shanghai, stayed only a few months; Joan realized Wendy was stealing. The second one also stole; Joan confronted her when she discovered silverware missing. This time Joan asked *why* she stole.

"You have so much more," the woman said. She was from Guangzhou, in her fifties, with thin lips and mottled skin. Joan had hired her knowing she would speak terrible Mandarin and that it would have to be Joan who taught Jamie.

Her third attempt, Joan tried to solve the problem in advance, with both care and money. She interviewed seven candidates before deciding on her hire, a Cantonese woman named Li Zhou who preferred to be called Linda. Joan took the amount Linda requested per month and doubled it and gave her every other Friday off. Linda *also* stole, however, and was the most profligate—when asked why she had taken not only a coral necklace but also a set of leather-bound books of Chinese poetry, Linda only cried and beat at her lap. The next morning, she was gone.

"I don't get why they all steal," Joan said. "I'm paying so much more than other families already."

"I'm sure they don't *all* steal," Bill said. "I liked Linda. So what if she wanted some books? We should have just given them to her."

Bill was right, in his own way, though Joan knew it wouldn't have stopped with only the books— for she understood what really motivated these women was their belief that they were just like her, that nothing separated them except for bad luck in an arbitrary universe, and in taking from her they were simply evening the score.

I'm tired, Joan thought. But I can't tolerate a *thief* in the house.

Thus Jamie continued to spend his days with Joan. He could now sit unsupported and was particularly fond of a metal truck with an attached trailer which had once belonged to Theo. "Vroom vroom," Joan would chant, pushing it back and forth on the carpet. "Vroom vroom!"

In the afternoons Joan would walk outside with Jamie in her arms to examine Bill's cars. Bill had four he kept in meticulous condition, including a vintage Jaguar and a Porsche. He was precious about his vehicles and had a mechanic visit once a month to check their condition. The mechanic, Gene Sugimoto, was ethnically Japanese and had come from Peru. His wife, Patty, who was Japanese as well, prepared elaborate lunch boxes for Gene to bring to work. She also made her own beef jerky, which Gene occasionally gave to Bill. One afternoon when Bill came out to discuss the Jaguar, which had developed a slight rattling sound, Gene handed him a box of jerky, neatly labeled as medium spicy.

"From my wife," Gene said.

"Oh, thank you." Bill said, taking the package. "Does she like to cook?"

"Not really." Gene sat on the stone bench outside the garage. "But she's not working now and has too much time on her hands. She's the type who always needs to be doing."

"Right," Bill said. He sat next to Gene. The box was delicately wrapped, with red rice paper, and Bill opened it and ate a piece. It was delicious, as it always was, and he chewed as he thought.

———

"I don't know," Joan said when Bill shared his idea. "Has the woman ever been a nanny before?" The *woman*, Joan thought. I don't even know her name!

"Gene said she babysits all the time for their relatives."

"I don't know her."

"You didn't know any of the other nannies before you hired them. And Gene's wife is wonderful. A truly respectable woman."

I bet he hasn't even met her, Joan thought.

The following month, when Gene arrived for his appointment with Bill, he brought his wife. Patty was in her forties, with long hair and perfect English (she was third generation—her parents and she herself had been briefly interned); she was also the first Japanese person besides Gene whom Joan had met in America. Joan had grown up hearing countless stories of Japanese atrocities in World War II, and most of the Chinese students she knew had vowed never to purchase a Japanese vehicle.

"This is Jamie," Joan said, tilting him in her arms so Patty could see. She wished she could say it was due to Patty's entrance that Jamie was screaming, but it was just a bad day; his tearfulness and bawling had begun that morning. "I'm afraid I'm doing something wrong." As Joan tried to hush him, she spotted a large splotch of spit-up on her sleeve. "The nannies keep leaving, and he keeps crying." Joan could smell the stain's sourness on her; she felt as if *she* were about to cry.

Patty was dressed in loose flowy layers, a white skirt and peasant top. "How old is he?"

"Six months."

Patty held out her arms, and after a moment's hesitation Joan passed Jamie over to her. Patty rubbed his back. "Oh, honey. You're not doing anything wrong. It's just gas."

"Are you sure?"

"Yes."

Joan watched Patty rock Jamie. She cradled his head with her palm and swung him energetically—perhaps too energetically, Joan thought, though before she could tell Patty this, Jamie released a loud burp. He stopped crying. "You see," Patty said, "gas. Gas is usually the problem."

Joan was suddenly afraid. "You aren't going to leave, are you?"

"Why would I leave? I just got here."

How quickly events turn, how fast affection can wane or bloom. Days earlier Joan hadn't wanted Patty to come at all; now she was terrified of living without her.

"Gene told me you need someone to work with you. Someone to help with the baby," Patty said, still rocking Jamie. In fact, Gene had not said so much; he'd simply arrived home one afternoon and stated in his usual maddening straightforward manner that "Mr. Bill might need help." Help for *what*? Patty had replied. She wasn't going to make beef jerky and bento boxes for some rich white man all day! But she worked out that Bill had a new child (why Gene hadn't mentioned this earlier, Patty didn't know—she loved babies); even then Patty had been hesitant. She and Gene were unable to have their own children, which Patty accepted with the stolid grace she did most disappointments, and through the years she had accepted babysitting jobs for relatives and friends. In deciding on such jobs, Patty had since determined that it wasn't only the temperament of the child which was important but also the parent—one cannot gauge a child, without first gauging the *parent*.

"She's Chinese," Gene had added. "Mr. Bill's wife now."

Which was a detail that had interested Patty enough to visit.

Joan scuttled to the couch. She watched Patty and Jamie as they made loops around the room, Patty murmuring softly. Joan felt both relieved and fretful at the sight of her son so content in another's arms. "I want to be a good mother. But then I feel tired, and I don't get around to any of the big plans I had of being one."

"That's normal. You need help."

"I try to get help. But people keep leaving."

There was a stretch of quiet. Joan had the strange feeling Patty was actively thinking, mulling over a topic or question. Eventually she came and sat next to Joan on the couch. "People are jerks," she said.

CHAPTER TEN

Occasionally Patty slept over. There was a cottage on the property with a bathroom and kitchenette; when Joan and Bill had late outings, Patty would put Jamie to bed and then spend the night. Sometimes Gene would also stay, and in the morning Patty would help Joan with breakfast while Gene and Bill went out for fresh orange juice and good coffee.

Some afternoons, after Joan had been in the garden, she would return to the kitchen and find Jamie helping Patty roll rice balls for lunch. There would be cut seaweed on the counter, scrambled egg pressed and sliced into thin strips, fresh air from the open windows, and Joan would experience such immense pleasure that she thought she could drown in it. Move in, Joan wanted to beg. Please, stay with us always! She knew Patty was unhappy with her current living arrangements: she and Gene shared a house with Gene's mother and brother, as well as the brother's wife and children, in a compressed multigenerational arrangement. At the very least, Joan wished to offer them permanent use of the cottage. This was not possible, however, as at times Bill's family would visit, for which the cottage was required.

———

At least once a year, the Lauders gathered for a major holiday. The family defined only two holidays as major: Thanksgiving and Christmas. Come April, the negotiations began over who would host what—this process was decades old and had always been managed by the women, Bill's sister Bridget and sister-in-law Gillian. They never included Joan, though whether this was deliberately to exclude or they assumed she wasn't interested, Joan wasn't sure. Each summer she and Bill were informed whether they would host a holiday and, if so, which one. This year, Bill's family was visiting for Thanksgiving.

"What is he, five now?" Bridget asked about Jamie when they gathered the first evening. It was the meal the Tuesday before Thanksgiving, which the family referred to as a casual dinner. Joan had learned by now that the difference between a "casual" and a "festive" Lauder dinner was the former required one fewer meat dish; otherwise it was still held in the dining room with a dress code and copious alcohol. Bridget was tall and broad-shouldered and, despite her frame, often stuffed herself into narrow floral dresses; she seemed to Joan the sort of healthy American who should be off chopping firewood or riding horses, although she'd never seen Bridget doing either.

"He's two," Joan said. She wondered if this was a comment on her parenting. The Lauders did not believe in separate children's seating, and thus instead of eating at his low round table, as he usually did, Jamie sat propped up on pillows on one of the adult chairs next to Joan, while she kept her arm suspended in midair across his chest so he wouldn't fall. Joan had not served Jamie the adults' food, a practice she knew Bridget also disapproved of; he had eaten a pork bun and a bowl of steamed egg.

"Two!" Bridget reared back her head, as if children possibly appeared younger from farther distances. "Goodness, I don't remember my own being so large. Did you know he was two?" She looked to Theo.

"Yes, I was aware," Theo said tonelessly, staring at his brandy. Bill's son had arrived late the night before and gone directly into his father's study, from which he'd emerged with a check of a sum Joan was curious about but would never ask. Joan knew Theo usually called Agatha for money, as every few months Agatha would then call Bill to pay her back.

"I suppose it's just been so long since I had them," Bridget said. (Bridget had two adult children, both estranged, whom she never spoke of.) "It's funny, isn't it, a new generation."

"There were quite a lot at our hotel in Oahu," Juliet interjected. She had recently returned from her honeymoon. "Remind me to specify adult-only resorts on our next trip."

"*Tons* of Japanese," Juliet's husband, Paul, said. "So many they actually had sake on the room service menu."

"Paul guzzled a bottle our second night."

"I have some sake in the kitchen, if you like," Joan offered.

"Mmm!" Paul said. "Me likey sake!" Joan held her breath that he wouldn't pull his eyes into slits, as he had a penchant for crude racial imitations.

"Oh, for God's sake," Bridget muttered.

After dessert, the family moved to the living room. Joan opened the doors to the garden; she had rearranged the furniture so guests could easily move in and out. Juliet and Paul dropped onto a couch, her head on his shoulder, while Theo began to remove books from a shelf, setting the hardcovers on the ground.

"Can I help you with something?" Joan asked.

"No," Theo said shortly. He continued to stack books. Joan looked at Bill, who raised his eyebrows.

Once all the books were removed, Theo lifted the ledge on which they had been set. From the space underneath, he removed a bottle of bourbon.

"I forgot that was there," Bill marveled. He handed Joan a glass of port.

"Well, I certainly didn't," Theo said, and Juliet laughed. Jamie toddled to the bottle, interested in its conjuring. "Jamie," Joan called softly. She took his hand and led him to his room, to escape the next rounds of drinking.

Now: it wasn't like Joan was a teetotaler. Over her marriage to Bill, she'd slowly built her tolerance for alcohol, developing a particular fondness for champagne. The way the Lauders consumed, however, was on a different level: they drank and drank, with no discernible impact or joy, until they passed out. The year prior, Bridget's husband, Martin, had vomited onto Henry's new Turkish rug, which caused a minor uproar; Martin had stumbled about, shouting that Henry could simply get a new rug down the street since everyone knew he didn't actually purchase it in Ephesus, like he claimed, but rather some seedy local emporium. At such times Joan didn't understand why the Lauders made such a big deal about holidays; they always seemed so miserable throughout.

Joan read to Jamie in her lap until he began to yawn and rub his eyes. She then tucked him into bed. Once he fell asleep, Joan lay on the carpet, occasionally half rising to sip at the snifter of port she'd brought to the room.

There came from the hall the sound of footsteps and soft murmurs. "Where's Joan? Is she sleeping?" Joan recognized the voice as that of Henry, Bill's younger brother. Henry always wore a sport jacket, even in the mornings, and was prone to immature jokes which he bookended with a high, reedy laugh.

"He's big for two, isn't he?" This was Martin, Bridget's husband.

"The Chinese aren't known for being *large*."

"The thing I don't get is why Bill allowed it. He always said he was done after the twins."

"You've got to admire her persuasive powers. By popping out the little guy, she's set for life."

"You know," Henry said musingly, "I'd have thought Evie would have made a go at it. She never struck me as the self-sufficient sort."

"Oh, Evie must be *steaming*."

There was a burst of laughter and then the voices faded. Joan reached for the port and downed the rest in a gulp. She didn't swallow, but instead lay on the carpet with the alcohol in her mouth and let it burn the back of her throat.

Oh, go on, no point in holding back—there was no face to save, no one could see her. Joan swished the port in her mouth once more and then, finally, swallowed. The waves broke. And the shame—oh yes, it came. And it rolled. And rolled. Since her first encounters with Bill's family, Joan had been uncertain how they saw her. The Lauders never treated her with anything less than pleasantness, and yet she had always detected from their interactions an undertone of transience. There have been others before you, was how she received the message. And there will be others after.

The snifter in her hand was smooth and cool, of heavy crystal. After the wedding, Joan had been surprised to receive from Theo and Juliet a set of Baccarat glassware. She had prominently displayed the flutes and tumblers in the open cabinets in the kitchen until Bill informed her, somewhat embarrassed, that this had actually been his wedding crystal with Agatha—the pieces had gone to Agatha in the divorce and apparently at some point been appropriated by Juliet and Theo. Why, they must have meant it to be cruel, Joan had thought. But wasn't it also Joan's fault? She hadn't thought of Juliet and Theo's feelings when she married Bill, mostly because Bill hadn't. They were adults, he told Joan. Well, yes, Joan might have said. But they are still your children. They will always be your children.

Next to Joan, Jamie whimpered in his sleep. He flung out a hand, where it banged against the bed frame. Joan rose and gently placed his hand back underneath his blanket. She had recently purchased a pack of glow-in-the-dark stars which she'd arranged on his ceiling. The glow was fading; they only ever lasted a little while, no matter how much light you gave them in advance.

When Joan returned to the living room, Bill waved her over. "Where were you?" he asked. Next to Bill sat Juliet and Paul. Paul's face was red and sweaty, and he was kicking the ottoman, lightly yet steadily, with the tip of his oxford.

"I was putting Jamie to bed."

"Is he asleep now?"

"Yes." Joan poured herself a glass of Sancerre. "He wanted to hear some stories. From the *Frog and Toad* book."

"You were gone for so long. I was about to look for you."

"Bedtime stories. That's nice." Paul raised a glass in her direction. "Mommy speak good English!"

"Please shut up," Joan said. For a second her vision went gray and there was a roaring in her ears. She finished her glass without looking at anyone and went to bed.

———

She was drunk, was what it was, Joan said to Bill after.

"Is that so," Bill said. She hadn't bothered turning to face him when he climbed into bed, even though she was still awake, which she'd never done before. She normally greeted him. He stared at her head, her black hair flowing over the pillow. After a moment he reached out and stroked it.

CHAPTER ELEVEN

Besides Bridget and Henry, Bill had a third sibling, Misty. She was the youngest by thirteen years and, as such, had been raised essentially as an only child. Misty was the only Lauder sibling not to follow the rules for holiday gatherings: she appeared when she wanted and almost always without warning. She never hosted and did not bring presents for the host. In nearly all respects, she was not like the other Lauders.

Joan's first encounter with Misty had been two years earlier, at Henry's house in Connecticut. Misty had appeared on Christmas Day, citing a mix-up at the airport (no one could figure out what that meant), and brought with her a young Mexican man with gleaming teeth who refused to set down his guitar. They ate very little and left right after dinner; there was relief when they departed, and plus the rest of the siblings would now have something to talk about: conjecture about what Misty was doing exactly, at the current moment, to fuck up her life.

Joan had not expected Misty that year for Thanksgiving. Misty and Bill had the largest age gap and the least contact—they spoke at most once a year. And yet on Thanksgiving morning, when Joan woke and went outside, she found Misty already by the pool, spreading lotion on her legs as she sat on a deck chair.

"The gate was open, so I let myself in," Misty said. She had changed her hair from the last time Joan saw her—it was light blond now and parted in the middle. She extended a hand toward the water, as if inviting Joan to use her own pool.

It was strange for Joan to swim with someone watching. She was paranoid about Jamie being attracted to the water and thus swam in the early morning before he woke. Joan's favorite moment was piercing the surface, the cold shaking her awake. After a second's hesitation, Joan waded in. She swam thirty laps and then got out and wrapped the towel around her.

"Is the water cold?" Misty asked.

"Oh no. Quite nice, once you get used to it."

"Great." Misty yanked off her shirt. She wore a bikini underneath, and immediately Joan could see Misty's breasts were larger than last time, significantly so. Previously Misty's body had been thin, hipless, flat—she moved with gazelle-like grace, and favored necklines that dipped provocatively low. Now each of Misty's breasts was the size of a smallish cantaloupe. Joan struggled to look away, as the image was both perfect and confusing.

"Nice, right?" Misty asked. Her hair shimmered against the sun, and as she lifted her arm, Joan could make out thin pink scar lines below her elbow. Misty winked and leaped into the pool.

———

Misty's breasts caused a commotion among the Lauders. It was an unspoken family rule that one did not acquire (obvious) plastic surgery before fifty; it was on the long list of Lauder taboos, along with split ends, tattoos, tube tops for women, and cravats for men. If the breasts had been a bright light to Joan, they were like a nuclear waste site to the other Lauders—they couldn't even *look* at them without seeming to incur personal damage.

"I don't know why she got them," remarked Bridget the next morning to no one in particular. Behind her was Henry, who was noisily making coffee. "Have you ever seen breasts like that?" Bridget asked Joan. "I wouldn't think they're common in China, are they? Isn't it the opposite, that they used to be bound? Or was that feet?"

"I'm not sure," Joan said. She didn't want to say that it was both breasts *and* feet, as that would invite more commentary.

"I think it's fine," said Henry. Henry liked to disagree with Bridget; Bill said this was just their relationship, as Henry was younger. "She's got herself some big ol' knockers."

"Don't be immature," Bridget said. She glanced at Gillian, Henry's wife. "Is he always this crude?"

"Yes," Gillian said happily. She was forever concerned that Bridget didn't like her; here was her chance to build a bridge with Bridget.

"Who paid for them?" Bridget asked.

"She did." Henry poured himself coffee. "Or maybe her boyfriend, what's-his-face."

"She's not still living with him."

"I don't know. She asked if she could bring him to Maine next year."

"And you said no."

"I said we'd think about it." Henry stirred sugar into his coffee. "It's always a pain to manage Misty's dramas."

"You don't do anything to manage them. Was it you who had to send thousands in traveler's checks to Madrid? Or what about when she bought that motorcycle?"

"Well, I do *listen*," Henry said. From outside, Misty waved.

———

Only Misty stayed past Saturday. She didn't say how long she'd be around, though Joan wasn't concerned, as Misty on her own was more manageable than the rest of the collective Lauders. So far in her cleanup,

Joan had discovered wine stains (carpet, marble), as well as a missing Christofle vase (Theo, taken as a Christmas gift for Charlotte).

"Still, it'd be good for her to inform us of her planned departure," Bill grumbled. He was often grouchy after holidays; he needed time, he said, to recover from his family.

"I think she'll leave soon." Joan looked out the window toward the pool. Misty liked to swim in the late morning, marveling at the warm weather in November. Afterward she would lie with her back to the sun on a lounger, where she often fell asleep until Joan called her for lunch.

"You never know," Bill said. "She always does the least desirable thing in any situation."

"Not always," Joan said.

After lunch, Misty asked Joan if she wanted to go shopping in San Francisco. "Retail therapy," Misty said.

"Sure." Joan liked shopping.

In Union Square, Misty strolled the streets with familiarity, exclaiming when a boutique had moved or closed. At Saks, Misty went first to the fur department, where she tried on a coat of silver fox.

"Do you like it?" she asked, looking at herself in the mirror.

Joan petted the arm. "It's soft."

Misty examined herself from the back. "Maybe I don't need it. Vegas is scorching." Joan hadn't realized Misty was living in Las Vegas. Had she said so? Or was she moving there?

"But people do still wear fur." Misty adjusted the collar. "You think Bill would be mad if I charged it to your card?"

"He would notice," Joan said. "I don't usually buy fur coats."

"Well, you should," Misty said frankly.

On the next floor, Joan went to the sales rack, where she found a floral cardigan on deep discount with red lace along the collar. It was pretty, but when she tried it on she could only picture Helen Wu, the imperious wife of the owner of Lotus Garden, who had tight permed hair and barked at the staff if she thought they gave away too many napkins. How did some people dress so well? Misty, for example, wore a chunky gold necklace, a long navy coat, and a black dress with brown leather sandals. The outfit didn't necessarily convey elegance but did show she had money, which had its own effect and power. Perhaps sensing the same, a saleswoman named Penny had latched on to Misty on the second floor; Penny now followed them up the escalator.

"This is our European level," Penny said. "Here we've got all the French, the British, the Italians."

Misty went straight to the new arrivals. She asked if they had a brand, a blur of syllables Joan couldn't discern.

"Oh, *yes.*" It was clear Penny considered the question proof of exceptional taste.

Misty chose some pieces and entered a dressing room. She took so long that Penny drifted to the other side of the floor, where she stood chatting with the cashier.

Finally Misty emerged in a light blue dress. "It's so hard to find clothes. I hate how everything looks on my body." She waited expectantly.

"You look very good," Joan said.

The dress was fitted, and Misty twisted and pulled at the jersey. She adjusted her breasts so gratuitously that Joan felt it would be impolite to look elsewhere—it was like when Jamie brought over his finger paintings, using both hands to point at the colors.

Misty smiled at Joan in the mirror. "I had them done in the spring. Recovery was a bitch. Did they talk about it?"

"Not much."

"I'm sure Bridget said something."

"Maybe a little. My English, I don't always understand."

"Oh, I think you do understand." Misty sat in the chair opposite Joan. "I think you understand quite a lot. And I understand you. I didn't feel that way about Bill's other wives. You know about all of them, right?"

"Yes. I am aware."

"You shouldn't let Bridget or the rest make you feel bad, you know, that you're his fourth. They're just like that—their whole thing is figuring out what makes them better than everyone else and then talking about it. They can't handle not feeling like they're on top. Hey, can I see that ring?"

Startled by the abrupt change in subject, Joan lifted her right hand, on which a small gold panther leaped over her index finger. Misty ran her thumb over the metal. "From Bill?"

"Yes," Joan said uncomfortably. "My birthday."

"Nice. I'd love to see your collection."

"Oh, it's very small."

Misty released her arm. "You know what's creepy? Just now I got a feeling I was going to die." She made a throat-slitting motion. "I get it all the time. I guess I'm scared. At night, sometimes I remember I'm going to die one day, and then I can't sleep anymore."

"You're very young." Joan didn't believe in telling people they would never die. It was what everyone wanted to hear, but it just wasn't true.

"It's why I did my boobs. I said: Misty, you've always wanted to look a certain way, so why don't you? It's the same with these clothes. Why *not* feel good, is the question. And I do feel good. I'm feeling incredible, actually. The death feeling is gone."

"Why don't you buy something and then we can go." Joan was beginning to tire of shopping. She guessed at how much the blue number Misty was wearing might be, if it was worth buying it for her and potentially annoying Bill in exchange for getting to leave the store. "Do you like that dress? I saw they also have it in red."

Misty didn't respond. Instead she hopped from her chair and came near, so close that her head almost touched Joan's. Joan could make out the individual glitter of Misty's eye shadow; she smelled Misty's perfume, which was something like a spring day, orange and lilies of the valley. "I have a secret," Misty said slowly.

"Oh?" Joan wasn't sure she wanted to hear. She liked gossip but suspected Misty might drop something awful. And what if Misty asked for something? Money or a favor from Bill. What if Bill was right, that they'd been too welcoming, and now Misty was going to ask to live with them indefinitely?

"I'm having a baby," Misty said.

CHAPTER TWELVE

Misty showed Joan the bump in the dressing room. She had to jut out her stomach for Joan to discern the curve; Misty estimated she was four months along. Though she wasn't certain. The identity of the father was not resolved, as she wasn't in contact with any of the possibilities.

"That doesn't mean I was dumped, to be clear." Misty ran her hand along her stomach. "Things just didn't work out. There's only one I think would make a decent father, anyway. Now, maybe I say this because he already is a father. But I don't actually *like* him."

"We should have noticed," Joan said to Bill that evening. "She's been in that swimsuit this whole time."

"We must have been distracted," Bill said. "By her huge knockers." Like his siblings, he had the habit of resorting to childish behavior when stressed.

"I don't think she's ready," Joan said.

"Ready for what? A baby? Is she keeping it?"

"She says she's going to give birth and then decide."

"Oh, *that* sounds like a great plan. I wonder who the father is," Bill mused. "She didn't say?"

"I don't think she knows." After Saks, they'd had to stop on the street so Misty could use a pay phone. The call had begun with seductive whispers and ended with Misty hysterically screaming—Joan had been forced to take her to the Taj for a drink of water, where she had ordered a martini at the bar. And this was Misty "feeling incredible"!

"Still," Bill said, "there could be worse mothers."

"That's right," Joan agreed. There were various ways one could be a bad mother—endless ways, really.

They heard Misty enter the house, as she often did at night, to bring food back to the cottage. The door slammed, and Joan held her breath. Sometimes Jamie would wake up when there were loud noises and come dragging his blanket into their room. He was afraid of monsters, he said.

"It seems awfully unfair," Joan said. "Not to try to arrange anything in advance. For the baby."

"There is no baby," Bill said. "Right now it's just Misty."

———

Misty left the next morning. This wasn't surprising, as her visits were usually brief. What was a surprise was when Misty returned four months later. She was driven to the house by a man in a white convertible. Joan and Jamie came upon them on their way home from the library.

"This is Johnny," Misty said. She pronounced his name breathlessly: Jeooohny. Johnny acknowledged Joan with a nod. He had hair nearly to his neck and one of those melty-looking faces with thin lips and a wispy beard. Misty exited the car, and Joan saw she was waddling in that way of heavily pregnant women. "We're on a road trip," she announced.

"From Mexico City," Johnny added.

Is he *staying?* Joan wondered. But minutes later, Johnny drove off; he was going to visit friends, he said.

"What's she doing here?" Bill asked Joan as she prepared dinner. "And no notice?"

"We have plenty of food." Joan scooped some spaghetti and meatballs into a bowl and added a liberal dusting of Parmesan. Misty had pronounced the steamed fish Joan had originally prepared for that evening "nausea-inducing." It wasn't that she wasn't familiar with Asian food, Misty said. It was just she currently found a lot of it gross.

Bill knelt on the floor, where Jamie was playing with a toy tractor. Bill set a box of crackers on the ground. "This is a bale of hay," he said. "Try and pick it up with the grapple."

"Fun," Jamie said. He pushed the tractor into the cracker box, knocking both against the wall.

"Or you could just do that," Bill said. "That's the nice thing about being a kid. Kids can act on impulses. Adults, on the other hand, should manage them. That's how we have a functioning society."

"I don't think our society is so functional," Joan said.

"That's a Massey Ferguson tractor, by the way, son."

"Massey Ferguson," Jamie repeated in his babyish way.

"I thought her boyfriend was returning soon," Bill said, standing. "What is soon?"

Joan didn't know. After dessert, she put fresh towels in the cottage. Johnny didn't return that night.

The next morning, Misty ate breakfast and then sprawled on her usual lounger by the pool. "Is that a cocktail?" Bill asked Joan as he splashed leftover coffee into the sink. Joan hurried behind him to rinse the porcelain so it wouldn't stain.

"I don't think so." She looked out the window. "Probably water."

"It's pink."

"Maybe juice." They watched Misty light a cigarette. Patty, who had been outside with Jamie, scurried him away.

"I don't think she's supposed to do that," Bill said. "Smoke."

"You can tell her," Joan said. She herself was feeling woozy; she sat and tried to massage the pressure from her brain. After her head cleared, she went out and joined Jamie and Patty in the sunshine.

———

That night Joan served steak and fries, a favorite of both Bill and Misty. After remarking that it sure would be nice to have mustard and pickles, Misty asked Bill for money.

"Nope," Bill said. "No gifts. You're an adult."

"This isn't a gift. It's an investment. Johnny has a great opportunity. Franchise-related."

"What is 'franchise related'? It's either a franchise or it's not."

"It's a restaurant," Misty answered sulkily.

"You're talking about, what, a McDonald's?"

Joan escaped to the kitchen to fetch Misty's condiments. When she returned, she set down the jars as quietly as possible. Even Jamie seemed to sense the conversation had soured; he was looking anxiously between the ends of the table in the way he'd been taught to cross a busy street.

"What sort of rate of return are you and Johnny offering on my investment?" Bill asked.

"Now you're deliberately being vulgar," Misty said. She started to cry.

"I can't speak to you when you're like this," Bill said. "I can't stand it when someone won't have a productive conversation."

"We just need some funding. You have a lot. I have less. It would be very helpful. In my situation."

"Oh, so it's the *baby* who needs the franchise."

Misty shoved back her chair from the table. She may have intended to storm out, but given her size, she was reduced to shuffling at a normal pace.

Bill resumed cutting his steak. He pointed his fork at Joan. "I hope you aren't thinking what I think you might be."

"I don't know," Joan said faintly.

"I write her checks every year. For her birthday. For Christmas. She's thirty-nine years old, for Christ's sake."

"I'm thirty-eight, you shit!" Misty screamed from the front of the house. Jamie put his hands over his ears.

After dinner, Joan found Misty inside the cottage. "Johnny said he was coming," Misty said. She was already packing. "He left a card game to get me." It was clear she considered this a significant victory.

"You can always stay here."

"No way. The only reason I came was because I was getting self-conscious with Johnny in the car. He hates how I look. And who can blame him? *I* hate how I look." Misty swept her toiletries from the top of the dresser into her bag. "I don't want the baby. I've said it and no one listens. They just say I'll change my mind. But I'm not going to."

"There are options," Joan said hesitantly.

"You wanted yours," Misty bleated. "Didn't you?"

"Yes." Although that was too rosy a picture; it had not been a continuous line of certainty. There'd been times when she and Bill fought—nothing important, everyday squabbles—after which Joan had wept bitterly over her distended belly, convinced she must be the loneliest person in the world. Flabbergasted that she was tethering herself forever to this person through the creation of life—how foolish she was! How utterly stupid, to believe karma would just go on unfurling options before you, opportunities to start over, to erase and renew. But such agonized moments had passed, as all moments do – and as Joan met Misty's shiny, bloated gaze, she sensed this was where she should emphasize her more motherly qualities, as it were. "I had a lot of energy. They say energy is important, that it foretells very much. It is a Chinese saying." Joan also knew Misty liked Chinese sayings.

"Well, I don't have energy. I don't have any feelings at all. And I don't have any money either."

"I'm sorry Bill didn't give you any."

"He thinks he's so tough. He doesn't get that some people just aren't built for making loads of cash. It isn't how I *think*!" Misty inhaled. "I should have scheduled an abortion. Now it's too late."

"You won't hurt yourself or the baby," Joan said quickly.

"No. I only know it isn't how things ought to be." Misty gripped her head between her hands. "Do you understand what I'm saying? I refuse to accept that one mistake means I've got to change the whole rest of my life."

Joan continued to rub Misty's back. Her hand moved mechanically up and down, the dot of an idea thrumming at a higher and higher pitch in her head.

Yes, Joan said. She understood.

CHAPTER THIRTEEN

Misty didn't return any of Joan's calls. Joan waited until a month after what she calculated was the due date and sent a check inside a congratulations card. Misty had recently sparred with the rest of the Lauders, after she'd given their phone numbers to Johnny, who'd called each to solicit investments for an import/export business out of Vietnam. He could get his hands on some excellent chairs out of Hai Phong, Johnny said, if only he had the funds.

"We *have* chairs," Bridget said that Christmas at their home in Ross. "Who needs to keep buying them? Why would someone think they could make an entire business out of chairs?"

"There are furniture stores," Joan said. She thought Bridget was being a little ridiculous. "There are couch stores. There are kitchen appliance stores."

"Surely Misty doesn't think she should open a *store*," Martin said. "Being good at spending money in shops doesn't mean you'd actually be skilled at operating one. I like steak. Does that mean I should become a chef?"

Joan didn't know why she defended Misty. Misty still hadn't answered any of her calls; Joan's check had been cashed but otherwise no contact made. Joan didn't even know the child's name. Boy or girl? Good sleeper or bad? Surely the baby wasn't abandoned. Surely Misty wasn't capable of the gut-clenching neglect one occasionally spotted in tabloids: an empty crib, dirty clothes on the ground, a pacifier on the street—if only someone had raised the alarm!

"Is she neglectful to the point of being a baby murderer? I don't think so," Bill said when Joan pressed. "Although you never know."

"It's a child! They can't speak. They can't call for help."

"You sure are worried about this," Bill said.

Weeks later, Joan was outside with Jamie, this time admiring the camellia bushes, when a car slowed out front. A woman with blond hair was driving. Misty was on the passenger side, a baby in her lap.

"This is Ashley," Misty said, climbing out. "She's my nanny."

Nanny! Joan stood and took off her sun hat. It did not escape her that Misty had already managed to procure a nanny when her own search had been so difficult. Ashley was young, with brown eyes and small hands and feet; in many ways, she resembled a miniature Misty. Another surprise: Joan had not thought Misty would hire an attractive nanny.

"This is Joan," Misty said to Ashley. "She's married to my brother. She's also one of my best friends. And here's the little one," she added, thrusting her arms toward Joan.

The baby was crying. "Wait, wait," Joan said. She ran and retrieved from the house a dangling plastic rainbow that used to entertain Jamie. On her way out, she stopped in Bill's office and wrote Misty another check, which she stuck in a manila envelope. Bill wasn't home, and Joan figured that even if Misty spent the money irresponsibly, still she deserved it for having kept the child alive thus far.

"Thanks," Misty said when Joan returned. She took the envelope and handed Joan the baby, who was dressed in pink. Ashley stood to the side and observed Jamie with a professional air. Jamie was three now and engaged in one of his favorite activities, pulling weeds and dropping them into his truck.

"What's her name?" Joan asked. The baby was a nice weight in her arms. She dangled the rainbow, making it glitter in the sun.

"Leonie. Like a lion."

"It's beautiful," Joan said, although she had not heard the name before.

"We moved to the area," Misty said. "It's not *too* near, I can't afford your city. We're in Pleasant Hill." This was a town an hour away. "A rental until we decide if we like things."

Joan rocked Leonie. "Are you enjoying motherhood?"

"Oh, it's fine. Having created life. It's pretty cool."

"Are you tired?"

"No?" Misty looked puzzled. "That's what I have Ashley for."

I guess she's doing fine, Joan thought. I shouldn't have worried.

———

Joan loved to read. She'd discovered libraries her first month in Palo Alto, when a friendly librarian in the College Terrace branch helped her open a card. She'd marveled at the endless aisles of hardcovers, the plush chairs, the tables out front with signs touting an astonishing opportunity: USED BOOKS, 10 FOR $1. After she had Jamie, Joan brought him to the library too; he liked the story hour.

It was upon returning home after one of these visits and setting down her canvas totes in the kitchen that Joan saw the light of the answering machine. She didn't recognize the name of the caller, and it was only after Ashley identified herself as Misty's nanny that Joan understood.

It was rush hour, and it took Joan ninety minutes to drive to Misty's apartment. The complex was larger than she'd expected. There were long cracks along the walls, and the balconies were crammed with furniture and toys, with handwritten signs promising violent consequences were any contents to be disturbed. As Misty's apartment was on the second level, Joan took the stairs, which were comprised of concrete slabs that came through the center of the courtyard. As Joan climbed, she estimated the gaps between the slabs as around the length of her forearm. A child could easily fall in those gaps, she thought.

Inside Misty's apartment, Joan found Ashley seated at the kitchen table. Leonie appeared clean and calm, and she lay in a crib which Joan recognized as the one she'd had delivered from Babies "R" Us.

"I came to work yesterday morning," Ashley said. She looked at Joan but kept a finger on her page in *Vogue*. "Leonie was in her crib, but Misty wasn't around. I assumed she had just left."

"Why did you think that?" Joan felt like she was conducting an investigation.

"The windows were open. Misty always does that—she likes to air out. And there was a bottle warmed. So I just did my thing. But then Misty didn't come back. I've slept over before, but Misty usually asks in advance." Ashley shrugged. "Ezra never came either. I'm flying to Cancún tomorrow, so."

Ezra, Joan thought. What happened to Johnny?

"Anyway," Ashley said, closing her magazine. "She said you're best friends, right?"

———

"I'm taking a break," Misty said when she finally called a week later. A break, Joan mouthed to herself as she turned on the bathroom faucet. The baby had just stained another set of clothing, and Joan scrubbed frantically at the cotton. A break. A *break*!

"I was looking at her in her crib, right?" Misty's voice was tinny, as if she were far away—across the globe on a desert island, maybe, or someplace else Joan could never reach her. "And all of a sudden I had this thought: she's not really anything to me, she's just a problem I have to deal with, the same as a clogged drain or a car that won't start. And I don't *like* to deal with problems—after a while, I'd rather not drive at all than keep fiddling with a difficult car."

"When are you coming back? You are coming, aren't you?"

"Of course I'll *visit*. But I don't have that motherly instinct. I haven't thought about her at all since I left. That can't be normal, can it? Don't mothers always think about their babies? Though what am I supposed to think? She doesn't have a personality!"

Joan didn't disagree—she didn't think babies had too much of a personality either. For the last ten minutes, Leonie (Joan called her Lee) had been staring at the same spot in the ceiling. Joan had just been happy she wasn't crying, until she suddenly pooped.

"I may sound all nice and light now," Misty went on. "But just so you know, it hasn't been that way, not for a while. For a long time it's only been *dark*. When I was pregnant, there was no one interested in my baby. Do you know how awful that feels?"

"I was interested."

"Oh? The same way Bill was interested when *you* were pregnant? I'm telling you, no woman should have to feel that kind of alone. Like you're the only person who cares about the baby inside of you. Because what does it mean when the baby comes out and you still don't care either?"

"A break implies you are going to return," Joan said.

"I think you know what I mean," Misty said softly.

Joan turned off the water. She wanted to argue; she wanted to say she didn't understand. But the truth was Joan did. Certain events passed, things happened, and people wanted you to be upset, or stew, or be sad. But sometimes you just went on with your life. Misty had said from the start she didn't want a child; she was only following through.

"I call her Lee," Joan blurted. She didn't know why she said it, as she hadn't really considered changing the baby's name. But Joan wanted Misty to understand that there would be differences between Lee's world in that apartment, however brief, and whatever life Lee had with Joan. The name Leonie rolled awkwardly in her mouth; whenever Joan called it, Lee never looked up.

"Lee." Misty paused. "That's nice."

This is crazy, Joan thought. This can't be real. But she didn't say anything.

CHAPTER FOURTEEN

For a long while, Joan had trouble saying Lee was hers. She was waiting around for Misty, was what she said. Even when the adoption papers came through years later, when Nelson brought them to the house along with a set of stuffed dragons for the children, she refused to let the idea stick. She peeked once in the folder at the original birth certificate: there was Misty's name, with no other parent. Joan didn't look at the new certificate, which listed her and Bill. She folded the papers and put them away in the butter-cookie tin, underneath her checkbook and passport.

"I don't like the baby phase" was what Bill said at first. But he couldn't protest too much; after all, he needn't *do* much. He had not objected to Lee as much as Joan feared; whether he'd simply been overwhelmed by the speed of events or was resigned to helping Misty, Joan never asked. She compensated by trying to make his life as easy as possible: she did not ask Bill to change diapers or get up at night. Lee was at an age when an abrupt change wasn't traumatic, or at least Joan hoped; Lee didn't cry excessively, and when not eating or sleeping, she mostly lay in the nursery with her eyes open. Sometimes she would rotate to stare at a spot on the ceiling. No matter which way Joan turned the crib, Lee would rotate back, her body arranged in the same position.

She must be looking for something, Joan thought. Is she searching for Misty? Joan went and retrieved a photo from Bill's first wedding that he kept in a drawer. Joan used to sneak looks, studying Agatha's tiny waist and ballerina posture, but now she didn't care about that. Joan used blue painters' tape to cover the faces of the other bridesmaids and showed Misty to Lee. But Lee only examined the photo for a second before squirming and averting her gaze. It wasn't that she was avoiding the photo—it just didn't hold her interest.

———

Eventually Bill's siblings heard about Misty's disappearance. First Bridget called and then Henry.

Bridget: "Where is Misty? Doesn't she care about the baby?"
Henry: "Maybe she's having the implants redone. Or a tummy tuck. Heh heh."
Bridget: "It's incredible that she would just leave. And the father hasn't appeared?"
Henry: "I wouldn't come back if I were her. And you shouldn't want her to. You think Misty is bad on her own? How about Misty as a *mother*?"
Bridget: "Does the baby seem a little odd? Infants can become disoriented in a different environment."

"I'm not doing anything *different*," Joan replied to Bridget's last query. "I'm keeping conditions exactly the same for when Misty returns." She did not mention she was calling the baby Lee.

"We're not saying what you're doing is *wrong*," Bridget said. She'd become friendlier after Misty had disappeared and dumped Lee on Joan—Bridget now spoke to Joan as if they'd experienced something significant together, like high school or a stressful cruise. "No one's suggesting the baby was better off with Misty. Whatever your and Bill's routines are, it's got to be an improvement."

"We're just waiting for Misty to return."

"What does the baby look like? Do we have any idea of the father? I remember the Spanish one, what's-his-name. He was, what do they call it, swarthier."

"Lee looks fine," Joan said. "She's got light brown hair and green eyes."

"Everyone thinks their baby's eyes are green. Do you know how rare green eyes are? They'll change into brown. We don't have the genes."

"Genes," Joan repeated. It was one of the Lauders' favorite topics, genetics. How they evolved as families grew larger, the traits distilled, the freak outcomes possible. Anything could happen when one made irresponsible choices.

———

A month after Joan retrieved Lee, she received a call from Misty's landlord. "Remember talking to me? You were Misty's reference," he said.

"Oh," Joan said. "Right. Yes." She wondered if Misty had bothered faking her accent.

The apartment needed to be emptied, the landlord said. He could do it, but did she want him to throw everything away? "Also," he added, "from what I've seen, she isn't getting any of the deposit back."

The landlord was a miser, Joan decided once she got to Misty's. Given the state of the unit, Misty should have been entitled to some of the deposit. Sure, she had left some furniture, but otherwise the apartment was clean (if dusty). Nothing seemed broken or in disrepair.

As she walked through the unit, Joan took an inventory of the remaining items. A coffeemaker, a beaded shawl. A small television and VCR. The fridge held a rotted apple and a lemon.

In Misty's bedroom, there were several perfume bottles on the dresser. The closet was empty, which Joan expected—she knew how Misty liked her clothes. Only an oversize T-shirt remained, on a hanger attached to the top of the door. It was white with a black skull and cross-bones, and on the bottom, in red lettering, was the word PESSIMIST.

Joan sniffed the perfumes, deciding to keep one bottle which was half full (Guerlain Shalimar), and then left the room. A minute later she returned and looked again at the shirt. She knew from her reading that babies preferred black and white, as they liked stark contrasts.

Joan gathered the beaded shawl from the kitchen and the T-shirt and dropped them into her bag. When she returned home, she went to the garage and retrieved a hammer and nail. She found a hanger and hung the PESSIMIST shirt up on the wall of Lee's nursery.

"Lee," she called. "Lee!" Hearing her name, Lee looked up. Her eyes locked on the shirt, and she brought up her fist and shook it.

———

Fall came and the weather stayed hot. Temperatures reached eighty in October and there was still the odd seventy-degree day that leaked into November. Joan felt, as she often did, very lucky to live in California. She began to think of Lee as truly her own; she used Jamie's stroller, and Lee received all of Jamie's old toys. Jamie began to spend full days at preschool, and now it was Lee whom Patty took to roll rice balls and stroll the garden.

At times Joan received strange looks from people in the neighbor-hood, although it wasn't as frequent as she'd feared—she supposed word might have spread about the situation, or it was assumed she was a babysitter. On occasion there would be someone who would ask how she, a Chinese woman, might have a young blondish child, upon which she typically deployed one of the following:

1. Her father is Caucasian.
2. Her hair is very pretty, isn't it.
3. I no speak English well.

As far as Joan was concerned, these were all true; besides, she wasn't deliberately obfuscating the situation—she didn't know what it was either.

Jamie and Lee played together or, rather, in proximity. Lee was too young to really participate but could at least observe—whenever Jamie was in a room, Lee watched him. Joan was thankful Jamie had been so young when Lee arrived, as he appeared to accept Lee as his sister the same as if Joan had been pregnant herself, although that wasn't possible anymore, at least with Bill. He had undergone a vasectomy shortly after she brought home Lee. He told her only after the procedure was done.

"I hope you don't mind," Bill said. "And I truly hope this doesn't hurt your feelings, but I do feel quite relieved at the idea of no longer fathering children at fifty-six."

It didn't hurt Joan's feelings. Some who come from big families may wish to re-create the experience, but Joan had not particularly enjoyed her own big family. She also knew Bill was worried about his older children. Juliet had dropped out of residency, was getting a divorce, and had started dating her marriage counselor. And Theo still called for money. "I need it for rent," he usually said. He only ever asked to speak to Bill.

"How were you paying before?" Bill asked.

"We were at Charlotte's place."

"And what's wrong with staying there?"

"We had to leave," Theo said shortly. It was clear that relations with Charlotte's parents had deteriorated, though Charlotte remained stead-fast, and sometimes she called as well.

"I'm thinking of birthday gifts for Theo." Charlotte's voice was light and wispy.

"When's his birthday?" Joan asked. She realized this was information she should already know, but the Lauders were not sentimental about adult birthdays.

"Next week," Charlotte said. "I want to get him something great. Theo's been doing so well. He's going to the gym every day. You should see him, Joan, he's the most handsome one there."

Handsome! Joan was boggled that Charlotte should mention this, though yes, Theo was objectively handsome; he possessed the sort of striking good looks that made people stop to take him in, reconfirming his appearance as they might with a celebrity. Still, it was incredible to Joan that looks, even excellent looks, could bring Theo so far; that his height and facial symmetry could mean an attractive, charming girl like Charlotte, who by normal rights should be living a nice life with a nice, responsible husband, could instead be passing her days with Theo, scuttling from apartment to apartment, eating at cheap diners while he rang his parents for money and listed all the ways the world was against him.

"He wants to be a ski instructor now," Bill said to Joan. Thankfully Joan had not answered that call, as she had been at the library, shopping the book sale.

"Why doesn't he become one?"

Bill shook his head. "It's not a proper career. He should be doing something in business."

Joan didn't agree: she thought Theo should pursue ski instruction. He liked the outdoors, and it seemed to her a more productive endeavor than the other jobs Bill suggested (money manager, consultant). Though she didn't say this. Theo already had a mother and father, and who was Joan to Theo? No one, really—it was just one of those unfortunate circumstances of marrying a man who's already lived a whole other life before meeting you.

CHAPTER FIFTEEN

For a while, Lee's hair was the exact shade of Jamie's. As she grew older, her hair became lighter while Jamie's deepened to an espresso. As Lee generally worshipped Jamie, in the manner that older siblings are worshipped, she often requested to wear his old clothes. Thus Joan began to purchase all of Jamie's shirts and sweaters in neutral colors, gray and navy and white, and the children appeared as slightly different versions of each other, like two sizes of a matryoshka doll.

By now Joan was used to being mistaken for their nanny. She was occasionally approached downtown by mothers impressed with her handling of two charges—and she was so engaged! She didn't loaf around; she didn't just stand and speak to the other nannies.

"There's this one park," a mother said. "The Chinese nannies there are always gossiping. It's fine, of course, to talk. But you also have a *job* to do."

Which park? Joan wanted to ask. What Chinese nannies?

One of their favorite spots to visit downtown was a bookstore. What was particularly nice about this shop was the child's section, which had lots of cozy corners to read in—it had been designed so that even little children could reach any title which might interest them. Once a week there would be a performance of some kind, a magician or balloon artist. Afterward, Joan would allow Jamie and Lee to each choose a book.

While the kids browsed, Joan would chat with the manager, Trish, who was in her late thirties with striking red hair. When not at the register, Trish could be found reading for story hour or reshelving books. Joan thought it wonderful that a beautiful person worked at a bookstore, as she knew how much young children prefer a pretty face. "Don't you think she's beautiful?" Joan asked when Bill came with them once.

"Who?"

"Over there."

Bill studied her. "That's quite a pronouncement," he finally said.

"She could be a movie star."

"Oh yeah? What sort of a movie?"

"She's just nice-looking. And young."

"She's not that young. And you think everyone is nice-looking," Bill said, nuzzling her cheek.

Trish looked over, and Joan waved. Joan still thought Trish was stunning, but maybe Bill was right that she was no one special; perhaps Joan only thought so because Trish was white and young, and Joan did seem to find many young white people beautiful. There were young Chinese people as well, of course, and Black and Mexican and Pakistani and Peruvian, but when Joan encountered such individuals, they often averted their gaze, as Joan did. On the street they appeared distracted, as if concentrating on a problem or some physical pain. She'd once tried to explain this to Bill, but he didn't understand. "It's in your head," he'd said. "We're all the same."

Joan knew they were not all the same, but it wasn't the sort of thing you can explain to your sixty-year-old husband, not when he's convinced otherwise. Besides, everyone treated *Bill* the same—as in they treated him nicely. He was trim and handsome in that way of certain older men when they dress well and have kept most of their hair. He was confident and had pleasant manners. Though it was Joan who brought the children to and from school each day, it was Bill whom the teachers spoke to at parents' night.

The following month, Joan brought Lee and Jamie to Los Angeles, where they visited Disneyland before stopping in Ojai to see Misty, who was housesitting for a friend. The Spanish-style compound had a pool and a tennis court, and Lee and Jamie, who were five and seven now, ran outside day and night. After they returned, both children had to stay home from school for a week to recover from bad colds.

So when Joan finally did make her way back to the bookshop, nearly two months had elapsed from her last visit. She'd come to buy a present for a birthday party—these damned birthday parties! Joan could not recall any such parties in Taiwan; her parents had never held a celebration for even her brothers, besides some cake at home. But in America, at least Joan's America, there were lavish events with petting zoos and waterslides seemingly every weekend. Each party also required a gift—the perfect gift, Joan was learning, as there would often be a public unveiling.

When Joan and Lee and Jamie arrived at the bookstore, it was already late afternoon. Joan looked at her watch and said they could browse only a short while.

"But there's a magic show," Jamie said, reading from a flyer. "At five."

"We can't make that."

"We never get to see magic," Lee complained. She was in a phase Joan didn't like, a *whiny* phase.

"Maybe we can watch the first five minutes," Joan said, which both she and the children knew meant at least twenty.

While the children browsed, Joan selected a C. S. Lewis collection and a plastic archery set (the recipient was a reckless blond named

Francis, who had once stomped on her tulips; Joan thought likely only the bow and arrows would see any use). "Oh!" Trish cried when Joan reached the register. "I haven't seen you!"

"The kids were sick," Joan said, flattered their absence had been noticed. She thought Trish looked especially lovely today: she was wearing a lavender sundress, which emphasized the auburn tones in her hair, and a little gold necklace. She should get a necklace like that, Joan thought. Last night at dinner, Dina had worn a similar piece, layered with a bold chain of onyx.

"Oh no. I didn't realize that."

"They're fine now," Joan said, gesturing toward the children. Jamie was throwing a stuffed boa constrictor at Lee while making hissing noises. Lee batted it to get it away.

"Still. It must be so worrying. Those poor darlings."

Joan smiled. That Trish was distressed was touching, as she had never shown particular interest in the children before.

Trish was slow wrapping the presents, and a line formed. The man directly behind Joan, a businessman type, kept looking at his watch. When Trish finished, Joan zipped her tote and prepared to leave.

"Hold on," Trish said. "I just thought of something." She went to the back and returned with a set of fruit-shaped erasers and a metal Slinky. "Some get-well gifts. For the kids."

"They're already well," Joan reminded her. The man behind Joan sighed.

"Then these are for them *getting* well." There was something wrong with Trish's voice; it was all wobbly, as if she were about to cry.

"I'm sorry I'm crying," Trish said a moment later. She wore powder blush, and her tears left coral tracks as they ran down her cheeks. She met Joan's gaze for only a second before looking away. "I really don't know what's wrong with me today."

"Sometimes we cry and have no idea why," Joan said, unzipping her bag and handing Trish a tissue. Although Joan thought she had a pretty good idea.

———

"I thought we said no more toys after Disneyland," Bill commented when he came down for dinner. On the table, on his linen place mat, were the gifts from Trish.

"They're from the bookstore," Joan said. "I took Jamie and Lee today." Joan recalled when the children had been sick. She'd not been able to sleep and had crept out of bed to check on them throughout the night. When Lee's fever went above 103 degrees, Joan wanted to go to the hospital, but Bill had stopped her. "She'll be fine," he said. He was right, naturally. Bill excelled at risk management.

"What's this, erasers?" Bill examined the box. "Banana-shaped? School supplies are a lot different than I remember, that's for sure."

Oh, he's so calm, Joan thought. He's so cool and easy. She reached for the bottle of soy sauce and drizzled a ribbon into the wok. "They were a gift from the manager. You know, the one I showed you before. Trish. She seemed very affected when she learned the children had been ill. It was almost as if something heavier, more significant, were weighing on her."

Joan sprinkled on some white pepper and ate one of the noodles as a test. As she stirred, she could feel Bill studying the back of her. She took a deep breath and held it before exhaling. That goddamn cheating *bastard*!

"Are we going to talk about this?" Bill finally asked.

"Later," Joan said. She turned off the heat. The noodles were done, but she kept stirring. She couldn't look at him.

———

"I wasn't lying about not finding her attractive," Bill said once Lee and Jamie were in bed. Joan and Bill had gone up separately to wish the children good night. When Joan came back down, Bill had been waiting at the table in the kitchen.

"Why did you do it?"

"I don't know." She saw that Bill was being honest, that he was puzzling through the question himself. "I went once to buy some magazines, while you were volunteering at the school. I suppose I paid closer attention because you said she was so beautiful. And then we got to talking."

"How many times were you with her?"

"Three."

"In public?"

"Only once. Lunch because she was hungry. At a diner by the office complex in Santa Clara. It's over, obviously."

He was remorseful, she saw; he was usually willing to admit fault. Joan had found it an attractive trait, as she herself could not apologize so easily, but now she realized Bill was this way because he'd always, always been forgiven.

"What if she doesn't think it's over?"

"I'm not responsible for how she thinks." Bill shrugged, as if he could not be held to account for the unpredictability of women.

The phone rang, and Bill reached to pick it up. "Henry. Let me call you back," he said into the receiver, looking at Joan.

"No, you talk to him." Joan went upstairs and changed into a black dress, one she had bought with Misty, which had a deeper V than Joan would have ever selected on her own. She fluffed her hair and found a pair of silver sandals and returned downstairs.

Bill was still at the kitchen table. She saw him register her change of clothes, her dark eye shadow. He watched her leave.

Joan shut the garage door and sat in her car. She wanted Bill to believe that in her dress and heels she was going out someplace; she wanted him to fear that in her rage she might sleep with someone. And yes, oh yes—there were times she'd been tempted. When she'd looked at Bill and smiled at him warmly, tenderly, all the while thinking: This, this, and *only* this? And nothing else? Ever again?

She turned on the car and sat with her hands on the wheel. Her breath was steady and she counted in and out. One. Two. You know why you're so calm. Three. Four. You're calm because you aren't surprised, because it's already happened before, maybe during our marriage but certainly earlier; it's part of why he's divorced so many times. You just never wanted to admit it. Because it would be inconvenient. You like this life, yes, and you like him reading *Narnia* to Jamie at night, the way he dotes on Lee. And there's no easy solution without ruining a good part of that, and so why think about it now.

Five. Six.

"Joan?" Bill stood in the doorway. He wore his long navy coat, the cashmere one she had thought so beautiful when they first met. "Joan, I don't want you to sit there. It's not safe. The exhaust."

He thinks I'm trying to kill myself, Joan realized with a start. He thinks him sleeping with someone is enough for me to end my life! She gaped at him, suddenly furious, and opened the garage door and reversed.

"Joan, wait!"

But she was already off, zooming down the street.

Now, where to go? The realization that she had no actual destination made Joan feel pathetic; she really had made pitifully few connections so far in America. She had dedicated all her efforts to Bill, she had believed their relationship was everything she required. How embarrassing to assume that he felt the same.

Down down down the long avenue. She wound up on the expressway, which in the late hour was empty, and she zipped on through the dark. Joan chose an exit and the following side streets at random.

The road she drove on was narrowing, with no option but to turn back or continue. Soon a long driveway was revealed, one blocked by a metal gate, and Joan recognized where she'd driven. It was Dina and

Trevor's house. She'd been here just yesterday, admiring Dina's jewelry. By this point, Joan had been visiting their home with Bill for eight years.

Joan parked though left the engine running. She must have come here deliberately. But no, more out of routine; the streets were familiar, but only vaguely, because it was always Bill who drove. She debated ringing the gate. Joan knew Dina would be sympathetic; she would listen and invite Joan in for a drink. Bill cheated on me, Joan could say. I'm so sorry, Dina would tell her, or something similar. She would want to hear all the details.

And of course Dina would tell Bill, maybe not right away but eventually; she would do it discreetly though in a way that made Joan look a little foolish, naive. This too Joan knew about Dina.

Thankful to have caught a bad idea before its execution, Joan shifted into drive. She had just started to make the turn and was passing the gates when they opened. A man in a gray sweater appeared from the driveway, wheeling a garbage can to the curb.

He waved, and Joan braked. She saw it was Trevor.

Joan rolled down her window. "Hi," she said. "Hi. It's me. Joan."

"I know who you are." He seemed amused by her introducing herself. "In the neighborhood?"

"Yes," Joan said. And then, not wanting to appear rude; "I was driving around."

"Ah! I do that sometimes." It was the friendliest Trevor had ever been to Joan. He usually ignored her, including last night, during which he'd spent most of the dinner speaking with Bill about something-something bond yields. Joan occasionally tried to engage Trevor on music, the one topic she knew he liked, but even then his answers were sparse. He was polite, and always asked her something back, but it was clear he didn't really care.

Joan realized he was waiting for her to explain her presence. "I thought I might talk to Dina."

"Right."

"So," Joan said reluctantly, "is she here?" She hoped not; she hoped Dina was out, maybe at one of her "girls' nights." Dina mentioned these periodically, describing them as necessary to pierce the monotony of marriage, and Joan always laughed, although it was a little awkward (though perhaps only for Joan) that Dina never invited her.

"Yes, she's here," Trevor said, but he didn't say he would get her. Instead he opened the car door and sat inside. At the door's opening, the light went on and his gray sweater was revealed to be a cable-knit cardigan on top of pajamas.

"What's going on?" Trevor asked. He shut the door.

The entire situation was so bizarre that Joan figured she might as well continue. She had come to speak with someone, after all. And Trevor was someone.

"Right," Trevor said when she was done telling. He massaged the back of his neck. "I see."

"What?"

"Nothing."

This was the maddening thing about him, Joan recalled, how he often lapsed into quiet, though he always seemed to have plenty to say to Bill. The silence stretched until Joan couldn't take it any longer. She kicked off her sandals. "He does cheat, doesn't he? He must do it all the time."

"Well," Trevor said again.

"Don't just keep saying that. What do you think?"

He sighed, the irritated noise of a man being put upon by a woman. "I don't think the interactions matter to him. I know it's not easy, but I wouldn't take it personally."

"This might surprise you, but I'm having a bit of trouble *not* taking it personally."

"Bill's crazy about you. From my experience, these sorts of aberrations—they often mean less to a man than a woman."

Joan sagged. Oh, she was so tired of being a woman. No matter where in the world she might be, Taiwan or California, the odds always seemed stacked the same way. Joan wondered if there was a specific point in each young man's life when he realized just how much had been tilted in his favor. When he looked at himself in the mirror and simply thought: Thank God.

"It might sound naive," Joan said, "but I really didn't think this would happen. Bill's been married so many times. I suppose I thought it would be out of his system."

"It's never out of your system. It's just how you manage it."

"What do you mean?"

"I mean that you keep having the same thoughts and urges; it doesn't change just because you got married. It's only now you aren't supposed to follow them. The problem is, you don't get a gold star for *not* cheating. And then the thought arrives: I'm going to die one day, I'm going to be lying on my deathbed knowing there's probably nothing coming next, and I'll have missed out on all of this."

Joan raised her eyebrows. He was talking to her, frankly, in a way that Milton or even Bill never had.

"I've felt that way before too," she said cautiously. "But I know it might hurt my children, so I wouldn't do anything."

"Well, but that's you. Bill might be older, but you're more mature."

He stared off, back in the direction of the house. Trevor was closer to Joan's age than Bill was; he had young features, round eyes, and smooth skin—a baby face, they called it. I could kiss him right now, Joan mused, and she was surprised by the impulse, its suddenness and ferocity. Was *this* the desire that Bill experienced? The thought didn't soften her toward Bill but did increase her understanding of him—some of the questions he might have been answering for himself. Is it worth it, to be good in such moments? And the next moment, and the next? Forever? Better to be a bad husband, then; better not to be good and to wring more pleasure from life.

Joan continued her observation of Trevor, who appeared to be regretting his decision to enter the car; his back was slouched in a posture of resigned endurance she recognized from squabbles with Bill. How ridiculous Joan was. Just moments earlier she'd been thinking how it was only out of choice that she hadn't cheated, but it wasn't as if she'd had any opportunities. No one wanted her; it was only because she was still (a little, barely) young that she assumed people did.

Suddenly bereft, Joan closed her eyes. A moment later there was the sound of the door opening. Great, she thought. He's leaving. She sat up and saw that while Trevor had opened the door, he was still seated. He was closer to her now and grasped her right hand between both of his.

"If you stay with Bill, I don't think you'll regret it," he said. Joan was focused on her hand. Even though he'd never touched her, the gesture seemed so natural as to be part of his usual communication, the same as pulling out a chair at dinner.

"Try to be the bigger person." His eyes were light and his skin tan; she had never noticed how naturally tan he was. "As we've established, you're the mature one."

"Yes," Joan said, breathing shallowly.

He ran his thumb lightly against her palm. "You're okay, aren't you?"

"I'm okay," Joan said. She felt a brief, gutting stab of disappointment when he released her hand. Their interaction, while oddly intimate given their relationship, was fleeting in her thoughts that evening, though she would think about it many times in the years to come. That's how it is with such moments: we don't always know which will stick around, and sometimes they are so vivid we must pack them away for a while. Joan would think about this later—how few truly surprising, lovely moments one receives in a lifetime. Surely there must be ways to have a new connection, a *satisfying* connection, without resorting to what Bill did. Joan would devote a great deal of herself to this question; it would become one of her life's obsessions.

But. That was to come. For now, Joan watched Trevor return to his house. He walked stiffly, as if he knew she was watching. She glanced away, to afford him privacy, though she believed he would not look back. It was dark and the moon full, a fat white button in the sky.

In the car, Joan's thoughts returned to Bill. She pulled forward and began down the road to home.

——

There would be others over the years. A radiologist, a baker, a substitute teacher. Each time Joan discovered a new betrayal she went to Bill and asked why. To the best of her understanding, it was because such women were there: he fell in lust, and while he knew it would be brief he still thought it'd be fun to have the experience. He would try to be better, he said. He always promised he would try.

Many times Joan considered leaving him. She was disgusted by him, she wished him gone. In her worst moments she wondered what it'd be like if he were dead. How free she would be! She compared herself to Bill's other women and did not know what separated them, why he should be married to her when others had been discarded. Was it because she had gone to Stanford? That she had been hesitant to sleep with him? It was the slim margins through which life's significant victories were won that kept her awake at night.

"What if we divorced?" she asked him once.

Bill was startled by the question, though not as much as Joan hoped. "I would be devastated, of course. You're an incredible woman."

"Why did you divorce before?"

"If I'm being honest, I suppose I've never been too good at compromising."

Well, I don't like compromising either, Joan thought. I've compromised enough.

Could she be divorced again? Joan had yet to meet another Asian woman who'd been divorced, although Joan supposed they must exist, they just didn't speak of it (she never offered up the fact about herself either). But to be divorced twice seemed to indicate some greater personal deficiency. Would she have to move? Find a job?

She should have a job, Joan thought. She should have a career, something she knew how to do. Joan had never considered that she might not work; her life until Bill had been defined by money, or specifically the lack of it, the immigrant's perpetual quest for survival. She'd been so awed by the abundance of Bill's life, the ease and pleasure of it, that she had simply fallen into this place—and now she was in this other unfortunate space, the one where her husband lapsed and lapsed and somehow still she stayed.

"What do you want to be when you grow up?" Joan asked Lee and Jamie one afternoon.

"I don't know," the children answered simultaneously. They were busy with their latest game, which involved a low hexagonal building they had built out of a vast pile of plastic bricks in the corner of the playroom. The two had been building for some time; the structure was nearly up to Lee's waist. There was no discernible color scheme, and the children appeared to have used whatever pieces were immediately at hand. On the building's side was a paper sheet, and Joan crouched to read.

PLANET INFINITY

RULE #1: ONE TICKET TO ENTER

RULE #2: AGE 6 AND OLDER ONLY

"What is Planet Infinity?" Joan asked.

"A place," Lee said. She jammed a fireman into a carousel and shoved it into a corner. "A nice one. With lots of rooms."

"What do you do there?"

"Fly to Jupiter. Eat chocolate bars. Or anything else you want. It can create it. Infinitely."

"It's kind of like a portal," Jamie said. He removed the sign, careful not to rip the clear tape. On the bottom, he wrote: RULE #3: NO TOUCHING OTHERS' ITEMS WITHOUT PERMISSION and then taped back up the sign. Jamie had a collection of model cars and was upset when Lee took one, as she was a rough player.

"So is it really a planet?" Joan asked. "Or maybe more a theme park of some kind?"

Lee and Jamie exchanged a look; Joan was pleased by their unity, even though she was aware that any tacit communication was likely a shared annoyance toward her.

"It's *our* space," Lee said with finality.

Yes, it was true that it was their space, Joan thought. They were free to play and pretend as they wished.

That evening Joan straightened the house as usual but was careful to leave Planet Infinity intact. The children had built it up farther; there were multiple levels, and a rocket pad had been added to the roof. They explained they were capturing all their good ideas now so they wouldn't forget them later.

"Like when we're older and have other things to think about," Jamie said.

"Right," Joan agreed. She read them their bedtime stories in Lee's room. Afterward she went to sit in the backyard, under the veranda.

"Good night, Papa," she heard Lee and Jamie call. Their windows were open.

"Good night," Bill said, and then Joan could hear him launch into one of his occasional evening routines, a pantomime called ATTACK in which he played from a rotating list of villains and pounced. Joan had asked him not to work up the children before bed, but he always forgot; he was the playful parent, the imaginative one, and as he roared from room to room, she could hear Jamie and Lee laugh and shriek in an uncontrolled manner they never did with her.

Joan bent and scratched her leg. The wicker couches were dented near her calf, injuries from Jamie launching trucks against the furniture in earlier years. The rattan screens bore similar scars. When they visited Bridget's home in Ross, Joan always admired the decor. How everything seemed to be of such nice quality but not brand-new. "Oh, this old thing?" Bridget would say. "I can't remember where I got it, I've had it for years." (Bill said Bridget was lying, that she knew the provenance of everything she owned, but that wasn't the point.) The point was that Joan had been with Bill for many years now, long enough for her furniture to develop a patina as well.

Joan removed from her pocket the scrap she had found in Bill's coat that morning. The piece of paper, unevenly ripped and the size of Joan's palm, looked to be from a junk brochure. On an empty corner, Bill had written: *Kathleen (receptionist—dentist)*, followed by a number. It was one of his quirks that he seemed to recall women by their jobs; to Joan's knowledge, he cheated only with women who *had* jobs. She theorized it was because that was where Bill met them—at their work. Joan recognized the area code as from the next town over.

It's not that Bill isn't bad, Joan thought as she carefully folded the paper into a little square; she waited until the familiar hurt had settled in her stomach before she stuck the paper in between the wicker of the chair. It's just as bad as he is, there's always the possibility out there of worse. And I've already been so fortunate. He's not perfect. But neither am I. No one gets perfect.

CHAPTER SIXTEEN

Yes, Joan was fortunate. But she knew this only meant danger, because eventually good luck turned to bad. And really, there was so much to go wrong in a life: you could cross the street and be hit by a car; a random bubble might travel into your brain and then, well, you needn't worry about anything anymore. This worry, this anxious terror, extended to her children. Because naturally Joan loved them most; should a karmic balancing descend, she knew it would come for Lee and Jamie. This was how God would break her heart.

"I thought you were supposed to love me most," Bill said when she confessed her fears.

"Of course I love you."

"But you love the children more."

"Well, yes." Joan didn't think this was controversial. In China, in Taiwan, you were always supposed to love the next generation more, or at least say you did.

Both Lee and Jamie were now attending the John Jay School, otherwise referred to as JJS, a private school with a bloated endowment and sprawling buildings of red brick. Bill had gone to JJS, as had Juliet and Theo. When Joan first saw the school, she had thought it was a college, that's how large it was. The swimming pool was Olympic-size (though it was not an institution that was known for athletics, besides tennis); in recent years a second auditorium and glassblowing facilities had been constructed. Joan had been impressed by JJS at first sight (to her it resembled a mini Stanford), but over time she'd become increasingly anxious about the place—angry mothers and opulent birthday parties aside, it just felt *weird*. The campus was too grand, its promotional literature overly bold, she felt, in its promises that graduates might never meet the vicissitudes of life, an unfair teacher or a bad boss.

Many mothers volunteered on campus, and Joan had recently been conscripted by Candace Uhlfelder, the lower school's "parent community director," into a weekly commitment. Joan had chosen cafeteria duty, thinking a service job would lessen her anxieties, but she found the juxtaposition of the dining hall's glossed walnut tables and stained-glass windows with the children's shouted demands for cheese pizza even more perturbing—the spilled milk and impatient shrieks and aroma of hot carbohydrates and soft vegetables all congealing into an unsettling, out-of-body experience. On those days when the worry crept too sharp, Joan would linger until the end of school, waiting for the children at the front entrance instead of in her car by the curb. They would then do an activity together.

"The mall?" Lee asked hopefully when she and Jamie came out one afternoon and saw Joan. The three of them walked to the car.

"No more malls," Joan said, passing each a granola bar. "We're going on a hike."

This announcement was met with restrained silence. The children were used to Joan's hikes, as she was going through a phase of liking them. She had taken Lee and Jamie to REI and bought them hiking shoes, which they had enjoyed at first, in the way of children liking new things, but now they'd had enough of both the shoes and nature. Joan, however, had not. She'd recently purchased a local map and begun marking interesting spots around the Bay Area. How fortunate they were, she said. To live near all this beauty!

Today Joan drove them to High Rock Park, a hiking area outside of Marin. The park was cliffside, facing the Pacific, which meant nearly all the trails wound to a view of the ocean. They began on a narrow uphill path, one new to them, edged with boulders and ice plants.

"Can we collect rocks?" Jamie asked when they reached a plateau.

"Five each," Joan said mechanically. She was distracted by the sight of the water. Prior to Bill, Joan had never been on a beach holiday. Even if she'd had the funds, which she didn't, she'd considered it a waste of money to travel so far only to bake in a chair in the sun. Over a decade later, however, Joan loved to be by the water: in Maui she could watch the waves break for hours.

The ocean here was a different sort of stunning from Maui, a cooler, rougher beauty. She was entranced by the sounds of the water and didn't realize how close they'd veered to the cliff until she looked down. The edge was only a few steps away; beyond that was at least a hundred-foot vertical drop onto the rocks below.

Lee and Jamie were a step ahead, sweeping the ground for interesting stones. Joan didn't call out, not wanting to startle them, and instead crept forward and placed a firm hand on each of their backs. "Let's move," she said, heart pounding. They obeyed, shuffling backward. Once the children were a safe distance away, Joan went forward again. She couldn't believe it: anyone could simply slip off the edge, dropping to their likely death.

On their way back down the trail, Joan noticed a rusted metal bar and what appeared to be broken latches attached to a boulder. She had missed these on their ascent and realized that at one point the path must have been gated. She normally would have been in support of the gate's removal—Joan thought Americans too litigious in general, and if you were the sort to eat plastic fruit or hold a chain saw on the wrong end, then surely you deserved what was coming to you. The cliff, however, was a different matter; there should at least be a sign, a warning to pay attention ahead.

Back at the parking lot, Joan spotted a park ranger exiting his booth. She informed him of the cliff. "It's dangerous," she said. "We didn't realize how close we were to the edge."

The ranger nodded disinterestedly, his eyes pinned to a group of female hikers in sports bras. "Right," he said when Joan pointed to the trail. "Yeah. I remember there being a gate. It must have broken at some point."

"Are you going to fix it?"

"These things are eventually gotten around to." His attention remained on the hikers.

Joan wished Bill were here. This was precisely the sort of situation she normally asked him to manage—the kind where everyone, Joan included, preferred the conversation to go from white male to white male.

The ranger returned to his booth. "Wait," Joan said. She pointed to the map of the preserve. "Here's where it is. Where the gate was."

"We'll have someone take a look."

"Will you *really*?" Joan asked desperately. "Because it's dangerous!"

"Oh, sure," the ranger said. "We'll put in a work request. We have a procedure for these things." He was in his early twenties, with floppy hair and a beautiful smile, though Joan was not assuaged.

Perhaps to hurry her along, the ranger gave each of the children a palm-size zipper pouch with CALIFORNIA STATE PARKS printed on the back. Once in the car, Joan turned and gave Lee and Jamie the rocks they'd collected.

"Put them in the pouch," she instructed. "And then put the pouch in your backpacks." It was then that Joan realized Jamie didn't *have* his backpack. "Where is your bag? Did you forget it at school?"

"I'm not sure."

"Do we need to go back to JJS?"

"I think," Jamie started, but then didn't say anything.

"*What* do you think?" Joan asked, trying to conceal her impatience. The interaction with the ranger had unnerved her; she was in a hurry to return home, to rest and stew. "Did you leave it at school? Jamie, you've got all your books in there. Your homework."

Jamie was silent. "I don't know," he murmured. Joan groaned and hit her head against the seat.

"Someone took it from him," Lee said.

"What?" Joan asked at the same time Jamie said "I don't know" again. Joan turned. "Who took it from you?"

"A kid!" Lee shouted. "A big kid."

"Someone took your bag on purpose?"

"Yes," Jamie said. After a second he added: "Greg Zimmer."

"Is Greg in your grade?" Jamie was ten now, in the fifth grade.

"He's a year above."

"Did he do anything else? Has he hit you? If he has, you should hit him back," Joan declared. "That's the only way to deal with these people."

"Hitting isn't allowed. And anyway, I don't want to. We could get expelled," Jamie said miserably.

Oh, Joan thought. Oh no. My heart. Her son, she well knew, was both a believer in rules and an ardent follower of them, and it was clearly stated that at JJS there was to be no hitting. Now, of course there were rule breakers and bullies at every institution; Joan was under no impression that what Jamie endured was unusual. Nor did Joan believe boys a more aggressive breed of tormenter than girls. She knew both her children would eventually encounter unpleasant people; it pained Joan to imagine their pain, and yet she believed such experiences necessary, so as not to carry unrealistic expectations into adulthood. But still Joan felt guilty. Because she was thirty-seven now, and Bill sixty-three, and when they walked into the annual JJS spring fundraiser there were knowing glances exchanged between Candace Ulfehlder and the others on the event-planning committee; because Lee was Jamie's sister but looked so different than him, because of all the baggage Joan had loaded onto her young son and sent him into the world to bear.

"I want to move him to a different school," Joan said to Bill that night.

"Let's stay calm." Bill poured himself a glass of merlot. He brought out another glass for Joan in which he'd poured just an inch, as was their routine.

Joan accepted the wine. "Lee too. She's getting older. Girls form close friendships. It's best we pull her out before she has a regular group."

"It's only schoolyard antics. The children will have to learn to handle problems on their own."

"*And* I'm going to write a letter. To the state parks authority. The cliff we hiked today was dangerous. And I don't think that ranger is going to do anything about it."

"You sure are worked up about this," Bill observed.

"Do you know what Greg Zimmer looks like?" Joan asked Lee the next afternoon. On Tuesdays and Thursdays, Jamie had soccer practice after school, during which Joan often brought Lee with her on errands before swinging back to JJS to collect Jamie. "Is he tall or short? Big or little?"

"He's right there," Lee said.

Joan looked. There was a hulking student in front of the main building who, even slouched, was nearly Joan's height. He had curly blond hair which ended over his eyes and a face bearing strong testimony of its rocky transition to preteen: the soft round fleshiness of the cheeks nearly gone, tapering to a jawline studded with acne.

Another student ran down the steps. This boy, roughly the same age as Jamie, was terribly normal-looking; he appeared to Joan as someone who likely had a good number of friends and played tennis. The boy passed Greg, and in one smooth motion Greg casually grabbed the handle of his backpack so that the boy was yanked backward. He stumbled, arms windmilling, and Greg released. Without looking back, his target quickly righted himself and ran away.

Greg then strolled to the parking lot, stopping near the handicapped spots to straighten his polo shirt. Why, he's a run-of-the-mill bully, Joan thought. He's just a little *goon*!

"He sings sometimes on the blacktop," Lee said. She was watching Joan, as she could tell when her mother was intensely focused on a subject. "He shouts at Jamie and a few others."

"What does he say?"

"'Chinese, Japanese, dirty knees.'" Lee held her breath; she knew it was bad, but she didn't know *why* it was bad. "What does it mean?"

"Never you mind," Joan said. She wasn't sure either. A black Mercedes had entered the lot, which caught her attention. Greg approached the passenger side.

"Who's that lady in that car?" Lee asked.

"Shh," Joan said.

"Hey, buddy!" A woman Joan presumed was Greg's mother leaned out the window, high ponytail bobbing. "Guess who came too?" If Joan shifted, she could make out a man speaking into a phone in the driver's seat. "You have a great day at school?" Joan couldn't hear Greg's answer. A yellow Labrador darted its head out the back window, mouth open, tongue lolling.

The Mercedes continued to idle, presumably while Greg's father finished his call. The sedan looked freshly washed, and Joan knew enough of cars now from Bill to discern this was a particularly expensive model. Before Greg climbed into the back, he lingered by the open door, scanning the lot.

He's *proud* of the vehicle, Joan realized with a start. He wants the other children to see him going into it!

Joan shut off her engine. Should she speak to the parents? Somehow Joan didn't think Greg's mother would be of assistance; she looked to be the sort who drank afternoon margaritas with girlfriends, shouting after her children to "Take it easy, busters!" as they lit insects on fire. This kind of woman could be gregarious and friendly but didn't like to be embarrassed; she might even try to make things more difficult for Jamie.

The following week Jamie had soccer again. Joan lingered after drop-off as she searched for a lipstick which had fallen between the seats. Once Joan finally wedged loose the tube, she sat up and spotted Jamie walking toward the field. He was with friends, laughing and joking in that self-conscious swaggery way of young boys; amid the red buildings in their soccer uniforms, they appeared as a moving mass of dark green. Halfway through the field, Jamie separated—he had forgotten something, Joan assumed—and reversed back to the school.

As Jamie ambled, Joan noted with alarm that his projected path appeared to directly intersect that of Greg Zimmer, who had appeared out of the main JJS building like a goblin-ish apparition. *Move,* Joan wanted to shout to her son. Run and stay away from that bully! Jamie had a way of strolling with his head down, lost in thought; he was a dreamy child, and both Joan and Bill would sometimes grow frustrated as they called him to dinner over and over, to no response. Joan's heart jolted when she saw Greg shoot out an arm once Jamie drew near—Greg did not yank on Jamie's backpack but crammed something into the side pocket, which normally held a water bottle. Greg then seized the top of Jamie's jersey and spoke into his ear. Throughout this Jamie stood frozen, head down, until Greg released him. Before Jamie returned to the field, Joan saw him remove the item Greg had shoved into his backpack, look at it for a long moment, and then toss it into a garbage can.

For a period, Joan struggled to breathe—it was as if she had forgotten how, and her heart fluttered in panic as she gripped the wheel. When her breath returned, it was ragged and painful. She sat with her rage, and when it didn't cool, she rose and stormed from the car. Fortunately the garbage can was a nearer target than Greg Zimmer, who now sat crouched by the school's entrance. If it'd been Greg who was closer, Joan felt she could very well have stormed *him*.

The garbage was nearly full, so Joan easily plucked out the item. Her heart again began to pound as she flattened the magazine page with her palms. The woman featured was East Asian, on her hands and knees, entirely naked but for a red lace thong. She was looking directly at the camera, her mouth open in ecstasy, presumably at the sight of the penis belonging to the two hairy legs straddling the right and left borders of the image (as in the video store downtown, here too the man did none of the marketing, Joan thought with frustration).

Joan did not know how long she stared at the image. She did sense it was too long, and yet she couldn't stop. The composition was neo-classical in that more details were revealed the longer she looked: the rough chunky yarn of the camel rug, speckled with orange and yellow; the woman's long thin brown nipples, which made double Y's from her breasts as they sagged toward the ground. Below her breasts was the caption: *Brenda, our Asian Siren.*

Oh Lord, Joan thought as she imagined Jamie looking at the image—oh Lord, what had *Jamie* thought?

Joan had always been aware that there were very few Asian mothers at JJS. Though until now this had never struck her as a problem. Because there was Bill. And Bill *did* look like many of the fathers (albeit older). He dressed like them and spoke their language and thus, Joan believed, assured a smooth entrance for them all. Joan had never considered what it might mean for her children that she herself acted and appeared differently. Even volunteering in the cafeteria—Joan had chosen it because none of the other mothers wanted the job. Jamie and Lee had never complained that she didn't volunteer for the Fall Harvest, one of JJS's signature events, which most of the other mothers *did* sign up for. Jamie and Lee had never said anything about her showing up to school one day with a little net in her hair as she passed out chocolate milk next to Beth Ellen, the actual JJS lunch lady.

Joan examined the page again. Behind "Brenda" was a leather couch with a rounded imprint on one cushion, as if she had been seated for some time before climbing down to be photographed. There were red lacquer chopsticks in her hair.

Have I embarrassed my children? Joan thought. Through my choices, have I made their lives more difficult?

She looked up as Greg rose and began to cross the parking lot. He was not a particularly fast walker: there was a lackluster tension about him, a lazy bully's scanning of the periphery as he moved. Still clutching the page, Joan watched him and then, on impulse, ran back to her car. She rolled slowly across the lot, tapping her foot on and off the brake. Once she drew close, she stopped and lowered the window.

"Hey!" she shouted. She threw the page at him. Joan had misjudged the density of the paper—it didn't smack him, as she'd thought it would, but merely bounced off.

Puzzled, Greg stopped and picked up the wadded sheet from the ground. He didn't appear to recognize it at first. It was only when he opened the page and looked at her again that a sly wariness crossed his face.

"My son is ten years old," Joan said. "Do you think this is a nice thing to show him?"

"I don't know what you're talking about," Greg shot back. His backpack strap slipped from his shoulder. Joan felt a flicker of admiration that Greg could defend himself so easily to adults; having been raised in the Confucian tradition, she found his insubordination quite novel. Here was a boy who'd been taught to firmly defend his behavior even in the face of authority—who believed he had the right to stand firm, occupying an immovable central spot in the universe. A big *American* boy.

She leaned out of her window. "You said something to Jamie. When you gave him this picture. What was it?"

"I don't know." Greg darted a few spaces down to a black car—*his* black car, Joan recognized. It was the one from a week earlier, with his mother and father. Joan steeled herself for a confrontation with rich white people. I'll just have to remember what Bill would do, she thought. After all, he's a rich white person himself.

Joan realized the car was empty at the same moment as Greg; after jiggling the handle, he pressed a hand to the glass. Joan guessed his mother must be somewhere in the school—Lee had mentioned Greg had a brother in her year. A pleasant breeze blew through the lot, scattering cherry blossom petals across the concrete.

Greg turned to face her, his body against the door. Joan crept her car forward. She was so near she could spot the emergence of a painful-looking whitehead on his chin.

Greg scowled. "Stay away from me. You're crazy."

"I *am* crazy," Joan agreed. "And I feel crazy too. When I see someone being bad to my son, I get filled with a hot, dark feeling. A crazy thing I might do in such a situation is crash into this nice vehicle of yours. Do you want to see?"

"No!" Greg cast a desperate glance across the lot, and Joan checked her mirror. The few parked cars were static, with no signs of life; the only movement came from the soccer field, the players' bodies crisscrossing in the distance.

Joan released the brake. The engine purred as it moved. Her little BMW was a diesel, and she liked its low sound.

"Stop!" Greg cried. "What are you doing?"

She let the BMW creep to within a few inches of the Mercedes. "What did you say to Jamie?"

"I don't know!"

"Try and remember."

"No, I really can't!"

"Well, then I'll just have to keep going."

"I asked if you liked to get on your knees and suck dick." Greg flushed and kicked the ground. "He doesn't know what it means!"

"Get on your knees and suck dick," Joan whispered. "Chinese, Japanese, dirty knees." She repeated the lines in her head; the words were like soot in her brain.

"It was a joke! I didn't mean it."

"But you gave him the picture."

"I've got tons. They're from these magazines."

"What magazines? Where did you find them?"

"Upstairs, in my dad's—" Greg caught himself. He looked hopefully beyond; at something, or someone, coming near.

Joan didn't bother to see what it was. She released the brake. She didn't stamp on the gas but let the car roll forward until there was the crunching of metal. She felt sorrow only for her own vehicle: she had nearly given it a nickname, something Chinese she could repeat to herself, and now was glad she hadn't, otherwise she would have cried. The little maroon BMW had served her so well over the years. It had been temperamental at times, being German, and as the BMW pressed into the long black Mercedes, Joan felt as if she were committing mechanical fratricide.

It would be Bill who dealt with the insurance. The impact and damage were both greater than Joan expected—the car was in the shop for months, and Joan had to drive Bill's Jaguar, which made both her and Bill unhappy. Greg Zimmer would not bother Jamie again, and in fact Jamie would enjoy a rather unbothered existence for the remainder of his years at JJS. There were times when teachers would pause at the sight of his name on their roster the first day of school, thinking it sounded familiar; Greg's mother liked to tell the story, broadly and in great detail, of how Jamie Lauder's mom had nearly killed her son in the parking lot.

"Asian drivers," Lainey Zimmer would conclude with a sigh.

Greg would not speak further on the incident. When his parents asked if he knew the child of the mother who'd hit their car, he shook his head. Though of all parties, Greg would be the one who recalled the incident most deeply, as sometimes Joan appeared in his dreams. She would haunt him in this fashion even into adulthood; he adopted the habit of being excessively polite to older women, especially foreign ones with dark hair.

As for Joan: she mostly mourned the car. Bill offered to buy her a new one, given how easily it had crumpled, but she insisted on driving the repaired BMW once it returned from the shop. It never ran completely the same—the motor made a putt-putt-putt sound as it started up—but she continued to drive it, and after a while Jamie and Lee became used to listening for its metal stutter as Joan approached. The noise meant that their mother had arrived, and they would come out front to be taken home.

II

THE HOUSE
WAS PROMISED

CHAPTER SEVENTEEN

New businesses were opening all the time. Not just restaurants but supermarkets too, Indian and Japanese and Korean. Fancy new stores appeared in the malls, and traffic on the freeways seemed to double overnight. It was what Bill always said would happen in Silicon Valley—he was, after all, in real estate, though he was retired now.

In August, they met Trevor and Dina for dinner. The restaurant, called Seasons, was Vietnamese, one of the slick new breed of Asian restaurants with flattering lighting and a separate menu just for wine.

The server arrived shortly after they were seated. "We're waiting for friends," Bill said, and the server nodded. He appeared slightly older than Joan, in his early forties maybe, with slicked-back hair, and there passed between him and Joan the silent exchange she always experienced in close proximity with another Asian person. He looked at her and Bill once more, and for the first time in a long while Joan felt embarrassed. I'm a serious person, she wanted to say. I'm not what you think!

"Sometimes I wish I had a place like this," Joan said once the server departed. The interior had been decorated with care, with sheer drapes and golden panels and artful photographs of the Mekong River. It was the sort of restaurant where Joan could imagine dining alone with a book, which she never did.

"You do?" Bill looked surprised. "A restaurant? Do you even like cooking?"

"Of course I like cooking," Joan said, insulted, although in her heart she knew she was not a particularly talented or even interested chef. What usually spurred Joan to return to restaurants was not the menu or decor but the interactions to be had: Cindy, the head waitress at Olympia Grill in Cupertino, who would sit and chat when dessert came, but only if you had ordered the lemon orzo soup which was her grand-mother's recipe; Big Chan, who owned the tofu shop in San Mateo and would always call out when he saw Joan: Ah, here she comes, it's my very best customer! On those afternoons when the chores ran tedious or the children were difficult and Joan felt that boxed-in anxiety creep, she would visit one of her favorite institutions and come home feeling, if not outright happy, then at least reassured.

Could she open a place like this? Joan wondered. Some little spot that brought out that feeling of contentment? What would she serve there? How would it be?

"Restaurants have tight margins," Bill said. "Didn't you take that small-business course?"

"Yes," Joan said, distracted. Her head was still filled with ideas.

"Well." Bill cleared his throat. "You know I'd be supportive of any-thing you wish. But something like a restaurant, it's a total commitment. You'd be gone all the time. You'd hardly see the children."

"It's just a silly daydream," Joan said after a moment, sad that Bill's feelings were so transparent, especially since they both knew she would never follow through. For most of their marriage—with two major exceptions—Joan had bent her choices to Bill's convenience. But Lee and Jamie had been two *major* exceptions indeed.

Dina and Trevor arrived. Dina was wearing a burgundy dress that flattered her coloring. "Happy birthday to Jamie," she said, kissing Joan and then Bill on the cheek. Jamie had turned twelve last week.

"He loved the video games," Joan said sincerely. Dina always remembered the children's birthdays and purchased terrific gifts.

Food and drinks were ordered, and soon after Dina and Bill were talking, as they remained great friends. As she often did when left with him, Joan asked Trevor about music. "Do you really like concerts so much?"

"Yes." Trevor sipped his beer. "Why would you think otherwise?"

"Maybe you changed your mind and can't stand live music anymore, but people keep asking because it's all they know about you."

"Is that all you know about me?"

"It's a lot of it," Joan said honestly.

"What do you not know?"

Joan thought about this. Bill and Dina were still talking, but not animatedly; the restaurant was also a quieter sort of place.

"What do you listen to when you want to feel sad?"

"Tom Waits." He paused. "Now I get to ask you something. Do you like to know the end of movies before you watch them?"

"Never," Joan said, enjoying both the question and him for asking it. She thought she could smell his cologne: something with neroli, maybe some sandalwood.

Joan and Trevor had never spoken about their conversation in front of his house. Joan had relived that memory many times over the years— in particularly sad, lonesome moments, she had positively *dined* on it. It had taken on a significance in her head that she knew had no basis in reality, yet this didn't diminish her pleasure. She wished she had recorded every bit of the interaction: how Trevor had smelled and if he'd really pressed his fingers to the center of her palm. There was a brief period when Joan had been somewhat obsessed with Trevor himself, surreptitiously asking Bill question after question, scraping information that ultimately proved useless for her fantasies (Trevor had two brothers named Alan and Joe; he liked pinball machines and wasn't good at golf). With time, however, Joan had stopped thinking about Trevor. It hadn't really been about him.

Still, maybe I should have tried something, Joan mused. I could have been worse, given how bad Bill has been. I don't know what I was holding out for.

It was a nice evening—a fun evening. Bill wasn't as hungry as he usually was, whereas Joan was the opposite: she ate all of her rice and grilled shrimp and the rest of Bill's beef. She also drank too much and was massaging her temples by the time they arrived home. Joan had said she'd go for a bicycle ride with Bill the next morning—she wished to monitor his road safety, as he had a way of rolling through stop signs that worried her—but now she wasn't sure she could wake up in time. "Such a delicate flower," Bill teased. He poured her a glass of water. "Hydrate, my love."

Even after years of marriage, Joan had not acclimated to the Lauder routine of very early mornings; it was usually Bill who woke first. She heard him as he got dressed to go on his ride, and then she returned to sleep. She was embarrassed when she went downstairs an hour later and saw Lee and Jamie at the kitchen counter, Bill already back, spreading apricot jam on croissants.

"I don't understand how you have so much energy," she said. Bill only shrugged, a little smug.

The next weekend, when Joan woke, she found Bill asleep next to her. Aha, she thought. Finally. After Joan finished making breakfast (she did a "fancy" breakfast on Saturdays, a berry French toast), she went upstairs and saw Bill was still sleeping. When she opened the drapes and he woke, he rubbed the back of his arm over his eyes. "I'm tired," he said.

"Did you go to sleep late?" Sometimes Bill would stay up and read. The light had bothered her when they were first married, but now Joan could snooze through it.

"No, I went to bed when you did." He yawned and stretched, making a V with his arms. She could see his stomach when his shirt lifted, and his skin appeared pale yellow in the light. "Is there coffee?"

"I can bring you a cup. And I'll take the kids today. You relax," she added. Bill nodded.

Both Lee and Jamie had birthday parties to attend that morning, at a skating rink and an arcade twenty minutes apart. Unlike in earlier years, Joan could simply drop them off; no more forced socialization, no more inquiries as to her husband's whereabouts (Bill never came). After the children were deposited, Joan drove downtown. There she strolled with no real agenda; she passed the bookshop and on impulse went in and bought a German motorsport magazine for Bill. Trish wasn't at the register, though if she had been, Joan would have said hello—it surprised her how often she forgot the history between the store manager and Bill. When Joan did recall, there was only a ping in her head: *oh.* Joan didn't believe those who cheated were automatically bad people. If she did, it would have been miserable staying married to Bill.

The florist was next door, and Joan splurged on a bouquet of anemones. Afterward she visited the bakery, selecting a box of pastries. While waiting for the pedestrian light to walk back to her car, Joan gazed across the street at a storefront renovation. The light blinked, and she realized it was the video store.

Joan crossed and went to the shop. She had seen the space only a few times over the years; it was on a side street she rarely visited but was where she had by chance parked. The place was gutted: the black curtain was gone, and while the shelves which had once exhibited such titles as *Wet Crimson Nights* and *Oriental Schoolgirls* still stood, they were empty now and exposed to the world.

Joan had never returned after her altercation with Milton. After graduation she had not seen Milton again, and rarely thought of him, though at times she still thought of the video store and its owner. She wished, rather improbably, that she had kept in touch with the man and wondered if she ever crossed his mind.

Well, that's silly, she thought. I'm sure he doesn't think of me at all.

She brought her hand to the window. More details were revealed: the cashier's stand by the left corner, a large storeroom in the back. Joan recalled how the sun had dappled at the entrance, settling on the carpet (the red carpet, she noted, was still there). An old childhood feeling rose, of not necessarily liking a thing but mourning its absence once it was gone.

After lingering another few minutes, Joan returned to her car and retrieved Jamie and Lee. As usual after such excursions, they were tired and sulky (these damned *birthday* parties, Joan thought again). When they arrived home, the house was silent. Joan sliced an apple and a mango into thin crescents and then called Jamie and Lee over to eat and went upstairs to change. It wasn't until she was folding her "outside" clothes and changing into the loose linen pieces she wore at home that she saw Bill was still in bed.

Joan froze, her jeans in her hands. Her heart jolted as it did when she came upon one of the children sleeping and they were completely still. She used to creep up and place her finger under their noses, just enough to confirm they were breathing. A second later Bill moved and she exhaled; she put a hand on his forehead and felt its coolness. She wasn't sure if it was *too* cool—it was a colder day—so she knelt and pressed her forehead against his.

Bill opened his eyes. "Is it the morning? I'm still tired."

Her heart began to pound. "No. It's the afternoon."

Bill blinked at her. "I'm tired," he said again.

CHAPTER EIGHTEEN

Life changed after Bill's diagnosis. The disease, oncologists said, was aggressive. Joan and Bill stopped going on bicycle rides and began to measure time as the waiting period between appointments. At first Bill was hopeful: there were a million ways to solve a problem, he said. Specialists to call, treatments to try. The trick was to remain calm and methodically work toward a solution. It was simple, and yet most people couldn't manage this. It was why he'd been so successful.

When the expected reversal didn't come, Bill became depressed and then angry. He was angry about many things: why the doctors had not given him a body scan earlier; why Joan had not nagged him to obtain one. Why he had drunk alcohol and smoked cigars and indulged in all the other pleasures that season life but supposedly shorten it. He lost energy and was resentful when others had it. Gene and Patty learned to keep out of his way—he would sometimes snap if he felt one of the cars wasn't done to standard. It was only the children, Bill said, whom he was always happy to see now.

"With the little ones, I have a few glimmers where I think it might be natural," he said to Joan. "That it might be time for me to go. The cycle of life.

"Of course," he continued, "you don't know anything about it. Being younger. Sometimes I think it would be better to endure this with someone my own age who'd understand."

"I'm trying to understand."

"You have no goddamn idea. You're not even forty, for Christ's sake."

"I'm thirty-nine," Joan said, knowing how stupid she sounded.

"Do you know how it feels to be sixty-five and about to die? Do you know what it's like to watch people around you who are older, who've treated their bodies far worse, go blithely about their days while you sit with this over your head? Sometimes I want to go up to people and tell them: You're going to die. You're going to wake up, and something's going to be wrong, and when you go to fix it, they're going to tell you there is no fix, that it's all over and the only thing you can do is prepare." Bill dropped his head in his hands. "It's so fucking lonely."

Joan rubbed his back. She willed herself not to cry; she knew both she and Bill would hate it. "I don't want you to be lonely."

"Despite what you may wish, I am."

"Do you want me to call Juliet and Theo?" Joan had tried to arrange some gatherings with Bill's family, to share the news and to spend time together. Bill left these dinners irritated, however, and his family seemed in denial, Juliet droning on about her holiday plans in Morocco. Only Theo appeared to understand that something was wrong; last week Joan had found him inside Bill's office, staring at a shell-shaped dish Bill kept on his bookshelf.

"Are you okay?" Joan had ventured. "Do you want—"

"You have no idea," Theo had said, cutting her off. He'd left after that.

Bill waved a hand now. "I don't want to see anyone. Like I said, you wouldn't understand."

Would a wife Bill's own age really be better? Joan wondered. What if she'd become sick first? Would he have cared for her? Would he have thought events so *natural* then? Bill had never minded her age before; really, if Joan were to state matters bluntly, it had been precisely her lack of age that had attracted him. Perhaps if they'd been married longer, he would have eventually left her, as he had the last three; he'd spun the wheel of wife roulette so many times, and it was only by random chance that he had landed on her for what was to be his last round.

But Joan couldn't say such things. Bill could be frustrated with his life, his health, and his marriage—she could not.

———

Joan tried to take Bill out, to restaurants or museums or back to Stanford. Occasionally he would consent, but once they arrived he would stare off, not listening, until he said he was tired and wished to leave. Finally one morning Bill announced he did want to do something: see a movie.

"A movie! Let's go today," Joan said.

"And I want to eat sandwiches," Bill added.

"Sandwiches!" Joan exclaimed.

She went to the deli first, without Bill. He tired easily now, and she wanted to prepare as much in advance as possible, like she did for the children. She regretted that it was a school day—perhaps she should have picked Lee and Jamie up early, but that would have been strange, missing school to watch a movie—they knew Bill was sick, but so far they had kept their activities as usual. Papa isn't feeling well, she told them. We all hope he gets better.

While she waited for her order, Joan rested the back of her head against the glass of the deli fridge. She was tired, not only from the work around Bill's condition but, if she were being honest, Bill himself. Dying people are not excepted from being unpleasant; they have more reason than most to be such a way. Joan reminded herself of this, and then her number was called and she retrieved the sandwiches.

At the theater, Bill didn't eat the sandwich but said he was happy with it; he liked its smell. During the trailers, he grasped her hand. The movie itself was nonsensical, something with trains and hostages. There was no part of it during which Joan was surprised, but due to the sheer joy of being out, engaged in something ordinary, she found herself gasping and laughing all the same.

In the middle of the movie—right at the point when the bumbling and gregarious teammate was revealed to be employed by the foreign-accented villain—Bill walked out.

Joan assumed he was going to the bathroom. "Bill?" she whispered, to see if he needed help, but he didn't turn. "Bill?" she whispered, louder this time.

"Quiet!" someone called from above. Joan ducked and raised her hand in apology and darted out of the theater. She spotted Bill walking away. "Bill!" she called.

She walked faster—it felt almost disrespectful to outpace him so easily, but she needed to catch up and didn't want to keep yelling. "Bill! What's wrong? Are you in pain?" She rounded the corner and stood in front of him and pressed a hand to his forehead. He shoved it off and stalked to a bench.

"I can't be with you when you're like this," he said.

Joan sat next to him. Absurdly she thought of their popcorn and soda left in the theater. All the tiny bubbles popping in their drink, turning it into a sick syrup. Soda was satisfying only for a little while; if you left it longer, it wasn't any good at all.

"You're being insensitive," Bill said.

"I'm trying to understand—"

"I think about dying," Bill cut her off. "Of everything I know and love being erased, my own consciousness going dark. Forever. And you're sitting next to me in that theater and *laughing*!"

Slowly, gently, Joan petted the back of his head. He still had his hair, although it was patchier. The skin underneath was pink and soft.

"It breaks my heart that I'm going to leave and you're going to stay here and keep on going."

"The treatments could work."

"Let's talk realistically," Bill said. "I married you because I liked that side of you."

They sat facing a poster that featured a starlet in a long gown, opposite an exceptionally attractive farmer. Joan didn't like most new movies these days; she didn't understand the storylines, which she found illogical. "If I could, I would give you ten years from my life."

"You have no idea what you're saying. You don't know how much you really want to keep going at the end."

"Still. I would."

He clasped her hand. "To tell the truth, I would probably take it." A movie was being let out; the doors opened and the audience streamed forth, blinking in the light.

"Motherfuckers," Bill whispered, watching them.

———

Bill continued to diminish. At night Joan would bring him a cup of cranberry juice, his favorite drink from childhood, and if he was asleep, she would leave it by the bed and kiss his cheek. She became religious about kissing his cheek; she felt she was showing bad faith to the gods if she didn't do so (though Joan was undecided what gods, if any, she believed in).

"Do you regret marrying me?" Bill asked one evening.

"Of course not."

"Even when I saw other women?"

"There's no reason to talk about that now."

Joan was no longer bitter about Bill's indiscretions. Perhaps in his position, she might even have done the same. It seemed to her a blessing that she had not left him, as she would only have had to return and visit, as each of his ex-wives had, and witness how little she meant to him now. Agatha and Evie had come days apart; Joan had seen how they arrived expecting some significant farewell from Bill, tears or heavy words, because there once was a time when he had loved no one more than each of them—but in the end he'd waved them away with the same emotion that he might have for an acquaintance. You tried hard to make yourself matter to others; you chased after and thought of them, and then you didn't. You cared about people in the moment, and then they dropped away. Children were the only exception to this, and even then, not always.

Pointless, was the word that kept coming into Joan's head. Pointless, pointless, pointless.

———

"Do you think you should just kill me?" Bill asked another night. It had been an uneventful evening, one without much pain or nausea. He had not required assistance on the toilet, nor in the shower that morning.

"No."

"It's something we should at least discuss."

"I don't think that's a good idea." Joan didn't look up from her book. It was the same method she'd used to deny his requests for an extra slice of cake, another order of fries, over the years. She had worried over his cholesterol and heart, and for what?

"I've been doing research. We can get morphine."

She set down her book. "You're serious?"

"Yes. Absolutely."

He'd married her because she was calm, she reminded herself. "I just go to the store?"

"You ask the hospital. It's part of palliative care."

"And then what do I do?"

"You inject it." He closed his eyes. "And I get to leave."

———

"I can refer a nursing service that'll keep you comfortable," Dr. Marcus said when Bill reiterated his request for morphine. Joan sat next to him in the hospital room—she accompanied him whenever he left the house now. Dr. Marcus was Bill's general physician whom he'd seen for years; Bill preferred his care managed through him. Joan thought in general Dr. Marcus should be sadder about Bill, as they were friends and occasionally socialized. They'd dined together multiple times, and Dr. Marcus had once shown them what he claimed was a Renoir at his house in Hillsborough.

"In my situation, a nursing service is table stakes," Bill said. "You know it and I know it."

"What else are you looking for?" Dr. Marcus cast a quick glance at Joan, which for some reason made her nervous; she bowed her head and searched her tote for the container of grapes she had packed for Bill that morning.

"Something that will actually help. Something that gives me a real choice in all this."

"The nurses will help you."

"Al," Bill said. "I'm not asking you as my doctor. I'm asking you as my friend. As a *human*."

Dr. Marcus studied Bill carefully and, when he didn't relent, released a sigh of frustration. He removed a white pad from his pocket and rolled his stool to the counter. "Morphine isn't what I'd recommend, at least not for beyond pain," he said in a clipped voice, his back turned. "I'm writing here a prescription for a certain sedative. Don't fill it down-stairs. Take it to the Longs across town." He swiveled and handed Bill the paper.

"I appreciate this," Bill said. He seemed in command, calm; he appeared more lively than Joan had seen in weeks.

"What I just gave you, it's powerful and needs to be carefully managed. Whether for pain or what you're asking. It should only be used if and when absolutely necessary."

"Of course," Bill said. "That goes without saying."

"Well, let me be clear right now that I *am* saying. And that I'm surprised by this request, Bill. You really don't seem like the type. I usually have a good feel for such matters." When Dr. Marcus said this last part, he didn't look at Bill but, rather, Joan. His eyes were hard and his mouth tight.

Does he think *I'm* who gave Bill the idea for drugs? Joan thought. Given that they were technically friends, this shocked her, though she supposed Dr. Marcus had encountered many difficult situations over the years. It had been only months since Bill's diagnosis; Joan could see how after years a caretaker might yearn for relief.

Bill asked Joan to fill the prescription, and so she did, and received a white bag with an amber bottle containing shiny red pills. Bill didn't say anything about the pills afterward, and neither did she. A week later he felt good enough for a walk. They called Theo after. Bill spoke to him for half an hour and then gestured Joan over and handed her the phone.

"Hello?" Joan said. Theo hung up.

Juliet was on vacation in Marrakesh, so they recorded a tape of Bill speaking to her. This was Joan's idea, as she had done the same with Lee and Jamie when they were little, recorded their small voices knowing that one day those voices would be gone and she would miss them. She figured Juliet would miss her father's voice too. Bill spoke for a few minutes and then Joan asked if he would like to say something to Theo. "We could record another."

"No."

"Maybe something short. A favorite memory together. He'd want that."

"I've heard enough of what he wants already. That's the only thing he talks about these days. What he wants from me after I'm dead."

They watched TV that evening. Bill fell asleep after ten minutes. He slept twelve hours and the next day he stopped eating. The palliative service Dr. Marcus referred sent a nurse to visit. "We'll glide his way when the time comes," Debby said. The nurse was no-nonsense; she had seen this conclusion many times. On weekends she worked as a pottery instructor. As she spoke, she casually picked up the bottle containing the red pills from the dresser. She read the label and shook the bottle and then set it back down.

That night Joan sat on the bed and looked at Bill. She wouldn't be able to do this, be with him on their bed, for much longer, as Debby had said they'd need to install a hospital recliner. Bill was emphatic that he wanted to die in his own bed. A hospital bed at home was the same as dying in the hospital, he said. Joan opened the amber bottle. The capsules inside were the sort she could easily open and mix the contents into cranberry juice. Put a straw in the glass, lift it to one's mouth.

Oh, Joan had her regrets. She regretted each time she had been deliberately difficult: when she'd refused to dine with Bill's oafish friends; when she'd said she was too tired for sex; when she'd interrupted him mid-explanation because she was bored of listening to Bill go on and on when she had other things to do. All these actions had been related to her pride; she'd thought they were essential to her well-being, a line in the sand. In her mind's eye, if she squinted, she could see the justification in her rebellions—she had believed, in acquiescing, that she would be giving something of herself away.

But. Your life was the most terrible thing to give away. Day after day, when you passed it not as you wanted, when you spent it as a compromise.

"We're all in one state of dying or another." Who had said this? Was it the nurse? No, Debby wouldn't have spouted such foolishness—it'd been Dr. Marcus, Joan recalled. Well, Joan didn't buy it. From what she'd seen, there was a time when you were living, and it ended for most before their heart actually stopped. It had already ended for Bill, she knew. If she did this for him, what he wanted with the pills, it would be the most loving, heroic act she was capable of.

Bill opened his eyes, but there was nothing there. She stroked his face. She was ready with the juice but understood there was no need. His breaths had become further and further spaced. She held his hand and was remorseful: for every moment she'd mused about life apart; for every dream she'd had of another man grasping her arm, bringing his mouth near. She held Bill's hand and waited; he did not breathe again.

CHAPTER NINETEEN

Theo informed Nelson of Bill's death. He'd been calling nearly every week after Bill's diagnosis. He was subtle at first but turned direct toward the end.

"I want to know about the house," Theo had said. "And whatever else I'm supposed to get."

"Let's have a meeting with your father. Once it's the right time." There was never a right time in these situations, and yet Nelson always believed one might still come.

Nelson hung up after Theo told him the news. He'd been in bed when he picked up the phone; for some foolish reason he'd given Theo his home number for emergencies, information Theo regularly abused for nonemergencies. Nelson had been reading a book as he reclined against pillows (a CEO's autobiography, which he kept rereading sections of without absorbing the content) while his boyfriend, Adam, watched TV.

Nelson informed Adam that his client of two decades was dead. He felt a heaviness about himself, as if something were being pressed across his face. "I feel strange," Nelson added.

Adam took his hand. "I'm sorry. You knew it was coming, though, right?"

"I don't think I believed it would actually happen. He was just so dynamic. I remember how exciting it was when Phillip retired and made me the partner on the account. I thought maybe Bill wouldn't keep me, but he did."

"Who called just now?"

"His son." Nelson paused to let the laugh track drain off. He was mildly irritated that Adam had not bothered to mute the TV. "Who's obsessed with whether he's going to inherit the house. And God knows what else he wants. Everything, maybe." This was a common expectation, as well as a disappointment, in Nelson's line of work. By certain logic, children might expect to be the main inheritors from their parents, but all this went out the window when there were multiple marriages. New loves that bloomed in later decades. The children of these loves, who were smaller and cuter and less bitter than the adult children.

"Gosh," Adam said. "When the death bit happens, things do seem to get wonky."

Wonky? The *death bit*? Nelson tried to suppress his annoyance. It wasn't as if Adam had ever experienced death close hand; he had an almost perfect family, a *healthy* family, and each time they called, Adam would try to put Nelson on the phone. "Just say hi," he'd whisper. "They want to hear from you!" Adam had no idea how complicated death could be, how it might be only the start of problems.

Adam passed him a joint. Nelson took it and inhaled. There was a slight lemon flavor, and he sat up and pretended to read more of his book, and then a new episode came on TV, this time *Seinfeld*, which Nelson liked. "I'm sorry about your friend," Adam said during a commercial.

"Hm?" Nelson said. He'd momentarily forgotten. And so the passing of Bill Lauder was recorded in the Das household.

———

Nelson's last memory of Bill:

Six weeks earlier, Bill had asked him to the house. It was only after he arrived that Nelson realized Bill must have timed it for when Joan was out. The front door was open, and when Nelson entered, Bill was seated at the kitchen table with a cup of water.

"Dead man walking," Bill said as a greeting.

"Don't say that."

"I'm sure I look it."

"You actually look fine." Bill did. He was paler and thinner, but his clothes mostly hid it. Nelson was impressed by those who naturally defaulted to slacks and a button-down each day, even if they were just hanging around the house. Nelson had a closet filled with beautiful clothes, but at home all he wanted to wear was pajamas.

It was Nelson's first time visiting Falling House. Bill had invited him before, to birthday parties and Easter brunches, but Nelson had never come (he liked Bill, but did not enjoy many of his type crowded together). At Bill's request, they moved to the covered patio, which he called the sunporch. The light splayed through the many windows onto the walls and floor.

I can hear all the birds, Nelson thought. It's like being seated directly in nature.

Nelson handed Bill the documents he'd requested. Bill took them and then moments later shoved them back to Nelson. "I can't read this. Just tell me the highlights."

Nelson put on his glasses. "A set amount goes to each of your siblings. Some other gifts, like your bequest to Patty and Gene. The majority to your children. Theo, Juliet, Jamie, and Lee. Four equal parts." Though there wasn't much, certainly not as much as Juliet and Theo likely thought, as Bill had not managed his funds so well over the years. Juliet's new home in Belvedere, Theo's ongoing "capital infusions," decades of alimony and school donations and a few overleveraged investments—the inflows simply hadn't kept up with the outflows. No matter how exotic the circumstances, the financial problems Nelson saw always came down to this equation.

"And Joan?"

"She's taken care of. If she spends responsibly." This last part Nelson didn't emphasize; he knew Bill wouldn't like to hear that Joan would need to live more modestly. Men like Bill had to believe they would forever be regarded as titans, great benefactors—any dent in that conviction, and the idea of death became unbearable. "Your prenuptial agreement states she receives the house if you've been married over ten years and you pass. You've been married thirteen." He recalled the lunch where Joan had asked for Falling House. In case Bill changes his mind, was what she'd said. But Bill hadn't changed his mind, at least not about Joan.

Bill nodded. He yawned, and for the first time Nelson thought he did look sick—and old. Bill directed a sharp look at Nelson, as if he knew his thoughts. "I never believed it would happen. I thought I would outlive you. I thought there would be a time when you got too old and slow, and I'd have to get a new lawyer."

Nelson nodded. He knew Bill was beyond pleasantries. "I understand why you may have thought that."

Bill stood, pressing himself against the table to push himself up. "I've got a bit of energy. Let's go outside."

Bill leaned on Nelson and clutched his arm. Once they were in the garden and could look back upon the house, Nelson was struck again by the elegance of the property. The Bay Area was changing: most of his days now were spent advising technology businessmen and the infrequent woman, people convinced they were uniquely important because they had built a company. I made this, they boasted. Without me, this (software, gadget, whatever) would not exist. But these sorts of projects were everywhere, and usually far more miraculous than whatever Nelson's clients did. They were the great volumes of water collected into reservoirs from storms, the lanes added to freeways, the museum exhibits curated. How many people had worked on Falling House? Who had set the great cedar beams inside and the flat stepping stones in the garden just so? Nelson wondered how it must feel to wake each morning in this place, to reside within such beauty and expect it as your natural habitat.

Bill coughed. From where Nelson stood, Bill appeared almost like his old self; his frailness was shaded and his eyes were young in the light. "I forgot what it was like out here," Bill said. "It's astonishing, isn't it?"

CHAPTER TWENTY

There were nearly two hundred in attendance at Bill's funeral. The crowd appeared as Nelson expected, the oldest resigned, the middle-aged freaked out. Nelson was also middle-aged, but then he had quite a lot of experience with funerals.

There was a good deal of crying. This surprised Nelson, as he had not thought of Bill's family as prone to emotion, even in extreme cases. Nelson spotted Joan in a black dress with long sleeves, her children beside her. Lee and Jamie each clutched a book, which Nelson thought smart; it was an excuse, an escape from having to speak with adults, who tended to say horrible things at funerals.

Theo was by the closed casket in a pin-striped suit. He had sobbed during the funeral's only reading, Juliet's recitation of a Yeats poem. After it was over, Nelson slipped out and called Adam.

"I wish I could be there," Adam said.

"You know you hate driving." They both did. They were staying for the season in a rental in Healdsburg while their place in Hayes Valley was remodeled. Nelson could have made the trip back, but Joan had offered him a room at a nearby hotel.

Nelson had made fifty copies of the will, far more than necessary, but he always printed extras as a policy. He brought them to the family reception, held at a Greek restaurant in Palo Alto.

"Aren't you staying for dinner?" Juliet asked when he didn't take a seat. He could feel her new boyfriend's eyes on the folder in his hand.

"No," Nelson said. "I just came to say hello. And to communicate Bill's wishes." These were the magic words. The parties were shy, or wanted the appearance of such, but one by one they came. He handed them the papers and slipped away.

———

Nelson regretted his decision to stay the night. He could have already been halfway home, though he knew that had he been driving, he would be tired and regretting things the other way around. The hotel was clean but sterile, with a king-size bed and shampoo and bar soap for toiletries, one of those chains furnished with a businessman's needs in mind. More out of curiosity than desire, Nelson opened the minibar and found it empty. He would have to remember that—to make sure the room was not charged for drinks upon checkout. He would not want Joan to think he was someone who drank from the minibar when another party was paying.

On impulse, Nelson went to the lobby bar. Unlike the rest of the hotel, the bar was dimly lit; there were records on the wall, for no thematic reason he could discern, as there wasn't music playing. There were a few others seated: a bearded man in a pink polo and two women who were clearly expecting to be approached by men. When Nelson entered, they glanced at him and then quickly returned to their conversation, their backs a wall. Was it because he was older? Or Indian? Or maybe they simply didn't like his face. When he was younger, he'd always been on the hunt for offense—there were, after all, so many aspects of Nelson for others to find offensive.

He considered picking someone up. Not to sleep with (but maybe? maybe?). He hadn't done that in years.

The bartender took his order, and Nelson briefly locked eyes with the man in the pink polo. Polo Man wasn't Nelson's usual type, and if he and Adam were compared in nearly every vector (physical, personality, taste), Adam was likely to win with embarrassing margins. And yet Polo Man was new, and newness was interesting.

A hand grasped his shoulder. "I knew it was you." Nelson recognized the voice without looking. "I'm staying here too."

Theo dropped onto the empty stool beside him. He already had a glass in hand. The two women across the bar eyed him with hope; even shiny-faced and drunk, Bill's son resembled some sort of Greek god, his blond hair pushed back, skin smooth and jaw defined. Imagine having all of that, everything Theo possessed, and still being so miserable, Nelson marveled. For Theo did look miserable.

"I bet you're happy that's all over," Theo said.

"I'm just tired. And sad. I was fond of your father."

"I noticed you didn't stay for dinner. Everyone was reading the will. But you knew that. You knew what was in there the whole time I was asking about the house."

"I'm sorry for your loss," Nelson said softly. He caught the bartender's attention and tapped a finger on his water glass. The bartender nodded.

"I really thought he would leave me the place. After all, he bought one for Juliet. And what do I have? Fucking nothing."

"You have so much, Theo."

Theo scooted closer, the stool making an ugly noise against the floor. "Do you know where Joan lived before she met my dad? Apparently she was some sort of *servant*. Whereas I grew up in Falling House; it's where

I was born. And Ava Castillo is dead in the ground. It's not like she can build another one."

"You can design your own place." Nelson nudged the water glass toward Theo. "You can make it however you like."

Theo stared at the glass, which Nelson still held. Theo moved his hand over Nelson's and then, very slowly, gently ran his pinky up and down the back of his hand. The movement was ticklish. After a moment Nelson set both hands in his lap. Theo laughed.

"Please," Nelson said, clearing his throat. "Drink some."

Theo picked up the water. In one quick motion he tilted both his head back and the glass; the ice hit his teeth and the water flowed from his mouth over his chin and neck. He continued to drink like this, the water soaking his shirt, until there was only ice.

"Are you okay?" Nelson asked, knowing it was a stupid question.

"I know people think I'm a failure. They see me, and in their head they go: *Loser.* Which really hurts my feelings! Didn't you ever fantasize about proving everyone wrong?"

"You aren't a loser."

Theo wiped his mouth. "I *told* him the house was my only wish. One fucking wish! What kind of father doesn't even give that?" He began to cry.

"Sometimes that happens," Nelson sighed.

———

That night, Nelson couldn't sleep. Theo's wet face, the water running down his neck, the comics clutched by Jamie and Lee as they stood in the pews—the images haunted him. He recalled his last meeting with Bill at Falling House. Did Theo really want the place out of sentiment? Or just for its monetary value? In Nelson's experience, these were rarely simple questions. People believed they wanted one thing and became fixated: on a divorce, a settlement, a company. They desired it to the point of obsession, and most of the time it was impossible to talk them out of it. And at the end, those instances when Nelson did manage to obtain it for them, they were rarely satisfied.

The whole business was extremely depressing.

Nelson closed his eyes, but sleep continued to elude him. This was unusual; he could normally nap in the most cramped airline seat or at a raucous party. Adam said this was just genetics and Nelson shouldn't be judgy about people who required lots of melatonin.

A chilly wind blew into the room. He'd forgotten the window was open. Damn! He didn't feel like getting out of bed. Nelson grabbed the covers and shivered: a foreboding, a tickle of paranoia.

His thoughts drifted again to Falling House. It wasn't a magical elixir; it wasn't a panacea or a fountain of youth. It was just a house. And yet people seemed to treat it as more. Nelson recalled again that lunch with Joan so many years earlier when she'd asked for the house. Someplace I can think of as my own, she'd said.

The house. The house. The words rang in his head until they formed an annoying little chorus. The house, the house! Nelson shivered again and rolled to the edge of the bed. He fumbled for the phone, his hand on the headset, as he debated whether to dial. He finally did, but no one picked up. He dialed again.

He was aware he was calling a widow, the phone shrilling through her rooms in the far too late hour, over and over on the night of her husband's funeral.

Joan still didn't answer. Nelson sat up and turned on the light. "Shit," he said.

CHAPTER TWENTY-ONE

Lee spent much of the funeral in confusion. She was ten, old enough to understand her father was dead, though not its implications. She asked her mother: Does this mean we are going to be sad the rest of this year? And the next? Joan didn't know. All day relatives had approached, making murmuring sounds; Juliet in particular had paid Lee close attention, asking in a sugary voice if she would like to be read a story, as if she were a little kid. Although it was a reminder that Lee had her book, and she'd shuffled to a corner with her newest Calvin and Hobbes. She assumed she'd be told to stop reading at dinner, but no one seemed to care. When they returned home, her mother put her and Jamie to bed.

"Close your eyes," Joan said.

"But I'm not tired."

"You've had a long day," Joan said robotically. "Just close your eyes and you'll fall asleep."

Lee closed her eyes. She tried to sleep, but that was when she thought of her father. How he lounged at the table in his striped pajamas and glasses each morning, coffee and newspaper at hand;

his fondness for beef jerky; his (impatient) attempts to teach her and Jamie chess. How impossibly little he'd felt when she hugged him through his blanket these last weeks. She hated to recall this, and yet the more she resisted, the more her brain summoned forth the memory. His bones, his loose skin, his medicinal smell. These were her last memories of Bill.

After what seemed to her like hours, she crept out of bed and went to the kitchen. There was a box of macarons on the table, which Misty had brought from London. She had flown in for the funeral with her boyfriend, a sullen-looking playwright. Lee knew by now she had been born to Misty, but Lee did not consider this significant. After all, Joan and Bill were her parents. Jamie was her brother. And Misty certainly didn't *act* like her mother.

Misty had been chipper and excited as always, softly chatting and joking at the funeral while most of the others were crying. Halfway through Juliet's poetry reading, however, Misty had abruptly risen and strode out of the hall. She had not been at the reception but appeared at the house after.

"God," she'd said, going to Joan. "It's not like I didn't know it would happen, but still. I can't believe he isn't here. It's just so fucking sad."

"Shh," Joan said. Her eyes slid toward Lee and Jamie.

"You sure you don't want me to stay over? It's no problem. Me and Keegan in the cottage."

"The hotel is better for everyone," Joan said diplomatically.

"Bridget gave me a copy of the will. I thought he might leave me our mother's earrings, but I guess Agatha snatched those in the divorce. Not that I'm not grateful for the money. I never actually *expected* anything from him, you know?"

"Uh-huh," Joan said. She made a minuscule gesture with her head to the living room, where Keegan sat, his fingers drumming an impatient beat against the side table. "Maybe you don't tell others about it."

"I'm not an *idiot*," Misty said.

Before she departed, Misty had brewed a noxious herbal concoction, touting its soothing powers. Only Jamie had dared a sip (he'd said it smelled like a box of silkworms). The full teapot sat on the counter, and Lee opened the lid. The liquid inside was murky and brown. Lee poured herself a glass of milk instead. As she took her first sip, Theo entered from a side door.

Lee could tell he was expecting her to yell or make a fuss, since he already had his hand out to stop her. "What are you doing?" she asked.

"Come here," Theo said. He grinned with only half his face turned up and teeth bared—it appeared more like a grimace, on the edge of grotesque.

Now Lee did consider screaming. Then again, it had been an odd day, and she knew Theo was part of her family, though it was only recently that she'd realized Theo's father was also *her* father. Oh, the interesting things adults managed to get up to! Lee understood she should act a certain way with Theo: polite at the very least, but also more, because they were related. This was something Jamie would do. Jamie was considerate of other people. But Jamie was sleeping—he had gone to bed when their mother said to. This was something else Jamie did (follow orders).

"I'm getting a drink." Theo reached above the fridge and opened one of the tall cabinets that historically only Bill could access. He brought down a bottle.

"What is that? How did you know to open there?"

"I used to live here, duh. There's secret spots all over the house. Though your mom did manage to find some. I opened the one underneath the stairs and found a bunch of gross snacks from China."

Lee was silent. She liked those snacks, the dried cuttlefish and haw flakes; she liked nearly all the food Joan purchased, and the meals she made too, except for the one with miniature sardines and eggs. She didn't like how there were so many little eyes, though of course Jamie always finished his plate.

Theo dropped into a crouch and stared at her. He grabbed her face with both hands.

"Ow."

"You look like him. That's the freaky part. Although I suppose you are related. In your own messed-up way." He let go and filled a glass nearly to its rim. He drank gloomily and silently. "Hey," he said when Lee turned to go. "Don't leave." She stopped. Her cheeks were flushed from when he'd pinched her.

Theo sank to the floor, massaging the sides of his neck. Next to him was a backpack, which he'd been wearing when he came in. "Check this out," he said, reaching into the bag. He brought out a gun, a dark metal object that covered his palm.

"Is that real?"

"Hell yes."

"What do you use it for?"

Theo appeared stumped. "Self-defense." He paused. "I have a lot of enemies."

"Oh." Lee didn't have any more questions. The situation in the kitchen, like at the funeral, had turned simultaneously bizarre and boring. She wondered if Theo would let her go now.

"Hey," Theo said again. "You ever heard of Russian roulette?"

Lee pressed a toe to the floor and made a circle with her ankle. "No."

"I first learned what it was around your age. I thought: Wow. A man who can do that is someone I want to talk to. My father would never dare, of course."

My father, Lee thought. "How do you play?"

"I could show you," Theo said, looking suddenly alert, "if you really want to know."

"I don't think I'm too interested."

"Well, jeez," Theo said. He put away the gun and leaned against the cabinets. He seemed a little sad about her saying no; Lee thought perhaps she'd hurt his feelings.

Lee yawned. She found she missed her father, and a swell of emotion rose. Its violence frightened her, and she pressed herself against the wall to squeeze it from her body. She dropped next to Theo on the floor. "Do you miss him?"

"No." Theo stared ahead, hair falling into his eyes. "It's mostly a blankness. The issue of the house has been consuming me as of late, anyway. Do you know how much it's worth?"

"This house? The house we're in?"

"Millions. The land alone. It strikes me as quite unfair that if he'd just changed one name in his will, all my problems would be solved, but here we are. Do you know what I'm saying?"

"Not really."

He rolled his eyes. "I'm saying Dad should have given me the house."

"But then where would we live?"

"That's probably what *she* said," Theo whispered. Lee didn't know who *she* was.

Theo had begun muttering to himself. He jammed his hand into his backpack, moving it noisily through the pockets. "It's not her fault. It's not her fault. You can't blame the kid."

"What are you talking about?"

"Ngghnnn," Theo moaned. "Fuck. Won't you shut up?"

"No," Lee said obstinately.

"What if I give you a present?"

"What is it?"

"Close your eyes and open your hand."

Lee unfurled her hand. Theo peeped at her and saw that she hadn't fully shut her eyes. "Smart girl," he said softly. He removed something from his bag and drew his hand level to hers.

Lee looked down. Her palm held a golden coin on which there was a woman sitting astride a lion.

"Pretty cool, isn't it?"

"Yeah," Lee agreed. The coin was cool. It had come from the collection of Louis Kincaid, the father of Theo's ex-girlfriend Charlotte. Louis had collected rare stamps and coins for decades (the lion was a particular favorite and worth quite a lot). When Louis noticed his box was missing, he would immediately think of Theo, but by that point Theo and Charlotte would have already been split for a year.

"It's shiny," Lee added. She held it by its tip between her fingers.

"Careful. It's worth a lot of money. I got it specifically for you."

"No, you didn't," Lee guessed.

"In exchange, I want you to do something for me."

"No."

"Fuck. You sure do say no a lot." Theo cradled his chin in his fingers. "Is it because you're pretty?"

"Well—"

"You shouldn't let it get to your head. Trust me, it only makes things more disappointing later." Theo sighed and spun a finger in the air. "Jesus, what a trip. There are bad vibes in here. Evil energy. It's probably what killed my dad."

"It won't kill my mother, though," Lee said, alarmed.

"Noooo. Not your mother. She's got that survival instinct, baby."

"Or my brother."

"Fine. But that's why you've got to listen to me, agreed?"

"Agreed," Lee said, since Theo was starting to make sense, or perhaps she was just tired.

Theo rose and went out to the backyard. He beckoned, and Lee felt she had no choice but to follow. He gestured toward the house. "Who's inside? Bridget and Misty and the rest left, didn't they?"

"Yeah. It's just my mom and brother."

"What about that lady you hang around with sometimes? Your babysitter."

"Patty's not my *baby*sitter. She helps with a bunch of stuff."

"Well, where is she? Isn't she usually in the guesthouse?"

"Not right now. No one's there. I'm *tired*," Lee added. "I want to go." She felt as if she could fall asleep while standing; though the grass was dry and poked through her slippers, she imagined it would be nice to lie down right there.

"Just one more thing. And then you can sleep however long you want."

Theo went and Lee followed, tripping across the lawn past the pool and to the cottage. She was surprised to see, at the cottage's back door, the red plastic gas can normally kept in the garage. Joan had purchased the canister, as she was paranoid about running out of gas and the sort to race to a filling station once the fuel gauge reached the half-full mark.

Theo picked up the can. "Do you know how to use this?"

"No."

"Fuck," Theo said. "It's so slippery." He placed the can between his feet and began to fuss with the nozzle, twisting and pulling.

Lee leaned against the wall of the cottage and closed her eyes. She recalled how Bill had taught her to climb a fence, his beautiful smooth leather shoes pushing into the metal links at the park as he called to her, saying, Lee, Lee, try it, I promise it will be fine. Everything will be fine, would I let anything happen to you? I'm your father. I'll be here forever. There came into the air the sharp, slightly sweet scent of gasoline Lee knew from trips to the Exxon station down the street.

She squeezed her eyes shut tighter. A smell wasn't anything to worry about; the world often smelled strange. Her father had too at the end. She hadn't liked it; she was sensitive to scents. Bill and Jamie had teased her, saying she was like an animal. The memory was as clear as if it had just happened, as if Bill were before her right now, calling her his little fox.

She opened her eyes. It was only the dark before her, the black sky and white stars.

The smell was stronger.

The little cottage was like a fairy tale in the light. Her favorite spot inside was a nook on the second level, too high for children to sit on without fear of falling, though she had sat there plenty of times. Perhaps Theo had done the same.

Lee shoved her hands in her pockets. Her fingers touched something solid, and she brought out the coin. The metal was dull without direct light, and she had to tilt it to see its face. The woman wasn't riding the lion, she saw, but walking alongside it.

Theo appeared from around the corner. "Up," he said.

"Look at this lady," Lee said, not moving.

He yanked her roughly by the arm. "Hey!" Lee exclaimed.

Theo brushed a hand through his hair; his eyes were unfocused, and he was breathing heavily. "No time to look now, all right? Just get up, pretty baby, rise and run. Run back to the house and open the front door, and then I want you to scream."

CHAPTER TWENTY-TWO

And so Joan would lose both her husband and her home in the same week. Nelson arrived as Joan was evacuating—together with Lee and Jamie, they watched the brave firefighters face the burn. It was Nelson's first time seeing a live fire. He felt the same primal fear he imagined animals must experience, and he wanted to cry.

Joan booked herself and the children into an extended-stay motel near JJS. Entire wardrobes had to be rebuilt, toys restocked, and she gave Lee and Jamie cash to purchase what they wanted at the mall. The authorities would eventually determine the fire was arson, which was fairly obvious to everyone. It also seemed obvious who'd *set* the fire, but there'd been no movement on Theo. When brought in for questioning, Theo said Lee was mistaken, that he'd merely been out for a walk, reminiscing about his father, and had encountered Lee. All Lee could say about that night was she'd been tired. Joan had asked Lee to try and recall more but was wary of pressing her.

As for Joan: well, she had never been a despairer, nor an overanalyzer, nor much of a crier. She had accepted, clear-eyed, the knowledge that Bill would die and worked to ease his passing. And yet now that Bill was gone, Joan found that she was, in fact, a weeper. She cried *all the time*. She'd sat crouched, sobbing into her knees the first time she saw the exposed bones of Falling House: the charred wood, the broken glass; the waste and destruction of something uniquely precious that would never exist again. Joan wept even more than she had after Bill's passing, but also because the house had been Bill's, and she'd found comfort in existing in the rooms he had, in touching the surfaces he'd touched. So many memories of him were connected to a physical object: the navy coat he wore on their first encounter; the matching commemorative sweatshirts they'd purchased at the annual tulip show in Amsterdam. The two of them in the white tops, Bill smiling at the camera without a trace of self-consciousness. FLORIADE! scrawled in bright alternating colors. And now the sweatshirts, the photos, the navy coat—all of it was gone. Joan had cared so much about the house, she had wanted to live within its rooms and gardens for the rest of her life, but she would have given it all to Theo in exchange for it to be still standing. For Joan too knew it was Theo.

Do I even want him to be caught? she debated. Does it matter? Does anything change? It did not escape Joan that burning down a house was a terribly violent act; it did not seem to her rational that she should bring her pocketknife "just in case" on morning walks through the park but not consider Theo, moving freely about the earth, as a threat. Yet the truth was that something in her brain didn't want to go further. For the first time she understood the Lauders' historical fondness for "sweeping things under the rug," of hoping a large, inconvenient matter might simply disappear.

"He's Bill's son," Joan told Nelson. "I don't want anything bad to happen to him."

"That's a nice sentiment," Nelson said, who was helping Joan with the authorities and insurance. He didn't add that it was questionable whether Theo felt the same way—whether he didn't want anything bad to happen to *her*.

"The only part I worry about is our safety. Should I be concerned?"

Nelson paused, as he was trained to be cautious. And yet what could Joan do? She had lost her husband and house; anything Theo could have wanted was already gone. "I think he's learned his lesson," Nelson said, knowing that most of the time this wasn't actually true.

———

Though Theo would retain an attorney and be questioned multiple times, he would never officially be charged with the act of arson. For most of his adult life, he'd been convinced he was singularly unlucky—that the fates, his father and mother and a string of stepmothers and siblings and potential employers and girlfriends—had all conspired against him. Theo didn't know why else he would have been given so much for it to come to so little; he did not understand why he was told he was attractive, and privileged, and rich, only to be fired from jobs and for girlfriends to leave him. It should come easily. He had, after all, seen it come easily to many others.

Since childhood, he'd vacillated between logic and frenzy. The weeks after the fire, he would enter a period of lucidity; he was fearful but calm, and as the days passed, he realized that if he escaped punishment, it would be the greatest luck of his life. And his fortune held. There was no breakthrough in the case, no persistent investigator with time and curiosity on their hands; it was simply inaction on the part of the authorities, a combination of laziness and ineptitude, that ultimately allowed Theo to escape prosecution. These things happen more often than the public thinks, and certainly more often to people like Theo.

On the one-year anniversary of the fire, Theo would ask Nelson to recommend a therapist. The significance of the date was not lost on

Nelson, who took care to find the ideal referral, an older man Nelson knew came from an East Coast family with money. A year later, Theo began a new career as a ski instructor in Maine. He no longer wore tailored suits or requested the sommelier at dinner; he shopped discount stores and drove an old Toyota (though Theo would always be a little snobby—his favorite put-down, almost to the end of his life, would be "nouveau riche"). One afternoon, when he was returning from a sailing expedition on Casco Bay, his tire blew out and he nearly rolled his truck off the side of the road. The woman who pulled over and taught him to change a flat was named Gretchen Peters. Many years after their first meeting, when Theo and Gretchen were on a road trip through California, he would drive on a whim to that old address in Palo Alto. Gazing at the lot, he noted the familiar marks of fence posts in land and the stump that was once a flowering acacia. The white birch, still standing, where he and Bill had hung a birdhouse.

As he parked, his gaze was caught by the glint of a foil wrapper in the wild grass. What could it be, broken glass? Or perhaps that coin he'd given Lee? He recalled the long smooth mornings of childhood, waking early and crawling into his parents' bed. The glow of his mother's jewelry on the shell-shaped dish atop the bedside table in the shards of morning light. He would never again feel so protected, so immortal. After a minute Theo stepped out with Gretchen and, with his hand, shielded his face from the sun.

"This is where I grew up," Theo said.

CHAPTER TWENTY-THREE

In the years after the fire, Joan became someone who celebrated Christmas. She, who'd secretly thought the holiday a wasteful spectacle before, now approached the weeks after Thanksgiving with zeal. She hung lights. She purchased a big balsam fir, nearly to the ceiling, and then in later years added miniature pines she openly referred to as the Christmas babies. She shopped year-round for ornaments. Each time Joan and Bill had traveled, he'd purchased an ornament. All those pieces of glass and porcelain from Munich and Tokyo and Vienna had been lost in the fire.

Joan and the children were living in a townhome now, one of fifty-six identical structures in the closest multi-unit zoned housing near JJS (it wasn't *that* near). Joan thought it indicative of the local real estate bubble that all fifty-six units were occupied, because they were designed in a crazy way. The homes were extremely skinny and tall, as if a regular townhouse had been pressed between two hands, and a bathroom directly faced the entrance on each level. The garage was on the first floor, and you lived on the second and third floors. There were many young families in the complex. The mothers carried their strollers up and down the stairs.

Starting in early December, Joan hung lights in nearly every corner of the townhouse, on all three floors. Coming home after school, Jamie and Lee thought it was like entering an enormous lit shoebox tilted on its side.

"You're going overboard," Misty told Joan one year. She was not staying over, as they no longer had space for guests, except for a futon in the living room which Misty found unacceptable.

"Lee and Jamie like it," Joan said without turning. Jamie had brought home a nutcracker from woodshop, which she was trying to display in a way that didn't make it look too lonely.

"You need to get back to a nicer place. Aren't you rebuilding?"

"Not yet."

"Why not? It's been what, five years?"

"I'm fine for now." In the months following the fire, Joan had been unable to stomach the idea of rebuilding Falling House. She didn't even like to visit, as the sight of the razed lot hurt her heart. The insurance payment was sitting in an account, earning negligible interest, and for some reason, Joan—the sort to scrutinize each utility and credit card bill in detail—simply threw away the bank statements unopened in their envelopes when they arrived each month.

Misty shrugged. "It's all right to be in the in-between."

"Yes." Joan liked this term, the *in-between*. "That's exactly where I am."

"Right, so." Misty straightened. "Who cares if you're in this weird house. Your damn mansion got burned down! You've got nothing to be embarrassed about, living here."

"I'm not embarrassed," Joan said, startled.

"Sure, sure."

"No, really." Joan felt strongly that Misty should know this, that she wasn't embarrassed. Or rather: Joan was embarrassed, but not for the reasons Misty believed: she was embarrassed because she had once been married, and lived in a grand house, and believed she'd figured life out—no, not just figured it out, *excelled* at it—only for her husband to pass away and her home to be destroyed.

A year after Bill died, Joan had gone to Lotus Garden. She'd thought it unlikely that Sam Wu, the owner, might still be around, but when she walked in there he was, in his yellow button-down and black slacks, and when she said she used to work there, he neither affirmed nor denied recalling her. "You want a job?" he repeated. "Doing what?"

"I was a hostess," she said.

He squinted at her a long moment. "You would not be reliable," he pronounced, upon which Joan believed she might just combust from shame, right on the spot. For it was true that even with Bill gone Joan lived a life of privilege; she had a roof over her head and enough to feed herself and her children. She had no real incentive to work at a place like Lotus Garden—nothing, that is, but her own desire to feel needed. All this Sam Wu could decipher within seconds of their meeting.

Joan adjusted the nutcracker and placed a sprig of holly in its arms. "I invited Juliet and Theo to Christmas dinner," she said. The extended Lauder holiday gatherings had tapered and then ceased after Bill's passing; Joan sometimes spoke to Bridget on the phone, although rarely.

"Oh, great," Misty said. "The terrible two. I hope *this* place doesn't end up in cinders." (Misty always made casual reference to Theo burning the house down, as if it were a fact accepted by all.) "When are they coming?"

"They aren't." Theo never responded to her invitations, whereas Juliet seemed to possess some special ability to call and have it go straight to the answering machine. Once she had sent a card: *Best wishes*, she'd written, beneath her letterpressed initials. After Bill's death, Juliet had returned to medical school. She was busy with residency, she said. She'd probably be busy for a long time.

There was that toy Jamie and Lee had made one winter. What was the name? Planet Infinity, Joan recalled, their mantra being that it would fulfill their infinite desires, though in reality Jamie and Lee had often been unhappy while playing. The children had built and demolished and rebuilt and argued until usually Joan had to step in.

"I'm supposed to feel *happy* on Planet Infinity," Lee cried after an argument, brought about after she dented one of Jamie's model cars. In revenge Jamie had knocked down a section of the structure, the plastic unicorns and firemen tumbling to the floor. "That's why we made it. So everyone can be happy."

"Sometimes that's just not possible," Joan had said, recalling her own dream as a child, the little world of the Satisfaction Café, which even as a fantasy had never reached anywhere near the dizzying heights of what her own children imagined for themselves. "Sometimes it's good enough to be content."

Joan didn't know if Juliet and Theo were happy now; at times she wasn't even sure about Lee and Jamie. But she did hope they were at least accepting and not bitter about their place in life.

"Why do you keep inviting the twins?" Misty asked.

"Bill would have liked it," Joan said. She knew he really would have. Just as he wouldn't have been surprised that Theo and Juliet didn't come.

III

THE DEMON ROCK

CHAPTER TWENTY-FOUR

When Joan dreamed of Taiwan, she usually dreamed of it in summer. The ovenlike heat and humid wetness on skin; rows of single-speed bicycles, metal white in the sun. The place was fading in her conscious memory, though when she dreamed, the scenes from childhood were clear, the people dimensioned and bright.

Many of Joan's former Stanford classmates visited Taipei. She could as well: her passport and papers were in the same butter-cookie tin. The tin, which also contained her jewelry from Bill, was one of the few items she'd saved the night of the fire.

Her entire childhood, Joan had lived in the same apartment in Taipei, near the electrical utility where Wen-Bao worked. Their unit was on the first floor, and they shared a wall with a family with six children who fought all the time. At night their shouts and screams pierced the air. The father liked to gamble, and first the mother would begin wailing, and then the children would join. Occasionally the father would lose his temper, violently slamming the walls.

Joan's mother loathed the noise, but what Mei truly hated was that the neighbors' apartment was nicer than her own—their unit had not been improved since they moved in, and there were many things wrong with it. The paint on the walls was chipped, and the door had come slightly off the hinges in a way that meant in the summers, when the wood expanded, it didn't fully shut. Why don't you fix it? Mei would shriek at Wen-Bao. Don't you feel shame, letting others see your wife and children come in and out of this place? But no, you don't care. You go across town and spend money on your mistress.

"Shut up," Wen-Bao would roar. But he never hit her, as the father on the other side of the wall did to his wife and children.

In the complex was a lovely courtyard with a lush square of grass in the middle. Because they were the closest unit to the courtyard, it was unofficially theirs (or so they considered it); Joan and her brothers would often run on the grass, on the edges of which were scattered large stones. They played a version of a game enjoyed by children all over the world, one where the grass was lava, the stones safety.

There was one strange aspect to the courtyard. The rumor was that, years earlier, a young woman had been murdered in a unit by her husband and his parents. Dissatisfied with her performance as a wife and daughter-in-law, they had chopped her body into little pieces and cooked them in a large pot. What remained, they buried in the courtyard, next to the loquat tree. Often when Joan played, she could not help but glance at the spot of dirt where the woman was supposedly buried. On the surface was a boulder, as high as Joan's chest, its surface streaked with brown and red.

Though the story was long denied by others in the complex (perhaps due to a fear of its impact on property values), still it persisted; as a little girl Joan imagined the woman's blood had somehow risen into the boulder, and had nicknamed it in her head "the demon rock." When Joan played, she was careful not to press against the rock. When her brothers dared her to climb it, to escape their lava monsters, she refused and let herself be caught.

Directly across the courtyard was one of the nicest apartments in the complex. The man who owned this apartment was named Joseph. He went by this Western name—rarer for men of his generation—because it was said he did business with Westerners. Joan thought Joseph's fancy name matched his apartment: it was twice as large as her own, though he lived with only his wife, a hardworking nurse who rarely socialized. Joseph was younger than Wen-Bao, and he was tall, extremely tall—after work he often stopped and chased the children in the courtyard. Upon catching them, he raised them onto his shoulders, which made the children feel like they were giants.

Joan often wished Joseph were her father. He was so different than her own, so much more dynamic and funny and interesting. Once he made a stray remark about her height, as she was relatively tall for her age, causing her to obsess over a possible familial link for weeks. She engaged in elaborate fantasies in which he was revealed at school to be her father, striding into her classroom and interrupting the lesson to announce he was taking her to an amusement park. How impressed her teachers would be! She would go and live in his apartment; she would visit her brothers, and they would be a little more careful with her, for now she was important too.

One morning when Joan was eleven, she threw up at school and was sent home early. When she arrived—having walked the mile in some digestive discomfort—she found a young woman in the kitchen.

"Oh, hello," the woman said when she saw Joan. She was washing a teacup. She was small, shorter than Joan, though a full-grown adult, with bright lipstick—when Joan saw her, the image that came to mind was a porcelain doll. "How are you?"

Before Joan could answer, her father appeared. "Ah, it's you," said Wen-Bao. He was hastily straightening his sweater and looked almost fearful.

"I wasn't feeling well," Joan said as explanation.

"Oh." Wen-Bao coughed. "This is Ling. She is, ah, helping me do some work."

"Okay," Joan said as she waited to hear about this work. Ling seemed to be holding back laughter, but neither she nor Wen-Bao elaborated further, and so after a few seconds Joan went to her room. The rest of the day proceeded as ordinary—so ordinary that Joan forgot to tell Mei she had been ill—until at dinner, while looking at Wen-Bao, Joan had the sudden thought that she hated her father. But that was *strange*, wasn't it? Why would she feel such a way?

"Have you ever seen anyone at the apartment?" Mei asked the following week. "Anyone who isn't a member of this family?"

"Yes," said Joan.

"Who?"

"A woman. Wearing lots of makeup."

Mei narrowed her eyes and Joan prepared to be slapped. There passed a long silence. "Your brothers lied to me," Mei said. "I've asked them many times. Only you dared tell the truth."

Initially the implications of the exchange were lost on Joan, as in the moment she was only relieved not to be hit. That evening at dinner, however, Mei served Joan first, right after Wen-Bao: she received five thick, tender pieces of duck, as well as the largest sesame ball for dessert, and finally Joan made the connection. How wonderful it was to have her mother's approval! How easy life was once you were liked!

And thus the first time Joan saw *Joseph* in the house—and now it was Mei who emerged from her room in a robe, flustered and hair mussed—Joan kept her mouth shut. Joan liked Joseph, after all, and he always had some pleasant words, inquiries about her schoolwork; often he would leave a snack for her on the counter, dried squid or seaweed crackers. Once Mei came out and saw her eating.

"Just be sure to finish before your father returns," Mei said. It wasn't a distinct order of the sort Joan was used to Mei barking but rather a light, private request, as if they were in friendly conspiracy.

Because her brothers stayed late at school for tutoring, it was only ever Joan who was home when Joseph visited. "Come try these chocolates," he said to her one Friday. "A business partner brought them. From France." Joan thought the shells, milk swirled with white chocolate, were the most delicious dessert she had ever tasted.

By now Joan had more of an idea of what Mei and Joseph did in the bedroom when she was sent out to study in the courtyard. But even when it was sweltering and Joan was forced to seek shade under the thin branches of the cherry tree, she didn't mind—Mei was the nicest she had ever been, and Joan closer than ever to her dream of an amazing father. Perhaps Mei would leave Wen-Bao, Joan mused. Joseph would move in. Or better yet: they would move to his place.

Weeks later, it was Wen-Bao who questioned Joan. He trailed her as she took out the garbage one morning.

"Have you seen anyone in the apartment?" he asked once they were outside. "Anybody new?"

"No," Joan said quickly. She could feel the sun tilting onto her face as Wen-Bao studied her, and she shifted her gaze, which landed on the demon rock, radiant in the light.

"Right," Wen-Bao said after a long moment.

There were small changes after that: Wen-Bao kept the same hours at work but no longer stayed every other weekend with his mistress in Shilin; he remained home for entire Saturdays. Mei did not appear bothered. In fact, she was happier than ever. And Joseph continued to visit.

The days stretched into summer. Taipei summers, so sticky and hot: funny how you could live someplace your whole life and never get used to the weather. Joan hated sweating into her clothes and was constantly searching for shade and fanning herself. She had a threadbare set of pajamas she was embarrassed by but wore openly come July. It was two pieces, a top and shorts, of the softest cotton, and little holes had been worn along the seams from all the use over the years. One afternoon Joseph surprised her in the kitchen as she was putting away dishes. She startled, not realizing he was inside.

"How old are you now?" Joseph asked. He was tying his robe around his waist.

"Twelve."

"You shouldn't be running around in such clothes." Joseph looked pointedly at her shirt, and then his gaze went to her legs. He drew a sharp breath and put his hand between them. His fingers were still; the cotton of her shorts was so thin as to be nearly nothing, and so Joan felt the full heat of his palm. Joseph looked at her while he did this, peering down from his majestic height, and she saw for the first time that his face was not perfect, as she had always thought—his eyes were uneven, and on his right eyelid was something small and white, a wart or some growth.

He brought his mouth closer to hers, the human scent of his breath pushing heat into her face. He did not kiss her but lifted his free hand to the side of her neck and parted her lips with his finger. Pressed it in slowly until his nail touched the back of her throat.

At that moment Mei came out from her room. She did not speak but stopped and looked first at Joan and then at Joseph. Joseph removed his hand, wiping it against his pants, and Joan stared at the floor. She could still feel the heat between her legs and on her face. Wordlessly Joseph and Mei returned to the bedroom. Once they left, Joan went to her own room, changed into slacks and a sweater, and rushed outside.

She was miserable in so many layers but concentrated on putting the event out of her head. Most important was that the day continue as normal: it was normal, yes, just an ordinary day. She looked at the demon rock, which did not appear more vivid in color—she had the theory that it fed off misery—and was gratified to find that, if anything, it was less red, as if the heat had sucked away its energy. And indeed, in another hour, when Joseph came from the house, he nodded and smiled at Joan as he always did and proceeded back to his apartment.

Good, Joan thought. She smiled at the back of him, making sure her eyes smiled too—a genuine smile, as if he could see her.

That night at dinner, Mei said one of her dishes was missing, the large tray with an inlay koi pattern that had come from Japan. Before Joan could deny touching it, Mei had already launched at her. After a while Joan gave up protesting and simply crouched with her hands over herself, knees to her chest. In between blows Mei stopped to shout: about Joan's irresponsibility, her ungratefulness—and if Joan turned her head, she could see that even her brothers had become nervous, and Alfred in particular was looking at Wen-Bao. But her father kept eating.

Eventually Mei tired, and after delivering a final kick, she returned to the table. When Joan went to her room, she saw her stomach was already blooming with red and purple. The next morning she noticed the demon rock appeared darker as well, mottled with old blood like her torso. The rock looked not just alive but *healthy*—as if it had received a transfusion of life.

From then on, Joan avoided Joseph. When he visited, she would immediately exit to the courtyard, where she sat at the very edge, out of sight. Occasionally she went to the back of the complex, where there were a few broken wicker chairs surrounded by cigarette butts and no shade, but was also where Mei and Joseph never ventured. There were more beatings from Mei—dissatisfactions ostensibly to do with some missing item or incomplete chores—but these instances lessened until they reached the same frequency as before Joan's encounter in the kitchen with Joseph.

And then Joseph stopped coming. Joan wasn't certain when this break occurred, except that for a while Mei's beatings increased; they would happen in the evenings and sometimes on those Sunday mornings when Wen-Bao hadn't returned yet from Shilin.

At some point Joseph disappeared entirely. The rumor was that he had left his wife for a wealthy Japanese widow; his abandoned wife, the long-suffering nurse, moved out in the middle of the night, and one day a group of men came and removed furniture from the apartment. Joan watched as they carried out dressers and chairs. One of the men, clumsily handling a table, hit the demon rock, and Joan gasped as a chunk fell from the boulder. It was impossible—the chair was wood, the boulder rock—it didn't make sense! Once the movers were gone, she ran over and examined the shard, which was the size of her fist. Pick it up, she commanded herself. Don't be an idiot; there is no ghost or monster or demon!

She dithered some more and then bent and picked up the shard. The next second she dropped it, shocked by its heat. It was winter; it had not been a hot day. But the rock was warm, as if it were alive.

When Joan dreamed of Taiwan, the demon rock was always present. It was there in her dreams when she was fifteen and when she was forty-five. She knew that if she ever returned, it would be there, waiting for her.

———

In the spring Joan received a call asking her to come to JJS for a meeting. At this point Joan had been driving to JJS for fifteen years, as it went from elementary to high school. Joan had been tempted to switch to the local public school on numerous occasions, usually in the midst of one of JJS's aggressive fundraising drives. But JJS had been Bill's preference, for all his children.

For the conference, Joan parked in the same lot where she'd once struck Lainey Zimmer's Mercedes, and walked to the administrative building. There, sitting outside on a chair, was Lee.

"Hi," Lee said, looking up. "Were you busy?"

"I just came from the post office." Joan had been mailing a package to Jamie, who was now in his second year at the University of Pennsylvania.

Joan had no idea why he had chosen to move so far, as Jamie had never expressed any interest in the East Coast before, and thus she'd convinced herself that he had selected the college specifically to get away from her. She would sometimes announce this on the phone, even though she knew it made her sound paranoid and naggy. "It's a good school," Jamie would reply. He'd usually say he had to go right after that.

"What'd you put in the box?"

"His winter coat. And snacks. Socks, even though he won't care about them." Joan recalled she had meant to include bedding. Well, she'd just seen on a flyer that Macy's was having a sale—she could go after she was done with this JJS business. She peered down at Lee. "Why am I here? Aren't you supposed to be in school?"

"I don't know," Lee said, even though she did know. She started to cry.

———

Trauma as a word, a concept, became popular sometime between Lee's sophomore and junior years in high school—to her it appeared quite suddenly, its adoption in the student lexicon fast and broad, and utilized to explain away all sorts of unpleasant matters, like shitty grades or fighting. Second semester, her chemistry partner was allowed to skip lab and given the midterm to complete at home because her grandmother had died. When Heidi Frazier returned to class a week later, completed midterm in hand, she told Lee about the funeral.

"Her body was in the coffin, but it wasn't Nana anymore," Heidi said. She still wore all black. "I can't stop thinking about it."

"Right," Lee said. She exercised all her resolve not to slap Heidi across her smug sad-girl face.

Though the truth was, none of the hardships Lee endured ever bothered her the way people thought they should; none of them made her more likely to cut school, or shoplift, or drink. When she did do such things it was because she wanted to, out of the usual reasons: boredom or curiosity or desire. To use, say, her house burning down or her father dying as an excuse for smoking would be tilting the universe out of balance, incurring a cosmic debt. Lee would rather be punished.

She was unique among the girls she knew in high school in that she did not have a best friend. If the weekend came and Lee had no plans, she spent those hours alone, reading or watching TV; other times she would go out with her brother or mother. Lee knew it was not cool to spend time with your family. Then again, maybe *this* was Lee's trauma, because she was acutely aware that one day her mother would be gone, and she knew how that would feel and what it would be like to regret. To hold remorse for all the ways you didn't love your parents enough while they were alive.

The morning Lee was found with Charlie Brooks, it was not their first time sleeping together, though it was the first doing so on campus. She had arrived early that day, had pushed him into meeting her, because, well—afterward she wasn't too sure. She supposed part of it was she would be graduating soon. For the past thirteen years, Lee had spent the majority of her waking hours within the school's halls. Even in her earliest memories, JJS was there; it was the scene of her most vivid triumphs and humiliations.

Charlie was not a student but a teacher. He'd recently graduated from Columbia and taught advanced math. Lee had met Charlie by chance at the park, where she had been walking Athena, the bad-tempered beagle from next door. As Lee often did in such interactions, she wondered whether Charlie found her attractive or repellent; these were the two modes she seemed to occupy as a seventeen-year-old. When it might be the former, it became a challenge to see how far she could take it—could she get him to say she was pretty? To touch her? Their first few meetings, they did not speak of their personal lives. When they finally did, it was in short, direct statements: Lee told

Charlie her father had died. He told her his brother was dead. She asked if he thought it was worse to lose a sibling than a parent.

"Yes," Charlie said bluntly. He added: "He was my twin."

This level of loss impressed Lee. As did the fact that Charlie did not bring up his brother again. He did not use it as a topic in poetry, as the only other student Lee knew at JJS with a dead parent, Lawrence Kelley, did repeatedly in AP English. Charlie did not reference his brother in the late hours of a house party in which earlier he'd poured endless shots of cheap vodka, proclaiming Lee a cocktease when his ridiculously long tongue came at her ear and she shoved him away (Lawrence Kelley again).

Charlie had dimples and spoke with genuine affection for his family dog (a full-size poodle). He gifted her copies of his favorite comic (*Transmetropolitan*) and poured Lee her first glass of Sauternes. When they slept together, he had a way of reaching his right hand behind his neck and yanking off his shirt in one smooth motion. For the rest of her life, Lee would be a sucker for small masculine acts done well: the loosening of a tie, a one-handed reverse parking job. The sight of a man putting on cuff links could leave her out of breath.

Charlie served as the yearbook adviser, and his working quarters were the small office behind the journalism room, which was where Lee met him that morning. Who could have known Gwen Stein had been coming in early Tuesdays and Thursdays to use the school's desktop editing software in her furtive attempts to pad her college applications by launching JJS's first "literary magazine" (*Waves We Break: Voices from JJS*)? That Gwen had a slight crush on Charlie, Lee was sure, was part of why Gwen narced—but she was also a do-gooder. In her written complaint, Gwen noted the *power imbalance* of the relationship, which Lee knew Gwen considered modern thinking, some real hot feminist stuff, and which Lee believed truly dumb. There were so many greater levers of power besides age: wealth, looks, instinct; there were certain people who would always hold the upper hand in relationships, no matter how old—they simply understood how to operate.

After that grim conversation with Cindy Watling, the head of the upper school, Lee followed her mother to the car. Throughout the conversation with Cindy, Joan had sat mutely with her hands in her lap; she had not even objected when a suspension between five and seven days was proposed (Arnold Zimmer, the younger brother of Greg, had recently been sentenced three days for breaking a classmate's arm). At the end Joan had merely ducked her head toward the administrator as if half bowing in apology.

In the parking lot, Lee and Joan sat side by side in the car without the engine on, the way they had years earlier while waiting for Jamie to finish soccer.

"I hate it when you don't talk," Lee said. "You seriously don't have anything to say?"

The panther on Joan's finger stared at Lee with its even green eyes. Joan continued to look straight ahead, hands on the wheel.

Finally Lee broke. "I'm scared of you dying." She was surprised as she said it to discover it was true. When Lee was little, she had asked Joan over and over to promise she would not die. Her mother had never acquiesced, not even right after Bill had gone.

Joan snorted. "Who says I'm dying?"

"Dad died."

"Your dad was older."

"But you're going to die. One day. Right?"

"Everyone has a difficult life. Everyone has a tough time. Your dad died; I am sad about it. I know you are sad too. But it's not an excuse. You don't need to date teachers."

"Charlie's only twenty-three. He teaches *calculus*," Lee added, instantly regretting it. She herself had not qualified for Calculus BC; it would serve only to remind Joan of yet another failure.

"I hope you feel stupid. In the future, if you want to do something, you should ask yourself: Would I feel stupid? After all, you have a very nice life."

A nice life. Lee thought it presumptuous to assume her life was nice—and she was tired of *being* nice too, she was sick of being considerate, and appreciative simply because her dad was gone, and she understood one day her mother would be too. She knew enough of Bill's history to infer how he'd indulged (though some of her classmates' parents were divorced, no one she knew had a dad who'd been married *four* times); she also suspected Joan had in the past indulged in her own secretive ways. "You must have done things you knew were stupid. How could you have had any fun otherwise?"

"Who said I've had *fun*?" Joan asked.

———

Finally Joan started the car. When they approached the house, she didn't park in the garage but pulled up alongside the driveway. "Go in," she told Lee.

"Where are you going?" Lee asked.

"Macy's," Joan said. There was that sale she'd seen earlier—she could find sheets for Jamie. She reversed and didn't say bye.

Lee went to her room. One of her windows faced their neighbor, Mrs. Kim, and Lee could hear Athena whining from the yard. Given the unanticipated disruption to her schedule, Lee hadn't taken out the dog yet today. Joan wouldn't let her accept payment for walking Athena, as she claimed Mrs. Kim had already endured enough bad karma, given that she had two children whom she'd worked long hours at the dry cleaner to support, including scrimping to buy a Honda Accord for their use in high school, only for them to grow up and move away and never visit. At the moment Lee was angry enough that she could imagine never visiting *Joan* again—it's because you were a terrible mother, was what she would say. You were emotionally stunted. It's a miracle I turned out so normal.

Lee had a phone in her room, a slim clear handset in which all the wires and inner workings were visible. She also had Charlie's number, though she never used it. They always simply met at his apartment. Her fingers drummed the phone's plastic.

"Oh!" Misty said when she heard Lee's voice. Misty and Lee didn't talk much, though Misty always sounded pleased to hear from Lee. Her mother spoke with Misty more often; on occasion Lee would return home from school and see Joan with the handset, her voice sounding disgusted as she insisted: "I don't want to go on *dates*."

"How are you?" Misty asked Lee.

"I'm fine." Lee twisted the phone cord between her fingers. "I, ah. Wanted your advice on something."

"All right," Misty said, clearly interested, and already Lee felt better. Misty had always held a distinct, if faint, fascination for Lee. She understood Misty was biologically her mother, but Misty seemed to live so differently—it wasn't only her energy, her clothes and hair, but also the practical elements Lee observed. What would it be like moving around all the time? Or having a mom who was really fun for a stint but could abruptly descend into hysterics? The boyfriends too, and there were so many, had always seemed suspect—Lee could not conceive of having her personal space constantly invaded by a rotating cast of construction managers and novelists.

Joan had told Lee about Misty when Lee was eight. "People will talk" was how Joan explained things. And over the years people did talk, but usually not to Lee—they assumed she was adopted, which they were sensitive enough not to refer to directly but alluded in circles around, waiting for Lee's confirmation. Sometimes when other mothers saw Joan with her at school, Joan's face blank and back stiff, Lee's hand and hers near but not touching, Lee could detect a hint of dismay, of nosiness shrouded in what the women might claim was concern—they did not think someone like Joan could truly have Lee's best interests at heart.

It wasn't that Joan didn't have her best interests, Lee knew. It was only that she didn't understand; she had come from an ocean away, from Taiwan. She'd never had casual boyfriends; she'd basically married the first guy she'd ever dated (Joan's children didn't know about Milton and never would).

Lee told Misty what had happened. She tried to be honest: she included even the details that made her look bad, like asking to see Charlie's apartment. When she finished, there was a stretch of silence. "Why are you telling me this?" Misty asked.

"Just to get your perspective."

"What did your mother say about the whole thing?"

Lee told her.

"Well," Misty said, "she's completely right."

"Right," Lee repeated. Her heart pounded; she had not considered that Misty might agree with Joan. "Right about what?"

"All of it. It's some old dude you were with, right? Sounds like a wack job."

"He's not that old. And he's been through a lot." Lee paused. "His brother died."

"Everyone has issues," Misty said without sympathy. "Jesus, you and a teacher. Your mom must have been out of her mind when she heard."

"No. She just sat in her car and then drove off to go shopping."

"That's when she's really pissed, don't you know? The only thing worse would have been if it was Jamie. Though your situation is bad enough, don't get me wrong."

"Why would *Jamie* be worse?" Jamie was the golden child; Lee was constantly paranoid about being compared.

"Because if it had been him hooking up with some crazy old witch, she might have gotten pregnant. And then what if she wanted to *have* it? Jamie wouldn't have any control over that decision. It could literally ruin his life."

Throughout the conversation, Lee had been winding the phone cord around her finger; she pulled it tighter now, to the point where she thought the cord might break. "Just to be clear," Lee said, watching her finger purple, "you're saying it would have been worse had Jamie hooked up with a teacher, because if the teacher had gotten pregnant, he wouldn't have had any control over whether she had the baby."

"Yeah. Exactly."

"Uh-huh." Lee's finger had gone numb. She released the cord.

"Listen to your mother. Do what she says."

"She doesn't say anything."

"What, she's not punishing you?"

"No. At least not yet." Lee left a long space as if to imply Joan might still punish her, though Lee knew she wouldn't. Joan rarely punished either her or Jamie; it was like she didn't know *how* Americans punished children and was afraid to get it wrong.

"Why are you bent out of shape, then?"

"I don't know."

There was the sound of the garage door opening. "I have to go," Lee said. After hanging up she stared in the mirror and found her reflection looking unnaturally healthy: her hair was shiny and her eyes and face clear. She forced herself to think of Charlie, to relitigate their time together. How special she had felt that morning, as she had every morning these last weeks, as if in possession of an exclusive, precious secret; the shock of Gwen entering the room, Charlie recoiling from her as if she were something repellent, the few seconds afforded by the light being off not nearly enough time to recover. The slow, wretched understanding that some humiliation—Lee just hadn't been sure what sort—would soon be visited upon her. Joan's look of disappointment (and disgust? had it been disgust?) when they were called into Cindy's office and Joan was informed of the transgression.

With all this in consideration, the tears sprang easily enough. Lee wept and felt her face swell and then went to the living room, where Joan was unpacking shopping bags.

"Clearly you had a good time at the mall," Lee said, sniffling.

"Yes." Joan didn't look up. "I found a matching set. Duvet and pillowcase. Sixty percent discount."

"So you're completely fine with everything."

"What, you don't want me to be fine? You want me to be angry?"

At times Lee thought her mother either a horribly callous person or a master strategist and manipulator. She dropped onto the couch. "Fine," she said.

"Fine," Joan echoed, unzipping the clear plastic duvet cover (useful for storing objects) and setting it aside, as she knew Jamie would just throw it away otherwise. Though, in fact, Joan was not fine. Roaming the sale aisle at Macy's, as she attempted to locate a flannel set for Jamie and half a dozen other nice-to-haves on her bedding list, she had been flooded at once with rage; not at anything in particular, but rather everything. Her son, residing across the country in a state he had never visited before deciding to move there, a foreign, Eastern place with cold people and freezing temperatures; the sadistic bedding merchandisers at Macy's, whose faulty logic had spurred them to purchase an unreasonably optimistic quantity of red plaid pillowcases, forcing her to dig through a mountain of Ralph Lauren–branded product to access the sole pack of gray at the bottom of the bin. As Joan had waited in line to purchase, she'd found herself behind a mother and daughter from which either or both emanated a strong, headache-inducing vanilla scent. The daughter was around Lee's age and wore a flippy miniskirt with sequins on the hem which had clearly just been purchased, as there was a price tag still hanging from the side. The mother had bent back her head and admired her daughter's outfit from behind. "The boys will go crazy over you in this," she'd said, squeezing her daughter's shoulder.

When Joan went shopping with Lee, Lee always came out looking older than her age (Joan's last selection for her had been Donna Karan pants from Loehmann's, which were charcoal and shapeless, albeit very comfortable). Joan had never held up a skimpy dress and said: You will look sooo gorgeous. She had never said: The boys will go crazy. She had never spoken of sex at all with either of her children. Even though Joan knew—oh yes, she knew!—that sex was all around.

In short: Joan was a rotten mother.

Because Joan couldn't say any of this, what she did say was: "Are you okay?"

"Yes," Lee said with dignity. "I'm fine."

"It's only it isn't normal. For someone so old to be interested in a high school student. The age difference isn't normal."

Age difference, Lee said. That was rich, coming from Joan.

Oh, how children could pierce you! But Joan deserved it. What an incredible experience parenting was: all the ways one could suffer—endless ways, really. Those nights back in Taiwan when Wen-Bao didn't return from his mistress's apartment and Mei would sit and despair, Joan recalled the disdain she'd felt toward her mother. She didn't see why Mei had married Wen-Bao to begin with; how silly of her to have made such a poor choice, and then continued to stay around and suffer for it.

"Your father and I were both adults," Joan said.

"*I'm* an adult. You don't think I've been through a lot?"

"You know you can always come to me with a problem." Joan wondered what Lee meant by "been through a lot." "I promise I won't be mad. I will help you."

"I'm fine, really. There is no problem."

"You understand I love you and Jamie. I will never not be here for you."

"Jesus, Mom." On impulse, less because she wanted to and more because she thought she might regret not doing so in the future, Lee bent and kissed Joan on the cheek. Joan blinked, startled, and then kissed Lee back. Joan's lips were dry and smelled of roses; it was an awkward few seconds for both.

Later, Joan would regret having promised Lee she would always be there. She understood how fearful Lee was about death, but it wasn't true, as one day Joan would be gone, and Lee would have to manage. The urge to give her this had been overwhelming in the moment; at times it was worth it, Joan thought, to enjoy a mutual delusion. Though she shouldn't give in like that again. The demon rock, after all, was a monster with infinite appetite—it needed to be fed, it needed misery. Sometimes you had to lie and say it wasn't there. But it was. It was coming for everyone eventually. You could only hope it wouldn't be for a little while.

CHAPTER TWENTY-FIVE

In college, Lee would date a string of older men: restaurant managers and law school students and the occasional lecturer. When she graduated, she went to work for an accounting firm, and after two listless years at a Big Four, she answered a job posting for a brand called Peony, run by a former professional tennis player with a penchant for ruffles and lace named Sugi Atkin. Sugi had no actual design experience and instead dictated her ideas to a team who executed her visions. Sugi hired Lee after learning her mother was Chinese; she claimed it was because Lee spoke Mandarin, although Lee never used it at work.

Peony was funded by Sugi's husband, a pleasant software executive named Tim who made quarterly inquiries as to how Sugi was spending his money. Sugi always directed such inquiries to Lee.

"You tell Tim whatever he needs to hear," Sugi said. She seemed in a constant state of irritation with her husband. "What we do is serious, it's a serious business. He doesn't understand."

It was serious; fourteen months after Lee began working for Sugi, Tim withdrew funding, and the business shuttered. Lee could no longer

afford rent on her apartment in Oakland Hills. Lee was also dumped
by Kenneth Agha, a venture-capitalist friend of Tim's who resided in
a six-bedroom historical Tudor in Piedmont and—by rather suspicious
coincidence—had broken up with her the day she was fired and in need
of subsidized lodging. Lee went home to Joan, who was thrilled enough
to have a child near (and no longer dating a forty-two-year-old) to com-
partmentalize Lee's unemployment.

Back home Lee settled into a routine, buying a monthly pass to
Sunrise Pilates and applying for a new library card. Lee was surprised
that a single decision which had appeared fine at the time (quitting
accounting) could leave her jobless and single, sleeping in her high school
bedroom; it seemed to her she should have at least received some type of
warning, of bad outcomes ahead. But Lee was not a whiner (or rather,
she knew Joan hated whiners) and, that as long as she was home, she
should hand-wash her dishes and escort Joan to the Chinese supermarket
without complaint.

Besides, there were some interesting distractions. After much delib-
eration, Joan had finally begun work on Falling House, hiring both a
builder and an interior designer. Lee particularly liked the meetings with
the designer, a Swiss German named Leonard Spruch who appeared
to subsist entirely on avocados and protein bars. He and Joan had a
sibling-like relationship and constantly squabbled. Recently they'd been
debating bathroom walls, with Joan balking at the price of Calacatta
marble.

"It's just so expensive," Joan said.

"It's not that much," Leonard countered, "compared to what the
entire *house* is going to cost."

"That's what you say about everything."

"Because it's true." Leonard unwrapped another one of his bars. He
had once been very big, he said, and now ate very little. He was a large
man, tall and quite broad despite his strict diet; he exclusively wore

black athletic clothes and white sneakers and costly watches. Lee would never tell him, but she thought Leonard might look better with a few extra pounds; his face was slightly gaunt, and he seemed constantly on edge.

"There's something strange," Joan said, "about spending so much on a place for only one person. I suppose it feels selfish."

"It cost at least this much to build it the first time. And you were fine living there before," Leonard said without mercy.

"When I was younger, I thought I would be happy for the rest of my life if I could just stay in Falling House. But now that it's just me, I wonder if it's a waste."

"It's not just you. Lee will be there too, won't she?"

Joan and Lee had both gone silent then; Lee didn't say she didn't intend to live with her mother forever—and she certainly didn't want to know if that's what *Joan* believed.

———

Brent, the general contractor, called. The building permits had been approved. He drove to the townhouse, and Joan gave him the check for the deposit.

"You'll be glad to get out of here, I'm sure," Brent said, looking around.

"It's not so bad," Lee said hotly. She didn't like Brent. He wore visors indoors and had a way of speaking to Joan very slowly, overly enunciating his words. When Joan asked clarifying questions, he often addressed the answers to Lee.

"Why does he talk to you instead of me?" Joan asked. "Does he not understand my English?"

"Your English is great, Mom."

"He doesn't *like* you, does he?"

"Gross," Lee said.

With the deposit paid, Joan launched into one of her organizational sprees. She began to pack and sort, lining the sturdiest of her cardboard-box collection along the walls.

"Why are you doing that?" Lee asked, watching Joan tear through a closet. "They haven't even started building. It's going to be years before you can move."

"I like to be organized," Joan said. "We have too many things."

"Maybe I'll go to Japan," Lee mused. She was getting tired of Pilates and trips to the Chinese grocers and cleaning out broken Christmas decorations from the garage—it made her feel old, as if she'd made a wrong turn and detoured straight to retirement. Her job applications so far had yielded embarrassing results, and a light but pervasive malaise had descended, which she was desperate to shake off.

"What's in Japan?" Joan asked suspiciously. Joan didn't like Japan, as she said the Japanese had not apologized enough for the war. Because of this, Joan had a comprehensive yet rather porous embargo against the country: she refused to purchase a Japanese vehicle but enjoyed sushi. And of course she adored Patty Sugimoto, whom she still met for coffee.

"The food. The sights. I always wanted to visit the temples in Kyoto."

"The food," Joan repeated. "You know, some Americans say they don't like Chinese food because it is greasy. There is greasy Japanese food too. Just like there is light and elegant Chinese food."

"Right," Lee agreed. She watched Joan open a large file box containing what looked to be all of Lee and Jamie's art projects from elementary school and dump the contents into a garbage bag.

"I've never seen Japan. I think I should go at least once, shouldn't I?" Joan knotted the bag. "I will come on your trip," she announced.

"Oh, wow," Lee said helplessly. She had not anticipated this.

"Do you think we should ask Patty and Gene for an itinerary?" Joan regarded Lee with an eagerness that Lee understood with doomed gravity meant she would indeed be traveling with her mother.

"I'll plan it," Lee said. "I can ask friends. Patty and Gene are in their sixties, they haven't lived there for decades."

"Time passes faster than you would imagine." Joan stiffened. "You don't think they have valuable insights?"

"I'll talk to them." Lee had imagined her trip as a solo endeavor, one where she would eat and shop and, if she were lucky, have a fling with an exciting stranger. Maybe it isn't so bad if Mom comes, she thought, but she was already planning what indulgences might come after—how she would reward herself for spending this time with her mother.

———

There were advantages to traveling with Joan. The yen was strong; a dollar went only so far. Over the years Joan had managed her money with care—she spent modestly but invested in companies whose names she recognized, Coca-Cola and Home Depot and Procter & Gamble. Before their trip, Joan had asked Nelson where they should stay. Nelson had pondered for some time (he enjoyed these sorts of questions) and finally recommended the Okura in Tokyo. The hotel was fading in its grandeur, but the Imperial and Four Seasons were more nouveau. And Nelson believed Joan was at heart an old-fashioned sort of woman.

Their first days in Tokyo, Lee and Joan spent most of their time in Ginza. Shopkeepers and waiters spoke little English, directing their commentary to Joan in Japanese. "I'm not Japanese," Joan would explain.

"Are you annoyed?" Lee asked. Joan had so far refrained from speaking about World War II.

"No. They are Japanese. Why would I be insulted they think I look like them?"

More disconcerting for Lee than the lack of English were the stares; she'd forgotten how their pairing confused strangers. Were they friends, coworkers, Joan an eccentric wealthy Asian, Lee her white assistant? Back in California, when they went out with Jamie, it was often assumed that

Lee was Jamie's girlfriend. That was the only way the equation made quick sense to strangers (which was disgusting).

Out on the street, Joan tried to decipher some of the signs with Chinese characters while Lee stared stupidly at the crowds crossing the intersection. "You should have studied more in Chinese school," Joan remarked.

"Well, I didn't." Lee consulted her guidebook for where to eat. According to Fodor's, there was a $$$$ French restaurant, a $$$ Japanese restaurant, and a $$ café within walking distance.

"Why are you looking at the dollars? Just choose what is good."

"Everything is so expensive," Lee said.

"It doesn't matter," said Joan, the same woman who at home rinsed out plastic sandwich bags to dry in the sun; who kept a bucket in each of the showers as well as beside the kitchen sink to collect water for her plants.

"How about this place?" Lee had found an upscale okonomiyaki within a kilometer. "It's supposed to have a nice sake selection."

"Lee! We are still recovering from jet lag. Don't you know alcohol isn't good for that? It dries your skin too."

What I need is to find people my own age, Lee thought. I need to connect with someone who isn't my mother!

On the few occasions Lee did sight younger tourists, she would strain for the sounds of English. So far she had spotted at the Okura a group of Australian women with deep tans and massive jewelry, and then the next morning several Americans at breakfast. The Americans had exchanged pleasantries with Lee but quickly moved on once Joan appeared, which was embarrassing. Some of the issue was that the eateries and shops Joan selected were expensive (not that Lee *minded*—not exactly). The next evening they dined at an Italian restaurant.

"Maybe we should pick some less expensive places," Lee remarked. "Some spots normal people would eat at."

"What's normal?" Joan asked. "I thought this was normal. You like Italian."

"Yes, but we're in Japan."

"The concierge said this was a favorite place for locals." This appeared true; the space was filled with Japanese. "What kind of place do you want?" Joan pressed.

"Somewhere with ordinary people."

"So you want to be with people with less money? Can you explain?" Joan was genuinely curious; it hurt Lee to see how *much* her mother was trying to understand.

"Forget it." Lee studied the dessert menu. "Are you having a good time?"

"Yes. I am having a good time. Why do you ask like that?"

"Nothing, nothing." Lee sighed.

———

Joan was having a good time. This was the most fun she'd had in a long while, perhaps years. She'd forgotten how pleasurable it was to travel. When the children were little, it had been stressful—the tracking of items, the sleep schedules, the snacks and picky eating. But now, with Lee as an adult, it was like being on a shared adventure, the sort Joan had enjoyed with Bill.

So maybe I don't like being alone as much as I thought, Joan mused.

She had not, as her children assumed, been entirely devoid of male companionship since Bill. For now that she was a widow with children, Joan felt she understood with real clarity the cycle of life—the ultimate end and all that currently lay in between and the eternal problem that there didn't seem to be enough there. And so Joan had been open to relationships with a casualness that would have shocked her earlier self. Her courtships usually began with something like coffee and ended with lunch. Almost never dinner. A few times, an overnight at the Sheraton.

In the end, these encounters had not been fulfilling but, more importantly, not been absent of fulfillment; it was exciting to have someone to think of, to wonder over, to look forward to. Joan knew not every activity would carry the color of an international trip to Asia. But it would be nice to have a steady drip of companionship, of conversation, of whatever the opposite of loneliness was. Just enough to bring her along day by day.

But for now Joan was with Lee. In Tokyo! The sights! The fashions! Even the food, Joan could admit, was quite decent (though overpriced).

"Nelson did a wonderful job with the hotel, didn't he," Joan remarked one morning. "I especially like the furniture. This bedside lamp."

"You should ask the hotel where they found it. Get one for Falling House."

"Maybe." Though since arriving in Japan, Joan had trouble imagining Falling House. She didn't know if it was being in a different country, the foreignness of it—because when she thought of Falling House, it seemed foreign now too, as if it weren't Joan who was building it but someone else. She had the feeling of purchasing a beautiful gown without a proper occasion, of a potential serious misallocation of resources.

You're being ridiculous, Joan chided herself. A house is so much more than a dress. Remember how devastated you were after the fire? Remember how much you loved the camellia bushes, the sunroom in the early evening?

They went to Takashimaya that afternoon, where Joan purchased gifts for back home: lacquer teacups for Patty, pearl earrings for Misty, a handmade umbrella for Mrs. Kim next door. She found a beautiful navy coat for Jamie that reminded her of Bill and lifted it for Lee to examine. "Do you think Jamie would like this?"

"I don't know where he's going to wear it," Lee said. Jamie no longer worked in finance but had moved to San Diego, where he was in training for the navy. His decision to join the military had been shocking to Lee and Joan; each privately believed he was undergoing some form of personal crisis, though neither had voiced this out loud. When they visited him in Coronado, he had worn T-shirts with cargo shorts all weekend, which he said were provided free as part of his "gear."

Joan didn't like to think too much about what Jamie was doing in San Diego—and what he *would* be doing once deployed in an active war zone. Joan had felt as if her heart would break watching those buildings collapse in New York. She had never imagined, however, that the tragedy would have led to Jamie—quiet, obedient Jamie—voluntarily placing himself in danger. She was faced with the idea that either her son had drastically changed once leaving her home or he'd possessed something unknown to her all along.

"I'm going to get the coat," Joan declared. That way she could imagine presenting it to Jamie when he came home. Maybe next year they could have Christmas at Falling House. Joan and her children back in its rooms, drinking eggnog and strolling the garden at sunset. Wouldn't *that* be nice!

In the evening, after dinner, Joan suggested they visit the bar at the hotel. Nelson had said the Okura had a famous bar—a "scene" was how he described it. The space was sleek and cool, and in the dark the white chairs resembled petals strewn on the floor.

"I didn't know," Lee said, "that you were the sort of person to go to bars."

"You don't know everything about me." Though Joan had never gone to a bar on her own. She'd only ever visited them with Bill.

There was a group of Americans at a table, the same ones Lee had met earlier at breakfast. Joan saw Lee's glance. "Do you want to be with younger people?"

"No, it's fine."

"You can go."

"Well, maybe just for a little," Lee said. And then she was gone.

Joan watched Lee across the room. There was one American in particular she seemed engaged with, a clean-cut young man with dark hair. At least this one looked to be in his twenties. Joan had once made the mistake of telling Lee she should date men her own age, that there was nothing a fortysomething could give her that a twentysomething couldn't—at least nothing that would matter to Lee later.

"It's nothing serious," Lee had said. "It doesn't mean anything." She was still young enough to believe every avenue was open, that every bad decision could be mitigated. That recklessness was simply fun, another good memory added to your scorecard without trade-off.

Lee was laughing now. Her hair swung and was sleek and shiny, complex with dimension and color. Ah, how pathetic to be jealous of your own daughter. How nice it would be, though, to feel that sort of possibility again, if only for a while.

She'd dreamed of Bill last night. This time they'd been back at Stanford, at their usual bench watching the Screamer, although the Screamer wasn't screaming but, rather, sharing a Chinese fruitcake with his audience. "It's just so much lighter, don't you think?" Bill remarked, even though he hadn't liked such cake when he was alive. He'd preferred the heavier sorts, with layers of chocolate fondant and marzipan. And the Screamer said yes, it was very nice indeed . . .

Joan had been sorry to wake from her dream. When she read about the latest technology innovations in Silicon Valley, she often wondered why those big brains couldn't invent a device that let you continue a dream. There'd been times where the only joy in her life came when she was unconscious—and given that she'd had such a *nice* life, with plenty of enjoyable moments, she knew this must be true for others. It was this conviction of a global deficit in satisfaction that had obsessed Joan as of late; she had been thinking of it more and more.

She decided to order a drink. This was how uninitiated with the world Joan was: she had not planned on drinking. But drinking was what people *did* at bars! Someone took the seat next to her; it wasn't Lee but another woman.

The bartender came. "Chardonnay, please," Joan requested, and then waited for some judgment, confirmation that he knew she was a pretender. When the verdict didn't arrive, she felt encouraged and studied her neighbor, a young Japanese woman. She must work in business, Joan decided. She had that sort of air; she wore a sleek black dress and a Chanel tote, although what Joan really noticed was her black jacket. Where did these Japanese women find their beautiful clothing?

Joan tapped her lightly on the shoulder. "Can I ask where you bought your jacket?"

"Jacket?" The woman repeated the word slowly.

"Yes," Joan said. She motioned to the garment, though she was careful not to touch it.

"Ah," the woman said. She removed from her bag a little gold pen and a notepad. She wrote: "Oscar de la Renta."

"Thank you," Joan said.

The woman's name was Tomoko. After replacing the pen and notebook in her bag, Tomoko smiled in a friendly manner at Joan, though the smile was only polite instinct. Tomoko was adept at smiling when she did not feel happy; she was also not a businesswoman, as Joan assumed, but a hostess, at an establishment called the Silver Pearl. At the Pearl, where Tomoko was one of its top earners, she entertained customers—who often paid the astronomical bills using their corporate expense accounts—with Dom Perignon and elaborate fruit plates. When Tomoko first felt Joan's tap she thought it was another client, which would have been a disaster, as she was meeting one of her most important relationships, Rex Fujihara, a senior executive at Mitsui Bank, that night. When she saw it was another woman, she felt the same light pulse of revulsion and panic she normally experienced when encountering a female she couldn't immediately classify (wife, heiress, worker) in an expensive setting. Within moments Tomoko had identified Joan as a tourist, however—a noticeably older one—and relaxed.

They began to converse. Tomoko spoke enough English that they could communicate, and in a few instances when there was difficulty, Joan translated the word into Chinese in her head and then retranslated via a different route back to English. She found it hard not to stare at Tomoko as she spoke. Joan thought she looked like a doll, not just doll-like but a real manufactured toy, as if she had been designed by a maker whose aim was feminine perfection. Joan had always believed she took rather good care of herself—she cut her hair every three months and had amassed a generous array of cosmetics as a result of her weakness for Clinique and Lancôme "gift with purchase" promotions—but looking at Tomoko she understood that there were all kinds of details she had neglected, and that by doing so she had been existing in a secondary tier, as a less than optimal woman. Tomoko's ears shone with diamond studs (and each ear itself was beautiful, round and smooth with a perfect lobe); her nails looked as though they had been painted yesterday; there was not a visible pore on her face.

"It probably doesn't seem like much to you," Joan said at one point. She had been describing her landscaping plans for Falling House, which did interest Tomoko—the hostess had dreams of operating her own inn, a luxury ryokan someplace like Niseko, where she had once been taken on a getaway by a former boyfriend. "My deciding between persimmon varieties must seem so silly, given that you probably manage accounts for a famous bank or something like that."

She thinks I'm a *business*woman, Tomoko realized with a start. She thinks I work at a *company* all day!

Tomoko was cheered by this thought and began to act how she thought a businessperson might, professional and warm. Which wasn't much different than how she acted at work—she had to be warm there too, and interested, asking the men all about their body aches and how their business mergers were proceeding. She kept the conversation on Joan: she heard about Bill and Joan's children and how she'd come to be in Japan. Joan enjoyed the conversation so much that when Tomoko eventually did leave, she didn't feel lonely, as she had before—Joan was still alone, yes, but now she was a *satisfied* alone. Her isolation was bearable again, even pleasant, as if her time with Tomoko had set a luminous haze over the rest of the evening.

Later in the night, Lee returned. The young man she brought with her was medium height with glossy hair; he had classical features and was clean-cut in his clothing. "This is Marc," Lee said. Joan said it was nice to meet him. Marc gave Joan a short introduction on himself: he worked in finance and was in Tokyo on a month's assignment. His company's office was across the street, and they often had meetings at the hotel.

"I was just talking to the loveliest young woman," Joan said. "I bet *she* was in finance. She had the nicest clothes too."

"Mom," Lee said. "She wasn't in finance."

"What do you mean?" Joan didn't like Lee's tone; sometimes Joan noticed Lee could be rude about Joan's friends. Lee claimed Joan had been the same way with Lee's own friends in high school, but when had Joan been anything but very nice?

Lee nudged Marc. "Tell her what you told me."

"No, no," Marc said. "It's okay."

"No, tell her."

"Yes, please do." Joan finished her chardonnay, unconsciously adopting Tomoko's easy, loose style of holding the stem.

"She's a hostess," Marc said apologetically. "She works at a host bar."

"What's that?"

"A friend at Nomura took me to one. In Ginza. I saw her there. It's not the kind of place where they, uh, have sex with you," Marc added hastily. "Though they have those here too." He reddened even more.

"Yes, but then what do you actually *do*?" Joan asked impatiently.

She did not think this young man was a pervert; she simply wanted
to know!

"They talk to you. The hostesses. They play drinking games if you like."

"What else? Do you eat?"

"Yes. Well, I had some grapes and strawberries."

"Why so many questions? Do you want to go?" Lee asked, looking
curiously at Joan.

"To one of those places? Why?"

"I don't know. You asked to visit the bar tonight. Who knows what
else you might want to try?"

Lee was teasing, Joan knew, although she could—she could go. She
wasn't as shocked by Tomoko's employment as Lee and this man likely
thought, but rather she was turning the idea around in her head, trying to understand all its angles. Tomoko had asked so many questions
about Falling House. Not just any questions but *good* ones—insightful
queries that proved she'd been listening. Answering them had been
one of the first times Joan had felt enthusiastic about the project, but
now she realized her excitement hadn't been about the house itself but,
rather, explaining it: which rooms had been hers and which Bill's; her
favorite reading corner, the creative pockets of storage. It was one of
those conversations when you don't feel you've said anything wrong,
where every cue is understood and returned—an authentic connection
with another person.

Although maybe it wasn't *so* authentic. But did that even matter?
Joan wondered about the place Tomoko worked, if it was filled with
charismatic women just like her. And not only women—why not men?
Gorgeous interiors, and maybe one could order food as well, a rich slice
of chocolate cake or maybe a bowl of beef noodle soup, although since
it was Japan, Joan supposed it would be soba or udon . . .

And with that Joan knew she would never go to the place. It was
best left in her head.

Perhaps that's how Falling House should be, she thought with surprise. Left in my head.

Lee coughed, and Joan looked up, startled. "Well?" Lee asked. "*Do you want to go?*"

Perhaps confusing Joan's silence with hesitation, Marc commented: "You probably need a reservation. It's overpriced, anyway. The place I went, a bottle of champagne was a thousand dollars."

"It's a little sad, don't you think?" Lee said. "To pay so much just to talk to someone."

"They're lonely, I guess," Marc said. He looked uncertainly at Joan, who stared down at the glass between her hands. It would be near impossible, she knew, to explain to these young, beautiful people how difficult it could be not to be lonely. Young people like Lee and Marc imagined loneliness as a consequence—something you did or didn't do to end up on your own. There was truth to that; sometimes it really was the miserable who were alone and the deserving who were surrounded. Sometimes. Youth didn't understand, however, how much luck played into it, that loneliness wasn't always a choice. Whereas at Joan's age, you knew it was always somewhere ahead, waiting. It could happen to anyone.

IV

HOW TO START A CONVERSATION

CHAPTER TWENTY-SIX

When Joan informed Leonard she was halting work on Falling House and wished to redirect his efforts to a small commercial project, the designer didn't believe her. Even when she told him she had signed papers, that she was in possession of a real address, he treated it as a whim. When she asked him to meet her at the location, he arrived ten minutes late (he was usually extremely punctual) and informed her she was having a midlife crisis. "All kinds of people like you have them," he said. "Ladies who want a shop that gives them purpose in the morning. Some cute little boutique with a name like Afternoon Treats or Peaches and Cream."

"I'm past midlife," Joan informed him. "And I don't want a boutique, I want a café. A special one."

Leonard sighed. He stared at her imperiously, and when that didn't work, he sighed again and produced a notebook from his leather satchel. "Tell me exactly what sort of *special* this café is."

So Joan told him. She wanted the café to be a place one visited for conversation. Not conversation with just anyone, but rather a trained host, with the specific personality needed at that moment. One of those pleasant, easy presences others gravitate to at parties. Or a calm, quieter sort to whom those under stress tell secrets. A beautiful woman or one of those men who is not necessarily handsome but somehow—by toeing the line between humor and thoughtfulness and confidence—exudes a powerful charisma. Someone snooty for those who strove to impress. An older woman for motherly approval.

"Or customers could *not* talk," Joan added. "Sometimes it's nice to be quiet but have someone near. Like when I was home and knew my husband was somewhere inside too." Oh, how she still missed Bill!

"It sounds," Leonard said, "a little seedy."

"Well, it can't be that way. That's what I need you for. I want lots of natural light. And enough space to fit—oh, say, thirty customers. Forty, maybe."

"You do know you need tables for that. And chairs."

"You said there were liquidation sales." Leonard had informed Joan in passing of such events, where treasures could be found at below whole-sale. The idea had captivated her ever since.

Leonard touched the tips of his fingers to his temples. "Why here?" he asked, closing his eyes as if he couldn't bear the sight of the space any longer.

"I just like it."

"No special reason?"

"No." Though even with his eyes shut, Joan was certain Leonard could sense she was lying. For there was a special reason for the location: it was the very spot the Chinese video store had stood so many years earlier.

Now, Joan hadn't meant to have the café here. Really—she hadn't been thinking of it at all! The idea for a café had first arrived as a hazy thing; she had her childhood daydreams but little else. To find the loca-tion, Joan had first enlisted a high school friend of Jamie's, a young man who Joan gathered was attempting to recover from a failure-to-launch situation by obtaining his real estate license. She hadn't liked any of the sites the agent showed her, however; it was always either a problem with the location (size, parking, neighbors) or a disinterested emptiness she felt when she looked upon the space. Desperate for an alternative, she had thought of the video store. The agent had looked it up and brought her there in his mother's Lexus the next weekend. "You know," he'd said, his voice slightly hysterical at the thought of a potential windfall, "it's not only available for rent, the *entire site is for sale.*"

Gazing at the space now beside Leonard, Joan was reminded of its flaws. The site appeared to have been transformed at least once more before being abandoned yet again—there was a small kitchen where the storeroom had been, and the interiors were painted a burnt orange.

"We'll need to do something about the walls," Joan said. "The color."

Leonard opened his eyes. "Uh-huh."

"And the kitchen, you'll have to change the equipment and layout. The floors too, and—well, we'll have to change a lot."

"Are you even allowed to make these renovations? Landlords have strong opinions about such things."

"Oh, they're very understanding," Joan said quickly. "A—ah, a very nice man. Extremely flexible."

"I don't know how, given these parameters, you expect to make any money."

"I don't expect to make money."

Leonard looked skyward in a manner Joan knew indicated he was exercising extreme patience. "I wish we could go back to selecting marble for Falling House."

"I'm not doing that now."

"When?"

"Maybe never," Joan said quietly.

There passed a stretch of silence. "Didn't you already pay a deposit on the build?"

"Yes." Joan was touched by the worry in Leonard's voice (and he didn't even know she'd *bought* this place yet!). There was a time when the sunk money would have kept her up at night—sometimes it still did (Joan *hated* to waste money). She had calculated with Nelson that after the lost deposit, the remaining insurance funds from Falling House would be just enough to purchase the lot, start the café, and finance it for a few years. Joan knew many might consider this reckless. She knew the practical, expected thing would be to continue with Falling House—to smash the idea of the café and let it wither, as she had other dreams over the years.

She did not doubt her decision.

Leonard was inching closer to the shop and reaching into his bag. He removed a tape measure. "That wall will have to come down. To expand the kitchen."

"Fine, fine." Joan tried to keep the hope from her voice.

"And there still might be some use for the marble. Or perhaps some terrazzo?" He directed at her a crafty look. "We'd have to rip up that awful carpet, anyway. You say this so-called *landlord* of yours is flexible?"

Joan looked off, deliberately not answering (she didn't know what terrazzo was, and the marble really was expensive). Her gaze landed on the carpet, which was rough-looking and stained. Whichever business had come after the video store hadn't bothered to replace it, and Joan suspected it contained unspeakable germs. And yet she had the urge to run in with Leonard's utility knife and cut a piece to take home—to store in a box someplace, and to preserve for eternity.

Ah, once the video store, and then something else, and then maybe something else again. And now the building would become a café. Time was truly unstoppable. Joan recalled an old dress of Lee's that she had ripped up for its fabric and sewn into a quilt. Lee hadn't been using the dress—it had long been outgrown, in storage for years—and yet when Joan presented Lee with the pretty new blanket, Lee had cried. You've ruined my dress, she said. I'll never have it again.

In another dimension, perhaps the video store remained open. Or maybe there was an alternate world in which Joan was still married to Milton. And perhaps in a faraway galaxy not only was the video store open but the Satisfaction Café as well, and she and Bill were together. Bill still sprightly, still alive. Joan knew none of it was possible, at least not in this life; she understood a person couldn't have everything they wanted without trade-offs. But wasn't it nice to think it was possible, at least once in a while?

———

On a Friday afternoon in April, eighteen months after Joan and Leonard first met at the site, the Satisfaction Café opened for business.

It was what is referred to as a "soft opening." Joan was renting the furniture (light gray tables and chairs, inoffensive, popular for weddings), as she and Leonard had yet to agree on the final pieces; the exterior had just been painted days before. The interiors were a warm blush, a shade Leonard swore was flattering to all skin tones, with large windows which let in sun. All around the space were riots of color in the form of fresh flowers, tulips and peonies spilling from vases, interspersed with green.

Standing out front alongside Joan for the opening was Patty. After the children outgrew babysitters, Joan and Patty had kept in touch, but Joan had been surprised when Patty asked if she needed a manager.

"I thought you were retired," Joan said, not daring to ask whether Patty might be too old.

"I've been selling jam at the farmers market, remember?"

"Do you have restaurant experience? The position has a lot of responsibilities."

"No problem," Patty said.

Patty dressed in the same loose, free-spirited fashion; on opening day, she wore a paisley blouse and a long lavender skirt that caught the air when she moved. Joan had to admit Patty wasn't what she'd originally envisioned as a café manager. Then again, Joan was aware she herself didn't present much like a café *owner*, either.

Isn't that funny, Joan thought. Because of course people can do many things—I'm sure Misty could have been a CEO of some big company in another life, and Nelson a famous artist, and the list went on. Joan had found most people were more talented than the opportunities they were presented with, but on the rare occasion when someone did try and muster a change, they were told: Well, where's this degree? or: Not enough experience.

Petty little bureaucrats, she fumed. Small-minded gatekeepers!

Also at the café on opening day were the hosts Patty and Joan had hired thus far, three women and two men, whose ages spanned twenty-five to seventy. Lee was in the back, helping to prepare drinks and plate dessert; Jamie was in training and unable to come. Joan had also invited the local newspaper, *The Palo Alto Gazette*. They had run an article about the café's opening weeks prior, a result of her first and only attempt to seek "press."

Nelson came to the opening. He showed up on time, as he knew how terrible it was to throw a party and have everyone decide to arrive fashionably late while you paced the house and the food got cold. As he'd feared, he was the first guest, although Joan didn't seem to mind. She said hello and led him to a table.

"It looks wonderful done up like this," Nelson said. He'd visited the space months earlier, when he'd reviewed the business paperwork with Joan. "I'll be honest, when you first told me the idea, I was worried. But it's not so different from paying a therapist for an hour, or chatting with a stylist while they cut your hair, is it? As long as everyone feels it's a suitable arrangement." Nelson spent most of his own days assuaging clients, making them feel good, more prepared and less anxious. And he didn't get to eat club sandwiches and drink tea while doing so.

"Yes," Joan said happily. "You understand."

Suspended over their table was a chandelier from which dangled white iridescent shells. Nelson told Joan he liked her dress, which was deep green and went to the calf. "You should wear more color."

Joan asked what he thought of the furniture, which she said she was renting. "I wonder if I'm being too picky."

"I like the chandelier," Nelson said diplomatically. He did not like the tables or chairs—it was precisely their unoffensive nature that he found off-putting. As they sat together, Nelson was aware, very much so, of no other guests arriving. How awful it would be if no one came! He kept up a steady stream of prattle while observing Joan; she didn't seem nervous, which he admired, for he knew she must be very nervous and was only trying to save both of them from the emotion.

And then: finally! The door did open—and a person entered, a *new* person, a man wearing eyeglasses and a soft jacket. He had a dry cough which drew everyone's attention.

The man took a few steps. "Is this the Satisfaction Café? I read about it in the paper. Is it for real? You have some food and a conversation?"

There went through the café what felt like a collective exhale. "I'll let you attend to business," Nelson offered, but Joan waved this off.

"They don't need me," she said. She watched Patty settle the man at a table, after which she brought over one of the hosts, a former trucker named Tracy. Tracy possessed a high energy, as well as an unending string of exciting and bizarre stories from the road. Tracy greeted the customer, and after a few minutes Patty delivered a bottle of sparkling water and a generous slice of lemon cake. Soon after, the customer was laughing.

"I bet you're feeling wonderful," Nelson said.

"I am," Joan said. And she was. Joan had worried that when the café opened, she would feel deflated, as if it might have been only the concept that interested her, an idea which lost all its fizz once the various compromises and practicalities were revealed. How awful it would be to invest all this time and then feel nothing! But no, she had so much joy. Not only that, but her joy was spilling out into the very air around her—she had so many ideas! Perhaps one day they could offer a service for hosts to teach social skills— because Joan knew how unfair it was when a perfectly lovely person missed out on all sorts of things in life simply because no one had ever taught them how to behave. Or lessons on flirting, or how to walk up to a group of strangers already in conversation and successfully insert yourself. And how about a special service, a confidential and objective means of assessing how good-looking you were! Joan had always wondered whether she was good-looking; it would be nice to settle that (although she ideally would have learned this earlier). Wasn't that a smart idea? And perhaps they could expand the menu, add some of her favorites, like fried chicken—but they'd have to buy more equipment, maybe extend the kitchen. How much would *that* cost?

"Do I have enough money?" Joan asked suddenly.

"Joan, you know I am not a financial adviser," said Nelson, who nonetheless knew she did have enough money. He had confirmed with Joan multiple times: Do you understand you are giving up Falling House, not just now but likely forever? Do you understand how *hard* owning a business can be? But she had insisted, and so he hadn't pressed further.

Ah, well: Joan had made her choice. Nelson had certain clients who were always comparing, going back in time, litigating whether they'd received the best of all possible outcomes. If only I hadn't married so-and-so, they said. If I'd just closed that big deal. Optimizers, Nelson called them. He attributed it to human nature—if there existed a hundred universes, it was understandable for people to want to live in the best one. To be the most happy. Though in Nelson's experience, happiness was only a concept, anyway: a clever, slippery creature that slips through your hands right at the moment when you think you've finally caught it.

———

Later that evening Nelson was surprised to discover, looking around, that the café was full. Most of the tables were occupied, and Joan had resumed greeting customers. Adam called, and Nelson went outside.

"Where are you?" Adam asked.

"My client's opening. The Satisfaction Café. I told you about it." Adam never remembered anything.

"Oh, right. How many cocktails have you had?"

"There's no alcohol. They have tea and coffee and pastries."

"I thought there were going to be champagne fountains and exotic dancers. Men in jackets without shirts."

"It's not that sort of place." It seemed to Nelson that Joan had deliberately designed the café to prevent anything untoward. While the tables were far enough apart for private conversation, the arrangement was open, observable, and the entire space well lit, with the refined but asexual air of an English garden.

"You're not actually going to have a conversation or whatever it is, are you? You hate talking about yourself."

"I might," Nelson said, surprising himself, and he could tell that his answer surprised Adam too. Well, I *should* surprise him, Nelson thought. He'd known for months, maybe years, to be honest, that they were becoming stale—age had crept in and instead of putting up a fight both of them had settled into its soft crevices. They went shopping at warehouse clubs now and had specific seating preferences for air travel. It wasn't bad, but sometimes, even if you weren't lonely, it was nice to have different.

When Nelson went inside, Patty informed him there was only one host available, a young, somewhat sullen-looking woman with dirty-blond hair.

"Is that acceptable?" Patty asked, looking curiously at him. Nelson shot a millisecond's look at one of the occupied hosts, a surfer sort who resembled (only a little, but it was enough) a young Paul Newman.

"It's fine," Nelson said.

His host was named Gina. "How do you know Joan?" she asked as they took their seats.

Was she supposed to ask that? Wasn't she supposed to treat him like any other customer? "I'm her lawyer."

"That's cool." Gina opened the menu and placed it flat before him. "I've already eaten, so just get whatever you like."

"What qualifies you to do this?" The question came out harsher than intended, but he was irritated, for both himself and Joan, as Gina didn't seem professional at all.

"I'm not usually a host," Gina said. "I was hired for the kitchen. But we're only doing dessert today, so I'm helping out up front."

"Then you're a chef?"

"Yup. I used to work at Mountain House."

"Huh," Nelson said, opening the menu while he collected his thoughts. For Mountain House was Nelson's favorite nice restaurant in San Francisco; he'd been trying to land a reservation for months. The place utilized a rather maddening booking system—requests were taken at precisely eight p.m. on voicemail, and the line was always busy. What kind of chef had Gina been? Why had she left? And, more importantly, could she get him a dinner booking, preferably a four-top near the back corner?

Gina knew what Nelson was thinking. She recognized from prior interactions with the moneyed and fussy that sometimes they had to release a certain amount of hostility before settling down. "I was a pastry chef," she said once he'd ordered. "Though before that, I did savory. Sixty-, seventy-hour weeks for *years*. The head chef, Dion, he's all right. But he leaves all the operations to his partner, and Fredric is a jerk. He harassed a bunch of the staff and finally we all quit."

"It seems terribly unfair that one bad apple could cause so many problems."

"That's how it usually is, in my experience."

Nelson thought about all the bullies and jerks he'd encountered over the years. "The world is so disorganized," he said. "It drives me crazy to see someone throw an aluminum can in the trash when there's a recycling bin two feet away. But what qualifies me to complain about the terribleness of humans? I do all the things I hate, I can be wasteful and uncaring; it's only that when I do it, I've always got an excuse, and I just assume everyone else doesn't care."

He hadn't meant to say so much—it simply slipped out. Nelson was always aware that when he spoke, his clients expected to derive value. He was never able to blurt his thoughts; everything had to be weighed, to justify his fee.

The lemon cake arrived. "Did you make this?" Nelson asked. Gina nodded, and he took a bite. "It's incredibly delicious," he said, and found he wasn't as embarrassed as he usually was when giving an effusive compliment. In fact, he wasn't embarrassed at all.

Later, Nelson would look at his watch and discover an hour had passed. During his conversation with Gina, there had been no great revelation; it was more a pleasant conversation, one that took little effort on his part, the way he might converse with his favorite cousin over brunch. He searched for Joan, locating her by the entrance. She was smiling, and he was surprised to see lines around her mouth, as he still thought of her as a young woman. It would be nice, Nelson mused, if the café were open for many years. Then you could visit those hosts who knew you earlier; they could remember you in the way of old friends.

So. Was this it? Was this what Joan wanted? Though he'd enjoyed conversing with Gina, Nelson couldn't decide if it—whatever "it" was—was enough to sustain a business. He couldn't decide if there was enough to draw him back, or if it was like being seated next to someone at a wedding reception where you have a pleasant enough evening, but don't care to keep in touch after.

It was enough. The café wasn't perfect: there was the issue of the furniture, which didn't fit the ambiance; the chairs and tables didn't seem like permanent residents. It took Joan some time to figure out the food as well (the menu would never make much sense; it would always be a collection of baked goods and sandwiches and Joan's favorite Asian dishes). There were also customers who visited for the novelty and never came back; customers who came hoping to fall in love and have love returned. The café's first week of operations, Joan had to eject two men who came in drunk and a woman who tried to grab a host's crotch. The female hosts, at least in the first months, were free of any sexual advances; this was accomplished via close management from Patty as well as the chef, Gina, who said she possessed a special sense for perverts. "They usually look ordinary" was Gina's statement on the matter. "You've got to look for those who look *deliberately* ordinary."

Joan recalled enough from her hostess days at Lotus Garden that she was able to manage the café's opening and closing. She also hired well, or rather Patty did, and Joan was generous with salaries and benefits. And so they hired more hosts, and more customers came.

The following month, Leonard received a call from a liquidator he regularly did business with, concerning an estate. It was rare that Leonard's contacts worked with estates, as typically the collection from a single person was sparse and scattered. This had been an unusual case, however, of a woman who'd collected a certain style of table made in the 1950s, designed and manufactured by an Italian company. The tables, which were constructed of cast bronze aluminum, came in a variety of lacquered-top finishes. The woman had hoarded the tables, purchasing piece after piece, which she'd kept first in her home and later in a storage unit. When she died, her children had not wanted even one of the tables, the same as how they had not wanted her paintings or letters. All the children did want was her jewelry, which they quickly flipped to a consignment shop in St. Helena. The rest they called in a liquidator for, to carry away.

"The tops aren't all the same color," Leonard said when he brought Joan to inspect the tables. "So the aesthetic may not appear entirely cohesive." But secretly he hoped she took the lot; he had grown fond of the pieces and didn't have another client he thought would require this quantity.

Joan examined the tables. The tops were slabs of white and black and bronze and green and azure and yellow. In the back, she spotted a brilliant crimson. "One woman bought all of these? Why?"

"Obviously she was a fan of the design. What led her to buy so many, I have no idea."

Joan thought she might understand. There had been times when she'd been tempted to gorge on beauty like this—if she happened to be in a particularly depressed period and found a coat or dress she liked, she'd had the urge to gobble up every version or color, to multiply her pleasure. She tried to imagine the tables in the café and whether her customers would find the colors jarring. Or perhaps they would grow attached to a table: I always have my conversations on the blue, they might say. But was that childish, the way Lee and Jamie used to fight over the purple place mat at dinner? Though lately Joan had the feeling that people her age were reverting back into little children: ditching their spouses for new loves, learning to fly airplanes and getting drunk in the morning. Personal gratification was all the rage.

"You'll have to get chairs that match," Joan said finally. "For continuity."

"Yes, yes!" Leonard said. "I'll find the perfect ones." He felt pleased that Joan had agreed, since he had not expected her to. And Leonard did find chairs—he had them custom-made, off a vintage French design of dark curved wood. The chairs' soft lines offset the modernity of the tables, and they were smooth and comfortable to sit in for long periods. Leonard was proud of the chairs and would reproduce them for other clients, but his admiration for them would never exceed his admiration for the tables. In the future, whenever he visited the Satisfaction Café, he would feel a frisson of pleasure upon seeing them, as if they were a family he'd kept from falling apart.

———

Six months passed. Spring came and with it, rain. Joan wrote a letter to Nelson, who was on an extended trip to Europe. He had written to her first, a postcard from Lausanne, where Adam was taking a course at the design school, saying he hated the food. You would hate it too, he wrote. The only Chinese place is six miles from the city center, and all they serve is Peking duck. Nelson was going to Düsseldorf next, and he didn't know if the food there would be any better. Joan went to Ranch 99 and purchased shrimp chips and rice crackers and then visited the Indian grocer next door, where she asked the cashier for his favorites. She brought everything to Kinko's for shipping, as she wanted the package to arrive by the time Nelson was in Düsseldorf.

There was a short line to the cashier. The woman directly in front of Joan, maybe a decade older, wore a yellow dress and was talking to herself. "Now I have to mail these," the woman murmured, "and then I have the cards, and I need a few more of those envelopes, and if I have time maybe I'll go to that coffee place, the one over on San Antonio, and pick up some of those cookies for . . ."

Joan closed her eyes. Something in the woman's voice; it was so smooth and melodic. She tapped her shoulder. "Excuse me?"

The woman's name was Adele. "It's a special kind of café," Joan explained once they were finished with their packages and she and Adele outside. "I'm looking for people who like to speak to other people."

"Oh, how *interesting*," Adele said. She seemed to understand the concept or at least did not seem perturbed by it, as people sometimes were. Adele was a health care executive with a busy schedule, so she did not have time to work at a café, she explained. Besides, she enjoyed her job. "But I'd like to come visit," she added.

"Oh," Joan said, "please do!"

Never one to idly chat at a school pickup, to make friends at dinner parties, to organize the neighborhood barbecue, Joan now found herself falling in love all over the place. Just walking down the street, she would encounter two people in conversation, the friends laughing in such synchronicity that Joan would have to stop and marvel that such compatible souls had found each other. She would see an old Chinese man walking his dog and carefully scooping its waste into a bag and think: Is someone praising him for cleaning up? It wasn't necessarily something people of her generation knew to do, pick up after their pets. Was he receiving credit for being a good citizen of the neighborhood?

While earlier she'd relied on Patty for the café's hiring, Joan became a seasoned recruiter herself. She found a slightly snotty academic, a postdoc in economics who could speak for long stretches to recently retired men; Joan also hired a stand-up comic, Bobby Henderson, who could be outrageously funny but whom she had to be careful not to overschedule, as Bobby could lapse into sullenness when tired. She even found a candidate to bring to fruition her idea of a third-party assessment of attractiveness, though after user testing Joan modified the service to include only positive feedback. Pierre had been a casting assistant on Hollywood films, and his IMDb spanned *The Forever Promise* to *Demon Scream 5*. Your posture is so elegant, Pierre told his clients. You have electrifying eyes. There is a leading-man quality to your jaw.

At the year mark, Patty came to Joan. She said that since Joan was doing such a good job managing the hosts and customers, she wanted to focus on back-end operations.

"Don't you like your job?" Joan asked.

"Sure," Patty said. "It's just I want to learn something new."

"Are you tired?"

"Nope," Patty said in an insulted voice, although she was tired—she was over seventy now. Her back hurt in places it didn't before, and managing the front meant a lot of standing. And yet Patty could not contemplate retiring. Without the rhythm and purpose of work she felt uneasy, bloated with time and adrift within the day's many hours.

"We can try it," Joan said, and Patty set off. She possessed a seemingly endless appetite for administration and, in her new role, tracked the café's energy usage and the cost of ingredients and maintained a list of furniture in need of repair. In December, after reviewing their prior year's tax returns and discovering their accountant had missed basic deductions, Patty bought a textbook on accounting and asked Joan if she could file the café's taxes the following year. The IRS would give Patty plenty to obsess over; in the agency's instructions and forms, Patty felt she had all the work she could possibly wish for.

Often when Joan left at night, Patty would be at her desk. "Shouldn't you go home?" Joan asked late one evening.

"I'm fine." Patty didn't look up. "There's so much to do, and they keep changing the damn rules."

"Who are they?"

"Everyone," Patty said. "Everyone is changing the rules." She had assumed a gruffer persona in her new position and yet Joan knew in her heart that Patty was content. Joan knew it because she knew Patty, the same as she knew all her staff and many of her customers. Only a few years earlier Joan could not have conceived that she would be bone-tired at the end of each day but not wish for any other existence. That she would believe, ardently, that she had found her life's work.

Not that everything which came before wasn't important, Joan thought. I would have wanted all of it, the good and the bad. After all: pain is necessary. Loneliness is necessary. For the first time in a long while, Joan knew she was truly satisfied, and like all parents who are finally happy, her most ardent wish was that her children could be happy too.

CHAPTER TWENTY-SEVEN

Once Jamie Lauder was old enough to drive, he would sometimes do a very dangerous thing: he would wait until he was on a long, empty stretch of highway and then close his eyes. Sightless, he'd count to ten. If out of fear or impatience he hurried the count, he would force himself to start over and do it properly. One one thousand, two one thousand. There were a few close calls when another three or four seconds would have meant he'd hit a median. But still he continued. It was the only way he knew to get rid of the feeling, the urgent heat that would appear in his stomach without warning. The sensation that if he didn't do something, anything—only he didn't know what that anything was—he would explode.

The feeling had started when his father died. For months prior to Bill's diagnosis, Jamie had sensed something was wrong; Bill simply seemed *off*. He was tired; he didn't eat as much and his skin looked strange. There was a stale, almost medicinal scent to him at times.

"You don't smell good," Jamie said at the dinner table. He had meant it lightly, the way the family called Lee "piggy" because she hogged dessert.

"I don't like that," Bill said. "In fact, I think that is an incredibly rude thing to say." When Bill stood, to refill his wine, Jamie caught Joan staring at him with compassion and looked away. He worried she understood not only the depth of his mortification but also that he didn't hold her in the same awe as he did Bill. Shortly after, they discovered Bill was sick.

The morning after Bill died, Joan woke Jamie and brought him to Lee's room. "Your father passed away last night," she said. Lee immediately started crying. Jamie tried to summon tears but didn't have any and felt that trying to fake them would be doing something awful. He returned to bed, and that afternoon he ran to the railroad tracks, where a senior at JJS had committed suicide over college admissions the year before. Jamie touched the dark metal of the tracks, waiting until he could hear the train's faraway approach, closed his eyes and counted, and then ran home.

It was Bill who first piqued Jamie's interest in the military. On a random weekend afternoon in his office, Bill had described for Jamie the roles of the navy, marines, and air force—though in contrast to Jamie, Bill's study of these subjects was merely casual, a subset of a greater interest in American history. He lacked Jamie's penchant for niche obsession; he did not particularly care, for example, why the U-2 required special fuel. "It flies at the edge of *space*," Jamie said, reading from a magazine.

"Mmm," Bill replied. It was clear he wasn't listening. Joan and Lee never even pretended to listen.

After Bill died, Jamie's interest in the armed forces intensified. He was small for his age, and like many small boys, he liked to imagine what he might do with big machines. When it came time for college applications, he debated between enlisting directly or applying to the Naval Academy. The same month, Joan came home from college information night with pamphlets for Stanford and the UC system.

"Your choice," she said, dropping the brochures on the kitchen table. "I don't want to pressure you like other Chinese parents." Though Joan was more a typical immigrant parent than she claimed. Jamie knew she had not even entertained that he might not attend a traditional college or have a practical major (Bill always said Theo should have studied business) and a practical career.

His entire life, Jamie would have trouble with his desire to please.

He was surprised when Joan was upset about his going to Penn. It had the best business program, and he knew she cared about the "best."

Because most of the UPenn campus seemed to want to work in finance, soon too so did Jamie. Senior year, he accepted a job in New York at Goldman Sachs. He entered into a serious relationship with Chloe Carter, a fellow analyst with a perfect body and anger issues. His second year at Goldman, Jamie was proofreading a pitch book for Ray Kollani, a sadistic vice president with the face of a movie idol, when the towers fell. The air outside reminded Jamie of Falling House the night of the fire, acrid and thick with poison. A year later, he quit to report to Officer Candidate School, to enter the pipeline to become a Navy SEAL. Jamie didn't tell Joan he'd left his job until he was already in Pensacola for training. When he did call to tell her, she hung up on him.

"I don't understand where this is coming from," Joan said. She'd been dismayed to discover that when presented with stressful news, she'd reverted to her own mother's habit of ending a phone call. Joan had pressed her face into an oven mitt—the nearest soft object—for several deep breaths before calling Jamie back.

"I've always been interested in the military." While Jamie had anticipated Joan's disappointment, her hostility took him by surprise. "I was obsessed with the special forces as a kid."

"No, you weren't."

"I think," Jamie said, "that I'm the authority on my own childhood."

"And I just hope," Joan said, "that you don't get yourself killed. I will pray every day that you are safe."

It seemed to Jamie that Joan's accent always grew heavier in such conversations. It wasn't that she didn't already have an accent, but it became blunter, more pronounced. "You aren't religious," Jamie said, keeping his tone stern.

"I know how much you don't want to listen to me," Joan said, voice rising. "No one wants to listen to their parents!"

"If I don't try now, I'll never be able to do it. You don't want me to have some big regret later in life, do you?"

"There are lots of things you won't accomplish in life," Joan said plainly. *Her* choice of career for Jamie had been scientist or physician—she did not find investment banking an admirable profession either.

———

It was during Hell Week, the brutal five days of operationally taxing, unbearably cold and wet training when candidates were allowed a total of four hours' sleep, that Jamie first fantasized about quitting. In the Grinder, the concrete grounds in San Diego where physical training was conducted, there hung a brass bell the size of a basketball. It was tradition that any member of the class who quit had to ring this bell, and its chime would echo through the courtyard.

Jamie had never seen the bell anywhere but the Grinder until Hell Week, when it was mounted on a truck's hitch to follow them up and down the beach. Hell Week began on a Sunday evening, and by Tuesday afternoon Jamie was imagining his hands against the rope. Thursday, he became afraid he might ring the bell unconsciously, that in his delirium he would wander over and pull. They were allotted a two-hour block to sleep that afternoon, their second of the week—hungry and feverish, Jamie dreamed that an enormous cheeseburger chased him through the surf.

Friday night, when it was all over, Jamie went to the barracks, where the passing class would be under observation for the next forty-eight hours. Years earlier there'd been a graduate who'd needed his arm amputated after blood pooled as he lay in a heavy sleep, his arm limp over the side of the bed; as a result, the mattresses were now arranged side by side on the floor.

All week, Jamie had fantasized about sleeping on a real bed. Despite his exhaustion, he dragged the mattress up onto its frame.

"Nope," a staffer said, and kicked the mattress back to the ground.

His best friend in training, Nick Bregman, pointed a finger and laughed. "Try again."

"I just want to sleep in a regular bed."

"You know what I've been thinking," Nick drawled. Seconds later, he was snoring.

Nick's feet were elevated, as there were drawers placed under the mattresses to keep their legs from swelling. When the staffer had dropped Jamie's mattress, he hadn't replaced the drawers, which lay yards away. Jamie, who was already on the floor, felt he could not move an inch farther.

"Are you going to set up the mattress like it was?" Jamie called.

"You're a big boy," the staffer responded.

Nick let out another snore. That loud fucker, Jamie thought, dragging his mattress. How am I going to sleep? Staring down at Nick, who often slept with his mouth open, his arm flapped over the side of the mattress where, yes, it could have led to a dangerous amount of swelling had he been on a raised frame, Jamie felt something close to love: not just for Nick but for the whole training class he'd endured Hell Week with, even the sociopaths, even the jerks. There was something about being pushed to their physical limits that reduced people to simple machines, and it was easy to love a machine. On weekends there was a group of six or seven who usually went out, including Dave Strum, who everyone knew was heir to an oil fortune but became extremely sulky if you referred to it; John Cruz, referred to as JC, who had played football for the University of Alabama. Nick, whose rather distasteful nickname in the platoon was Ted Bundy due to his persuasive talents, was often dispatched to approach the best-looking women: "Come meet my friends," he'd say. It really was that simple. And more often than not, the girls would come, and it was all so easy, it was as if Jamie had been waiting to become this person who threw himself into the cold surf; who blew up C-4; who hated cynicism, he realized, he hated it even when it was smart, because Jamie understood now that such cynicism came from behind a desk, a desk meant to reinforce one's superiority above other, more rudimentary souls, a desk he himself had occupied for three years at Goldman.

Nick snored again. It was louder than Jamie had ever heard, almost one continuous saw.

"Is he all right?" one of the staffers asked.

"He always sleeps like that," Jamie said. The sound was familiar: it was an amplified, harder version of waves crashing to shore.

Six years later, both Jamie and Nick would be in Iraq. It was their second operational tour, and a routine was quickly established: on weekends they swam at the recreation center, after which Nick would visit the internet café to email his girlfriend and message other women on Myspace. Five months in, they flew intra-country, driving armored Ford Explorers onto C-130s to escort one of Iraq's vice presidents to his home in Erbil. There the platoon was taken to the bazaar by the vice president's personal security; Jamie purchased a scarf for Joan and helped Nick select an elephant figurine for his mother.

They returned to Baghdad, the short trip enough to add texture to the otherwise *Groundhog Day*–like consistency of their deployment, and a week after, Jamie and Nick were on a roof conducting over-watch for the same vice president's arrival. Somehow their position was compromised and a grenade tossed onto the roof. Hours later, Jamie was on a helicopter to a field hospital in Balad. Though his leg was shattered, he felt fine because of the morphine, his memory periodically wiping clean the events of the last hours before reassembling itself in gentler colors. As the rotors spun, a song wormed into his brain that matched the rhythm of the blades as they chopped: Well I *am*, well I *am*, well I *am*. Ba da boom, ba da boom, ba da *boom*. Well I am, Jamie sang in his head, happy to be alive, until remembering again that Nick wasn't.

CHAPTER TWENTY-EIGHT

Joan packed two containers of Patty's beef jerky to bring with her to see Jamie in the hospital. After Landstuhl in Germany, where the worst of his injuries were treated, he'd been transferred to Bethesda and then to California. Joan flew down to San Diego to meet him.

Jamie had a private room with butter-colored walls and wood chairs for visitors. When Joan arrived, he was seated in bed with the TV on.

"The jerky isn't as good as before," Jamie said, chewing. He muted the TV. "I think Patty used to make it spicier."

"It tastes the same to me," Joan said. The jerky was drier, but she would never admit this.

She had rehearsed what to do on the way in: how she would behave, the casual manner with which she would regard his injury. In one smooth motion she lifted the blanket to reveal Jamie's knee. He had not walked in over three weeks at that point, and she quailed at the pale and twisted flesh. To her it did not resemble a knee but rather something moldable, like clay. Joan could feel Jamie watching and kept her face still.

"I'm starting physical therapy," Jamie said.

"Good, good. Listen to everything the doctors tell you."

"They said if I work hard, I could walk again."

"Of course you will."

"They'll take me back, won't they?" he burst forth. "They'll let me deploy again?"

Why would you want to go anywhere for these people? Joan wanted to shout. Look what they've done to you!

After she returned to her hotel from the hospital, Joan sat on the bed with her hands clasped. The entire half hour–long drive back she'd been disturbed—the tall palms, the neon sport utility vehicles, the distant glimpses of the ocean through traffic—all these shining colors had darkened in her consciousness and then hung there, a rolling storm cloud of unease. But why? Jamie's injury had been terrible, but ultimately it meant he had come home. While not the best of scenarios, it was also not the worst, and the worst was what she'd so feared. And yet there was a narrative neatness to the situation that Joan disliked. She had felt, strongly, that something would happen to Jamie in Iraq. That he had returned home with what was, in the end, a serious but not catastrophic injury, well—it felt to her as if the universe had taken something else instead.

Nick Bregman's mother, of course, had been dealt a different narrative. Joan had struggled with how to contact the woman, whom she had met only once, although it had been a *nice* once, at lunch after navy graduation. Joan recalled how Jamie had been so nervous—he'd pulled her aside less than a block before they arrived at the restaurant.

"You have to behave," he said.

"Behave?"

"Nick's mom is more conservative than you might be used to. So you can't do that thing you sometimes do."

"*What* thing?"

"You know. When you answer questions bluntly and pretend you don't know it's rude because English isn't your first language."

Joan had been indignant, and then just to prove him wrong, she'd had a lovely time at lunch, although she didn't have to try—it really had been easy. She and Carly discussed gardening and bonded over the fact that neither of their sons drank coffee. "Nick won't even chance *decaf*," Carly exclaimed, and the two laughed. Joan understood from Jamie's hints that Carly might not share her political views. She and Carly were around the same age, however; they had each been married and then widowed. They had more in common than Jamie realized.

Joan settled on writing Carly a letter expressing her condolences. Two weeks later, Carly called Joan. She remembered Joan from the lunch, she said, and how only the two of them drank coffee.

"That was one of the last times I saw Nick," Carly said. "At that restaurant. You know what's been bothering me is I can't remember what he ate."

"I could ask Jamie," Joan said, and then she regretted her words, as she shouldn't have mentioned her son was still alive.

"I keep thinking about God," Carly said. "Guessing at what His plans might be. Nick's father was Jewish, but after we divorced, I let that go. I visit another church now and I've come to see that it's a blessing, what happened to Nick."

"I understand," Joan murmured, even though she didn't, not at all. After they hung up she sat on the ground and cried, great gulping sobs.

Jamie was medically discharged from the navy and returned to the Bay Area. The apartment he found was two miles from the townhouse. Joan did not allow herself to go as far as to believe he deliberately meant to live near her.

"I'll cover the deposit," Joan said. "And rent until you've decided what you want to do next."

"No, I have savings," Jamie said. His right leg was weak, and he had a distinct limp as he helped unload the dishwasher. Joan recalled how strong Jamie had been as a teenager, his fast running and beautiful form. He had liked to watch nature documentaries after school and was quietly upset when the prey was eaten. She observed him putting away glasses in a high cabinet and did not offer to help.

Jamie did not speak about his time in Iraq or his friend dying. He would reference his injury, though not what caused it. My knee is messed up, was what he'd say. In a year his limp would go away, but it returned in cold weather. Within a few months he started work at a technology company called Atom, which Joan recognized from the news. She added it to her stock tracker.

———

After Jamie's injury, Joan became a quieter person. It didn't make much of a difference at the café—most customers were there to talk, not listen. The staff were used to not just listening but also watching, and unbeknownst to Joan, they began to watch for her as well. And so Joan too became a customer of sorts of the Satisfaction Café; Tracy learned to sit with her during quiet periods and tell stories about the customers; Patty knew Joan usually lost energy in the early afternoon and would bring over two mugs of black coffee and a plate of biscotti. Gina, the chef, decided to study Chinese food; she learned to make Joan's favorite dumplings, chopping and salting the cabbage just so.

Sometimes Jamie would visit after work. Joan bought big glass jars and filled them with all his favorite candies and snacks from childhood and displayed them behind the register. They were ostensibly for customers, but really it was to tempt Jamie. "What's this?" he'd ask when he came in. "Japanese rice crackers? Chocolate-covered gummy bears? Who's going to eat all these?" But he always helped himself to a scoop or two.

One afternoon Trevor Hall came in to see Joan. He was older now—well, they were all older. He appeared a tiny bit shorter as well, and his hair flashed mostly gray in the sun. Joan had seen Trevor and Dina on occasion over the years, though their contact had lessened after Bill died, and then the Halls themselves divorced. From Dina's telling, Trevor had quickly moved on, to a young blonde named Stacey. Joan learned this at lunch, to which she'd invited Dina several years back. They'd met at an Italian restaurant.

"Maybe we can do this again," Joan had said once they were done with espresso.

In response, Dina grasped her arm across the table. "We're too old to pretend, aren't we?" she asked, blinking her narrow blue eyes. It was the rudest thing Dina had ever said to Joan, and yet the two women regarded each other with genuine warmth. Outside the restaurant, they'd embraced for a moment and gone their separate ways.

Joan greeted Trevor and sat with him in a corner. He told her about the divorce and his relationships after, and she told him about Jamie. "I wish he'd never deployed," she said. "He could have just stopped at the SEALs. It would have been enough for his résumé." For some reason, maybe because he'd been an investment banker, Joan was under the impression that Jamie was extremely résumé-oriented.

"From what you describe, that wouldn't have made him happy."

"I don't know if he wants to talk about it. I try, and he just sits there." Joan realized this had been her complaint about Bill as well—that he didn't like to discuss emotions. It felt strange to be saying it about her adult son; she had the sensation of vertigo, of falling into a hall of identical patterns.

"He'll talk when he's ready. I don't mean to hurt your feelings, but certain topics, sons may not want to speak of with their mothers."

Naturally it hurt her feelings, but Joan believed him. She wished Jamie still had Bill to talk to: a parent who had grown up in America, as Jamie had.

Trevor rose to leave. "Dentist appointment. But I'll come see you again."

"Yes. Sure."

"No, I will. Soon." He grabbed her hand, and it seemed to Joan exactly what he had done so many years earlier—it was as if she were finally getting to relive a dream, to summon it forth as she might open a favorite chapter of a book.

Joan curled her finger over his thumb to hold it there. "Do you think it's a waste we didn't do this earlier?" she asked, her heart jumping a little. "You could have come over and seen if we got along."

"Well, you were married then. We both were. It would have been a mess."

"It could have been fun," Joan said lightly. Now that they were in the future, the suffering of a theoretical past seemed worth it, since it would be all over with by now.

"I should tell you," Trevor said quietly, "that I'm seeing someone."

Joan glanced at him, surprised he took her words so seriously, as if she were asking him to marry her. She had thought they were only flirting, being a little silly, two old friends happy to see each other. And now Trevor didn't look rakish and handsome, as he had just moments earlier, but more like an old man past his prime and then that's what he became: an old man. Part of Joan wished she hadn't seen this side of him; she wished he could have stayed as he was in her memory, a younger point of eternal possibility.

I suppose nothing stays as good as it might have been in your head, she thought. I should know that—half of the café's customers are here because of precisely this problem.

But Trevor came back to visit, as he'd said he would, and then visited again, and again. Because Joan still listened to an old-fashioned radio, the sort with a tape deck, he brought her a cassette, and Joan marveled at her first mix tape. She listened to the songs, paying close attention to their lyrics, and imagined the messages they might contain for her. Because Joan had never experienced it before, she didn't know this was an activity for the young. Joan took Trevor to the empty lot that was Falling House, filled with weeds and wildflowers, and they spoke of the memories they'd had there. At some point he was no longer in a relationship, and they saw each other more. On occasion they slept together, at either his home or hers, and it was easier than Joan had expected—he was considerate, and so was she. Joan didn't ask if he saw anyone else. Trevor didn't ask either (Joan wasn't seeing anyone else).

But not only this: over time she and Trevor became friends, and then *good* friends—she spoke to him about her business, and he gave advice. He sent her long emails, thoughts he had after a thrilling concert, or just musings, and she would think about them and respond. Some weeks they spoke constantly, multiple times a day, and then a week or more would pass when they didn't speak at all. It was fine. It flowed so easily. Sometimes there were people like this who might be a part of your life, who you wished could be a *bigger* part—but it wasn't meant to be, and you had only that limited share. Mostly when Joan thought about this she was accepting, but other times there was a hollowness inside. At the idea of having been with Trevor when they were young, of having watched the ocean roll against the crest in Big Sur, of going to a concert and planning together for the vast life ahead. Of all the things she would never experience because she was past that stage, and in such moments she would have to go and sit by herself for a while.

CHAPTER TWENTY-NINE

After Tokyo, Lee and Marc dated long-distance. Once he proposed, Marc wanted to live together. "We've been apart too much."

Lee was unsure. In her experience, relationships were rarely improved by being together all the time. "Should I ask Mom what to do?" Lee asked Jamie on the phone. "It's cliché, but I think it's crazy that I'm supposed to wake up and go to bed with the same person for the rest of my life. That can't be *natural*, can it?"

"Mom's only going to say you're complaining," Jamie said. Joan would have no sympathy—sympathy wasn't what you went to Joan for.

Marc was starting a new job in London. He worked in banking, like Jamie had, although in a different specialty, which was the extent of Lee's understanding. She wasn't sure she wanted to move to London. It was far from her family, and she didn't know how she would get a job.

"You'll find something," Marc said. "A company can sponsor you for a work visa. And until then, you can just kick it."

"I need to do something." Lee reached over and mussed his hair—she liked how he used phrases like "kick it." "I can't just do nothing."

"You won't be doing nothing," Marc said. He pushed her playfully and they rolled onto the couch.

They settled on her staying with him through Christmas as a trial. Marc signed a lease for a flat in Chelsea, and Lee brought three suitcases. Almost immediately she regretted the move. Late twenties, unemployed, living with your mother (when your mother was Joan) was bad enough, but soon Lee discovered that swapping the scenario with London and Marc brought its own distinct gloom. Every few days, it seemed she would receive a call from an old friend informing her of a new job, dog, house. "And what are *you* doing?" they would ask, and Lee, compulsively honest, would tell them she was doing nothing. She spent her first months learning the bus routes and occasionally walking to Waterstones and reading entire books in the aisle (an activity she felt was marginally less acceptable abroad than in the States). She overspent on lunch, eleven pounds for simple cheese sandwiches, and was in a rage when she discovered supermarket meal deals. And then at some point the guilt and anxiety fell away, and Lee woke one morning and found she was in love with London.

It's easy to fall in love with London in early summer. On most days Lee could walk to St. Paul's in clear weather and eat her tomato sandwich on a bench in the shade. She browsed the boutiques, where she had enough muscle memory from shopping with Joan to garner service from snooty salespeople, and occasionally allowed herself a late-afternoon cocktail at one of the chic bars on Mount Street. As she walked, Lee would surreptitiously raise her hand to admire her engagement ring in the sun. The ring was a modified square on a platinum band, and gazing at it was like looking down a staircase. When she returned to the apartment, sometimes Marc would be there. He worked long hours and at times sneaked home for a midday nap. Marc was an angelic sleeper who didn't sleep with his mouth open (as Lee did, embarrassingly); his long eyelashes were still, and he often slept with a smile, as if he had only good dreams.

In November, Lee made plans to travel to Virginia to celebrate Thanksgiving with Marc's family. Lee felt guilty about this, as she always spent holidays at home with Joan and Jamie. Joan didn't prepare the traditional dishes anymore; instead they would make hot pot, tossing in great platters of sliced beef and fish cake and tofu.

"Well, I hope you'll be here for Christmas," Joan said. "I plan to buy a very big tree. And I'll decorate the café with all sorts of goodies. It will be beautiful!"

"I might spend Christmas with Marc," Lee said, although she wasn't sure, she only wanted to hedge. "Or you could come visit me in London?"

"I'm busy with the café," Joan said. "Very busy. I'm there now." There actually was the sound of busyness, of dishes clinking and people talking.

"Is that Jamie? I want to talk to him."

"No, Jamie's at home. It's another host. Pierre."

"Another one? Do you have enough work for them all?"

"That is my policy. I meet a good host, I hire them."

This didn't seem to Lee a sustainable practice, but she didn't want to argue, as she would then risk Joan shouting "Huh?" and repeating loudly whatever Lee had just said.

There was a knock at the door behind Lee. "Housekeeping!" a voice called.

"What was that? Where are you?" Joan asked sharply.

"A hotel. Marc's parents treated us to a weekend away."

"Which hotel?"

"Claridge's."

Silence. Lee suspected Joan thought Marc's parents were snobs; she also knew her mother would never say so out loud. "You should send them a thank-you present. A nice one."

"I know."

"But with your own money. Maybe it's time you get a job. I don't know what you do all day."

"I'm exploring—"

"It's important for a woman to support her own living. It's a signal to herself as much as to others. Anyway, you get to see Marc's parents at Thanksgiving," Joan said. "So you will come visit me for Christmas." She hung up.

"All mothers are difficult in their own fashion," Toni said when Lee confessed her frustrations over Thanksgiving. Lee and Marc had arrived in Virginia on Wednesday, and Lee had warmed immediately to Marc's young, elegant stepmother.

"She's just worried," Lee said, acting the good child. She was fascinated by Toni, who was young but not too young, and who, like Joan, possessed an excellent jewelry collection. Her arms bore matching bangles in a watery silver, and when she gesticulated, they made a pleasant clinking sound.

"You should take time to find the right career." Clink clink. "Marc is obviously going to be successful. Why stress yourself?"

"It's not like I don't *want* a job," Lee said. She left out her chief complaint, that it wasn't as if Joan had made her own living for most of her life—since this applied to Toni too.

Lee and Marc had been placed in a bedroom on the first floor of his childhood home, next to what appeared to be former nanny's quarters. Having grown up in Falling House and visiting the mansions of her JJS classmates, Lee was no stranger to opulence, but the Lewis place was on another level. The house had three floors and what she'd been informed were eleven bedrooms. The interior had been chosen originally by Marc's mother, though half had already been redone by Toni, who Marc said was working through the house at the precise allowed pace of a new wife tearing down a beloved former regime's (Marc's mother had died a decade earlier) monuments. As a result, there was a disjointed feel to the rooms: a bedroom of French toile was followed by an office of stark white. The furniture was the same, a mix of acrylic chairs and heavy jacquard. Lee wondered if Marc was ever bothered by Toni's removal of his mother's footprint, but she never asked and he gave no indication of caring.

The Friday after Thanksgiving, Lee and Marc walked the grounds with Toni and Marc's father, Peter, before dinner. "Did you ever visit China?" Toni asked as they strolled through what was described as miles of preserved forestry. "I understand your mother is from there." Lee knew Marc had told his parents about Joan and Bill and a little of Misty (for she had told *him* only a little of Misty). Lee could tell from Toni's manner that she and Peter had discussed it privately and were resolved to treat the situation as completely normal.

"I went to Beijing and Shanghai when I was younger." Lee watched Marc and Peter up ahead. She was embarrassed that she sometimes felt jealous when Marc spoke to his father—they had hour-long phone conversations, and afterward Marc would recount the highlights, worship bright on his face.

"Peter and I stopped in Hong Kong on our way to Bali. It's a fascinating city. Do you speak?"

"Some Mandarin," Lee said, though in truth her fluency was poor. She was less adept than Jamie, although their schooling had been the same. It was only that people were impressed when Lee spoke any Chinese at all, and thus she had coasted for years.

"A valuable skill," Peter remarked. He and Marc had dropped back to join them. "Some might say the most valuable, given the direction of global economies."

"Oh boy, Dad swooping in with the opinions." Next to Peter, it was clear how close Marc was to his father physically—they not only were the same height but also had the same coloring and posture. "Careful. He'll debate your ear off."

"I'm sure Lee can manage," Peter said, smiling. Lee smiled back. She could tell Peter and Toni were determined to like her.

———

When they returned to the house, Marc checked his messages and said he had to fly to New York.

"It's the weekend," Lee said.

"I've been off most of the week." Marc folded a single pair of boxers and a white undershirt and dropped them into his backpack.

"But that means it'll just be me and your parents."

"I'll be back in less than twenty-four hours. Besides, my parents are *nice*," Marc said, nuzzling her shoulder. "Aren't they?"

The next evening, since it was only Lee and Toni and Peter, they ate in the kitchen instead of the formal dining room. Lee said she liked it this way because it was what they did at home. "The chicken is delicious," she added.

"I wish I'd had time to get the seabass," Toni said. "But work has been crazy. We're finalizing our holiday issue."

"Toni is extremely invested in her magazine," Peter said, standing to refill Lee's glass. "It's important to Toni that you admire her career."

Toni smiled beatifically in the resulting silence, maintaining an impressive show of eye contact which Lee struggled to return. Lee had noticed Peter was prone to statements like this, which, if taken with anything less than a generous spirit, were on the edge of jerkish. There was a flexing to them, a shaping of reality that Lee didn't care for. And yet Lee liked Peter, or rather, she *wanted* to like him. Lee was also used to older fathers; she knew how to handle them.

Halfway through dinner, Peter discovered Jamie had been in Iraq. Peter's company sold software to the military. "We're providing on-the-ground solutions," he said. "Though the technology has applications far beyond government."

"That's amazing," Lee said, although she knew Jamie would likely hold a dim view of whatever Peter's company did.

"We should have your brother here sometime."

"I'm sure he'd love it."

The pinot was finished. Another bottle was opened. By the time Lee went to bed, she was approaching sloshed. Back in her room, she sat on the covered toilet seat in the connecting bathroom. "I might throw up," she said when Marc called. "My head is all swimmy."

"I told you it's hard to match the Lewis drinking levels. Toni in particular is savage. It's even more impressive when you consider she doesn't eat carbs."

"When are you coming back?" She felt as if her head were splitting.

"I'm at the airport. We're taking off soon."

After they hung up, Lee dug through her makeup pouch, where she was convinced she had at one point stashed an old candy tin with painkillers inside. After a longish search, Lee managed to unearth a loose aspirin dotted on one side with eye shadow. She wiped it with a tissue and stuck it in her mouth.

"I thought I heard Marc," Peter said, knocking from the doorway. He held a magazine in his hand.

The pill lodged in her throat. Lee coughed and emerged from the bathroom. "I think he's on his way."

"Do you have everything you need?"

"Yes, thank you so much." The aspirin finally went down. Peter had changed into flannel pajamas of the sort Bill once favored. Peter reminded Lee of Bill quite a lot—he was near the age Bill had been when he died.

"Well then, good night," Peter said. Lee covered her yawn and accepted from him a kiss on the cheek. He sighed and wiped his hand over his brow. "Can I have another kiss?"

At first Lee thought Peter meant another cheek peck—she was still getting used to the air kissing in London.

"Like *this*," Peter said. He came forward and kissed her on the mouth. His breath smelled of garlic.

"You're drunk," Lee said, stumbling back.

"It's not a big deal," Peter said. "You get that, don't you?" When Lee shook her head, he laughed. "I forget what it's like to be young and believe everything is so important. Now, don't be *upset*." His mirth was so real, so light, that Lee wondered if she might actually be the one who was mistaken. "I'm just saying, once you've lived some, you realize all those solid lines you laid out earlier were only stopping you from being interesting."

When Peter came at her again Lee was ready; she shoved him, hard, and then slammed the door. After another second she put a chair under the doorknob; this was a technique she'd read about in detective books as a child. The chair wedged nicely underneath the knob, with two dainty white legs in the air, like a woman falling backward.

There was no movement or noise beyond the door that she could discern. Lee sat against the wall and kept watch until her boredom turned to sleepiness. She was still drunk but glad now for the drunkenness, because it allowed her to blot out the memory of Peter. His wet breath, his bits of beard against her chin. The sound he'd made in the back of his throat as she stood, frozen, when he pressed close.

She woke to the rattle of the door.

"What the—" Marc said from the other side. Lee sat up and discovered she was in bed. She pushed off the blanket. The chair had proved, at best, a minor inconvenience—Marc simply stuck his hand through the crack and pushed it away.

"That's weird, this chair got stuck." Marc dropped his bag. "Did I wake you? The lights are still on. Did you pass out? It's like you're in college."

"Wait," Lee said before he kissed her. She ran to the bathroom and brushed her teeth. She forgot to put water on the brush, and the paste stuck in her mouth.

Marc watched from the doorway. "My little drunkard," he said with affection.

She rinsed and spat in the sink. "Your father hit on me."

"What?"

"Peter kissed me. On the lips. Like how you would kiss me." Lee kept her eyes on Marc. She felt the fear and inarticulate numbness of an approaching confrontation—her head pounded and she had the urge to hide, a sensation she hadn't experienced since the night of the fire. She could still recall the sweat on Theo's face, the ridges of the coin in her palm.

Marc shoved his hands in his pockets and paced, stopping to move the chair. He began to change, unfolding the T-shirt he slept in and putting on shorts.

"It seems to me," Lee said, climbing back into bed, "that you aren't reacting how I'd expect."

Marc unbuttoned his shirt. "I don't know what you want me to do," he said, not looking at her.

"We're getting married. Do you think this is an acceptable situation?"

"Of course not." Marc came and sat on the bed. "I'm not saying it's *acceptable*."

"Well, what should we do?"

In response, Marc rose and once again began to pace. Lee watched him move. She wanted to cry as, even now, in her expanding rage, she couldn't help but see it from his side: how much you simply wanted to love your parents. His mother had died when he was in high school; Lee remembered the first time she told him her father was dead. How relieved he had looked that he didn't have to explain.

Was it a big deal? Lee could almost see Peter's side of things: your wife died and you got a new one. You had an urge and you followed. As Lee had told Joan before: she was an adult. Bad things happened. You recovered.

Lee sighed, and Marc came to her and held her hands. She stared at him—at his kind, beautiful face. This was the person she had moved countries for; this was who she wanted to spend her life with. She'd thought when she met him that she was done.

Marc's voice was soft and his eyes pleading. "Someday my father is going to die, and I think about that a lot," he said.

CHAPTER THIRTY

And so Joan would have Lee back that year for Christmas after all. In December she brought out all her favorite decorations, the ornaments and lights and Jamie's old nutcrackers from woodshop. Once these were arranged, she set up the camera's self-timer, and the three of them stood in front of the tree.

It was not the outcome Joan desired. That Jamie had returned home had been the natural order of things, given that if he hadn't, it would have meant something awful (though something awful *had* happened to Jamie). But this—Lee and Jamie both near, both defeated—this Joan had never wanted. Perhaps she had wished for them to be with her too much; perhaps this was Joan's punishment for all her desires.

Joan had liked Marc, whom she thought handsome and hardworking; she'd hoped the couple would have a very nice life together. Of course, you never want your children to be unhappy, but Joan worried that perhaps she'd taught her children to expect too much. She knew very well that even the best marriages could not always be satisfying. But how did you *teach* that?

Joan had prided herself on not pressuring Lee or Jamie for grandchildren. Now she wondered if she should have pressured more. I have
no grandchildren, she despaired. Neither of my children is even married!

"Don't talk to her about it," Misty said when Joan brought it up on
the phone.

"Have you spoken to her? Did she say anything?"

"We talked a little, but not about the engagement," Misty said, and
Joan could tell Misty wanted to know more too.

"He seemed like such a nice boy," Joan mused.

"Oh, please. Everyone's a nice boy. Until they aren't. Believe me, I
would know."

Joan was surprised by this. She hadn't known Misty to date nice
boys—she'd always assumed Misty liked her boyfriends precisely because
they *weren't* nice. "Do you want to come visit? The weather is good."

"I'm busy with the store." Misty had gotten married several years
back, to an orthopedic surgeon in Scottsdale whom she'd sat next to in
first class on a plane. Misty hadn't appeared too upset by the divorce,
which transpired a year later—she had stayed in Arizona and opened
a furniture store. She was already talking about expanding to a second
location. Joan had purchased an outdoor teak set when she visited in
February, though two of the chairs were already splitting from the rain.

"Do *you* know what happened?" Joan asked Jamie the next time he
visited the café.

"With who?" Jamie asked, scooping out malt balls from a snack jar.

"Lee," Joan said with exasperation. "I think something might have
happened over Thanksgiving. But what could it be?"

"If Lee doesn't say, it means she doesn't want anyone to know," said
Jamie, who did know something about it, or at least more than Joan. He
didn't have specifics, only that it had to do with Marc's parents. Well,
naturally a family of military contractors would be problematic, he
thought. Jamie really did have a bias against such contractors, especially

wealthy ones, though he had been in the military and his parents wealthy; it was one of the many contradictions within Jamie.

Lee showed no outward distress over having lost both a fiancé and an apartment in London in one week. As she'd already done once before, Lee moved back in with her mother. She spent her mornings accompanying Joan to the café—she never worked as a host, but helped with the cleaning, and if they ran out of Pellegrino midday she drove to Costco to buy more. Most nights she also made dinner, which she and Joan ate in the kitchen. Lee was always pleasant, never miserable, but Joan knew something was wrong. "Don't you think something is strange?" Joan asked Jamie. Although Joan thought something *strange* about Jamie as well.

"She needs more to do," Jamie said. "Maybe I'll take her shooting." He didn't tell Joan that he believed Lee might prefer an especially aggressive activity; he didn't wish to be drawn into that quicksand.

"*Shooting?* Do you even have a gun?"

"Yes." In response to her look, he added: "It's in safe storage." Which for Jamie meant the top shelf of his closet, underneath a stack of pillows. It was where Jamie had hid things ever since he was a kid.

On the day Jamie was to take Lee to the range, Joan moved about the café, half distracted by paranoia (her particular paranoia being that they would accidentally shoot each other). Lee finally called that afternoon. "Are you okay?" Joan asked in a hurry.

"Yes. It was fun. Relieved some stress."

Joan stopped herself from asking what sort of *stress* Lee needed to relieve. "No injuries? Everyone is safe?"

"Yes, everyone's fine. Do you want me to come over?"

"No," Joan said, a little peevish at Lee's nonchalance. "Why don't you keep spending time with your brother?"

"He's going to the gym."

"Why don't you go to the gym too?" There were men at the gym, weren't there? Or perhaps Lee could at least meet some friends, as it seemed strange to Joan that she didn't have many (never mind that neither did Joan). "Exercise is good for you," Joan added. "Please don't come to the café. It's not busy."

There was a pause. "All right," Lee said, and hung up.

Though Joan was busy, quite so. Most of her days were busy now; the café was at capacity nearly every weekend, and the weekdays had begun to fill as well. Despite her rapid hiring of hosts, many worked part-time, and Joan remained short-staffed. Nearly every day she'd have to sit with a customer to accommodate walk-ins or hosts who'd called in sick.

Over her time sitting with customers, Joan had begun to notice commonalities. Naturally each individual was unique, but humans also shared certain qualities, like ego and loneliness. On the break room wall Joan had taped a large poster board which featured her writing in block letters:

HOW TO START A CONVERSATION!
Ask questions—about them!
If they look troubled, ask what is bothering them!
Everyone is interesting—you just have to discover what it is!
And how about their *parents*?

For nearly everyone did eventually speak of their parents; in Joan's experience, the sole topic which regularly surpassed it was divorce, but then only a certain population was divorced, whereas everyone had parents. Joan was fortunate in this regard: she had relevant experience with both matters.

Joan had left room on the board for additional maxims; she first wrote them on index cards which she kept in her pocket, and only after she'd reviewed them days later and still found them relevant did she add them to the poster with black marker. *Ask*, she wrote over and over. Keep asking, she exhorted her hosts. Ask!

For Joan had discovered this was what people wanted, to be asked about themselves; often a few questions were all it took, and then an hour or two was gone. As time passed, Joan became increasingly convinced of a serious epidemic of lack of attention in the world: the old man throwing a fit at the post office when his package wasn't found; the young mother staring despondently at the wall in the hospital as her baby screamed and name after name was called. Come here, Joan wanted to say. Come, I can help! She had business cards made up with the address and phone number of the café, which she gave out; she left little piles at Neiman Marcus and the car wash, both places she'd witnessed customers behaving badly. Perhaps because she was so small and harmless-looking, people at least took the cards (though most threw them away right after). Some came, however. And then more and more. Until one Tuesday afternoon (usually her slowest period), Joan looked around and saw the café was full. The tables were packed with hosts and customers; they were drinking coffee and eating Black Forest cake and spooning chili paste on top of dumplings. Joan had recently added some of her childhood breakfast favorites to the menu, and she noted with pleasure a woman at a corner table dipping fried dough sticks into soy milk.

With success came worry over competition. Unknowingly Joan followed the paths of other chief executives in constantly iterating her product. She read business books and took notes. She agreed that only the paranoid survive. She reevaluated her menu and nixed the egg-chive pockets (while tasty, their aroma could be controversial). She also charted the demographics of existing customers and determined they should be marketing more to married people—though they should make it clear the café wasn't a *sordid* destination, simply a place to speak with someone different. Perhaps there would be fewer divorces if more husbands and wives knew of the café. People wouldn't be so desperate for variety that when any opportunity arose, they thought it was the excitement, the thrill, the meaning they'd sought all along. Sometimes one just needed a little release, to prevent a big explosion.

But was there a way to communicate this? Joan pondered. How did you possibly *market* such a feature?

Between all this brainstorming, Joan continued to fill in for hosting duties. Some clients enjoyed their conversations with her so much that they requested her again. Joan really didn't have time for regulars, though she was reluctant to extricate herself, as she knew from her business studies that one must always strive to Delight Your Customer.

Joan's most loyal client was a redhead with a ghostly complexion named Dustin. The first time Dustin visited the café, there had been no available hosts, and so Joan sat with him at a table. Dustin brought with him a green duffel which his hand kept meandering to and petting the top of. Joan had eyed it nervously during their introductions and was relieved when he pulled from it a large yellow hardcover.

"Do you know what this is?" he asked. She shook her head. "It's Greek mythology," Dustin said. "I'd like you to read it to me."

Joan had not studied the Greek gods in school. She knew who Zeus was (he seemed like a jerk?) but barely, and the others were strangers. Joan liked the book: it had clear prose and lovely watercolor illustrations. Each appointment Dustin had her read a chapter, after which Joan asked questions about the material. Joan decided Dustin's enjoyment was both in being read to and in playing the expert.

One afternoon Jamie happened to visit during her usual Friday session with Dustin. "This is my son," Joan said.

"Oh?" Dustin replied in a possessive tone. He was wearing what Joan had come to recognize as his lucky hat, a baseball cap with the word SORRY embroidered in yellow thread. When Jamie introduced himself, Dustin did not shake hands but hugged his book to his chest, as if afraid Jamie might take it.

"That guy seems like a creep," Jamie remarked the next morning.

He had recently begun accompanying Joan and Lee on their Saturday walks, as it was the most exercise his knee could tolerate.

"Which guy?" Lee asked. Jamie explained to her.

"It's just reading stories," Joan said. "It's not so bad." In truth, her time with Dustin was far preferable to some of her other conversations. While Joan had a rule that any host could drop a customer without explanation, she had an owner's sense of fiduciary responsibility when it came to her *own* bad customers. As such, she currently tolerated in at least semiregular rotation an unpleasant Korean woman who told long, complicated stories about her appalling behavior toward her own family; there was also an arrogant, fitness-obsessed mortgage broker named Lincoln who complained of his dating failures, uniformly characterizing the women as ungrateful bitches who would one day be sorry. Compared to such customers, Dustin was harmless, easy—if only her calendar could be *filled* with Dustins.

"Which book?" Lee asked. Joan told her. "I read that in elementary school. Why is an adult having you read it? I don't think it's normal."

Sure, Dustin's habits may not have been normal. But was Lee and Jamie moving home, spending so much time with their mother, normal? Joan felt she was losing her grip on *normal* day by day.

She could see Jamie and Lee up ahead, kicking stones the same way they had years earlier, the first time they visited High Rock Park. The sun was just cresting as they strode over the hill, and it lit the ocean so that it appeared filled with stars. It was a family joke now that despite Joan's many attempts, a barrier or sign warning of the cliff had yet to be installed. On their way back to the car, Joan took another comment form: THIS TRAIL IS <u>DANGEROUS</u>! *People may not know they are approaching an unprotected cliff,* she wrote, along with her phone number.

"Why do you keep writing those cards?" Lee asked. "You know no one reads them."

"But they have the box," Joan insisted. So it must be for something. She could not imagine a person would have created such a system—one that included printed cards and little white pencils and the green metal box—without having arranged for someone to open the box from time to time; to retrieve the words that someone had put down on paper for another to receive.

CHAPTER THIRTY-ONE

Of those who survived the roof in Baghdad, only Jamie required evacuation to Ramstein. The transport that took him to the hospital in Germany was not a regular ambulance but rather resembled an American school bus with blacked-out windows that leaked strips of day along the borders. Inside, Jamie lay next to a talkative marine who would end up losing his right arm, half of his left arm, and his right eye.

After two weeks Jamie was transferred to Balboa Hospital in San Diego. The navy physician examining Jamie's leg said they needed photos of its damage.

"For our records," the physician said. "So we can document progress. It would also be used for the disability claim."

"No disability," Jamie said, thinking of the marine.

The doctor regarded him with weary patience and handed him a packet. Jamie brought it home and stuck it on top of his microwave, where he usually placed paperwork he thought might be of some importance but required no immediate action. He would come across it months later, when he was moving out and tossing items into recycling. At the top of the packet was a blue sheet with a list of questions. Jamie first read the ones at the very bottom: *Who were you before combat? Who do you believe you are now, after?*

———

Even though he never answered, Jamie still thought these were valid questions—as it was only now, well outside of the navy, that he truly appreciated the resources previously expended into his believing his work had meaning: the training, the equipment, the ceremonies and medals. At Atom, Jamie was part of the business group, where his job was to manage a software release that would soon be overridden by the next software release, one he did not manage and had no input in. His desk was on the fourth floor, in a semi-open layout with low walls. There was a chatty data scientist who would often visit, Sandy Chu. "Coffee break?" Sandy would ask, her lips fresh with gloss, caramel highlighted hair swept over a shoulder. "Lunch?" Jamie did not want to have coffee with Sandy but didn't understand how to continually reject such requests and not be guilty of some form of reverse sexual harassment; when he saw Sandy approach, he would put on his headset and dial slowly until she passed.

Directly across from Jamie's desk was a single bathroom that locked from the inside. When Jamie first started work he'd been nervous to take even a half hour for lunch, so much did it feel as if he were stealing time from the company—but now he regularly ate ninety-minute lunches, and when there was an empty afternoon, would read a newspaper inside the little room. One morning Jamie noticed that a key card reader had been installed outside the entrance. He swiped, but the reader blinked red and the door remained locked. That afternoon, a tall East Asian man with hair gathered in a bun at his neck stopped at the bathroom door. He bent to swipe his badge. As he entered, Jamie saw a glimpse of his skirt; it was burgundy and flowing, longer in the back than the front.

"That's Ellison," Chloe informed him the next day. Jamie's ex-girlfriend had left Goldman two years after he had, to attend business school at Stanford, after which she'd joined Atom's venture arm. They'd been dating again for half a year, though they kept their relationship private. Jamie wouldn't have minded their relationship being *less* private, given Sandy's drive-bys—but Chloe found Sandy's overtures amusing. Chloe was an extremely secure person in general.

"Why does Ellison have his own bathroom?"

"Don't talk so *loud*," Chloe hissed. "I can see him." They were in the cafeteria, seated a collegial distance apart. "Don't look," she said again.

"Why?"

"Because you're so obvious. It's probably people like you who made it so Ellison needs his own bathroom," she added obliquely.

"Right," Jamie said, though secretly he was annoyed by Chloe's insinuation—as by "people like you," he was fairly certain she meant veteran. While in theory, Atom made an effort to hire veterans (for the past two years Jamie had been asked to record a video for the company's diversity showcase), in actual practice the population was treated in a similar fashion to large dogs or small children: valuable to society in their own right, but prone to embarrassing outbursts. Jamie compensated by behaving as benignly as possible; he avoided political discourse and did not volunteer his opinions on Afghanistan, the carried interest tax, or low-income housing. Occasionally the fact that he'd been a SEAL seemed to garner some interest from executives. Had he killed anyone? they would prod, and of course he couldn't actually say, they understood, but the answer was yes, yes, *yes*—wasn't it? But, as with Jamie's initial intake with human resources, such executives had no idea what to do with his experience; it didn't seem to translate to real life. At times Jamie felt people were embarrassed for him, that he had been in special operations, trained on a sniper rifle and explosives and interrogation techniques, and now had to make an ordinary living—it seemed to him they thought *he* might be embarrassed about his current state. At such moments, Jamie would open one of his many spreadsheets, the financial projections he was asked to calculate, and make an edit: $4 million in estimated revenue became $40 million; fifty thousand users turned into five hundred thousand. So far, the changes had gone unnoticed. Jamie theorized people cared only when the numbers became smaller—when they grew bigger, they simply believed their wishful thinking had come true.

As Jamie rarely left his desk, he became accustomed to seeing Ellison nearly every day when he visited the bathroom. Sometimes Ellison was in a button-down and jeans, his black hair neatly parted to one side—in such moments Jamie thought Ellison looked nearly identical to the Asian bankers he'd worked with at Goldman, all the mathematically gifted Steve Kims and John Changs. At other times Ellison would be wearing a skirt or wide-legged trousers, his height enhanced by sturdy heels. It wasn't until Jamie saw Ellison outside of Atom that he realized Ellison had left the company, and he knew *that* only because Ellison had started work as a host at the Satisfaction Café.

"He's a nice man," Joan said. "Originally from Singapore, but I have the feeling he doesn't speak to his parents. I'm sure he has his reasons, and who knows what one's parents are truly like? I should take their side, but I won't. After all, Ellison is my employee."

Jamie reached for a slice of scallion pancake. He was eating dinner with Joan since Lee was out that evening, with someone Joan hinted she found highly unsuitable. "Does he live near the café?"

"He lives in a nice house in a nice neighborhood." Joan tilted the dish and dumped the rest of the pancake on Jamie's plate. "Saratoga. He owns. I'm paying him more than he said he was making at your company. I certainly hope *you're* earning more. I would think it'd be irresponsible to live by yourself otherwise, instead of here with me. Do you like the pancake, by the way? I'm thinking to serve it at the café. With a nice dipping sauce."

"The pancake is fine. And I'm sure I earn more," Jamie said, although he really wasn't sure. He hadn't negotiated his offer from Atom at all. He'd known he might be leaving some money on the table but assumed it would be unethical for the company to shortchange him simply because he didn't care to argue (he'd since begun to suspect, from Chloe's cutting remarks on the matter, that this assumption was incorrect).

"Or you could live with your girlfriend," Joan said. "Although I would hope you'd introduce her to me first."

"I haven't brought her because I only want you to meet the serious ones."

"Please don't waste people's time," Joan grumbled. She rose and began to clear the table of dishes even though Jamie was still eating.

———

"I left Atom because I didn't like the people," Ellison told Jamie later. It was their first official introduction. Jamie had stopped by the café near closing and encountered Ellison in the break room.

"The stares and jokes were part of it," Ellison went on. He was drinking a mug of tea, and from the specific chrysanthemum flowers unfurling in the water, Jamie suspected Joan had brewed it for him, using her special blend from Hangzhou. "But the worst was the lady from human resources. Did I understand the impact of my appearance on the employee population? she asked. Perhaps clarifying my gender would put colleagues at ease? Clarify *what*? I asked. Because until I say otherwise, I am a man! But eventually the argument became too tiresome."

"Right," Jamie said. Ellison had already been talking for twenty minutes. He was one of those naturally chatty people, which Jamie assumed was part of why Joan had hired him.

"It isn't as if I haven't *thought* about becoming a woman," Ellison said. "But I'd describe it as my laziest fantasy, the kind I'm not willing to do anything about at the moment in real life. Sort of like opening a pizza parlor or becoming a tennis pro.

"Now, after Atom I thought I might do something with my hands," Ellison went on. He held them up for Jamie to admire; they looked like ordinary hands to Jamie, although the nails were nicely shaped and smooth. "I wanted to be a massage therapist. I took some classes, but it turns out I far prefer receiving massages to giving them. I was driving around a few days later and saw this place and thought: well, the Satisfaction Café. *That's* an interesting name."

Ellison set down his mug. He seemed to expect constant interaction; as a decent listener, Jamie had often found himself victim to such personalities. "Are you full-time?" Jamie asked.

"Nearly. I have a good number of customers. Though lately I've been getting a lot of wives." Ellison sighed. "I'm sick of these wives. All they want to talk about is their husbands. How they came home and he was wearing their dress or they went to Victoria's Secret and he tried on a bra. They're all trying so hard to be *understanding*. It's the consistency that's boring. How much they want to understand."

"How do they know to request you in the first place?"

"They see my photos. In the binder." This was a recent introduction of Joan's, a physical binder kept at the check-in stand. Each host had their own page, with their name, a few sentences of introduction, and a photo. Joan took the pictures: she allowed the hosts unlimited do-overs but insisted she be the photographer. As a result, when Jamie first flipped through the binder he'd been struck by its resemblance to a yearbook. The descriptions also had a flat consistency. *Ellison is a graduate of Yale and has fifteen years' experience in finance. He likes brisket sandwiches and recently returned from a holiday in New Zealand.* Jamie and Lee had told Joan to put the binder online, to attract more customers, but she'd refused. "I do not want an Internet sort of customer" was Joan's reasoning.

"Are you in the binder?" Ellison asked.

"No. I don't work here."

"You would make a good host. Joan told me you were in the military. Do you still talk to people from there?"

"A few," Jamie said, although it was more like none. Most of his former teammates were now married with children, with the attendant obligations, whereas the few single ones he'd met up with had all been kind of weird, outlining their personal branding strategies with the grim determination of a second-year MBA candidate or loudly boasting about past operations in bars. Jamie always left such encounters a little sad, a feeling he would try to crush by watching TV for hours.

When Lee was in an annoying mood, she would sometimes say the military had been a phase. Just something Jamie had to do, as if it'd been a jacket he'd tried on and then taken off. "Come on," she said. "Chewing dip? Guns and steroids? That isn't you." And yes, it was true it wasn't him any longer, but what Jamie couldn't explain was that it *had* been him—that while he was in, there had never been a moment when he'd thought he wouldn't live the rest of his life this way.

He saw now how it all looked. Moving through house after house in Baghdad, who do you know, what are you hiding, what have you seen? The sirens up high, explosions in the street, the staccato of gunfire—the silence of Hemin, Jamie's favorite interpreter, as they watched a grove of palms felled for a highway. The owner crying for his lost trees. Nick's face swept with dust, the delicateness of his last breaths. Lee had shown Jamie a photo of her ex-fiancé's family home. "Eleven bedrooms," she said. "The dad sells software to the military." Jamie had peered at the image, a turreted castle in the heart of Fairfax County. Six-car garage, custom stone and brick.

Yes, he couldn't help but see how it all looked now.

"There are so many movies about wars," Ellison went on. "People are interested in that. You need a *thing*, is what I've learned. Maybe it's not what you end up talking with customers about, but it's what you start with."

"I don't know. I was in Iraq. People have feelings about it."

"What kind of feelings do people have about Iraq?" Ellison asked innocently. He looked at Jamie with wide eyes. Jamie couldn't tell if he was fucking with him.

————

The next week, Lee called Jamie. "Guess what," she said.

"What?" Jamie answered. He could see Chloe in a conference room on the other side of the floor. They had been fighting recently: it wasn't that Chloe *wanted* to ruin her life and get married and have children, she said, but still Jamie should propose.

"I don't see why I have to propose if you don't want to get married," Jamie had said.

"I won't be in a relationship unless the man loves me ten percent more than I love him," Chloe said. "It's a personal rule."

Chloe was in a meeting with Mickey Kim from finance, whom Jamie didn't like. Mickey was always asking Jamie to play basketball (Jamie was bad at basketball, which both he and Mickey knew). And when Jamie saw Chloe like this, teasing with someone else, he thought he *did* love her ten percent more than she loved him—and yet even as he was seized with desire, mentally pricing out engagement rings, some lizardy part of his brain prevented him from going through with it.

Chloe saw Jamie looking at her. She laughed in Mickey's direction.

"Go to the window," Lee's voice said in his ear. "The one facing the lobby."

Jamie rose. "I don't see anything."

"You don't?"

"No." Jamie craned his neck, but there was only parking lot. He looked again at the conference room. Chloe and Mickey were sitting side by side now, facing away from him.

"Darn. Well, then go to the lobby."

First Jamie returned to his laptop, where he edited the research and development costs for Electron Cloud 6.0 from $12 million to $1.2 million. He immediately felt better. He then took the stairs to the lobby, where he saw Lee. She was professionally dressed, in a white shirt and black skirt. "I got a job!" she cried when she spotted him.

"Where?"

"Here, dummy."

"How?" He tried to hide his alarm. "When did you interview?"

"I didn't. I'm a contractor. I suppose I did interview with the staffing agency. But they only asked me, like, five questions. All behavioral."

That Atom's contractors were so easily qualified was disturbing; Jamie hoped Lee hadn't told Joan about her interview, since Joan held Atom in rather high regard. "What are you contracted to do?"

"Something with servers." Lee looked around. "Check out this building! Won't it be cool to lunch together?"

"Yes. Sure."

"Though I don't actually know what a server is. You can teach me." She peeped at him hopefully, the way she had as a kid.

"Yeah, of course," Jamie said, though come to think of it, he didn't know what a server was either. He, who once aspired to conduct major business deals as an investment banker, now had no idea how the company he worked for made money.

There was a quaking in his chest.

"Jamie? You look weird." Lee was studying him the way that had driven him crazy when they were kids—she was *always* watching him then. Because he was the good one, Lee said. And Jamie could admit that as a child, yes, he'd been good, in retrospect even embarrassingly so. At school, he cleaned up the yard after recess. When others fought, he gave up his share. Sometimes, rarely, when there bubbled in him that swell of resistance, he would go outside and run circles in the backyard or, later, the JJS campus, doing laps around the track until he was too exhausted to feel shame. Once, when Joan yelled at him for some slight, he had gone to her room and taken one of her necklaces and thrown it from the window into the street. Later he'd run outside to find it, but it was gone. The idea of a truck driving over it, crushing the pearls, had haunted him for years.

Lee was still looking at him. He began to gulp; he felt like he might run out of air.

Recognition bloomed in Lee's face. She walked him quickly to a small glass room called a privacy cube, meant for phone calls.

The door had been shut for only a second before he began to cry. And here he was, for the first time he could recall in his adult life, he was crying, no, actually sobbing. Jamie tried to keep his body still; he could see in the reflection of the glass the security guard behind his desk. Lee sat next to him, their backs to the lobby. She searched her bag and handed him a tissue.

"Jamie. What's wrong? Whatever it is, it'll be fine."

Jamie wiped his face. It was the start of the lunch hour, and in the reflection of the glass there began to appear employees walking in and out of the building. Some were holding food, their grilled chicken and passionfruit smoothies and spinach salads nearly spilling from their hands. Jamie had the urge to run out, to hit each one, to throw them against the ground. These stupid, condescending, selfish pricks.

"Jamie, talk to me."

Jamie didn't talk. There were more employees in the glass's reflection; it was as if they had all simultaneously decided to stop working at 11:50 and go out for lunch in the sunshine. They were laughing and smiling.

He hated them. He loved them. For bicycling to work and volunteering on weekends and all their good intentions.

Who were you before combat? Who do you believe you are now, after?

I was nothing. I am nothing.

CHAPTER THIRTY-TWO

Joan was always tinkering with the café. She carved out a little shopping area up front where she sold whatever caught her fancy, Meissen porcelain and white chocolate Toblerone and dazzling geodes of amethyst and citrine. She added new appetizers to the menu (Korean beef and radish soup, papaya salad); she had Leonard install a few booths in the back so that multiple customers could sit with a host. Sometimes there were small birthday parties for those who wanted to celebrate their special day but worried no one would show, or simply wished to spend the occasion at the café. Tracy or Ellison would bring out a cake, Black Forest or vanilla with fresh strawberries, and everyone would sing.

In mid-April, the Satisfaction Café turned three years old. The Saturday prior, Joan closed the café to the public and threw a big party. She ordered catering and gave each of the employees a red envelope, even though she was aware that Americans sometimes had feelings about cash gifts. "It's supposed to be the thought that counts," Lee explained. "People want to know you selected something specifically for them."

"I did put thought into it," Joan said. She'd spent over an hour browsing Palo Alto Shopping Center before deciding on money.

On the actual date of its anniversary, the Satisfaction Café recorded an intake that, if maintained, meant the business would soon be cash flow positive. "You could grow," Jamie said. "Make this space bigger. Open other locations."

But from Joan's perspective, there was no need to expand. She had gone from a daydream to a real business; she had created something from her mind and with only herself to report to. How narrow her path here had been! How many ways it could have gone wrong! And Joan knew it wasn't all her doing—she knew she'd been fortunate. Nelson confirmed this. "There's been luck, of course," he told her. "But you've also worked hard. No business like this thrives without work."

This, Joan knew, was as close to an endorsement as she could hope for; as a policy, Nelson did not approve of his retirement-aged clients opening small businesses with tight margins. And yet, even with Nelson's blessing, Joan fretted.

Recently, when Joan woke in the morning she would discover she was sweating, and not from the temperature; for the first time she was experiencing an emotion she had on occasion disdained in others: the ennui of everyday existence. The thought blaring in her head that something was wrong, wrong, wrong—if only there was some way to guard against whatever *wrong* was about to happen. She became alert for creaking in her house: a rotten beam collapsing on top of Lee, killing her. A gas leak in the café, undetectable, poisoning her employees.

She, who never had trouble falling asleep, who, even after Bill's death and the destruction of Falling House, had ended each evening unconscious moments after dropping her head onto the pillow, now found herself lying awake for hours. Joan visited her doctor, the same Dr. Marcus who had treated Bill, who prescribed her sleeping pills. Dr. Marcus was old now, as Joan supposed she was as well—he refused to use the new computers in the examination rooms and scrawled his prescriptions by hand. The Ambien he prescribed knocked her out, so she cut the tablets in half. On nights when she felt it would be irresponsible to take another pill, Joan lay in bed and stared at the ceiling and comforted herself with a list.

The list: that her business was well; her house was well; her health was well; that her children seemed well, or at least fine, and even Theo had recently sent a note of apology, an output of therapy, though the apology itself was vague and cut with sulky undertones (*Dad always spoke of the family home . . . I've come to question whether he truly regarded me as family*). That Lee and Jamie were both unmarried was a state Joan would have worried over earlier, but she'd relented. There were advantages to marrying young but also disadvantages. And one had to choose *well* there too.

Last month, a petite woman with dyed black hair had come to the café. Joan thought she looked familiar, but it wasn't until the woman introduced herself that Joan recognized her. It was her old friend Kailie, whose wedding dress Joan had borrowed for her ceremony with Milton.

"I heard you started a business," Kailie said. "I thought I'd come see." It had been at least fifteen years since Joan last tried calling Kailie, and Joan was no longer bitter about the dropped friendship. Sure, Kailie had distanced herself after Joan's split from Milton, but Joan understood how at the start of marriage you might believe you didn't need anyone else. Recently even Joan's memories of Milton had been fond: the way he used to skip without embarrassment when excited; how in the winter he hugged his peacoat around himself and his cheeks went pink from the cold. It seemed to Joan a terrible reality that this youthful Milton would never exist again. That were she to call and say, *Remember your scratchy wool coat*, at best she might receive some faraway nostalgia.

I suppose that's why I've got the café, Joan thought. I've got this place to make people feel better, and now look who has come to try.

Kailie wore a short-sleeved lavender sweater, and the skin on her arms was thin and crepey, like rice paper.

Joan had not kept up with anyone from Stanford or her life before. Her brother Alfred had called once, when he was on a trip to Los Angeles. Joan had offered to drive down and meet him in Monterey Park, where he was staying with his wife and children.

"Or you could visit me," Joan offered. "Bring the family." There was a short silence before Alfred coughed. "Maybe next time," he said. He hadn't given her his phone number and never called again. It was sad, Joan knew, but some families weren't made to stick together. They fell apart and stayed that way.

"I've been thinking," Kailie said. "About old times. All the things I might have done."

Joan thought she recognized the specific note of melancholy in Kailie's voice. "You might enjoy meeting Lila," Joan said gently. Lila was an amateur birder in her seventies and an excellent listener; she often said people her age had many stories, including new ones, it was just as they grew older it seemed fewer people had the patience to wait for them to start telling. She could be flirtatious without going overboard, and possessed a comprehensive memory that she utilized to ask thoughtful follow-up questions the next time she saw a client. "Please. Enjoy an afternoon on me."

"Oh, no. I couldn't."

"Just try," Joan insisted. And Kailie had been a regular ever since. Sometimes Joan would arrive at work and see Kailie already in the corner with Lila, the two of them with their hands curled over mugs of hot tea. On occasion Kailie brought sushi. Outside food wasn't technically allowed, but Joan let it be.

Kailie and Joan didn't chat like they used to. They weren't friends anymore, really; Kailie was a customer. Joan knew Kailie had judged her in earlier times, though Joan wasn't upset over this. After all, Joan had judged herself plenty. But now it was as if all the doors of her past were open and she could walk freely between. This was what the café had brought her.

———

Lee told Joan she should spend more time with Jamie.

"Why?" Joan asked. "I do spend time with him! He doesn't spend time with me!"

"Just ask him over more. I think he needs interaction."

"Why?" Joan asked again, but already her mind was racing: perhaps this was why she'd been worried. She knew Jamie was not completely well; he appeared the same, but it was as if he were acting a role. When the children were little, she had a way of extracting from them their problems; she would prod and ask until they became frustrated and confessed, and then she would tell them it really didn't matter, whether it be a bad grade or not being invited to a sleepover. None of it mattered. But what Jamie had endured, well—she didn't know what she could say. Except that life was senseless and unfair and it started over like this each day.

But really: life could be nice, too. It could be gorgeous.

The next day was Saturday. Early that morning, Joan called Jamie. "Why don't you come visit me at work today?"

"Why?"

"To, ah, taste some new menu items. Besides, Lee will be there," Joan added, slightly flustered. Now she would have to ask Lee to come.

"I'm heading to the gym," Jamie said.

"I don't think you're there *all* day, are you? Visit after. You don't even have to shower. Just don't stand around customers."

There was a pause. "Did Lee ask you to call me?"

"What about?" Joan asked innocently. Jamie sighed and said goodbye.

Joan pecked a message to Lee on her phone—better a message than a call, as Lee was less likely to argue—telling her to come to the café, and then left for work. She arrived an hour before opening and played the voicemails from the night before. First was a call from Dustin asking to move their appointment to Thursday. Next was a rambling message for a host named Blake, whose older clients liked to comment resembled a young Paul Newman. This particular message leaver, a young woman, said she wished to share with Blake a poem. "I won't say it *now*," the girl said, as if she didn't want others to hear. "But I'll read it the next time I see you, Blake. Okay?"

Joan replayed the message, noting the proprietary lilt in the girl's voice, and wondered if Blake would have to quit this customer. Crushes did occur; occasionally customers went so far as to outright declare their love. Blake had a way of listening with earnest attentiveness, no matter what silly thing you might be saying; there was also an intensity in his gaze, as if he were realizing something very flattering about you at precisely that moment. "It's like he's a beautiful vampire," Gina once said, sighing. "And I've got very delicious blood."

But. Wasn't it nice to feel that way at times (wanted, singular, interesting)? Joan recalled how, sometimes at home, she liked to replay scenes from romantic comedies (the desperate gaze, the long-realized kiss)—and in Blake's blue eyes, customers had a chance to experience a bit of that sensation, at least for a short while. The problem, as it had always been, for thousands of years, was that people wanted more. Good enough, after a time, became not enough at all.

There were tactics commonly deployed by hosts to deal with such attractions: the fake engagement ring, the sexual orientation. In some cases, hosts simply said they couldn't meet certain customers anymore. The customers were usually upset and sometimes angry. One had accused Joan of running a "whorehouse full of teases," which had flummoxed her until Lee explained the meaning.

Well, I suppose we are teasing in a way, Joan thought. But wasn't anything that eventually ended a tease? A job could be a tease. So could marriage. Life was the greatest tease of all. After writing herself a note to speak with Blake, Joan proceeded to the break room, where she encountered Ellison.

"You're here too early," Joan scolded. She knew Ellison kept late hours.

"I couldn't sleep," he said. Joan suspected Ellison came early to eat pastries in the break room, though she never voiced this.

After sharing an almond croissant with Ellison, Joan went to the supply closet. She had recently placed some orders for the boutique area up front, and shipments had begun to arrive.

As she stood and assessed the stack of boxes, Joan thought glumly that she should have exercised more control at "market." Market was a quarterly trade show held at a warehouse in San Francisco, where Joan had spent hours browsing with Lee. The wholesale prices, three or four times below retail, had been intoxicating; it had seemed like nothing to order a box of candles, a stack of architectural pot holders, some Lucite bookstands. Now that everything had arrived, however, Joan faced the problem of space. Where on earth was she to put it all?

Joan opened a box which was promisingly light, hoping it was the cashmere scarves she'd liked so much. When she opened the flap and spotted a flash of silver, her spirits sank. *Why* had she purchased sequined pants? She'd known they were awful, but the designer had looked so desperate that out of sympathy Joan had ordered a full size run.

"I told you those were a bad idea," Lee said from behind. So! Lee had received her message and come; Joan experienced the surge of pleasure that arrived whenever one of her children obeyed a request without fuss. She watched as Lee tried to fold the pants so they'd be decipherable as clothing and not a silvery blob; Joan had already concluded they were impossible to hang, as the clamp bit into the sequins. "You can't keep buying on impulse," Lee said. "No good businessperson makes decisions in this way."

Joan was silent. Had Lee always been this righteous, this inconsiderate of her feelings? Joan opened another box and unfurled from it a long dress made out of a slinky black jersey. "I think this would look nice on you."

"No. Never."

"I think you might *consider* it." Joan made an open appraisal; Lee was wearing one of those awful sacks that had recently become popular, which Joan imagined were manufactured in only one size. At least one size would pose fewer inventory problems, Joan thought. She had a new appreciation for inventory management.

"You have such a nice figure," Joan said.

"Don't say 'figure.'"

"I just think it wouldn't hurt for you to try some different styles."

Lee pressed her lips and sighed loudly. "Why don't you try the pants, then?"

"If I were your age, I would." Joan would try nearly anything if she could return to her twenties and thirties, whether it be a bikini or short shorts or purple hair. She would visit topless beaches; perhaps she'd even consider an orgy (given appealing parties). Why not?

"Ellison," Lee called, "what do you think of these pants?"

He came over. "They're extremely shiny."

"Would you buy them?" Lee asked.

Ellison was quiet (he also hated the pants). Stronger than his aesthetic sensibilities, however, was his loyalty to Joan. Unlike what he'd told Jamie, he'd first come upon the café not seeking employment but as a customer; he'd been a little high and looking to complain, and as it was a busy day and he had no reservation, he'd been paired with Joan. He told her his mother and father in Singapore were religious financiers (in fact, they were atheists, his mother a surgeon and his father a painter); that they had taken his ex-wife's side in the divorce and no longer spoke to him. Once Ellison started at the café, he'd waited until his third week to wear an oxford shirt and a slip skirt along with a red bobbed wig to work.

Joan had taken him aside during his break. "I didn't know you dressed like this," she said. "Is this why your parents are unhappy?"

"It doesn't impact my job performance or customers." He could feel himself shaking, as this was the confrontation he'd dreaded.

"Of course it impacts the customers, not that it's necessarily a negative thing," Joan said mildly. "It's just something you could have told me, is all. Your customers should know too that sometimes you dress like this. Some of them might not like it, and do you really want to be seated with a bigot? You can let me know what sort of picture you want in the host binder. You can have two, if you like."

Ellison picked up the pants now and ran his hands along the seam. "I'm not sure about the fabric," he finally said. "The stitching isn't even."

"Maybe they really aren't the best quality," Joan conceded mournfully. The ground was already covered in sequins, and she reached for the broom at the back of the closet. Turning to sweep, she spotted something near the entrance of the break room. She tilted her head. It was the demon rock, she realized with a start—the rock from the courtyard in Taiwan. Nothing else in the world had its shape and color; it stood waist-high, its dark jagged edges stark against the cream floor, proud and glittering in the light.

So! The rock had found her. Even though an ocean separated them, still it had made its way. A peculiar tremor went through her.

"Mom?" a voice said—from far off, it seemed. Joan continued to study the rock. The last time she had seen it was the day she'd left Taiwan. The boulder before her appeared the same as it had that morning, substantial and dazzling. She stared at its red streaks with pleasure, as if gazing upon the face of an old friend.

"Mom?" This time Joan looked up. It was Jamie, a gym bag on his shoulder. "Did you hear me?"

"What?"

"I said, where are these new dishes you wanted me to try?"

"Oh." There were no new dishes—Joan had made that up. She normally would have dodged, changed the topic, but now felt at peace with the deception. "There aren't any."

Jamie stared at her for a long moment, and then his gaze shifted to her hands, which still clutched the pants and broom. "What's going on? What is that silver thing?"

"Nothing, nothing," Joan said. "It doesn't matter. I'm just pleased you and your sister are both here."

Joan looked again toward the rock. It was gone, as she knew it would be. But she could still detect a shimmer in the area, as if it had left some of its essence behind. Ah, how exciting life was. How compelling, so that at nearly every turn, it was impossible to resist. Joan blinked, and the shimmer disappeared.

CHAPTER THIRTY-THREE

Ellison asked Jamie to go shoe shopping. He knew Jamie's weekends were free, since he'd recently been dumped. Chloe had done it a month before their anniversary, when Jamie was in the midst of planning a trip for them to Puerto Vallarta.

"I didn't want you to buy plane tickets, since those are hard to cancel," Chloe explained. Jamie had liked her when she said this; as had been the pattern with other girlfriends, he'd never liked Chloe *more* than when she was breaking up with him. He'd been reminded of all her good attributes, the most attractive of which was that she no longer found him desirable.

"I don't like shopping," Jamie said to Ellison.

"What? Who doesn't like shopping?"

"Why don't you take Lee? I don't know anything about shoes."

"But you're the one I'm friends with," Ellison said.

Friends. Jamie supposed he and Ellison were friends, although he wasn't certain how that'd happened; he hadn't made any friends in a long time. Ellison had a way of badgering—if he asked what you were doing that weekend and you said you were busy, he would ask *why* you were busy and then question your answer. "Errands?" Ellison would say. "And those are going to take *all day*?"

It was like he simply didn't abide by the normal rules of social engagement.

Jamie had always loathed shopping; as a kid, he'd been dragged to the mall with Lee and Joan, who seemed to possess infinite endurance for pawing through racks of clothing. They would move through store after store, holding up dress after coat after sweater: What about this one? Does this look good on me? Okay, but does it look better than the other one? No matter what Jamie said, they were never satisfied with the answer.

And now he was having to go shopping *again*! As an adult! When he had complete authority over his time!

Even worse: the boutique Ellison wanted to visit was an hour north, in San Francisco. And somehow Ellison had finagled it so that Jamie was driving. There was stop-and-go traffic the whole way. "I brought you because you project a certain presence," Ellison announced once they had finally parked and were inside.

"What presence?" Jamie asked quietly. They were the only customers in the store. He could tell the place was expensive: the interior smelled heavily of jasmine, and the walls were a checkerboard of glass and resin. Each pair of shoes was displayed on a small pedestal and lit from below, as if it were precious jewelry.

"Just something about you. The air you give off. Moneyed. Cultured. Though I wish you hadn't worn that T-shirt today. Yuck!"

The saleswoman returned with the shoes Ellison had requested. On the walk over, Ellison told Jamie he'd called the store in advance; he wanted to be sure they had his size. "Oh, these look *perfect*," Ellison said when the saleswoman opened the boxes. He waited until she walked away before trying them on.

The first pair were wedge heels made out of green patent leather. Ellison raised his foot and tried to pull down his pants hem so it draped over the shoe. "I like the look of these," he said. "Although they're so chunky. Really, I'm just trying them on for fun. It wouldn't be a good use of my budget."

"So you're getting the other pair, then."

"I'm not buying anything." Ellison took a lap around the carpet. He stopped at the mirror. "Surprisingly comfortable. You can feel the quality of the leather. It's hard to find good patent."

"Then why not get them? What are we here for, otherwise?"

"So I can be *prepared*," Ellison said. "For sale season. You really have no idea how much these things cost, do you?"

Ellison apparently thought nothing of having Jamie drive nearly three hours round-trip, simply to try on a few pairs of shoes. After they left the boutique empty-handed, Ellison said he was ready to go home. Jamie was determined to do something else to justify the drive. "Let's get lunch."

Jamie made Ellison walk with him until he found a bakery, an upscale one with a French name, where he purchased a ham sandwich. Ellison, who had nursed a glass of ice water while Jamie ate, bought a bag of chips from a hot dog cart on the way back to the car. "I worry about your mother," he commented as they drove. Ellison had a way of burrowing into the plastic bag that drove Jamie crazy. After each bite, he crumpled the bag's top, vowing not to eat any more, only to open it again seconds later. It made a tremendous amount of noise.

"You're always worried about Joan." Ellison was constantly fretting that people were after Joan—random crazies, perhaps, or angry former customers, perverts or rageaholics Joan had told to scram and never return.

"No, it's *different*," Ellison insisted. "She's loopy sometimes."

"She's getting old. Older people can be loopy."

"Your mother isn't that old. And she's forgetting things."

"I forget things," Jamie said. He was beginning to be irritated by Ellison's insistence on the matter; it was as if he wanted to prove that he cared more about Joan than Jamie did.

There was the sound of the bag uncrumpling again, and Ellison leaned back and tipped the crumbs into his mouth. "The other day we were getting ready to close, and she came in and said she couldn't find her car," he said, wiping his fingers and then folding the empty bag and shoving it into the cupholder. "She said it must have been stolen, because it wasn't where she left it. I went out with her, and we pressed the key until it beeped. The car was right in front of the café, Jamie. Everyone makes mistakes, but she was flustered. Joan said she didn't want to drive again, that she was sick of it. She said she was going to sell her car and take cabs everywhere."

"She loses her temper like that sometimes."

"Does she? I've never seen it."

"She's my *mother*. I've seen her at her worst. If she got impatient with you, it means she's comfortable."

"Well, I guess you do know her best," Ellison said.

Silence. Jamie tried to work out why he was so annoyed with Ellison. Well, he *is* annoying, he thought as he merged onto the freeway. Ellison was always asking for little (and sometimes big) favors and talking about Joan; he observed her with an intensity that seemed to border on paranoia. But there was something else bothering Jamie that he couldn't quite place.

"Sour worm?" Ellison asked. He'd brought a bag from the snack jars in the café.

"Thanks." Jamie pulled one and wiped the sugar onto his pants. He played back in his head something Ellison had said about Joan, the bit concerning the car. As long as Jamie could recall, Joan had loved to drive; she never complained about driving, even on long trips through

Oregon and Washington. She adored each of her vehicles and took care of them with the tenderness afforded a baby. And yet she'd told Ellison she didn't want to drive again, which Jamie knew she didn't mean—it was just something you said when you felt foolish or flustered.

But the thing was: Joan was almost never flustered. Nor was she foolish.

CHAPTER THIRTY-FOUR

They took Joan to see a specialist. Both Jamie and Lee came to the appointment. In the hospital, Joan walked the halls with purpose. She strode so fast she nearly left her children behind.

I created you, Joan thought bitterly. I raised you. She had bathed them; she had wiped their little butts and held them when they cried. There had been countless instances when she had wanted and gone without to make their lives as seamless as possible. This she had done without complaint. But Lee and Jamie were grown, and she was her own person again. And now they dared give orders about her body?

Joan was always fastidious about doctors' appointments, and taped on her fridge was an AARP mailer that listed recommended tests by age. She scheduled her mammograms, her colonoscopy, her physicals months in advance. She was structured about medical visits because she did not like hospitals and otherwise would avoid them. When her children were younger and asked if she would die, she said only that she hoped it wasn't soon. And when they asked if they themselves would die (Lee being the child most fearful of death), all Joan could offer was it wasn't for them to worry about. Either of them dying was unimaginable; it was the only event Joan could not bear to ponder.

And yet it seemed now her children were able to imagine her own death quite easily—in fact, they were bringing her to the hospital to learn even more about it. Joan strode faster and faster. By the time she arrived at the specialist, both Lee and Jamie had to run, to catch the door she'd flung open before it slammed shut.

The fury lasted until Joan was seated in a blue felt chair, a nurse before her with a list of questions. The questions were insulting: what day it was, who was the president, what year she had been born. She answered them clearly and accurately. They asked her to draw a clock.

"Of course I can draw a clock," Joan snapped. She drew a perfect circle—if she had used a stencil, it could not have been more perfect. Next she went to add the numbers but found she was stuck. Suddenly the request seemed impossible. When was the last time she'd actually observed a clock, the manual sort with hands? It was like being asked to draw a car engine!

But a little pulse began to beat: not normal not normal not normal.

After the test she waited, and at last the doctor arrived. His name was Dr. Chin—Lee and Jamie had deliberately chosen a Chinese doctor. Dr. Chin was around their age, with black hair which flopped evenly on both sides of his head. He asked if Joan wanted him to speak Mandarin, though she declined as she could tell it wasn't his first language. He inquired how she felt.

"I feel fine," Joan said. She waited. "Do I have a disease?"

"At this point we don't know. It could be anything. A bad day. We'll do some more tests and ask you to come back."

Joan said that was fine. He had an excellent bedside manner. She knew Dr. Chin's parents were likely proud of him, of the work he was doing. She knew it wasn't a bad day.

———

Even though it was her children who'd insisted she seek medical attention, the news that Joan was suffering from an actual disease of the brain—that she would continue to suffer, with no likely reversal—was stunning to Jamie and Lee. They discussed it privately and then went and confronted Joan together; this way, she was less likely to intimidate them with the usual tools at her disposal.

"You shouldn't live on your own," Jamie said.

"One of us can stay with you," Lee said. She had recently moved out, to her own apartment. "I can break my lease. Or we can *both* live with you," she added heroically. She did not look at Jamie when she said this.

"I don't want to live with anyone," Joan said.

"Well, you've got to live with someone," Jamie said.

Joan didn't want either of her children staying with her. It wasn't how she'd envisioned getting older, it wasn't the natural order. Wasn't that funny, though? Because of course people did get old; at a certain point adults needed to be taken care of, the same way as little babies. People never questioned that children should be kept secure, safe, protected from loneliness, and yet it seemed unnatural that it might go the other way around. And really, if you were divorced, or your spouse was dead, or you were simply alone, who else was supposed to take care of you? Children, after all, usually owed you most; they were the ones you could guilt into listening to all your grievances and fixing the sound on your television.

But still. Still. It wasn't right. Children weren't supposed to take care of their parents, not in that way. And Joan knew it wouldn't work. If the disease kept going as she had read it would—if she kept degenerating until she needed help to eat and bathe and dress—she would require the sort of patience needed for a young child. And that sort of love, that constant vigilance and lack of freedom should go only one direction, in her opinion.

Isn't it funny, Joan thought.

———

Jamie and Lee didn't move in. But they hovered. They asked annoying questions (When did you last eat? Is your vision clear?) and called. But after a few months the inquiries lessened; without an immediate catastrophe, the issue receded, and Jamie and Lee returned to their lives. Though it didn't fade for Joan. She knew what awaited her.

"I try not to think about it," Joan told Patty. Patty was the only employee Joan had informed of her diagnosis, as she wanted her to be alert for bookkeeping errors. Patty was so understanding, so discreet, that Joan often thought of her as a well: you simply whispered to her all of your secrets, and they dropped into the dark. The other employees also confided: Gina told Patty she was sick of baking carrot cake ("I know it's a bestseller and that it keeps well, but I should be allowed my preferences"); Ellison complained about his ex-wife ("She keeps calling, and I know it's only because she wants attention").

On Patty's suggestion, Joan went to a support group, held at a community center. The speaker recommended that everyone record events in a notebook to have proof of what had been done and said. "It's better to have your own confirmation," a woman commented, agreeing with this. She was jittery and clutched a highlighter. "My husband tells me when I've fallen. But how do I know he isn't *pushing* me?" The rest of the group nodded in sympathy. The woman wept loudly the rest of the session.

That lady needs the Satisfaction Café, Joan thought, staring at her with compassion. She believed quite a few in the group needed it, but they came from all over the Bay Area and she felt it would appear self-serving to suggest they drive out of their way for some coffee and conversation. After all, they were receiving free conversation in the support group, though Patrick insisting his wife was stealing his boxers at night wasn't really the same as tea and dumplings with Ellison, was it?

As the months passed, she began to forget more. She stared straight into the face of Patty one morning and introduced herself. "I'm Joan," Joan said.

"Hi," Patty said, extending her hand. She didn't speak of it after.

The following month, Joan fell at home. All she'd been doing was walking in the kitchen, minding her own business, and then suddenly had fallen over, hard, as if she'd tripped on an unexpected object, but when she looked down there was nothing but smooth tile. The entire left side of her torso was bruised, the darkest spots where her ribs met skin, and for the first time in a long while Joan wished she had a husband. I've hurt myself, she could have shouted. Come, honey—please help! She could always say such things to her children, but first she'd have to call, then wait for them to arrive, during which time she would have felt impatient and well enough to get up on her own, but would have to remain lying on the floor to justify Lee or Jamie driving over in the first place. And they would want to move her somewhere; there would be talk of strokes and head injuries. Of how her brain could no longer be trusted. But Joan was loyal to her brain—it had served her so nicely! She wanted someone to sympathize without consequence, who would respect her desire to remain home.

She went for a walk with Trevor. They still saw each other—she hadn't told him about the diagnosis, as they didn't have the sort of arrangement where she could call him if she fell. Or rather: she could call, and he would come, but their relationship wouldn't be the same. He would be upset by her condition but could not be counted on to manage the care of it—they had not reached that place, there hadn't been enough time.

The next week they visited a local winery. The winery had a large patio, and there was a concert there that day, some band Trevor had followed for years. Most of the music was fast, chipper, and folksy, but then they dropped to a ballad that the crowd seemed to know—quite a few sang along. The song was nostalgic, stirring, the way the singer's voice broke and warbled as she reached certain notes.

"Are you crying?" Trevor asked. "You are, aren't you? I just realized I've never seen you cry."

"It's nothing," Joan said. She searched her bag for a tissue.

"Is everything okay?" Trevor touched his hand to the back of her neck.

"Yes, yes," Joan said, folding her tissue. She could feel his fingers gently rubbing the skin right beneath her collar; it was one of those moments she had once dreamed of happening. Did she love Trevor? Had she *ever* had big love in her life? Big, romantic love? Joan thought so at times, and other moments she thought she'd only ever taken these little sips. But perhaps that was wrong. Pleasure doesn't keep so well as a memory. Everything fades.

She could sense Trevor waiting. Joan was afraid she would say something ridiculous were she to speak. I'm going to miss you, maybe. I wish we could have been together earlier. I think it would have been worth it.

"Do you want to talk about it?" Trevor asked.

Joan cleared her throat. "It's just a nice song, that's all."

———

After Joan forgot she'd already purchased a deep freezer, and had become angry when a second freezer she'd ordered appeared in front of the café, berating her favorite UPS deliveryman, she turned over daily management of the business to Jamie. It was Jamie who volunteered; she originally told him she was posting a job listing. "Patty's already so busy."

"Don't hire anybody," Jamie said. "I'll do it."

"What about your work?"

"Oh, they're fine. The company is super flexible."

Atom was indeed super flexible, not least because Jamie no longer worked there. He had quit months earlier, after Joan's diagnosis, although the two hadn't been related, not exactly. It was more that he'd had enough: the meetings, the projects, the recurring one-on-ones; the managers, the climbing, the gossip, the endless doomsday whispers of a looming "reorg." He had half a year of savings and asked Chloe if she might want to travel around the world: "We wouldn't be getting back together," Jamie said. "Just as friends." Chloe had said no.

Jamie hadn't informed Joan of his leaving, which he considered an act of benevolence. Joan attached a great deal of meaning to corporate work, possibly because she had never done it herself.

"There's nothing special about a company," Jamie once told Joan. "There's nothing admirable in working yourself to death for an entity that doesn't care about you."

"You should be proud just to *work*," Joan had said.

Whether Joan suspected and found it convenient not to comment, or failed to notice that Jamie now spent most of his days at the café, he never knew. He took over her managerial tasks: he arranged and rearranged the host schedules and kept track of the evening's receipts and maintained a list of banned customers. He swept the floors in the morning and evening, and when they still weren't clean enough for his liking, he began to sweep nearly every hour. He brainstormed menu additions and attended trade shows to select items for the shop.

All of this is *work*, Jamie thought. So much actual work. It staggered him that he had once thought sitting at a desk all day, staring into a computer, was work.

In contrast with Jamie's sweeping and scurrying, Joan appeared relaxed, carefree—her condition had fostered in her a tranquil disposition that Jamie and Lee had never witnessed. They realized that for their entire lives, their mother had always been so *stressed*. Even when happy, she had also been anxious, looking around for something to do. Jamie recalled when Joan had to stay home the whole day to wait for a repairman. He had gone to school, and when he returned, his mother had assembled an end table and regrouted the shower.

Now Joan was no longer in constant motion, cleaning or sorting; a languor had set in, that extended from her schedule to her body. She carried a journal, in which she scrawled notes that she showed no one. She sat at a table in the café and read her latest library selection, her notebook within arm's reach. When Jamie was free, he'd join her. He tried to intrigue his mother with anecdotes about his friends. This once reliably interested Joan: What's Darrell doing, you know, that handsome boy who was so good at math? And your ex-girlfriend Eunice, her parents, did they ever move to Korea?

In the evenings, when Joan stayed late, Jamie would sometimes bring her the plastic file containing all the day's receipts and any notes on unusual incidents or customers. One Friday after closing, Joan asked for the file; her left hand rapped against the table as she leafed through papers. Her finger went down a sheet; she was wearing her usual ring, in the shape of a gold panther. "Are you glad things are the way they are?" Joan asked without looking up.

"Things?"

"Yes." Joan flipped a page. "Your life."

Maybe she'd realized he was working full-time at the café. "To be honest, I didn't like Atom. I barely understood it."

"Eh?" She looked up and narrowed her eyes. "I mean about Lee. And her joining. Our family."

"Oh." Not once had Joan asked this of him. Jamie had been only three when Lee arrived. To him, it was the same as if Joan had given birth herself. "Of course."

"You didn't wish you had a brother, more siblings?"

"No," Jamie said honestly.

Joan peered up at him again. Her notebook lay in her lap. "Life is very strange," she said. "It turns out the things I thought would be difficult aren't so. It's what I hadn't thought about that's causing all the problems. Sometimes I wonder if I'd worried more, fewer bad things would have happened."

"I had a friend like that in the navy. He used to say out loud what he was most frightened of because he was convinced God was listening."

"What happened to him?"

"He was with me on the roof."

Joan showed no sign of understanding. "It was Nick," Jamie added. "The one who died. You met his mother."

Joan blinked. She held her hand in front of her face as if she needed to examine something on it. "I'm tired," she said. She pointed to the expense tracker. "I think you forgot to add the fee for the plumber." She went off to another table with her notebook, scrawling into it her mysteries, and Jamie wondered how much she would recall of the conversation.

———

Jamie and Lee agreed upon a routine: at least one of them saw Joan each day. They also tried to drive her whenever possible, though they hadn't broached the topic of Joan giving up her car. One weekend she said she wanted to go hiking, and Lee drove them to High Rock Park. Still there was no railing or sign at the cliff base. Lee had been afraid Joan might be angry—she was angrier these days—but her mother seemed resigned. "Oh well," Joan said. "What can you do?"

After the hike, Joan had been withdrawn, wordlessly staring out the passenger window during the drive home. The following Saturday, Lee thought it best to ensure a pleasurable activity, and Joan always enjoyed a good meal. To qualify as good to Joan, the food had to be Chinese, well priced, and the restaurant busy. Lee settled on dim sum.

When they arrived at Joy Palace, there was already a line. Customers were pressed against the fish tanks, the excess crowd spilling onto the lawn.

"I told you we should have come earlier," Joan said.

"We are early. We left the house at eleven."

"Look at how many people. So many Chinese here now. And even some white people."

Lee didn't respond. She knew Joan thought of her as a Chinese person. The crowd, however, did not, and when she went in to get a number, a grandmother elbowed her from behind. Lee didn't push the woman aside, not exactly, but she did square her body in front of the counter. To make a point, she asked for a table for two in halting Mandarin.

"What number are we?" Joan asked when Lee returned outside. Joan had found a bench, and she lifted her handbag so Lee could sit. The bench faced the Chinese supermarket at the front of the plaza. Lee watched the grandmother who had shoved her scurry into the market. There passed a set of twins in starched eyelet dresses with large bows in their hair, each holding a hand of their mother.

"I think if we hadn't had you, maybe I would have tried to be pregnant again," Joan remarked, looking at the twins. "Were you happy to be in this family?"

"Yes, of course."

"What if I'd had a baby after you and Jamie?"

"It would have been fine," Lee said carefully. "But I've always liked things exactly as they are."

Joan stared off. "I just worry that you miss another life you didn't have. I hope you really are happy."

She doesn't know what she's saying, Lee thought. She's just making conversation; sometimes when people get older, they just blurt things out. She glanced at Joan; her eyes were foggy, and she was breathing with her mouth slightly parted.

She's tired, Lee thought again.

Lee didn't know that, just days earlier, Joan had asked Jamie a similar question. Lee didn't know how loudly this idea of whether her children were happy rumbled through Joan's head. If Lee had thought a little more, she might have realized how strange, how out of character it was for Joan to ask about happiness. And if Lee were *really* thinking about her mother, she might have recognized certain patterns, such as Joan's routine of checking items off a list before starting a major task.

But Lee didn't consider any of this, which was what Joan expected. After all, it was natural for your children to think more of themselves than they did of you. That was what parents did too, as they aged—they thought of themselves. I've thought of myself plenty, Joan mused.

Inside Joan's tote was her notebook. On her desk at home, she kept a jar stocked with her children's old gel pens. As a result the pages were filled with different colors: blue and green and silver and pink. Sometimes she would open it and know exactly what she had written, and other times she would read and be surprised. She never doubted its contents, however. She did not doubt her intentions.

When Bill was dying, or rather, when Bill knew he was dying, he complained that people treated him differently. "They see me and think: Dead man walking," he said.

Joan was the opposite: she believed that her children and her employees weren't thinking about her mortality enough. They nursed foolish hopes and yearned for her to get better; when she had good days—and she still had them, good days—they thought it was like before. But she knew what lay before her.

And yet.

"Fifty-eight," the loudspeaker said from above. "Party of two. Fifty-eight," the voice chimed again, first in English and then in Mandarin.

"Okay," Lee said. "Let's go."

But Joan didn't move. She remained seated and petting Lee's hand.

Lee was wearing a dress, a light orange number that went nearly to the ground, and little white sandals. Joan used to have white sandals like that. She had kept them pristine, thinking they were too good to use, and then they had been lost in the fire. Wear those sandals all the time, Joan wanted to tell Lee. Wear them until they fall apart. Joan had loved Falling House, but she never thought of it now. It was just a building. Everything goes.

Their number was called again, and finally Joan rose and together they went into the restaurant.

CHAPTER THIRTY-FIVE

Jamie was in bed when Lee called. Next to him, an arm's length away, was Sandy, his former coworker from Atom. When Jamie had quit, he hadn't included Sandy on his farewell message— she wasn't the level of acquaintance who rated his personal contact details—so he'd been surprised when one afternoon she'd shown up at the café.

"Oh, it's you," Jamie said.

"It's me!" Sandy agreed. She looked incredibly pleased to see him.

Ellison did not like Sandy. He said her eyes held the light of menace and—Ellison added—possible psychosis. "She tries too hard," he said. "She's one of those girls who's always *trying.*"

"Sandy's nice," Jamie said. Though even as he spoke, he was suddenly cognizant of her resemblance to females of his earlier youth: the sort who, through sheer persistence and *Are you awake I'm so drunk are you hungry I can bring something over* eventually wore you down, because the men of his generation had been trained not in direct rejection but in indifference and increasingly shitty behavior, until they were dumped and released from obligation. But Sandy's joy at seeing Jamie again, the childlike purity of it, had moved him; at the current moment in Jamie's life (single, lazy), he found enthusiasm extremely attractive.

When Lee called, it was after his and Sandy's third time sleeping together. The prior evening—from the greasy, overpriced tapas to the bottle of room-temperature cava back at his apartment—had felt a little dirty. *He* felt a little dirty. Sandy, Jamie thought, was *also* a little dirty; her neck had a grayish cast that he realized, upon lightly rubbing his thumb against it while she was sleeping, was actually unwashed skin. For that reason, and also because he didn't feel like speaking to anyone, he sent the call to voicemail when he saw Lee's name. He did it again while he was getting dressed, and again saying goodbye to Sandy, while politely but firmly leaving no option for her to remain in the apartment. He was certain she was the sort to snoop while he was away; he suspected she'd already done so while he was in the shower. Lee called again in the car, which he ignored until he realized his sister was not the type to call over and over—it was Sandy, Jamie thought, who would do something like that.

Jamie called Lee only for her not to answer. He continued to drive but turned his music down. He nearly sped through a red light. When the phone rang, he answered before the ring was complete. The first seconds, all he heard was Lee's breath.

"Lee? What is it?"

"She's gone," she cried. He knew there was only one person Lee could be talking about.

CHAPTER THIRTY-SIX

On Wednesday morning, Joan had gone for a hike. She set off the way she always did, with a small bottle of water and a zipped bag of nuts in her nylon tote (she refused to use a backpack), sneakers securely tied and her hair in a clip. At some point on the walk, she sat down and lost consciousness. The area was relatively isolated, and no one found her for several hours.

All this Nelson told Jamie and Lee when he met them at the Satisfaction Café. It was Nelson who'd been called by the police after park rangers found Joan's body. His card was in her wallet, in the slot marked EMERGENCY CONTACT.

"She was in a remote area," Nelson said. He was seated across from Lee and Jamie in the back office of the café with the door closed.

"Where was it?" Lee asked.

Nelson removed from his pocket the slip of paper on which he'd written the name of the preserve. "High Rock Park." Jamie looked at Lee.

"The ranger remarked that it was near some unprotected cliffs, that they'd been intending to install signs to warn hikers."

"Are they doing the signs now?"

"They were putting in a work order when I left. In the meantime, they said they'd cordon off the trail with tape." Nelson found it curious that Joan's children were so interested in the signs. "Had you been there before? Was she familiar with the place?"

"She was . . . fairly familiar," Jamie said awkwardly. He and Lee looked at each other again.

That's all right, Nelson thought. You don't have to tell me anything.

Nelson was both touched and annoyed to be in this position. He was *older* than Joan, after all; it seemed a little insensitive to have him deal with her death. There was something almost unseemly about seeing a client not only through life but then past the end of it, although he supposed he didn't have many more years of this. He too was creeping toward that edge.

Nelson was mostly retired now. He had become the sort of senior citizen he would have mocked in earlier years: a personal trainer came by the house twice a week, and he and Adam were planning a cruise on the Rhine. Nelson was even working on his memoir, an activity he'd previously believed reserved for bores and the delusional. When the police had called, he'd been writing a new chapter as he sat in his office. He had just poured himself a cup of coffee.

"What do we do?" Lee asked.

"I suggest you go to your mother's," Nelson said. "Take care of anything there."

By the time Nelson arrived home, he was feeling morose. He wished he'd seen Joan more. He recalled the box of snacks she had sent him in Düsseldorf. How special he had felt, entering his hotel, when the concierge called his name and said he had a package. *From your friend*, Joan had written on the note.

At the door to his office, Nelson saw the full cup of coffee still on his desk, next to the legal pad with his scribbling. Honestly, who on earth was going to read his memoir (if he ever finished)? He didn't have children; he doubted Adam would be interested in learning *more* about him, once he was gone.

And yet, nearly every day, Nelson still wrote.

He went to his desk. There was a line he'd added that morning: *I've been thinking that relationships, like life, are*

Like what. Like *what?* He couldn't recall. Over the years Nelson had given and received countless nuggets of so-called wisdom; he had sat before billionaires and CEOs and fifth wives and third husbands. There were strategies plotted and abandoned, plans promised and secretly changed. There had been so much planning for certain events: divorce and marriage and death and children. People were always surprised, though. It never turned out how they thought. People changed. People died.

———

For most of her life, Lee had been a messy person. While Jamie straightened his room without reminder (a habit he continued into college, that was only exacerbated by his time in the navy), she was the sort who misplaced homework and dressed from a basket of unfolded laundry. Lee also lost things. She lost money and jackets. She lost key chains and employee IDs.

The day Joan died, however, was the day Lee would become not only a neat person but one who kept track of her possessions. Going forward, she would be unable to tolerate clutter; it would bother her in a way it never had when Joan was alive.

After leaving the café, she and Jamie drove to the townhouse. "She's been talking about that cliff for years," Jamie said, turning onto the street. "It just seems strange that she would—would fall unconscious right there. Do you know what I mean?"

Yes. Lee knew what he meant.

The townhouse appeared unusually crowded, and Lee began to inventory its contents. There were several Home Depot bags on the floor, filled with Joan's latest purchases, batteries and powdered bleach and a watering can. On the kitchen counter were her radio and several cassettes stacked in a metal tin which originally contained mooncakes. In the pantry were a pack of Chinese seaweed crackers, six different bags of Kirkland-branded nuts, and Japanese curry blocks.

After sniffing dozens of jars of old spices to test their potency, Lee's head began to hurt. She swallowed an aspirin without water and massaged her temples as she went through the house. It did not occur to Lee to sit and rest. If she stopped, she would have to face that Joan was gone. Lee would have to imagine her body on the side of that cliff.

Joan didn't believe in God. When you died, she had told Lee, it was like the lights going off.

Lee went to Joan's closet. Here was where she had spent hours as a kid; not the sort to actively entertain children, Joan had simply instructed Lee and Jamie to do as they wished inside without breaking anything. Lee had tried on Joan's clothes and jewelry until somehow she had managed to lose a pearl necklace, and then she hadn't been allowed in anymore. Or perhaps Lee had barred herself from entering. Joan had a way of turning cold, nearly to the point of cruel, when she was disappointed; it prompted self-regulation, even in children.

Where did Joan store her jewelry? It seemed improper to ponder, but that was what Nelson had asked them to do—identify sentimental items. What Lee wanted were some favorites she'd seen Joan wear over the years: the gold panther ring, a Chanel cardigan Joan had splurged on and then worn only on special occasions, usually when she went to lunch with women she described as "rich ladies."

Lee tried on a camel coat she had always admired, which was too small. There was a gray silk dress Joan had purchased because she liked the material, but had never worn; this fit Lee perfectly, though when she saw her reflection, she could hear Joan's voice telling her to take it, it fits you better—she shrugged it off and avoided mirrors after that.

With each minute Lee felt more and more pinpricks of a creeping hysteria; when she did finally break, she wanted her mother's ring. Surely something was wrong with her. Surely there was something grotesque about needing a physical item to hold on to. But she did want something physical, because if it was only Lee and her thoughts back in her own apartment later that night she thought she might drown.

Lee could hear Jamie on the floor above. Perhaps he too was looking for something—there was a set of art supplies Joan kept in a metal tool-box, including steel calipers and a protractor, that he'd always admired and which had survived the fire as they'd been stored in the garage.

Lee searched the closet again. Along the back wall was a collection of shopping bags. Joan had once told Lee that such bags invited clutter. "It doesn't matter how *nice* the store the bag came from is," Joan said.

Lee flipped through the bags. Joan had nested them with a large orange bag inside of another orange bag inside of a yellow bag. Lee reached into the last bag, which was navy. Inside were two gray cashmere sweaters and then, underneath the sweaters, a red velvet envelope. Lee opened the envelope and was relieved to find the panther ring. Also tucked in the envelope was a white index card with Joan's handwriting in clear block letters:

BE NICE TO EACH OTHER!

"Jamie?" Lee called.

———

They sat next to each other on the floor of the closet. Because Lee had tossed so many items on the ground, it was covered with empty boxes and coats and pants. Lee was playing with Joan's ring, which she had put on. It was loose on her finger, and Lee flipped the panther around and around.

"Nelson called," Jamie said. "The police asked him to pick up Mom's bag. There was an empty pill bottle inside. Nelson said the label was for a pretty powerful barbiturate."

"What's a barbiturate?"

"A sleeping pill. A strong one."

Lee kept spinning the ring. "Where did she get it?"

"I don't know." (In fact, it was the same bottle that had been prescribed by Dr. Marcus for Bill decades earlier. In the years since, such pills had become nearly impossible to procure. Joan had been worried they wouldn't work, given their age, and so she had taken half a pill the week before. An hour after swallowing, she felt simply incredible.)

"It smells like mothballs in here," Jamie said.

"I told her not to use them. They're supposed to be cancerous."

"I guess she didn't care about that."

Lee fingered the carpet. "What's with the note? We are nice to each other."

"Maybe just a reminder." Jamie recognized the index card from the stack Joan kept at the café to jot potential phrases for her poster board. He thought of her deciding on those specific words—*BE NICE*—and sighed and looked at his hands. His mother, who had only ever wanted him to have a stable job, who had so resented his time in the navy—what had she once called it? A waste of a nice boy like him. But he *wasn't* such a nice boy, he knew: Jamie was never as nice as he wanted to be. He had followed rules, that was all, but they hadn't brought him anywhere. It wasn't until he'd started working at the café that he'd felt any sort of peace.

He'd dropped little hints to her these past months. Jamie had told Joan the other evening, after a particularly busy Friday, that he hadn't known there were so many lonely people in the world. "Loneliness!" Joan had exclaimed. "Jamie, you must be brave! Living by yourself is nothing to be scared of!" At the time, he'd assumed she'd heard about him and

Sandy, but now he was unclear. His mother had been steadfast and also impulsive. She had been unhappy, and then happy, and unhappy and happy again. She'd been both the best mother in the world and the person who knew most what he hated about himself and, at times, like many mothers, when frustrated or angry, had pressed her thumb to that tender place. In the end, Jamie knew Joan would have known, when she'd taken those pills by the cliff, that he still needed her.

CHAPTER THIRTY-SEVEN

One of Joan's guiltiest pleasures over the years (though she really didn't feel too bad about it) had been not only her acquisition of items but how much she *liked* them. Even when she didn't have money, she had enjoyed shopping; she liked walking the aisles and touching with her hands and eyes. She adored the spangle of beads and the feel of good material and the heaviness of fine jewelry.

In her final weeks, Joan spent hours in her closet. She sat on the floor and gazed upon the prints and the solids. The brights and the neutrals. Among them she felt at peace, clearheaded and ready.

At first Joan had contemplated carbon monoxide. She was amused to recall that so many years earlier it was exactly this Bill had been fearful of as she sat in the garage. She ruminated on the idea but then forgot about it altogether, which only enraged her when she did recall it weeks later. She'd previously resisted writing on the topic in her notebook, worried her children might snoop, but now began a list:

Methods:

Carbon monoxide (bad for real estate value? can I ask Nelson?)
Hanging (same real estate problem?)
Charcoal fire (popular in Japan)

She debated options on her morning walks. Time was limited, as Joan knew that one day, likely sooner than she thought, her car would be taken and thus much of her freedom. She returned to High Rock Park with Lee and they went to the cliff. And there the idea came.

Initially Joan thought falling would be simplest. After all, you needed only two objects: your body and the cliff. She recalled a book Lee had purchased years earlier, a guide on how to manage all sorts of dangerous physical situations. Joan located the slim yellow volume, which indeed contained a chapter on cliff jumps into water, albeit surviving them: you had to clench your anus, it instructed, to keep water from flooding into your body. If possible, you should try to hold your nose closed.

As she read, Joan worried about internal sabotage. Her brain, having accumulated this knowledge, might conspire with her body and attempt to survive—and her body was *already* conspiring against her, or rather, it was whispering, giving strong hints as to the future. Joan and her brain and body in a room. Being fed. Being bathed. Dependent on her children, who would never again release her from their grasp. No more control.

No.

In the end, it was Bill who furnished the solution. The pills in her bag, turning her face from the sun as she lay above the cliff. The sounds of the ocean were so strong as to be almost physical. She could feel the blue with her eyes closed.

Wasn't it funny how the people who crowded your mind in such moments could be so unexpected? Here she was, pills in hand, about to say goodbye. You might assume she'd be thinking of Lee and Jamie, but she wasn't. Nor was Joan thinking about Bill or even her mother or father.

After Bill died, Joan had gone through a period when she liked long drives. She would open one of her maps and pick a city two or three hours away and set off after dropping the children at school. Joan passed through extended stretches of dusty roads, little towns, and lone farmhouses, and she would find herself overcome by all these worlds she'd never know. She'd had the urge many times to pull over and knock on a door. Who are you inside? she wanted to ask. We'd never meet otherwise, isn't that a shame? And so it was Dustin who floated in her thoughts as she sat by the cliff; by building the café, she had knocked on the door of the universe. And Dustin—still her most loyal customer—was one who'd answered.

The two of them had long graduated from the book of Greek myths and moved on to other tales. Their last meeting, Dustin had brought a Nordic volume, another one meant for children, the cover a dark red. They had sat at Joan's favorite table, the one with a turquoise top, and perused the book. She read quietly and slowly until Dustin looked at her with his pale eyes.

Joan stopped. "Are you okay?"

She knew more about Dustin by now: how he had an older sister who'd been his parents' favorite growing up; how, in the evenings, they'd often locked him in the basement while the rest of the family ate dinner upstairs. Some folks just get a rawer deal. But the admiration Joan had for Dustin's attempts to get better, to *feel* better, was so immense as to be close to love.

Yes yes, Dustin said. He was okay. "Please read on."

So Joan did. Baldr, she said —pronouncing it as *bald*—was a Nordic god.

"You say it like *Balder*," Dustin interjected. He knew Joan liked to learn. "He was the son of Odin."

"Baldr," she repeated. Dustin nodded.

Joan continued. When Baldr died, she read aloud, he was loaded onto a boat. A giantess came to his funeral, named Hyrrokkin, who was famous for riding a wolf. The boat was supposed to be launched in the water, but even Baldr's brother Thor did not possess the strength, and so the boat sat there, not moving, with Baldr's now mortal body on it. Until eventually Hyrrokin came to the water, her wolf waiting behind her, and pushed Baldr out to sea.

CHAPTER THIRTY-EIGHT

One aspect of her death Joan did not consider was her funeral. After all, she would already be dead. She had an estate plan, though she could not recall the precise directives, and feared that asking Nelson would alert him to her greater intentions. Also, she just didn't care about funerals.

If Joan *had* cared, she might have asked that the service not be held at a church. These instructions had been copied over from Bill's, who had not been a churchgoer either, but the Lauders believed that, like the royal family, they should conduct their important ceremonies at church. And certainly Joan would not have requested to hold the reception at Lotus Garden. Not due to any embarrassment over her prior history but because Sam Wu had retired and sold the business, and thus the restaurant she had known was no more. The cook was new, and the menu touted cocktails with names like "Sunset Dreams" and "The Pink Bubbly"; everyone knew that when a Chinese restaurant tried to pivot to serving Caucasians on first dates, the results were usually dire. But Joan had never told her family this (if she were alive, she might have argued that by not visiting, she'd already delivered her verdict), and so after the service, they all traveled to the restaurant where Joan had worked as a hostess decades earlier, as a young woman new to California.

Misty showed up at Lotus Garden. She sat right outside the entrance on the low concrete ledge, which was where Lee encountered her.

"I couldn't go into that church," Misty said. "I spent the whole time sitting outside staring at traffic. Funny thing is, I did the same for most of your father's."

"Oh?" Lee didn't remember much of Bill's funeral; it was a blur in her memory, though she could still recall the heat of the fire that night.

They walked inside. Misty looked strong; her hair was short and dyed red. She went first to Bridget and Henry, the three siblings forming a little knot, and then halfway through dinner returned to speak with Lee.

"She wanted to give you something," Lee recalled. She ran and retrieved the box from her car. Lee had found about a dozen such boxes, wrapped and clearly labeled with the recipients' names, on Joan's dining room table. She had resisted the temptation to open them, though Lee had a pretty good idea what was in Misty's.

Misty seemed to know too; she shook the box and didn't open it. "Your mother always had the greatest jewelry."

"Yeah." Lee glanced at the ring on her right hand. "I'm aware."

"She had *taste*. Like sometimes I thought Joan dressed too much like an old lady—I'd make fun: was she trying for the world's biggest collection of cardigans? But then she'd surprise me with something. A sexy dress. A bright color."

"Why couldn't you come into the church?"

"I didn't want to break down and cry everywhere. I mean, I just know your mother would have hated it."

"She wouldn't have hated it," Lee said, knowing Joan would have.

"You know what's funny." Misty was clutching the box, slightly crushing its sides in her grip. "From the first moment I met her, I knew she was a decent person. A *good* person. I used to tell her: Joan, if anyone deserves to live forever, it's you."

"What did she say to that?" Lee asked, curious.

"That she didn't want to," Misty replied. She wept.

——

Ellison drove Jamie to Lotus Garden. Ellison was dressed in a charcoal suit made of very fine wool; he seemed extremely pleased to be wearing it, perhaps to the edge of inappropriate, given that it was a funeral. He said he had been waiting for the perfect occasion for the suit, which he'd had made in Hong Kong by a tailor who worked out of the Peninsula. "I didn't think your mom was a churchgoer," he said.

"She had her own spirituality," Jamie said wryly. To his knowledge, Joan had never expressed an interest in religion, except to once comment that it was admirable churches distributed food to those in need. "That is, if they don't ask for anything in *return*," she'd added.

"Do you need a ride to the café?" Ellison asked. The employees would have their own event later that night, a tribute to Joan. Jamie had paid for the food and drink and given them the following week off, saying Joan would have wanted it.

"I can't go. I've got to stay here."

"What for?"

"Some paperwork." Jamie poured himself tea. "Family affairs," he said.

"What?" Jamie added a moment later. Ellison looked angry, and Jamie thought perhaps he was upset that Jamie hadn't poured him tea, as this was something hosts were instructed to do at the café, to be polite. "Why do you look like that?" Jamie filled Ellison's cup; he was hasty, and some of the liquid slopped over the edge, which Jamie tried to blot with a napkin.

Ellison snatched away the cup. "The way you say it," he exploded.

"*Family affairs*. As if I didn't consider her family. We had a relationship that was entirely separate from you!"

Jamie stared at Ellison. He felt exhausted, as he often did when someone was mad at him. He was confused that anyone was allowed to be angry with him at his mother's funeral. But it was true that Jamie had not considered Ellison would be in mourning too.

"I'm sorry," Jamie murmured. "I shouldn't have said it like that."

"Maybe I'm being too sensitive." Ellison sniffed.

"Well—" Jamie started.

"But we *did* have a connection. Joan told me I didn't have to speak to my parents if I didn't want. Whenever I felt guilty, I'd ask her again, and she'd tell me all over. I took her to Costco just a week ago. On the drive, she spoke about you and the navy. Honestly, I think she was a little proud."

"Well," Jamie said again. He was surprised to feel the lifting of some weight: that Joan's approval, even after she was gone, could settle over him like one of her perfect, cool blankets.

"You know," Ellison said, "when I was younger, I was a very jealous person. The thing I was most jealous of was beauty. Sometimes even now I'll watch Lee twist her hair around itself and stick in some old pen to hold it together and feel like I could die of envy. I'm almost never jealous of men, but I was when I started at the café and heard Joan talk about you. Neither of us did what our parents wanted us to. But how come your mom still loved you?"

"She wasn't exactly *approving*," Jamie said. "And I'm pretty sure she loved you too."

"You're my best friend. Don't say anything back, I know I'm only your very good friend. But that's because you're incapable of having real friends."

"I do want to have friends. It's just."

"I know, I know. You're working on it." Ellison retrieved from his pocket a silk square and gave it to Jamie, as if he expected him to cry.

I should cry, Jamie thought. I should fucking sob. Because Lee was in shock, Jamie seemed to be the only one so far who'd realized they no longer had a mother or father. He would work in the café, every day, and never see Joan again.

Jamie tried to cry, but nothing came out. He stuck the square from Ellison into his pocket and went to greet Juliet and Theo, who were seated with Bridget. His limp had returned, and he could feel the table make a show of not watching him as he walked. Only Theo looked at him straight on. "I always wondered how you'd turn out," he said, thumping Jamie on the back. For a moment Theo looked so much like Bill that Jamie returned to an old fantasy, that the last decades had been a dream. And it could all start over.

In the late evening, when it was just him and Lee and Nelson left at the restaurant, and Nelson's hand shook as he drank his water, Jamie saw that Nelson was getting older. And Jamie knew that one day Nelson would die, and Lee would die, and he himself would go. He stuck his hand in his pocket, where his fingers grazed the stitched edges of Ellison's handkerchief, and it felt so familiar, as if it were something he knew from before, a soft item placed in his fingers when he was born.

———

When Jamie was nine and Lee seven, Bill planned a trip to Las Vegas. The trip would be only Bill and the kids, as Bill had gotten it into his head that a dad's bonding weekend was a rite of passage. Though in truth, Lee and Jamie preferred to travel with *both* parents—Joan, after all, was the one who packed their underwear and made sure they had snacks. As a result, Jamie and Lee were somewhat agitated, although they were sensitive enough not to hint such to Bill. Lee especially couldn't shake the thought that something terrible would happen to them while away, that due to Joan's absence, a tragedy would strike.

The night before they were to leave, Lee sat on her bed and watched

Joan pack her duffel for her. "What will you do if something happens to me while I'm gone?" Lee asked.

"I'll cry." Joan dropped Lee's toothbrush and a travel-size toothpaste into a toiletries pouch. "But nothing will happen to you."

"What if Dad takes us to space and I get stuck on Mars?"

"I'll come get you."

"What if Jamie gets stuck there?"

"I'll go get him. What, you think I'm going to fetch one kid and not the other?"

"What if the three of us crash in the plane?"

Joan stopped packing. This, of course, had been Lee's aim to begin with. Joan set the sweater she'd been folding on the bed. "Don't say that. You have to knock on wood." Joan was not superstitious but had adopted a few American customs. She waited until Lee actually knocked three times on the headboard. Joan then knocked.

"But what would you *do*?" Lee pressed. "If all of us were dead?"

"I don't want to talk about it."

"You have to tell me. I asked you." This was a house rule: when the children asked a real question, the adults had to give a real answer.

"I would want the plane to just disappear. I wouldn't want it to be found. That way, I could imagine you were existing out there, that you had gone through a wormhole."

"What's a wormhole?"

"I don't know. An alternate life," Joan breathed.

CHAPTER THIRTY-NINE

There was a work conference, a three-day trip to Boston. When she'd booked her flight weeks earlier, Lee had not anticipated her mother dying. "You can cancel," her manager said. But Lee wanted to go.

Jamie drove her to the airport. He had to drive Lee's car because his own was in the shop—he'd had a wreck, he said. He'd accidentally drifted into a barrier exiting the freeway.

"The 280 by your place?" Lee asked. "But you drive that every day."

"Well, my eyes were closed," Jamie admitted.

"What? Why?" But a memory floated: Jamie staying late at JJS after Bill died, running lap after lap even when he didn't have track. How he nearly crashed into a tree until Lee called out his name, shouting, What were you thinking, didn't you feel the grass?

Lee drew a sharp breath. "You can't do that anymore, understand? Jamie, I'm going to be pissed if you ever do it again."

"You sound like Mom."

"You think I care if I sound like her? You can't do it. You have to promise."

"I won't," he said, sounding amused.

"I don't know if I believe you."

"Really," Jamie said. "I mean it. I got sick of it. Besides, it's annoying having the car in the shop."

They didn't speak after that. Jamie turned up the radio and Lee sat with her arms crossed. She lowered the window even though she knew Jamie didn't like it—the air-conditioning was more efficient, he said. They arrived at the airport and she retrieved her bag from the trunk. "I promise!" Jamie hollered out the window after she had already begun to walk away, and she thought then that she did believe him—he flashed her a grin, the same clean joyous expression they used to share as children, and she had to stop herself from screaming that she loved him.

"You *better*!" Lee yelled.

She went through security. The airport seemed to Lee the same all the time, regardless of season or hour; as a child, she had believed there was a certain population who lived at the airport, so much did the people, their patterns and colors, all appear the same. Shortly after Lee boarded her flight, a woman in a blazer and loose slacks arrived in her row and took the aisle seat. She nodded at Lee, and Lee nodded back. The tacit agreement had been struck: neither would attempt to converse unless absolutely necessary. They would be polite with the other's space and considerate if one needed to use the restroom. They would hope the middle seat remained unoccupied, and if it did, each would consume only their half of the space. Lee loved the etiquette of frequent travelers. It was as if they were engaging in the same dance all over the world.

Except that a moment later, the woman spoke. "I like your outfit," she said.

"Thanks. I like yours too."

"Where'd you get that shawl?"

"It's my mom's." Lee had found it in Joan's closet, a large green and blue cashmere square with a flying zebra in the middle.

Her phone pinged, and she grabbed it. She saw the messages were from Marc.

I'm in the Palo Alto office this week, he wrote. *Tell me when you're free. Whenever you want.*

Yes, Lee wrote. *Thank you.*

Are you sure you're OK? I'm worried about you.

I'm fine, Lee wrote. She and Marc had gone to dinner last night. They'd been seeing each other the last few months—he had been gentle and caring when she'd told him Joan's diagnosis. He had offered to come with her to Boston, to book a ticket on the same flight, in which case he would have been next to her in the middle seat. Their arms would have been touching; he would be speaking in her ear. There would be a warm body instead of this empty space.

Though space could be nice too. Lee could put anything in that gap: her bag, her shawl. She could raise the armrest and spread out a little more if she liked.

I miss you, came the next message.

I miss you too, Lee typed, and then after another second she deleted it. She sighed and shut her phone. This had always been her problem, when she could see an end point to anything, a relationship, a job, a place: sometimes there was an alternate track which looped back, but usually not. How stupid I am, she thought. How silly and immature to keep tossing things away all because I let something get in my head to the point where there's no return. But Lee knew she wouldn't change. She'd keep doing it this way, she'd keep trying new things and different people until she felt how she thought she should. And if it was too late for certain milestones at that point—if she ended up an old spinster, as Joan had once hinted threateningly—well. She'd just go to the café each evening and sweep the floors with Jamie.

Lee put away her phone. To her left, her neighbor perused a magazine. Lee found herself with the rare urge to talk, to have a pointless and meandering conversation. If she were at the Satisfaction Café, she'd be asking for an hour of conversation right now, a bowl of dumplings or a slice of lemon cake. Lee looked out the window. She realized the plane was already on the runway and accelerating. When had that happened? She hadn't even noticed they were moving.

They were rising now, the plane at a sharp angle against the sky, the trees and buildings and streets rushing past. Lee pressed her face to the glass. Somewhere below was Jamie, driving back to the café, past the place where Joan's ashes were buried, the plot next to Bill's. And now the plane was higher, over the bay, and somewhere in the area was Marc, and then maybe the next man she would meet, and the next. She squinted to see if she could spot the big lot overrun with grass and wildflowers that had once been Falling House.

Joan spoke in her head: I'm glad you took the shawl from my closet. Aren't planes so cold? These bright colors always look better on young people, anyway.

It looked great on you, Mom.

Why are you staring out that window? Don't you know the glass is dirty? I hope you cleaned it before touching it like that.

I'm trying to see something I recognize. Maybe I'll spot something or someone familiar.

Well, there's no point in doing that now, Joan said. Don't you know? From up here, they all look the same.

ACKNOWLEDGMENTS

With thanks:

To Michelle Brower and Kara Watson, who believed in this book and made it far better. I am so grateful.

To the team at Trellis: Natalie Edwards, Allison Malecha, Tori Clayton, Elizabeth Pratt.

To the team at Scribner and Simon & Schuster: Nan Graham, Stu Smith, Marysue Rucci, Jonathan Karp, Jaya Miceli, Kassandra Engel, Lauren Dooley, Laura Wise, Joie Asuquo, and Sophie Guimaraes. Also to Kate Lloyd at Broadside.

To Felicity Blunt and Anna Kelly for their work in bringing this novel to the UK, Australia, and New Zealand. Also to their colleagues at Curtis Brown and Little, Brown Book Group: Matilda Singer, Katya Ellis, Lilly Cox, Flo Sandelson, Emma Walker.

To the writers Cathi Hanauer and John Jay Osborn, whom I met when we were on a panel at the Tucson Festival of Books. Also to festival organizers, for introducing me to cherished friends who have enriched my life in writing and beyond. Cathi, I am grateful for your comments on an early draft. John, I miss you all the time. Also to Emilie Osborn, and the Osborn family.

To friends: Danielle and Astro Teller, Tom Moss, Janice Y.K. Lee, Lydia Kiesling, Philip Yen, and others who have informed, inspired, and moved me in creating this work.

To my mother, whom this book is definitely not about, but who inspires me endlessly.

To Tom. You have accomplished such incredible things and are the person least likely to brag about any of them. I admire you so much.

And once again to Daniel and Vivienne. I love you, now and always.